Finish Line

By

Kathy Mazalatis

Mazpie
Books

This book is an original production of

Mazpie Books

Summerville, SC 29485

Copyright @ 2015 by Kathy Mazalatis

Cover design by Lukas Cannarozzi

Text design by Diana Wade

Editor: Nicole Ayers

ISBN: 978-0-9861423-0-7

This book is dedicated to my husband Larry, my sons, Ryan and Kevin for their endless supply of love and support. To my friends and family who supported and encouraged me, even though I think they never thought I'd see it through. I didn't either! Most importantly, I dedicate this book to my biggest cheerleader of them all. Someone I would not have been able to get through writing this book without. My friend, Susan Minter. Thank you for always encouraging me throughout this entire process, reading page after page and lifting my spirits. I would have never made it to the 'finish line' without you! Much love!

Chapter One

"Laney! Are you still listening to me?" says Allie, my best friend since middle school.

"What? Yes, sorry. Sometimes I get caught up thinking about how miserable my life is right now. So, you were saying?" I force interest in the conversation.

"I was telling you about my latest doctor's visit. I swear, Laney, these menopausal hormones are getting the best of me!"

"I hear ya, sister. They are bogging me down too. I'm in such a funk right now. I really feel like I need a change—see new places, new faces. With the kids going off to college again in a month, I feel like there's nothing left here for me now." I say.

Allie lives back where I grew up, in the suburbs of New Jersey. It's a beautiful area; mountains, lakes, farms, but just nothing to do. After high school, I left and could never imagine going back. My cheating ex and I found a little piece of heaven in South Carolina. "Smiling faces, beautiful places" is the state's motto. Jim and I needed more than lakes and cows; we wanted to live where people went on vacation. We most certainly got that in Charleston. We felt like we were at home the minute we arrived almost thirty years ago. I moved here sight unseen. Jim had vacationed in Charleston as a kid, so he was well aware of its beauty. I truly love living in South Carolina, but a part of me always pines for my old life in New Jersey. Things seemed so much simpler then.

I especially miss my lifelong childhood friends. Their friendships are like no others I have experienced. I have met many acquaintances over the years. You know, the kind of people you think at the time could truly be lifelong friends, then they stab you in the back with a smile on their face? I can't tell you how many times the term "Northern Aggression" has been used in my presence or how many times someone has "blessed my heart." It's exhausting really. Someone once told me to feel lucky if in your life you have two to three true friends. The other friendships you have that end up fading away, merely exist to serve their purpose for that time in your life.

"Laney, why don't you get away? Take some time for yourself. You have nothing keeping you in Charleston right now," Allie says with her all-knowing tone. She is right. Allie usually is.

After the divorce from Jim (luckily, it was after the divorce), I received a substantial inheritance from my Grandmother Joan. My grandmother was a brilliant business woman. She was also super smart and savvy with her money. Thanks to Gram and her unselfish ways; I can live a simple life, work part-time if I want (just to keep busy), and really never have to worry about money. I'm very low maintenance, don't like a lot of bling. I'm simple and cheap. You would think I'd be every man's dream girl! So this money, this gift of financial freedom, will last me my lifetime. In an ideal world, I'll even be able to leave some to my children and their families. Although they made out just as well, since they were the only great-grandchildren.

After being with Jim for all those years, I craved time alone. I spent so many years taking care of others around me, and not me. I needed more space. To breathe. To do my own thing without being questioned. I spent too many years worrying about everyone else. I wanted to worry about me. I've learned to take the good days along with the bad days.

On a positive note, I'm in the best shape of my life. Exercising regularly, signing up for a bunch of 5Ks, actually participating in some. I've got quite the t-shirt collection. However, at this point in my life, I'm starting to feel lonely. I want to love again. I want to hold someone's hand, give them a kiss goodnight. It's been two years since the divorce, and really, I have no prospects. Don't get me wrong, I've seen plenty of hot guys, but when I say see, I mean in passing. Like when they run past me at races, over the finish line into the arms of their significant other. I need to have someone waiting for me at the finish line.

"Well, Allie, let me run. Got lots to do today," I respond, knowing damn well I have nothing going on.

"Okay, Laney, but really, think about getting away. I have an idea. You should come here! You can stay with me!"

Although I love Allie, I know from experience that, like fish, company starts to stink after about three days. Plus, Allie is adjusting to her new single life. She'd been married to a man much older than her. She got to a point where she wanted to be with someone she could be more active with, someone more in tune with her needs. I wasn't completely surprised when Allie decided to leave Adam. He was a super nice guy, but I never saw a spark between them. She's so full of life and outgoing. Adam was more of a sit back quietly and read the paper kind of guy.

"You're so sweet, thanks, Allie. I'll think about it. Talk to you soon!" I press end on my phone and I'm alone again. That is the frustrating part. It's amazing how the grass is always greener. I longed for alone time, and now that I'm alone, I need to be with someone. Not just anyone. Someone who will protect me, compliment me, and pamper me. Lord knows Jim never did that for me. Is this too much to ask for? Is there such a guy? Or am I dreaming? I'm beginning to lose hope. I'll be fifty in two short years; then who will want me?

Chapter Two

As I look around my adorable little cottage home nestled under the grand oak trees, I realize I have a lot to offer someone. I'm smart, funny, somewhat attractive for a "mature" woman. I'm active in my community, donating my time and my money to several charitable foundations. My chestnut, shoulder-length hair needs some coloring every few weeks and I have to use reading glasses now, but I'm ready to try something adventurous! Time to dust off the wounds and scars of love gone wrong and face the world.

But first, I need to check Facebook to see how wonderful other's lives are being made to appear. Why do I even look? Most times when I get on there I feel like there are so many people trying to paint a perfect portrait of their lives, hiding behind the mask of a computer. Hell, I was one of them at one point. Pictures of the happy couple, romantic getaways, gorgeous sunsets, decadent meals. Oh, how we tried, Jim and I, to convince ourselves and those out in Facebook Land that our life was ideal. We tried for a long time but just ran out of steam.

Once you lose someone emotionally, it's hard to get them back. I knew that. I knew Jim was gone. His infidelities were brought to my attention via text message. A fucking text. From a number I didn't recognize. A pissed off lover of Jim's, whom he had done wrong by. Here you go, lady I don't know, with two kids, a bright future, and retirement with the man you love. One text brought it all crumbling down. I tried to trust Jim again. I really did. Not just for the sake of our kids. For the sake of all the years I had invested into our relationship. The years of work building a foundation that I thought would hold us up during our twilight years. We attended endless therapy sessions, went on amazing family vacations. No matter how hard I tried, I couldn't let his cheating ways go. I was always so consumed with paranoia. Checking his emails, his phone calls, hell, I even followed him once. That was all it took. Followed him right to a hotel downtown. He told me he was going bowling with the guys.

I've always been a glass half full kinda girl. The divorce knocked me down, but I'm back up. I'm ready for the next chapter in my life. No matter what lies ahead.

Are you kidding me? Another migraine? Every time I go online, this chick has a migraine! Oh, wait, love these shots of the girls so frantically trying to hold on to their youth. Fake boobs, orange tans, big Jersey hair, dressing promiscuously, hanging out at the local bar. Girls' night out! What a bunch of skanks! And they're married! Okay, I'm jealous. A little. I wouldn't want my hair that big or my skin that orange, but damn, I'd love to look "hot" again. Sexy even. I need to work on that.

Scrolling, scrolling. Same shit, different day on Facebook. Wait a second, wait a second, what's this? Is this a sign? A girl from high school—I think I hung out with her. Who the hell can remember?

Status update: Stacy Foreman is looking for a house sitter. Leaving the country for two months. If you know of anyone looking for temp housing, let me know. :)

Ugh, smiley face. I click on the link—where is this house? Looks familiar. "Lakefront home, fully furnished, 3 BR, 2 BA, short-term rental, Sept – Oct on Falcon Lake."

Falcon Lake! In my hometown! So close to my best girlfriends! A change—a breath of fresh air after a smoldering hot Charleston summer. I could totally do it. I think. To not be within driving distance of my kids for two months would be tough. Although, I think I cramp their style anyway. The last time I visited Jake at Duke, I could tell by his tone that he was feeling like, okay Mom, are you headed out? I wasn't planning on leaving, but sitting across from him on his bunk, I couldn't help but notice him texting away and smiling at the texts he was getting back. He had plans.

And Kerry out at Clemson, I really only hear from her when the money is running low. Great-Grandma Joan was smart to not allow the kids access to their inheritance until after college graduation. My kids don't need me like they used to. I need to accept that.

Let me message Stacy. I'm sure the house isn't available anymore. After all, I haven't checked Facebook in, like, one day. I need a life.

> Hi, Stacy! Just saw your post about the rental. I have some serious interest. Is it still available?

Oh boy, do I really want to do this? What the hell am I going to do in Jersey? Party at the local bar with the orange skanks? I would love to spend some quality time with my oldest and dearest friends, but everyone has their own lives. Would they even have time for me? I haven't spent much time at Falcon Lake since my parents passed away. The memories overwhelm me. Why am I second guessing this? The kids leave to go back to school in three weeks, then I'm here...alone. Again. Okay, here goes nothing...SEND.

I'm not going to overthink this. I tend to do that. Talk myself out of things constantly. I wish I didn't live in such fear of living. I was raised to be very cautious, which led me to be anxiety-ridden. I tried so hard not to pass that anxiety along to my kids. Thanks to Jim's input, I think I was successful. See that! Jim did do some things well! Actually, very few things, but that was one of them. Our children have no inhibitions.

Okay, let me vacuum now. I'm sure by the time I'm done, there will be a response from Stacy. I wonder where she's going? Does she have kids? From the pictures of the house, it doesn't seem that way. The house looks too kept for kids. Very neat. Beautiful stone fireplace, picture glass windows overlooking the lake. Outside fire pit. Oh, how I miss those cool New Jersey nights. Sitting by a fire pit with a glass of wine, wrapped in a blanket—oh—sounds like a dream. Gorgeous dock. A hammock under the shade of trees alongside the lake. It doesn't get any better than that for me. Okay, now I'm getting excited! Let me just hit refresh before I vacuum. *Ding*...one new message. Seeing that little white message box makes my heart jump. Here goes nothing...*click*.

> Hi Laney! So great to hear from you! Yes, our house is still available. My husband's company needs him for an assignment in Germany for two months. I've decided to join him. We couldn't stand to be apart! We hate to leave the house unoccupied all that time, so that's why we were hoping to find someone to stay, keep an eye on things. Would you and your husband be coming? It would be a great

getaway. Just let me know if you are interested. We are looking for $4000 for the two months. That includes utilities and the use of our boats. Really, it's not about the money for us, we really just want some peace of mind. Talk to you soon! :)

Not about the money? Then why ask for four thousand? Not that four thousand is a lot to me anymore. I'm still not used to having so much money available to me. I see the number on my bank statements, but it doesn't seem real to me. I know it's real to Jim—oh, how pissed he was to miss out on that inheritance! He was counting on my grandmother's money for his retirement. Did he honestly think he would never get caught cheating? Sucks to be you buddy! Ha!

Okay, before I respond, I need to call my girls and get their input. First, Grace, my most level-headed, conservative friend. Of course, she'll want me to come. It damn near killed her when I left all those years ago.

"Yes, yes, yes!" Grace immediately responds. "We can go to the spa together. I can come spend a few nights at the house with you—yes!"

Wow, someone needs her own getaway! But that's great. Who am I kidding?

Elise will also want me to come. We are each other's comic relief in this stressful life. Elise has been on the same emotional roller coaster as me the past few years. Her marriage isn't what she thought it would be. The difference between Elise and I: I tell her everything. Everything! She's much more reserved and keeps a lot of things to herself. Almost like she doesn't want to burden anyone with her problems. So we resort to laughter when we talk.

"This is Principal Montgomery." She answers her phone in her stern principal voice.

"Yes, hello, Principal Montgomery, this is your favorite friend from South Carolina and I wanted to know if you think I should come to Falcon Lake for two months," I ask in a southern accent.

"YES!" was all I heard on the other end of the phone. "I need you up here!"

And I know Allie wants me up there; she already offered to take me in. Oh, the trouble Allie and I could get into. Just like the old days.

Here I go again, looking for affirmation from others. Why can't I just decide things on my own? I really do have nothing holding me back. My house will be fine for two months. My neighbors are the best. They can keep their eyes on the place. I have a landscaper to keep the yard up. Okay, okay, stop second guessing it. Just do it.

Wow, Stacy! What a great opportunity for you and your husband. I love Europe- have been several times!

I had to zing Stacy. She seemed too braggy, and I truly dislike braggers.

I am actually no longer married, so I would be staying alone in the house. Just looking to spend quality time in my old stomping grounds with some of my dear friends.

Old stomping grounds? Jesus, am I that old? Who says shit like that? I can hear my kids mocking me on that one. That's something my mom would say. But I leave it, too lazy to delete.

Do you need me to fill out any paperwork, lease, etc.? Can I have your address to send the check? Let me know what I need to do. The house looks great. So excited! Looking forward to it! :)

Smiley face back at you, Stacy. Oh boy, here it goes...*SEND*.

Holy crap, did I just do that? I did. And I'm glad. Fall is my favorite time of year in New Jersey. And I do miss my friends. So much. This may be just the change of scenery I need. Regroup. Focus. Live. Get back to the fun me that hasn't been around for a while.

Chapter Three

Jake and Kerry have packed up and left for school. I can't believe Jake is going to be a senior and Kerry a sophomore! Time flies. Too fast. I feel like it was just yesterday that I was getting them ready for preschool. The first few years we were married, Jim wasn't completely convinced he even wanted kids. I knew I wanted to be a mom from the time I was a little girl. Being on different pages about having kids was not a great way to start a marriage. I think Jim got to the point where he went along with me just to shut me up. I wouldn't have it any other way. I would not want a life without my kids.

Time now for me to start getting ready for my big trip. I'm going to drive to Jersey. Alone. It's okay. I'll take my time, stop to see some friends along the way. I know the route well. I would drive the kids up to Jersey about once a year to visit family and friends. Jim could never go with us. He had to stay home and run the business. Now in retrospect, I can only imagine what else, or who else, he was doing while I was gone. The thought makes me want to vomit.

As I load the Beemer, my one luxury purchase since the inheritance, I feel giddy. Just thinking of seeing my friends again, being on a lake, cool crisp night air…ahhh. I know I've made the right decision. No more second guessing myself, no more fear. I'm going to be a new me! Two months is the perfect amount of time. Over the years I have spent time with my friends, but not good quality time. I'm hoping to visit people that I normally don't have time to see on my short visits back home. It's going to be great! I turn and look at my house one last time. It's like a dollhouse, so adorable. I love it so much and I'm going to miss it. I take one last mental picture, get into my car, and pull out. I'm on my way!

Two days in a car is so much longer when you are alone. Alone. My new theme in life. I need to embrace it. What if my Mr. Everything isn't out there? That's a very possible scenario. I'm approaching fifty, and my skin is sagging. Although, I feel my skin has always sagged. Lines are deepening and increasing in number on my face.

It's okay to be alone, I try to convince myself. It's something I never imagined. I feel like I've always been in a relationship. Gosh, I guess I have. Jim and I started dating the summer after junior year. Before then, I just had a mad crush on Brady Gramble, no true relationship. Well, I did date one guy in eighth grade for about two weeks. But I wouldn't call that a relationship by any stretch of the imagination. We never even talked. Just declared that we were "going out."

A day and a half of driving and there it is. The bridge into New Jersey! If only when I drove over that bridge I'd be at my destination, but still three long hours to go. Yet, as soon as I cross, I feel like I'm home already.

I guess you can take the girl out of Jersey, but you can't take the Jersey out of the girl.

As I get closer to the lake and where I grew up, a bunch of memories flood over me, as they always do when I'm back in the area. It really was a beautiful place to grow up. Plus as kids we had the added benefit of not having video games or computers. We played outside. Nonstop. Endless games of tag, hide-and-go-seek, hopscotch. I wouldn't trade my childhood for anything. Once I became a teenager, the area got too boring for me. There wasn't enough to do in my eyes. The mountains and farmland were truly beautiful, but not pretty enough to keep me interested. I think these are just the right surroundings for me now as I reevaluate my life. Go back to where I started. Find myself again. This trip is all about me!

Chapter Four

The house is even better in person. I leave all my things in the car, because the excitement of seeing the inside of the home overtakes me. Stacy had a neighbor hide a key under a rock for me. On the front step is a huge basket of cheese, crackers, fruit, and my favorite wine.

Welcome home! Love, Grace

Typical Grace. Overly generous and always so thoughtful. I open the door and step in. Holy cow, Stacy is organized! Everything labeled and in its place. A note on the kitchen island reads:

Hi Laney! I hope you enjoy your stay! Please make yourself at home! In the master you'll notice a closet that is locked. That's where John and I locked up our personal and private possessions. So please, use everything else as if it were your own! :)

Jesus, she even draws smiley faces. Annoying, but really, a nice welcoming. Of course, now I'm wondering what's in that closet.

As I step out the back door onto the deck, my breath is taken away. The view is spectacular! Sun sparkling off the lake like little diamonds, the mountains surrounding the lake reflecting in the water. Two of the resident swans swimming by the end of the dock. I mean really, this is a dream. Oh yes, this is going to be a fabulous stay.

I head back out to the car to unload. I notice the neighbor, an attractive man, probably mid-thirties if I had to guess, washing his car. He places the hose in the bucket and begins to walk over.

"Hey, you must be Laney! I'm George Olsen…Stacy had me put the key under the rock for you," he says while drying his hands on his shorts.

I reach out to shake his hand and immediately check for a ring. This is a habit of mine now. No ring. "Hey George, great to meet you. What a great view of the lake from here! How long have you lived next to Stacy?" I ask, trying to remember what I looked like the last time I saw my reflection in the door window. Is my hair a mess? Do I have anything in my teeth?

"Oh we've lived here for about three years now."

We. Oh well. Next.

"Yeah, my brother and I thought it would be a good investment. Thought we'd fix it up and sell it, but no luck in this market. So we stayed. It's been fine; it's just not easy to live with your brother. Are you staying here alone?"

Okay, this just got interesting. A little young for me, but I've never been one to be deterred by someone's age. I wouldn't go much younger than George, but he's fine. "I am, yes. Looking to spend quality time with my best friends that live nearby. Did you grow up in the area, George?"

"No, my brother and I are from Vermont. Our parents retired down here and we followed them down. There wasn't too much going on where we were from."

"And you find a lot going on around here?" I joke, throwing my hair over my shoulder. Smooth.

"No, I guess not, but there are some fun things always going on around the lake. I could tell you some stories!" He looks like he is thinking back on one story in particular.

"Well good, I'm looking for some 'me' time, but I'm all about a good time as well." Shit. Sometimes I wish I could pull words back into mouth after they've slipped out. Beware neighbors! Single, forty-something lady from the South has moved in temporarily, and is looking for a good time.

"I'll keep that in mind if I hear of anything going on," George replies. "Did you need some help with your things?"

"Oh no, I don't have too much." Who am I kidding? I pack for every trip like I am never coming back. "You get back to your car washing. I'm sure I'll see you around."

"Okay, please let us know if you need anything. Abe and I work from home most of the time, so we're usually around."

"Thanks so much! I really appreciate it!" I watch him walk back to his driveway. Nice butt. I think he may be a runner, very long and lean. Typically not my type, but fun to look at. Seems like a nice enough guy. I wonder what Abe looks like? This is getting exciting now. Calm down, dirty old lady. I'm sure you are way too old for the likes of Abe and George. Abe and George? Good God, what's with people picking out such horrible names for kids? Is Abe short for Abraham? Like Abraham Lincoln and George Washington? Lordy, Lordy. I hope not.

Chapter Five

As I finish unpacking and settling in, I'm so thankful for Grace's basket. I do not have the strength to get my butt to the store to do any shopping. I'll save that for tomorrow. Ah, I feel so at home here. This place is really great. I kick my shoes off, plop on the couch, turn on my laptop, and return some emails. I post on Facebook that I've arrived safely, put the kids at ease. I'm sure they are super worried about their mom. Well, a mom can dream. Then, a quick call to Allie to let her know I have arrived.

"Hey Allie girl! Guess who's in town?" I ask with a gut full of excitement.

"Yay!" Allie shrieks. "Girl, we are going to have so much fun. Two wild and sexy single woman on the prowl. I'm jumping out of my insides!"

Oh Lord. Sexy? Yes, Allie is sexy. Always has been. Me? Yeah, not so much. Jim never made me feel that way, that's for sure. Sometimes I see men checking me out, but I am easily overlooked when placed next to someone very attractive like Allie. That's okay. I rely on my quick wit and friendliness to reel them in. It seems to be working like a charm so far. Ha!

"Girl, wait until you see the fine specimen that lives next door. He came over and introduced himself and offered to help me carry my stuff in."

"Did you let him?" Allie asks as if she was sitting on the edge of her seat.

"No, no. I didn't have that much. Plus, I was getting a little nervous and jerky. He was so young, no wrinkles. I almost felt like I needed to prove I was strong enough to lug my own shit." Allie and I laugh. It's so nice to have someone to go through this next chapter of life with. Even if I'm only here for two months. Our conversations have gotten me through some of the worst times of the divorce. So really, even with eight hundred miles between us, my lifelong friends have been my rocks through this whole ordeal.

Grace has been a huge support for me, but now, she may have a hard time relating to where I am. She's married to a wonderful man and seems to have it all together. She's even a grandmother already! That seems so bizarre, but she started earlier than the rest of us. I am by no means ready to be a grandma yet. Elise is me a few years ago. Right in the turmoil of it all. I'm so glad I will be here for her.

I finish talking with Allie and take my last gulp of wine. It always helps me sleep. What time is it? It must be at least eleven? Oh wait, nope. 8:45. Good God, I'm getting old. My heart stops when there is a knock on the door. Oh shit. Who the heck can that be? Is it someone for Stacy and her husband? Maybe someone doesn't know that they are gone? It's Sunday night. Isn't 8:45 late for a Sunday? Why am I such a chicken shit? Okay, toughen up and go answer the door. But grab a kitchen knife to put behind your back just in case.

As I flick on the front light, I see George standing in the doorway. "Hi Laney, I hope I didn't startle you," he says, peering around my shoulder to see the tip of a butcher's knife.

"Oh gosh, George, sorry. I guess I'm on edge. First night here and all. Plus, I saw a real creepy looking guy washing his car earlier." I hope he gets that I'm joking because a lot of people don't get my humor.

"Haha, yes." He giggles. "Well, my brother made these earlier and I thought I'd be a good neighbor and share." George handed me the most perfect looking brownie, covered in white powdered sugar, on a flowered paper plate.

"Why thank you, George, and please thank your brother for me. What did you say his name was again?" As if I couldn't remember George and Abraham!

"Abe."

"Abe, that's right. Great, thank Abe for me. Does he bake often? Because I could get used to these deliveries." Simmer down now, cougar, simmer down. You have to live next to these young men for two months. Need to get off on the right foot.

"He does do a lot of baking. I'll make sure I always save you some. Have a good night, Laney!"

"You do the same, George, and thanks again!" I call to his back as he walks away. Okay, is it me? Or did George look even younger in the night light? His sun-kissed, wavy hair (a little on the long side for me) glistened in the light of the front porch. Flip. If I find out he's in his twenties, I'll be thoroughly embarrassed. I swear I think George and his brownie just made me sweat a little. It could just be the brownie. Food does have that effect on me. Well, that was an interesting development. I think I'll save that brownie for tomorrow. This old lady can't handle sweets late at night; it will keep me up. Abe does "a lot of baking?" Hmmm. Wonder what that's about?

In the morning, I decide that I'm walking to this wonderful breakfast spot about two miles around the lake. Or maybe I'll run. Or should I bike? Stacy did leave a bike. Why can't my decisions be simple? I over think things! Okay, I'll jog. Then walk back. Perfect. Off to bed where I stare at that locked closet door. "Personal and private belongings." I want to know what's in there. What didn't they bring with them to Germany? Oh well. Time for sleep. It is 9:30 after all.

Chapter Six

W hat a great night's sleep with the windows open, hearing the lake. So peaceful. I wander over to the window, take a peek out of the blinds, and see what the brothers are up to. Looks quiet over there. Two cars in the driveway. I wonder what their deal is? I'm sure I'll find out. I have a way of getting information out of people.

I brush my teeth, get dressed, throw my hair up in a ponytail, put my favorite "Life Is Great" hat on, and lace up my running shoes. After I start out, I realize my running legs are not used to hills. The Lowcountry of South Carolina is pretty darn flat. The only time I really run hills is when I run the bridge downtown. But those hills are slow and steady. These lake hills are pretty drastic. Up and down. I'm starting to regret my choice of running, but I keep at it. I know it's the only thing keeping my weight down. I also know there's a brownie in my future and possibly some other baked goods. I arrive at the restaurant pretty worn out. Definitely in some pain. I sit outside for a moment, cooling down and rubbing my knees.

Gosh, this restaurant has been here since I was a kid. The original owner used to make me a smiley face with two eggs, sunny side up, and bacon when I was little. I loved that. I wonder if they would still do that for me?

As I enter the restaurant, I notice out of the corner of my eye two familiar faces. I know that I know them, but I can't place them just yet. I sit on the opposite side of the restaurant and think about it. A friendly older lady (hell, who am I kidding, she is my age) takes my order. I don't dare ask for the smiley face, plus, I am in the mood for an omelet. I can't help but look at the two guys across the restaurant as I drink my coffee. Okay, it's coming back to me now. I think, but it's hard to tell through the graying beard and large belly, it's my boyfriend from eighth grade, Pete Murdough. Damn, do I look that old? Who's with him? Looks good. Oh wait, that's Brady Gramble. Oh my, how I had a crush on Brady Gramble! All the girls did, but I think my lust was the most obvious in high school. Poor guy, I'm sure he thought I was crazy or a stalker. I really, really liked him. Never really spoke to him, but you know how teenage hormones are. He didn't need to speak or have a brain. He was just hot and the star of the football team. I have to say, the years have been very kind to my boy Brady. He looks quite good. No signs of balding, just some sprinkles of gray. Still very muscular. Oh crap, and I look like shit. Pony tail in hat, sweaty, gross. Maybe I'll get lucky and they won't recognize me.

Face down in my spinach omelet, all of the sudden I hear, "Laney, Laney Simms? Is that you?"

Frig. I look up and there, under the gray beard and behind the big belly, I spot him. My old boyfriend Pete.

"Pete? Is that you?" I pretend to act surprised.

"Laney, I can't believe it! I haven't see you in a long time. The last time you were up this way was about six years ago, right?"

"Yes, Pete, that's right! Wow!" I stand up to give Pete an awkward I'm-sweaty-and-I-don't-want-to-get-too-close hug. "Sorry, Pete, I ran here and I'm a little on the sweaty side." I pull away.

"That's okay, that's okay. Hey, you remember Brady Gramble from high school, right?" Pete gives me a shit eatin' grin, because he knew, as much as the next guy, that I had it bad for Brady Gramble.

"Yes, hi Brady. I'm Laney McGuire, er, Simms." Good God, he still has those eyes, that smile, those dimples…snap, I'm shaking his hand and not letting go as quickly as I should.

He finally breaks free from my grip. "Hi Laney, how are you doing?"

"I'm good, good. Just sweaty, sorry, I ran here." I say for a second time.

"Oh, good for you. I've been running too. Great exercise."

"Yes, yes it is," I say, trying to look up at him from under my hat while also trying to stop my upper lip from quivering. It does that when I'm nervous. I hate it. I feel like everyone can see it. Feels like my whole face is vibrating. Calm down, calm down, cougar.

"So what brings you back to Jersey?" Pete asks, breaking my stare with Brady.

"Oh yes, I actually rented a lake house for a couple of months…a little getaway for me." I am so self conscious speaking in front of Brady. Please, God, don't let there be spinach in my teeth.

"Where's Jim? Gosh, I haven't talked to him in years!" Pete asks from behind his beard.

Thank you, Pete, for the opening. "Oh, I'm surprised you didn't hear. Jim and I divorced a few years ago. It's okay, we're still friends, have two great kids." Rambling, I'm rambling. Did you hear that Brady? Your stalker is single. Yeah, baby.

"Oh no, I'm sorry to hear that. Brady here is divorced too. Been talking him off the ledge for some time now." Pete gives Brady a punch in what appears to be rock hard abs.

"Yeah, right, Pete," Brady says in an annoyed tone. Brady turns to me. "Divorce is not easy, that's for sure, but I look at it as one door closing to another one opening."

Sigh. So romantic. That may even be a line from a song.

"I agree. Once I got over the initial disappointment about my marriage failing, I decided I needed to embrace this next chapter in my life and make the best of it." I am pretty sure I read that in Self magazine, but I think he bought it. He shook his head in agreement. His gorgeous, beautiful head.

"Well, it was great to see you Laney. We need to head out to work. We own a dock building and repair company: Falcon Docks." Pete motions his head toward the truck parked out front. "We do a lot of other odd jobs to get by. It's been busy; it's good." Pete says, trying to convince me.

"That's great, Pete. I'm happy for you." I try to maintain equal eye contact with Pete so I don't stare too long at Brady. I give Pete another half-body, sweaty hug goodbye. "Maybe I'll see you again while I'm in town," I say to Pete, but in my heart I hope to see Brady again.

"That sounds great. Maybe Jean and I can have you over for dinner some time."

"Sounds great, Pete. Give her my best."

I went to school with Jean as well. I always got the vibe that she didn't like me because I dated Pete for thirty seconds in eighth grade. Really?

I raise my hand to shake Brady's while he approaches me for a hug. Flip! My arm hits his rock hard abs. I hold my breath, hoping the lack of breeze keeps the smells at bay, and go in for the hug. It's a quickie because I'm sure he is disgusted. "Great to see you Laney. Hey, if you're interested, there's a

5K around the lake a week from this Saturday. It's to raise money for autism. A bunch of us are signed up to do it. Then that night, there's a fundraiser banquet. You should think about joining. Lord knows my boy Pete here can't do it!" Brady laughs and shoots Pete a punch in the arm.

"Well, I can't do the 5K, but I can certainly attend the banquet! Brady's right, you should come, Laney. It's going to be like a high school reunion. Grace's friend Beth is running the event because her son is autistic." Oh yes, I've heard of Beth. Her daughter is in Grace's youngest daughter's grade. They've been Girl Scout leaders together and ran the PTO together one year. Grace made her sound like Mother Teresa.

"I will think about it for sure! Thanks guys! Have a great day...maybe I'll see you then," I say, already panicking about the number of hills I'd have to run. Is a week and a half enough time to train? Oh boy. But to be in the company of Brady, by any stretch of the imagination, would be fantastic. He's divorced! Holy cow, maybe he forgot what a crazy-ass stalker I was in high school. Could I get so lucky? Chill out, cougar. Remember you're only here for two months. Well, I'm going to make the best of it, that's for sure!

Chapter Seven

I have a leisurely walk home. No way I'm running after that meal. I almost feel like I'm floating. It's amazing how that little spark of excitement fills me with such hope. I think that all I need is hope sometimes. Makes you feel alive. I do miss the physicality of a relationship. I'm a touchy-feely kind of person. When you are without physical affection for so long, even a simple, smelly hug gives you hope. What a horrible—first/second impression. Last time I saw Brady, I was a junior in high school; he was a senior. I was walking toward him in the hall, not even aware of what was going on around me because I was in the "Brady" zone. I never saw Eric Manes running out of the classroom to my right. He hit me with such force, I went flying across the hall, and was knocked onto my ass. It was like a bad dream at the time. I could hear people laughing. Grace was nearby. She ran to my rescue and helped me up. All I saw were Brady's feet, walking by. Stalker down.

From that point, I decided I needed to find a new interest. After all, Brady was graduating that year. Once he left school, I knew for sure I would never stand a chance. Because I stood a chance when he was there...not! So I set my sights lower, at a more realistic catch...Jim McGuire.

As I approach the house, I see George outside getting his newspaper. "George, how are you doing this beautiful morning?" I ask with a spring in my step.

"Look at you up and at 'em so early in the morning. Did you have a nice walk?" George asks.

"Oh it was a third jogging, a third eating, and a third walking," I say, cracking myself up as usual.

"I'm guessing you went to Henry's for breakfast?" he asks.

"Why yes, I did! My favorite breakfast place in the area." Especially now.

"I've been going there since I was a little girl. Henry himself used to make me a smiley face egg plate," I say, as if Henry only made me that smiley egg.

"Yes, my great-uncle Henry was a good guy," George says.

"No way! Henry was your uncle?"

"Yes, ma'am. Well, my dad's uncle. My dad worked most of his summers there before he moved to Vermont to be with my mom."

Frig. Ma'am? Really? "That's so cool," I respond, feeling very young and hip, hoping to negate the ma'am.

"You have a nice day George, and thanks again for the brownie. I saved it for today." I stroll up my walkway toward the front door. "You're welcome Laney, and like I said, if you need anything, Abe and I are right here." Why thank you, young man, I think in my head. I can't help but admire George's chiseled face. He really is handsome. He still has his summer tan and that hair...umpf, I'd like to run my fingers through it...stop. You could be his mama! I'm sure I could. One day I'll find out how old George is, and maybe one day I'll even meet Abe. Wonder what he looks like?

Chapter Eight

With my cougar hormones all on fire from such an exciting morning; I decide to shower, grab a book, and head out to the hammock that's been calling my name since I got here. I have the whole day to go food shopping. There must be a shortage of men in South Carolina because I'm feeling pretty darn cocky here in New Jersey. The men seem to be everywhere!

The hammock is placed right along the water. It's like the trees grew here for that very purpose. I awkwardly get into the hammock, trying to look smooth because you never know who may be watching. Perfect landing. I got in that hammock like a pro. The lake is quiet and peaceful. Everyone is back to work; summer is wrapping up. Perfect time to relax and read the latest best seller.

Boom! Boom! Boom! "What the hell is that?" I think to myself, getting pissed at this noise that's ruining my moment. It sounds like an echo, but it's loud. I look around the lake, trying to find the source of this disturbance. There it is, at the end of the cove, about six houses over to the right. I see a huge machine. What is that thing doing? Looks like it's pushing something into the lake. Oh, I make sense of what I'm seeing. Someone's building a dock. Wait, what? Building a dock? Is it Falcon Docks? Oh my, oh my. I squint trying to make out the man operating the machine and the other man standing alongside the lake directing the machine operator. Could it be? I think I see a belly and a beard. That can only mean one thing—Brady is working the big, bad piece of machinery. My anger leaves my body, and now I feel all warm and tingly. Just like the girl in high school. I have no idea what this guy is even like. I'm still obsessed with the idea of him. He can be a total dick for all I know! But feeling this way again is fun and innocent enough. I'm an old lady. I need some excitement in my life!

I try to refocus on my book, but I can't help moving it to the side and peeking to see how that dock is coming along. The booming stops and I see the figure, who in my fantasy head I presume is Brady, jump out and walk down by the lake to check on his progress. Oh yes. It's him. Thank you, person with a house on the lake, for needing a new dock. I'm watching Brady and Pete discuss their next move, when behind me, a chainsaw is cranked. I turn to look, but can't see who is making the noise behind me because there is a row of tall hedges between my yard and George's.

When I turn back to check on the dock boys, they are both looking in my direction. I'm sure they are both trying to find the source of the noise like I was, but in my head, I think they are looking at me. So I give a nervous, hesitant wave. I'm sure they can't even see me. They both raise their arms wave back. Pete's yell echoes around the cove. "Hey, Laney!" Dang, for an old guy, he's got good eyes. I wave back and pretend I'm not impressed with their dock-building skills. I place the book back in front of my face to prove it.

After peeking over the top of the book nonstop, barely even reading a page, I realize it's approaching noon. I told Allie I would come into town and go to lunch with her. She owns an adorable little eclectic shop full of funky accessories and some of her homemade jewelry. The store is called "Bohemian Bling". It's a very successful business. Allie's good at whatever she does.

Chapter Nine

I see the guys pack up for lunch, so it makes leaving the view from the hammock a little easier. I hop in the car and head to town. It's so adorable here, cute Bavarian style homes and stores. Allie's shop is right in the middle of it all. Great location. Especially for all the wealthy Manhattanites who frequent this lake and own homes here. They love buying Allie's goods and passing them off as true treasures when they get back to the city. I'm happy for Allie. She's made a nice life for herself since her divorce. She's not dating anyone seriously; she tends to get around a little bit, but in a fun way, not a slutty way. I would never refer to one of my closest friends as slutty. She's fun! She always puts herself first, and I aspire to be like that.

As I walk in the store, these beautiful little butterfly-shaped chimes ring. There's Allie working her charms with a male customer. He'll buy anything she's selling by the looks of it. "Laney! Is it really you?" She drops what she's doing and runs to me.

"Allie! You look as beautiful as ever!" I say, hugging her. Gosh, I missed her.

"So do you, my old, dear friend. Let me just finish up here and we'll head out." She heads back behind the counter. Good God, she's tall, or am I shrinking? I look at her feet; she must be wearing six-inch heels! No wonder! I could never pull off a heel like that. Allie has style and the perfect figure. She can pull off any outfit.

I start looking around the shop. She really does have cute stuff. One necklace in particular grabs my attention. Two hearts intertwined. It makes me wonder once more if I'll ever find love again. Lord, I hope so. She finishes up the sale. As the customer walks out, I swear he shoots me a dirty look, like I just interrupted something. I'm sure I did on his part. Allie doesn't even seem phased by him.

"I'm so glad you are here. I need a break from this place. June!" Allie yells toward the back room at her ex-sister-in-law who still works for her. "I'm going to lunch, can you keep an eye on the store for me? Thanks! Hurry, let's go before she complains." We move quickly out of the store, giggling, and head down the street. "I love this little Italian place around the corner called Vito's. Does that work for you?" Allie asks.

"Of course, you know I can't get good Italian food in the South." We enter and Allie is greeted like a celebrity. "Geez, come here much, Al?" I say laughing.

"Well, yes, and see that guy by the oven?"

I peer over the counter and see a very attractive man, early thirties at best. "Yeah, I see him."

"I kinda had a little fling with him a few months ago," she says with a smirk on her face.

"Oh, wait, yes, I remember now! Is that Tony Bologna?" Allie gives her men nicknames. It helps me to remember them and keep all the stories straight.

"Ha! Yes! Tony Bologna!"

"He's hot. What happened?"

"Well, let's just say he was good for bologna and nothing else!" We laugh loudly and make a small scene while being escorted to our table. Tony glances over and smiles.

"So tell me, how's the house?" Allie asks while drinking her diet coke.

"It's really adorable. The best part: there's a hammock down by the lake. I'm so glad I did this, Allie. I think this is going to be just what I need to refocus and get going with living. I need to find my purpose and start setting some goals."

I fill Allie in about George and running into Pete and, of course, Brady. Allie's eyes are bright and enthusiastic as I tell her every single detail. "When I first realized it was him, I felt just like I did in high school, Al. Heat rose up my neck and I got goosebumps all over."

"Isn't that the best feeling...liking someone? I think that's the best part of a relationship. Those initial dates, the chase, it's so...sexy!" Allie says with a devilish look in her eye.

"It really is great. I'm sure nothing will come of it, but I feel happy, excited again. I haven't felt that way in a long, long time." I say, truly meaning it. Jim and I lost the excitement a long time before our divorce. I guess that's why he had to go out and find excitement somewhere else.

Allie snaps me out of my thoughts. "What do you mean, nothing will come of it? Come on now, I know damn well that Brady is looking and ready to have someone in his life. Don't forget, he and my sister are still great friends. She keeps me posted on what's going on in his life. His wife really screwed him over too. Cheated on him with their son's teacher! Can you imagine that? She kept telling Brady she was volunteering at the school. Meanwhile, they were in the janitor's closet getting it on! So you two have a lot in common to begin with."

Wow, that's horrible. I'm glad I didn't know Jim's lovers. I can't even imagine if it was someone we knew…That is so hurtful. Poor Brady, I just want to hug him. And kiss him. And…

"Laney! We need to get out and hit the town!"

"This town? Is there really a scene here? Seems awfully quiet," I say, like I have great experience hitting the town.

"Oh yeah, the weekends are hot with a lot of New York City guys looking for innocent country women like ourselves. It's really become a fun town since you left."

We both laugh uncontrollably. I can't imagine Falcon Lake being fun, but I'm open to it.

"So when are we hitting the town?"

Allie responds, "I was thinking Thursday night to start. There's a new bar in town that has half price drinks on Thursday night, so the place gets packed. Does Thursday night work for you?"

"Let me think…YES!"

Lunch with Allie is great. We walk around town a bit. She's like the mayor of Falcon Lake. Everyone knows Allie Fenway! "Well, time to get back to work. Wish I could see you again before Thursday, but I'm swamped," Allie says apologetically.

"No, no. It's okay. If I come to town, I'll pop in. I have my eye on a necklace I saw in there, that one with the intertwined hearts. I love it!"

"Yes, I created that one back in the Beggin' Greg days."

Wow…I had no idea Beggin' Greg had that kind of effect on you!"

"Oh, he did, but apparently he affected his wife that way too! Ooops!"

Oh, Allie, she is too much. My face and my stomach hurt from all the laughing we did at lunch. What more can you ask for in a friend?

Chapter Ten

As I pull away from the store, I remember that I still haven't picked up any groceries. Good old food shopping. But I guess it must be done. I drive to the updated (but still the same) Shop Rite. I swear the people working here are the same ones that worked here when I was in high school. It's weird; I feel like I never left at moments like this. Everything is still the same. I make my way up and down the aisles like a pro. I get the same staple items every week it seems. I guess it's easy to shop for one.

As I turn to head up the frozen food aisle, I look ahead and there he is. Brady. I stop dead in my tracks, like a deer in headlights. This is ridiculous. I'm a grown woman, not some horny high school chick. I know nothing about this man. All I know is for three years during high school, he looked at me in a confused way, if he looked at me at all. Like he didn't get me. That's okay, I didn't get me either. I still don't sometimes.

Back to the task at hand: food shopping. I continue walking up the aisle, looking at the food behind the doors to remember why I walked up this aisle to begin with.

"Laney?" he asks, not recognizing the well-kept, good-smelling me.

"Brady, hi. We meet again!"

He nervously laughs. "I saw you earlier in the hammock. That's a great house you're staying in. I know it well. I helped my friend Alan build it, well, rebuild it. It was nearly destroyed one winter. The whole roof caved in from a heavy snow. The owners decided to change some things about it, and that's where we came in."

Gosh, is he talking? His lips, so full. His short, dark hair. The scruff, not a beard, just two or three days of growth. Those green, green eyes. Those dimples. Snap out of it!

"Oh, neat! What a small world. I love the house. I don't know what it looked like before, but it's just perfect." *Just like you, Brady,* I think to myself, hoping I haven't said it out loud. He smiles.

"Well, great to see you again. Are you planning on running next Saturday morning?" he asks.

"I don't have any other plans, so I think I will. Especially since it's for such a good cause. With these hills, I'm more of a jogger. I live in a part of South Carolina that is very flat. Those hills kicked my butt this morning." I laugh and throw my hair over my shoulder in a "come and get me" kind of way.

"I bet. Well, hopefully, I'll see you there." He turns his cart to go around me.

"Okay, enjoy the rest of your day," I yell after him. Still practically the same body from high school. Wowza. Okay, I'm sweating again. I open one of the freezer doors just to cool down. Breathe, Laney, breathe.

Of course I continue to stalk Brady the rest of the time I'm shopping. He's gone in a hurry, though, and by the time I'm at the register, I see the Falcon Docks truck pulling away. I meant to pay closer attention to what was in his cart. Is he shopping for two? Is he a health nut? A drinker? I look at my array of foods on the conveyer belt and wonder what someone would think about me. Wine, pasta, ice cream. Quite the combination.

Chapter Eleven

A s I sit down to eat dinner, alone, I can't help but reflect on what was a very exciting day. If every day is like today, I may never leave. But I'd miss my kids too much. I'm going to have to get a FaceTime fix tonight if they have time for their old mom. First, I need to call Elise and fill her in on my day. Plus, I need a running partner. She's always been a better runner than me, but I'm going to beg her to stay by my side to make me look good.

Elise is just wrapping up her day at school. She's the principal at the high school the next town over. "Elise, oh Elise, I have so much to fill you in on. I can't believe it's only been one day!

"Oh boy, what is going on?" she asks, as if nervous to hear what I'll say. I fill her in on all the juicy details and beg her to do the 5K with me. She says she'll do it. Yes! We decide we'll catch up while running together since she has a busy couple of weeks ahead of her and is going out of town this weekend for a wedding.

I'm starting to feel guilty. I don't have a busy week ahead of me. I did for many, many years. Jim and I ran our own landscaping business. We put a lot of blood, sweat, and tears into that business and it was good to us for a long time. Until the market crashed. People didn't want to spend money on expensive landscaping. That was just about the time our marriage fell apart. The beginning of the end.

"I guess I'll have to wait to see you then." Yay, Elise, I knew I could count on her! "If you want, there's a banquet that night. You and Scott can come. They say it's going to be like a high school reunion!"

"Nah, that doesn't excite me like it would you, Laney. I see people from high school all the time. Too much really. Plus I can never get Scott to do anything social these days. We'll do something another time."

I saw Elise's point. If I saw all the people I went to high school with on a regular basis, the idea of a banquet with them would not excite me at all. I don't remember Scott ever being that social to begin with. Always made me wonder how those two have lasted as long as they have. At least I know that Grace will be there! She's one of the organizers, of course. I'm still trying to talk Allie into it, but I'm sure I'll be successful.

I hear some movement from next door. I hop up and move to the blinds, slowly so as not to be noticed. I use two fingers to spread the blinds and peek out the front window facing the road. There's George…what's he doing? I'm on my toes, trying to get a better look, when he sees me and waves. Shit. Real smooth. Stalker. I wave back and quickly scurry away from the window, wishing I had someone to share my embarrassing moment with.

I decide, since there's still some daylight, I'm going to head back to the hammock and see if I can actually get some reading time in. As I walk down to the lake, I can't help but glance to my right, as if Falcon Docks will be working at this late hour. They're not, but their equipment is still there. That's a good sign they'll be coming back. I don't think I'll get much "viewing" time tomorrow though. There's a cold front coming and we're supposed to have lots of rain and wind. May be a good day to see a movie.

I break open the book again, starting from the beginning, because after all the distractions this morning, I didn't retain one page of the story. I'm just about to delve in, when I hear, "Hey Laney…sorry to bother you. I was wondering if I could go under the house and borrow Stacy and John's wheelbarrow. We share some of our bigger items to save on space," George yells from his back deck.

"Oh, absolutely. Help yourself."

In the blink of an eye, George is standing by the hammock. "Wow, you're fast!" I say, surprised to see him there.

"Yeah, I have super powers. Didn't even have to move, just blinked my eyes, nodded my head, and bam, I landed here," he says, with a childlike grin on his face.

"Well, I'm impressed! Do that again. This time bring me a glass of wine, will ya?" I say, laughing.

"No, really, let me get you some. What kind?"

"Really? You don't mind?" I ask.

"Not at all," he says.

"I have a bottle of pinot noir open on the counter. Help yourself to a glass as well if you'd like." I say to be polite, not thinking he'd take me up on it.

"Sounds good, I'll be right back." And he's off again, into my house, well, Stacy's house. He obviously knows his way around the place because he's back in no time with two glasses (two very full glasses) of wine. He pulls up a chair alongside the hammock and I sit up, carefully balancing my glass. I've become very clumsy in my old age. I can totally see this ending badly. But all of the sudden, I'm feeling very confident. A young man fetching me a glass of wine while I lay in a hammock, lakeside—I like it.

"Thank you so much, George. So whatcha needing the wheelbarrow for?" I ask, with my ever-so-slight Southern accent.

"I'm going to make a new walkway on the side of the house and need to move some sand. Always some project with this old house." He takes a big sip of his wine.

"Home ownership, never-ending work, that's for sure," I chime in, all-knowing.

"So, Laney, tell me about you. I know you're from South Carolina, originally from this area, divorced, but that's it."

Well, really, what else is there to know? I'm a boring person.

"Well, let's see. I've done some traveling, love that. I owned a landscaping company for almost twenty years, so if you need some help with that sidewalk, I'm your girl."

He shakes his head, seeming impressed.

"I have two children. Kerry is twenty and Jake is twenty-two, both in college. The apples of my eye. Really, they are my greatest accomplishment in life."

"That's really nice. They're lucky to have you as their mom."

Thanks, George, I could probably be your mom too. "What about you, George, what's your story? What do you and Abe do all day?" I can't wait to hear this.

"We own a computer software company. Olsen Technologies. Have you heard of us? We're pretty huge in Falcon Lake," he says, laughing.

"Oh wait, THE Olsen Technologies? Holy cow! I can't believe it's you, sitting here with me. I'm impressed," I say, acting shocked and in awe.

We're both laughing now. He's a funny guy...kid. Still can't make out his age. Should I just ask him? I've got nothing to lose.

"So George, how old does one have to be to run such a huge technology company?" Too forward? Oh geez, I hope not.

"I'm thirty-four." Okay, so I've got fourteen years on him. Happens all the time in Hollywood.

"Wow, thirty-four. I haven't seen that year in a long time. You look so much younger. Do people tell you that all the time? I bet they do." Uh oh. The wine is kicking in. I get very talkative when I drink. Jim complained about that all the time.

"Yeah, it's an Olsen curse. We all look younger than we are. Come on now, I can't imagine it's been that long since you've seen thirty-four. I wouldn't put you a day over thirty-nine."

Smooth, Mr. Olsen. I almost spit out my drink.

"Why, thank you, George. I don't want to concern you, but I believe there may be a problem with your vision." I'm laughing; he's not.

"You shouldn't be so hard on yourself. I truly have no idea how old you are, but I can say, I think you look great."

Oh my. I'm blushing. I'm sure I'm as red as my pinot.

"I really appreciate that." I turn and face the lake. The sun is starting to set, and a group of geese fly over the lake. So beautiful. "You are so lucky to live on such a beautiful lake. I mean, does it get any better than this?" As I turn back, George is finishing off his wine and standing.

"I can think of a few things better than this, but I digress. I'll put the glasses back in the house, let you get back to your book, and grab the wheelbarrow." He takes my glass and does just that. Before leaving he comes back to the hammock, pushing the wheelbarrow.

"Thanks, Laney. I hope that's the first of many glasses of wine we will have together in the next couple of months." I think my mouth is open, but there is no noise coming out. I adjust myself in the hammock.

"Thanks, George, I really enjoyed that. Question, do your super powers work while your have a wheelbarrow in your hands?"

He laughs. "No, unfortunately, I haven't mastered that yet. Goodnight, Laney."

"Goodnight, George."

Is this still just my first full day here? Wow. I feel like the tides are turning. This is my time. This next chapter of my life is going to be exciting, damn it! I can feel it!

Chapter Twelve

Just as expected, it's pouring out. Even some thunder and lightning. I'm not good at sitting around, especially alone. I like to keep busy. Maybe I will go see that new romantic comedy that's out. I check the theater times online. There's a show at one. Perfect! I call Grace to see if she'd like to join me. Going to the movies together is our thing. We love to put chocolate covered peanuts on top of our popcorn.

"Laney, oh I wish I could. I'm watching the baby today. Kyle and Emily had to go to a funeral, and you know I can't say no to my kids. And certainly not to my grandbaby," she says in a cooing voice, obviously speaking to six-month-old Clara. "It is a perfect day for a movie, isn't it?"

"It really is. Next time! I'm here for two whole months. I can't wait to meet Baby Clara! I can't believe she's six months already!"

"You'll meet this angel baby the week after next. I can't wait for you to see her in person…the computer does her cuteness no justice."

"I can't wait either, Grace. Hey, I heard about the 5K and banquet next week. Are you running the 5K or just going to the banquet or both?" I ask.

"I'll be working at the 5K, not running this time. And yes, I'll be at the banquet. Put so much work into this fundraiser."

Grace puts so much work into everything. She's so creative and so giving of her time.

"I'm sure the banquet will be great. Love you, Grace, talk to you tomorrow."

Thank goodness I bought these new rain boots. These are something I know I couldn't wear around Jim without him mocking me in some way. What Jim lacked in complimenting me, he more than made up for in making fun of me. I don't know if it was just his way of showing me his love or if he really did look at me as someone to make fun of. Looking back, I realize he was just a real jerk.

Wow, the rain is really coming down. Thank goodness the theater is nearby. I park as close to the door as possible and walk through some puddles confidently in my rain boots. Part of me wants to jump in the puddles like I did when I was a kid. Then a sudden boom of thunder reminds me to get inside quickly.

I place my umbrella in the stand by the door and head to the ticket counter. This place is a ghost town. Makes sense. It's Tuesday at 1:00 p.m. The white-haired lady behind the counter sells me my ticket. How convenient, she's also working the concession stand.

"I'll have a small bucket of popcorn and some chocolate covered peanuts," I say confidently, as if she knows all about my and Grace's great concoction.

She hands me my food and I head into the theater. I'm the only one here. Perfect! I sit right in the middle, three rows from the back. This is so bizarre. The movie starts in five minutes. I may be the only one in here! Well, that makes going to the movies alone a lot less uncomfortable. I grab my water out of my purse. I'm not about to spend $2 on water when I have a twenty-four pack sitting in my refrigerator at home!

I'm comfortable, settled in. Ready for romance and laughter. The previews have started and all of the sudden, a bright light from the rear of the theater. Damn it! Someone is coming in, ruining my solo theater experience. I glance over my shoulder to see who it is. Please don't let it be a couple of lovebirds. That would be horrible. Nope. Just a guy, alone. Oh boy, hope he's not some kind of perv. Light flashes from the screen, giving me a better look at my co-theater patron. Holy shit…I sit up. Oh my, oh my. It's him. Brady. You have got to be kidding me. He scans the theater and spots me. He looks a little startled at first and stops in his tracks. He must have thought he was alone too. Then I see him squint a little, waiting for the light to hit me. When it does, he says, "Laney Simms? Is that you?"

I can't even believe this.

"Brady? What are you doing here?" In my theater, alone with me. Thank goodness I was here first, because if this had happened the other way around, I'm sure he would have thought I was back to my stalking ways.

"The storm's horrible, can't work today. Do you mind if I sit with you?" He asks as he is in the middle of taking the seat next to me.

"Oh yeah, sure, of course. Lucky for you, there are still seats available," I say, trying to break the ice.

He gives a little chuckle. Oh, there they are. The dimples. Gosh, they seem deeper than ever today. I want to kiss those dimples.

"The curse of living in a small town: only two movies playing and one is animated."

What? I'm sorry, did your dimples say something?

"That does stink, but I love romantic comedies."

I smile at him, hopefully not creepy-like. I feel like my smile might have been creepy looking. I need to relax. I've got nothing to win and nothing to lose with this guy. Just breathe and enjoy the moment Laney.

I pour my chocolate-covered peanuts on top of my still warm popcorn. I notice he has popcorn too. "Would you like some peanuts on your popcorn?" I motion, showing him my amazing popcorn bucket.

"Really? I never thought of doing that," he responds with a look of intrigue in his eyes.

"Oh yeah, it's all the rage. I highly recommend it. The salt/sugar combo of each bite is divine," I say, like a saleswoman.

"Oh really, divine?" He smirks.

"Yes, sir. You want to experience it or what?"

"I'll take you up on your nut offer, Ms. Simms."

"Here you go, Mr. Gramble, enjoy." I shake the remainder of my box of nuts onto his popcorn. He takes a handful and looks at me while he's chewing with a big goofy smile on his face.

"You are right, this is divine."

I smack his arm. We both laugh, but it's time to quiet down; the movie is about to start. This is going well. I'm hoping he doesn't view me as a stalker anymore. Hopefully, enough time has passed.

The movie is so full of romance and sexual tension I can't even stand it. At times, I'm squirming in my seat, even breaking out in a sweat at one point during the sex scene. I'm trying to keep my eyes on the screen, but I'm curious about his reaction as to what is going on. I look over at him nonchalantly. He turns from the screen and is facing me. Deer in the headlights. I smile; he smiles back and laughs a little. Oh, Lord, what is going through his mind? I know what's going through mine!

All of the sudden he's in my ear. "What do you think of the movie so far?" He whispers, like there are other people in the theater.

"I like it. A lot," I whisper back, looking straight into those beautiful green eyes.

Holy crap, the sexual tension. I don't know if he feels it on his side, but I'm about to jump out of my skin. Then, suddenly…BOOM! The whole theater shakes and the screen goes black. I let out a small screech. Then, without even realizing, I grab hold of Brady's entire arm and hold on so tight. About ten seconds later, the sound system makes a gargled sound, and then poof! The movie is back up. In the light of the screen, I realize I'm still clinging to Brady's arm like a scared little kid.

"Oops, sorry about that. That scared the crap out of me." I start to pull my arm back when he stops me.

"No, you can keep it there. Really." He squeezes my hand and wraps it back under his arm.

Holy crap, is this really happening? Tides are a changing, Laney. Time to take chances, make your move. You only live once. I lean in and put my head on his arm. Oh, is this too much? Am I going to weird him out? Am I being too aggressive? I am pleasantly surprised when he leans over and kisses my forehead.

No, no, no. The movie is over. Time to release my vice grip on Brady's arm. "Did you like it?" he asks.

"I loved it. How about you?" I respond, not talking about the movie.

"I liked it a lot too." We stand up, and I feel almost dizzy. It's been so long since I've felt this way or held on to a man's arm like that. I am on a high right now and I don't want to come down. We walk out of the theater and stand under the entrance awning. It's no longer thundering and lightning, but still raining.

"So, what are your plans for the rest of the day?" I ask, hoping he says all he wants to do is take me to bed.

"I actually have to pick up my son and take him to basketball practice. I have him every Tuesday and Wednesday, and every other weekend."

"That's great. What's his name? How old is he?"

"His name is Jeremy. He's seventeen, going on thirty. Thinks he know more than his dad," he says, smiling.

"They all think they know more than their parents. Jeremy. That's a nice name. Well, enjoy your time with your son. I know how valuable that time is."

"It really is. He's a good kid, but I can see how the divorce has affected him. As long as my ex and I remain in constant communication with him, I think he'll be okay. He tends to be a loner. We are constantly trying to bring him out of his shell. That's why he's playing basketball."

What a good dad, I think to myself.

"How about you? You mentioned at the diner that you have two kids."

"Yes, two. Jake and Kerry. They are the loves of my life, but they are both off at college now. I miss them terribly," I answer with a sad face.

"I'm sure you do." Brady pauses, then asks, "Laney, can I have your number? I would love to get together with you again, maybe dinner or another movie? After all, that popcorn concoction was divine," He grins.

"Haha. I knew you would love it! I'm sure you're going to do that from now on. Just remember it was me that introduced it to you. I have my phone right here. Give me your number, and I'll call it, and then you'll have my number." I reach for my phone and try to conceal my excitement. I'm worried my shaky hands will give me away.

After we confirm that his phone rings, we say goodbye. "It was great bumping into you, again," Brady says. Is he blushing? Oh my heart.

"I agree. I'm starting to think you're following me, Brady. Everywhere I go, there you are!" I would hope the huge smile on my face gives me away. He smiles in relief.

"Can't help it, Ms. Simms. I find you very intriguing." Someone put a mattress on the ground behind me, I'm about to faint.

"Well, I'm here to answer any of your questions," I say as I wave my phone at him.

"Bye, Laney," He steps forward and gives me a flash of a kiss on my cheek.

"Bye Brady, see you soon, I hope." Brady follows me to my car, and being a gentleman, he opens my door for me before darting to his truck. I back up and pull away. My face hurts from smiling. Oh, this is good. This is really good.

I go right into town and run into Bohemian Bling. "Allie!"

She runs out from the back of store.

"Isn't today the most beautiful day ever?" I ask while I'm floating on my cloud.

She leads me to the breakroom, where I fill her in.

Chapter Thirteen

"What the fuck? A kiss on the forehead? All the passion in that movie and he kisses you on the forehead?" Allie asks after I tell her about the movie interlude.

"It was nice. I felt safe, like he was protecting me and saying it was okay. I love that sense of security with someone. I've always wanted to be with someone who would protect me." I think back on how alone I really was in my marriage.

"I guess. I would just think, in that moment, that was his chance to shove his tongue down your throat."

"Allie! He's a gentleman…I think. Listen, I really don't even know anything about him. I'm just going to 'keep on keeping on' and see what happens. Again, it's a win-win for me. If I do 'hook up' per se, great! If not, no big deal either. Just experiencing these feelings is enough for me right now."

Allie shrugs, "All I know is I can't wait for Thursday night! Make sure you wear your dancing shoes, because we are going to get down!" We both laugh at the thought.

Thank goodness, the storm has passed. I still feel cold and damp. I look at the gorgeous fireplace in the middle of the room and I decide to start a fire. Perfect. I go out the back deck and down the stairs to a little shed in the side yard. Stacy told me they keep some firewood in there for the fire pit. She also bought me a few starter logs. Thanks, Stacy! :)

I get the fire started rather quickly and am feeling quite proud of myself. Now, what to eat? Hmmm, does anyone deliver around here? I check my phone for restaurants nearby. As I'm checking, I wonder if George would like to join me for dinner. Maybe even the mysterious Abe. I throw my favorite blanket that traveled with me from South Carolina over my shoulders and head next door. There's only one car in the driveway. I pause. Am I really in the mood to meet someone new? What if only Abe is home? I turn on one heel and decide to head back into the house. I'll save that introduction for another time.

"Laney?"

I turn to see George calling for me from the front door.

"Hey, I was walking past the door when I saw you heading over. Everything okay?"

"Oh, yes. Hi George. I didn't think you were home. I was about to order dinner and I was going to see if you wanted anything. Save the delivery guy a trip."

"Where are you ordering from?" he asks with interest.

"Oh, I hadn't really decided yet. Do you have any recommendations?"

"I do. Do you like sushi?" he asks.

"Yes, very much." I reply.

"Well, I'll tell you what. You head back home and I'll be your delivery man. As long as you don't mind sharing?" He looks at me with devilish eyes.

"That sounds good to me! Do you need me to do anything?" I ask politely, hoping he says no.

"Nope, I'm good. Looks like you have a fire started already, so that's perfect. Pinot noir, right?" Oh boy.

"Yes, that would be great." I'm worried where this is headed.

"Okay, I'll see you in a little while." He closes the door and heads back in the house. I head back into mine and sit on the couch, facing the fire. What is this young man up to? He can't possibly be interested in me? I'm too old, I mean mature, for him. I'm sure he's got girls chasing him on a daily basis. Plus, after the forehead and cheek kiss, I'm feeling pretty committed to Brady. I giggle to myself even thinking that. Oh, what the hell. I'm single and ready to mingle.

My thoughts are distracted by a *ding-dong*. A new text. Probably Allie. I head to my purse to retrieve my phone. A text from a number with no name associated with it.

My right arm is still sore from being mauled at the movies today, but I wouldn't have it any other way. Do you have any plans for Thursday night? I was thinking dinner. Let me know, Brady.

Oh my, oh my. My heart is racing. 'I wouldn't have it any other way.' I can't believe he texted me!! This is an exciting development. Okay, simmer down, simmer down. I feel like a teenager again. I need a clever response, but first, Thursday, Thursday…crap! I'm supposed to go out with Allie. Do I cancel on her? No, I can't. I'm looking forward to it too much. This may be the perfect opportunity to play a little hard to get. Make it interesting.

Oh, but I want to be with him so bad. Shoot. Okay, here it goes:

> That was my first time jumping someone in a dark theater, but I'm sure it won't be my last. I would have loved to do something with you on Thursday night, but I already have plans to go out with Allie. Another time for sure.

I am on fire. I feel like a guy magnet! What is happening here? This kind of stuff just doesn't happen to me. I am loving it. I'm just going to sit back and enjoy it. *Ding-dong…*

> That's too bad. Maybe we should go to the movies together again. I want to increase the odds of it being me that you jump.

I'm dying to respond again, but I want to play it cool. For too many years this guy saw me going gaga over him every day in school. This time, I'm going to be very adult about it. But for now, while nobody's looking, I'm going to jump up and down screaming. "Yayyyyyyy!"

After I come back down to Earth, I remember I'm having dinner delivered. I head back to the bathroom to check my face. Goodness, look at all those lines. I pull my hair over my forehead a little to cover the deepest of them. Put on some lip gloss. That's enough. I think I may even keep my throw over my shoulders. It's one of those nights.

Plus, I feel like I have zero pressure to be anything but myself in front of George. Thirty-four is awfully young. I'm sure if he knew my exact age, he wouldn't be as eager to get me sushi on a cold, rainy night.

There's a knock on the door and there's George, with a bottle of wine, the bag of food, and a bouquet of flowers. My stomach does a little flip. Crap. Does he think this is a date?

"I saw these flowers in the store and couldn't pass them up. Isn't that a great combo of flowers? I was hoping to get your landscape input because I want these colors along my new sidewalk."

Whew. Oh, good, not a romantic gesture. Just using my professional eye for his landscaping project. Pressure is off.

"I do like these colors a lot. And, depending on the color stone you use, you can really make them pop." I release the breath that I didn't realize I was holding. "Come on in. It was so nice of you to do this. You are really spoiling me, George. I may need to move you down to South Carolina so you can be my neighbor there!" I say, half-joking. A neighbor who likes to serve me wine, baked goods, and dinner. I could get used to that. He's also easy on the eyes.

"I love South Carolina. We used to go to Hilton Head on vacation when I was a little kid. It's beautiful there, but so hot in the summer," he says with a reflective look on his face.

"Tell me about it. That is the only thing I don't like about South Carolina. The hot and humid summers. But not having snow and cold winters makes up for it for me. I do not miss snow at all." I respond with absolute certainty. "Let's set up on the island."

"I think Stacy keeps some vases in this cabinet over here." George reaches into a cabinet above the refrigerator. I notice his calf muscles as he stands on his toes to reach the vase. Yep, those are runner's calves for sure. Nice. As George cuts the flowers down and places them in a vase, I'm setting up the island for a nice, not necessarily romantic, dinner. I open up the two boxes of sushi.

"Wow, this looks delicious. Good choices, George."

He joins me at the island and we dig in. "So, George, tell me more about Abe. Will I ever get to meet this elusive fellow?"

George laughs. "He's really not that elusive, Laney. You've only been here two days."

Geez, only two days. He's right. I feel like I've already experienced more in two days than I have in two years back home.

"That's true. I guess I just thought since you are brothers you would be more alike. I guess he's not on the welcoming committee, like you are."

"Abe is just more comfortable at home. He knows how to relax. Unlike me, I have to constantly be doing something. I used to always come over here and bug Stacy and John. So now that you're here, you're my new person to bug," he says with a cute little sushi smile.

"Well, so far you've brought me a baked good, served me wine in the hammock, and now this delicious dinner. You can bug me as much as you like!" We laugh and take sips of our wine.

"No, really, Abe is a good guy. Just much more reserved. I'm sure you'll meet him soon enough. I meant to mention to you; did you hear about the 5K next week on the other side of the lake?"

"I did!" I think back fondly on how I first heard about it. "I am doing it. What about you? Do you run?" I ask, knowing damn well that he does.

"I haven't decided yet. I've been having some foot pain and I'm thinking I may not want to push it. There are other races coming up that I would rather run."

"Then you should let your foot heal. I've had problems with my feet before and rest seemed to be the only thing to make it better," says the old lady who has tons of experience with pain. Part of me doesn't want George there. I want to focus all my attention on Brady. I wonder what his calves look like. Focus, Laney, focus.

We finish up dinner. Part of me would just like to be alone, but George suggests we move to the couch by the fire. George is really at home here. He puts another log on the fire and has a seat on the couch, not right next to me, but sitting sideways so as to face me. He must spend a lot of time here; he knows where everything is. Hmmm. "So, tell me more about your plans while you are here." George strikes up a conversation.

"Oh, nothing too exciting. This trip is really about spending some quality time with my friends. I don't get to see them very often, so I'm really looking forward to my time with them. I have the best friends," I say, smiling.

"That's great." George goes on to talk about his friends from Vermont and his friends from college. I just sit, shaking my head and acting super interested in the words coming out of his mouth. In the back of my mind, I'm only thinking about one thing. One person. One kiss on the forehead. One kiss on the cheek. Snap, here I go again.

Just like the girl in high school. Obsessed with Brady Gramble without knowing a thing about Brady Gramble, other than he's hot and he makes me feel things I haven't felt in a long, long time. I'm starting to think I haven't felt this way since then. I don't remember Jim making me feel this way. I can't imagine George having that effect on me. He's adorable, but he's young, so young. I hear our age difference in the conversation we're having right now.

Or should I say the conversation he's having right now? Gosh, this guy likes talking about himself. George wraps up and I'm pretty sure I've only heard about a third of what he's said.

"Well, this old lady needs some sleep. George, thank you so very much for dinner. Wait, let me get my purse. I want to pay for it. It's the least I can do." I stand and walk toward my purse on the kitchen counter.

"No, really Laney, my treat. Compliments of Olsen Technologies. You can get dinner next time." Oh, is there going to be a next time?

"Okay, thanks, George. I've got it next time for sure." I start walking toward to door to show him out. George awkwardly leans toward me. I give him a hug. A nice, motherly hug. "Thanks again, George, that was very sweet of you. See you tomorrow, I'm sure!"

"I hope so," he replies as he walks out the door. Whew! I'm so glad there wasn't a kiss involved there. I'm not ready for that. Well, not with George.

Chapter Fourteen

The sun is shining off the lake again like little diamonds. A beautiful September morning. I bring my coffee onto the deck, dry off a chair, sit down, and enjoy the view. What to do today, what to do today? Maybe I'll go out and do some shopping. I do need a new outfit for tomorrow night. I wonder what Grace is up to? I send her a text, unsure if she's awake yet.

> Up for some shopping today? Need a slutty outfit for a bar night tomorrow night.

I love pushing Grace's buttons. Although I'm a few months older than Grace, she's always been the more mature, proper, rule-follower. Very conservative compared to me. But opposites attract and that's why we've been friends since first grade.

> Oh my, I can help you with that. But not too slutty, dear, we don't want the locals talking.

> How about I pick you up at 11?

> That works for me, see you then!

Yay! A shopping day with a dear friend. I finish up my coffee, still in a waking-up daze, when I hear it. *Boom! Boom! Boom!* Oh my, the dock boys are back. There's Brady, working the big piece of machinery, Pete directing his moves. I wonder if Brady told Pete about the movies? Do guys talk about stuff like that? Knowing guys, they probably didn't. I head inside and start to get ready for my shopping day.

Grace's car was due to be serviced, so I picked her up at the local garage.

"Good thing you have an SUV. I'm ready to shop until I drop!" She enters the car with great shopping enthusiasm.

"Me too, sister!" We hug and sit back and smile at each other. The years have been annoyingly good to Grace. She in no way looks old enough to be a grandmother.

"So what have you been up to, single woman on the town?"

I'm almost hesitant to tell her. She never got my obsession with Brady back in high school. She didn't need to be obsessed with anyone, because so many guys were obsessed with her. Boyfriends were always available to her. Not me. I had tons of friends that were guys, but none of them obviously had interest in me in that way; otherwise they would have asked me out. Jim was the first guy who showed interest in me. He came on so strong, like the player that he is. And it worked. It's okay, I was always happy for Grace and interested in her relationships. I learned a lot just from watching her.

"Well," I start, "I bumped into Pete Murdough and Brady Gramble the other day at Henry's. I can't believe how different Pete looked!" I try to take the attention away from Brady. I cringe waiting to hear her reaction.

"Oh Lord, Brady Gramble! Remember how much you loved that guy in high school?" She giggles. "Is he still a lump on a log?"

What the…don't you talk about my Brady like that!

"No, what do you mean 'lump on a log'?" I ask, defensive.

"Oh, please, Laney, the guy obviously knew you had it bad for him and he never even gave you the time of day. He was so emotionless. Rude really. At least throw a girl a smile or something. Geez." She is all fired up. Grace has always been my defender: motherly and protective.

"Ah, he was a kid. I'm sure I scared the living crap out of him anyway. I mean, really, I acted like a total love sick puppy," I say, in an attempt to defend Brady.

"Whatever, he was a jerk to you. How's Pete doing? I see him every now and again. He's so sweet. Now there's a guy that had a total crush on you."

"Oh, please, that was eighth grade, Grace. We never even kissed or talked for that matter. Then a year later he was with Jean and that was the end of that," I say, dismissing her silly statement.

"It doesn't matter that he met Jean. Hell, he still had it bad for you on your wedding day. I saw the way he looked at you. He has never gotten over you; you were his first love!"

I never got those vibes from Pete. He always seemed very content with Jean. Grace is just trying to get my mind off Brady. I know how she rolls.

"Well, Brady looked as fine as ever. He even asked me to dinner some time." Take that.

"Maybe you should let him do the stalking now. Get a little payback."

"Not a bad idea," I say, but little does she know, that's already in the works.

Grace and I have a lovely day shopping. Laughing with my friends is the best. We really enjoy each other's company. I pick up a cute top that hangs off one shoulder and is slightly form-fitting, but Grace assures me that it's as slutty as I should get at my age. I agree. With jeans and some new strappy-heeled sandals, I think I look halfway decent. "How about tomorrow we get our hair done, manis, and pedis?" Grace asks with excitement.

"Well, that sounds divine, dahling," I respond with an English accent.

"Great! I know a fantastic salon. I'll make the appointments for us. Is anytime good tomorrow?" she asks with phone in hand.

"Yeppers, any time works for me!" The beauty of having financial freedom is so appreciated at times like these. Back in the old days, I was lucky if I was able to get a pedicure once a year. Not just because money was tight, but also because I just didn't have the time. Now, thanks to Grandma, I can live a very comfortable life.

Grace has always lived comfortably. Her dad was given a seat on the stock exchange as a gift from his father many, many years ago. He was a millionaire by the time he was twenty-five! Grace and her family have been so generous to everyone, but especially me. I didn't have much growing up. Came from a working-class family. My dad made sure we never did without, but we just never had too much. Grace's family included me in everything: vacations down to the Jersey shore, parties at their house. They really spoiled me and Grace still tries.

Chapter Fifteen

I drop Grace off at the garage and head back to the lake. I drop my purchases on the bed, grab my book from the nightstand, and head to the hammock. This time, I promise I'm going to get some reading done. It's around four o'clock now, and I don't hear any noises coming from the dock boys. Darn it. Looks like they've wrapped things up for the day. That's okay. I really do want to do some reading. An hour later, I wake up from what I guess was a needed nap. The buzz of my phone startled me.

> Hope you enjoy your nap. You sure do look comfortable over there. Came back because I forgot something—sorry to miss seeing you awake.

I look over to see if by any chance he's still there, but he's not. How embarrassing! He must think I'm such a bum. Oh well. I head back into the house when my phone rings. Elise!

"Want to meet me for dinner? My schedule has cleared and I can't wait until next week to see you!" Elise and Scott are new empty-nesters. Both of their girls are in college now. It's hard to believe. Seems like just yesterday our four little ones were playing board games together. Time goes by too fast.

I freshen up, grab my purse, and head out the door. I meet up with Elise at this cute, eccentric restaurant in the town next to Falcon Lake called Hanover. When I see Elise, it feels like I just saw her yesterday. We pick up right where we left off. Elise fills me in on some of the dirt going on with her staff at the high school, and I fill her in on my latest rendezvous. "I remember being your right hand man in your stalking efforts of Brady. Remember that time we drove past his house, and he was outside, and you ducked under the dash?" Elise laughs.

"I know, it wouldn't have been as bad if I wasn't driving!" I remember that incident well. We had to pull off the road after we were clear of Brady's house. We were screaming and laughing so hard, we could barely breathe.

"Good times, good times," I say, remembering it with a smile.

We spend the next two hours reminiscing.

"Hey, Allie and I are going out tomorrow night, some bar that has half-price drinks. Can you join us?" I know she can't, but I don't want her to feel left out.

"I wish. Wouldn't be responsible of a principal to come to school hungover." She seems disappointed.

"Well, next time we'll plan for a Friday or Saturday night. That way you can come. We'll be partying at the 5K next Saturday morning! Woo hoo!" I say swinging my arm in the air. "And thank you again in advance for running with me. I know that's going to kill you being that you're so darn competitive!"

Elise laughs in agreement. "Nah. I've lost my competitive edge, Laney. I'm a go with the flow kind of girl now." Elise looks tired.

"Everything okay, Elise? You seem, I don't know, tired?" I ask cautiously.

"I am, Laney. Exhausted really. This job is getting to be overwhelming, but with the girls gone, I guess it's good for me to stay busy. I can't wait for them to graduate and come back home!"

"I'm sorry you're going through this. Let me know if I can help you in any way, please. Take advantage of me being here and come hang out with me whenever you want!" I say, squeezing her hand.

"I will, thanks. But for now, I need to go to bed!" With that, we leave the restaurant and head home in opposite directions.

Chapter Sixteen

I wake up nice and early, throw my blanket over my shoulders, and head out to the dock with my coffee. The sun is just starting to rise. I sit on the end of the dock and just take it all in. It's so beautiful and peaceful here. I could live on a lake easily. Ducks flying in formation, birds just starting their morning calls, a few fisherman in the distance casting from their boats. Ah. I am at peace.

I think about my day ahead. Spa time with Grace. Allie's coming over for some appetizers; then it's off to the bar for us. I'm feeling very blessed right now.

As I'm finishing my last sip of coffee, I see a kayak headed my way from around the cove. Seems like it's coming right toward the dock. At the last second, it turns and heads to George's dock. Oh, it's George. I wave and he nods back.

Wait a second, I try to readjust my morning eyes. Is it George? Looks just like him, but in a different way. Is this the elusive Abe? I watch as he turns the kayak alongside his dock, hops out, and pulls the kayak out of the water. Doesn't even glance my way. I'm waiting eagerly for him to give me some kind of greeting, but nope. He walks across his backyard, up the deck, and into the house.

Are you kidding me? A nod. That's it? What a weirdo! How can you be so unfriendly? I know I'm only temporary, but geez buddy, you can throw me a wave at least. Oh well. I'm not going to let that jerk ruin my day.

I head back up to the house and get ready for my day. The thought of going to Henry's for breakfast goes through my head. Hmmm. That would be too darn obvious, wouldn't it? I decide I need to stick to my plan of playing a little hard to get. Keep him guessing. Have him looking over to see if I'm in the hammock or not. Yes, this is my time to be stalked. He owes me!

***

Well, Grace was right; she does know a great hair stylist! I got my toes and fingernails painted a really cool, fun, purplish color. Because that's me: cool and fun! Now off to the store to buy some appetizers for me and Allie. I scan the store as soon as I walk in, looking hard at people's faces. I'm sure I went to school with some of these folks. No, no one looks familiar. Too bad. I'm loving bumping into people from my past. Especially when my hair is looking so fine. I giggle on the inside at even thinking that. I head home with my groceries and get food ready for me and Allie.

Allie arrives in all her glory a couple of hours later. "Let's get this par-tay started!" She yells upon entering with a bottle of liquor in tow. "Look at you, Laney girl, you are smoking hot!" She holds my hand out and looks me up and down. "Tonight's your night, girl. You are going to get luckyyyy!"

I bust out laughing. "Ew, I don't want to get lucky. I want to have fun!" I must say, I am feeling pretty good about myself tonight. All of this running and only cooking for one has me comfortably fitting into my size eight jeans.

"You look great yourself! I'm sure you will be the one to get lucky tonight, woman!" I say to Allie, feeling very certain about that.

"Yeah, I know. I probably will. But just in case, I brought stuff to sleep over if that's okay. I plan on getting pretty toasted!" We laugh again.

"That would be great if you slept over. Just like high school!" But a lot different, because I think she plans on bringing a guy with her! "Well if you're planning on drinking a lot, make sure you eat some carbs," I push a plate to her, mothering her.

"I brought you some of your favorite sweet tea vodka, you Southern Belle." She hands me the bottle.

I do love this stuff. I quickly open the bottle, mix a couple of shots with some lemonade and crushed ice, and we toast to a fun night. Just then, the doorbell rings.

"Who can that be?" Allie asks.

I look over toward the door and see George.

"It's the cutie from next door, George."

"Well, let that little boy in!" Allie says in a hysterical tone. I open the door laughing. George takes a step back on one foot and laughs in return nervously.

"Hey, Laney, sorry to bother you. I see you have company." He leans his head in the door a little, just enough to see Allie waving at him. He waves back with a warm smile.

"No worries, George, come on in. This is my dear friend, Allie. We've been friends for about a hundred years now."

George walks over and shakes Allie's hand. "Hi, Allie, nice to meet you."

"The pleasure is all mine, George," Allie says in a sexy cougar tone. No wonder she's getting lucky all the time. She can really lay it on thick!

George turns back to me. "Laney, do you mind? I need to borrow Stacy's juicer. It's just over here in the closet." George makes his way to the hall closet and comes out with the juicer. "Another big item Stacy and I share. Hey, I just want to say I'm sorry for Abe being so rude this morning. He told me he didn't introduce himself or even say hello. He has been so out of sorts lately. Who am I kidding, lately...he's been this way a long time now. He's really difficult to live with at times, but rudeness is unacceptable and I just wanted to say I'm sorry." George looks down then looks back at me with these dreamy, puppy dog eyes.

"Oh, please, George, no apology necessary. Really. He was at the end of what looked like a very strenuous work out, and it was early. No big deal. Not a great situation to meet someone in. It's okay, another time. Can I get you some sweet tea, George?" I ask, desperately trying to lighten the mood.

"No, no, you get back to your quality time with Allie. I'm meeting up with some friends later, so I want to save my liver until then," he says with his boyish grin.

"Well, you have fun and be safe," I say in my motherly tone.

"So nice to meet you, George. Maybe I'll see you around." Allie shakes his hand slowly, almost purring like a kitten.

"Have a good night, ladies." George turns and leaves.

"Okay, you've been here for, like, four days and you haven't made the move on that young hot thing?"

"No, no. I'm pretty sure he's too young for me. He's great company, definitely easy on the eyes, but he's not doing it for me. You know what I mean?" I ask the relationship expert.

"I guess. Plus, you are still so hot for Brady. That doesn't help."

She's right. I may be denying myself a good time by overlooking pretty decent guys because of my obsession with the idea of Brady Gramble. It's high school all over again. But I do have to say, the texts from Brady have really made me like, like him. A lot. His texts are adorable. And the way he kissed my forehead at the movie theater. Ah.

"Snap out of it, Laney! You ready to go?" Allie snaps her fingers in front of my face.

"I am, what time is it? I have a little surprise scheduled." I say, checking my phone for the time.

"What is it, what is it?" Allie says like a little girl. I peek out the front window.

"Nothing major, I just got us a car with a driver tonight so we don't have to worry about driving." Outside is a black sedan with dark tinted windows. A gentleman with a suit is standing outside of it.

"That is so cool! We are going to be the talk of Falcon Lake for a long time, that's for sure." We head out, hungry cougars. I'm thankful that we're not orange or married, like the skanks of Facebook. The driver opens the door for us and we're on our way.

Chapter Seventeen

"Seriously, Allie, this is the bar? The Bird's Nest?" I ask, trying not to sound too skeptical.

"Oh, don't worry, it's safe. I'm telling you, this place is all the rage. Come on now, let's go make some memories."

The driver opens the door for us and we step out. We definitely get a couple of looks, but we act like it's completely natural for a couple of middle aged women, dressed on the slutty side, to take a limo to a bar called The Bird's Nest. As we approach the entrance for the bar, I can already hear the music blaring. Sounds like some good old country rock. Right up my alley. We walk in, and of course, it's a little on the dark side. We're getting bumped around a little bit, trying to make our way to the bar. Allie says hi to a couple of people she knows, but as of yet, I don't recognize anyone. There are tall bar tables surrounding the bar, plus stools all around the bar.

The place is hopping for a Thursday night, that's for sure. We finally reach the bar and order our drinks.

"Allie, the drinks are on me."

I give the bartender my card to start a tab. Allie knows better than to argue with me. She gives me a quick hug and thanks me. As we stand and toast each other, I take my first sip and glance around the bar. I see a table on the other side of the bar with some big guys around it. They catch my eye because I see a beard. Then I see the belly. I quickly scan the other faces. Yes! He's here. My heart jumps into my throat and I almost choke on my drink.

I lean over to the barmaid. "See that big table of guys over there, the one with the bearded guy?" She nods. "Send them over a round on me and throw it on my tab, please?" She nods again. No use speaking, you can barely hear a thing.

"Allie!" I shout. "You're not going to believe who's here!"

She looks at me with eyes wide open. "Brady? He's here?" She shares in my excitement.

I love that about her.

"I just sent his table a round of drinks," I say, smiling so big my face hurts.

"Oh, good one. Let's watch their reaction."

We both look that way just as the barmaid delivers the drinks. I see her head motion back our way as she leans in and tells someone at the table where the drinks are from. At that instant, all four guys at the table arch their necks to see who treated them to these drinks. I only see Brady's face. If I'm not mistaken, his face seems to brighten and he smiles. They all simultaneously lift their drinks as if to toast me and Allie. We lift our drinks in return and laugh.

"I think that's Paul Laryn and Steve Sulte with Brady and Pete," Allie informs me. I haven't seen Paul and Steve since high school. I considered them both pretty good friends. Paul graduated with Allie and I, and Steve graduated a year ahead of us with Brady.

I look back at the table and see that Brady has walked away. I quickly pan through the crowd, trying to spot him, when I see him walking toward us.

Allie grabs my arm and says in my ear, "I'm feeling the urge to have to go to the bathroom. I'm going to leave you two alone."

What? No, you don't have to do that Allie...he still makes me nervous, I think to myself. I haven't really even spoken to him. It's so easy to be clever texting, but this is the real deal. I give Allie my stink eye, but she says hello to Brady in passing and walks away. I have my back to the bar and he comes and stands right in front of me. The band has taken a break and the volume of the stereo is much more bearable.

He leans into my ear. "Looks like I get lucky and get to see you tonight after all. You look amazing."

I feel the hairs on my neck stand up and suddenly feel very hot.

I lean back into him, "Don't think this gets you out of taking me to dinner," I say with a smirk on my face.

"Oh, don't you worry, I'm still going to take you out." Just then, the music slows and my favorite country song is playing. "Will you dance with me, Laney?" he asks with sex filled eyes.

"I'd love to, Brady."

He takes me by the hand and leads me through the crowd to the dance floor. Gosh, I haven't even slow danced with a man in as long as I can remember. Who can remember anything right now? I'm lost in this man's eyes and dimples. I wrap my arms around his neck and he wraps his around my waist. I'd like for this song to last forever.

"I missed seeing you in the hammock today. Makes my work day a heck of lot more interesting hoping to see you there, and I have to say, it sucks when I don't."

Is this for real? He's saying all the right things. Everything I ever dreamed that he would say to me one day. I'm just taking it all in, trying real hard not to blush beet red. I hear Grace in my head saying, "Just thank him, don't say anything back, keep the upper hand…let him chase you." She's right. I have to play this cool.

"You are too sweet," I say, smiling at him. He's smiling back at me with such intensity. I don't even feel the floor under my feet anymore. I am floating. The song nears the last few notes. We stop moving but are still wrapped in each other's arms. He leans down and kisses me, so softly, on the lips. We part and we're both just beaming. I know that's what I've been waiting for, but he has a look on his face like he's been waiting for the same thing. I give him a hug and we walk hand and hand off the dance floor. As we approach the bar, I see Allie talking to some woman.

I squeeze Brady's hand and lean up to his ear. "I need to spend some time with Allie. I hope that's okay?" I say with a scrunched-up face.

"Absolutely. Just promise me you'll save me the next slow dance, okay?"

"I sure will."

He leans down and gives me another kiss and we part. Perfect, perfect dance.

I head back to Allie, feeling like my heart is going to jump out of my chest. I've got to cool down though. I don't want Brady seeing the effect he has over me. I need to play a little hard to get, but mostly I just want to jump up and down screaming!!

"I think that dance went pretty well," Allie says, elbowing me in the arm.

"Holy crap, you know I'm screaming on the inside, but really Allie, I want to play this cool. Like it was just like any other dance," I say, talking through my teeth.

"Good idea, because he's looking over here. Oh, so is the rest of the table."

I barely glance in that direction, when I hear over my other shoulder, "Hey Laney, hey Allie!" We both turn in unison and there stands George.

"Hey, George, long time no see," Allie purrs.

"I had a feeling I was going to bump into you ladies here. Can I buy you ladies a drink?"

"No, George, let me get you a drink. It's the least I can do since you bought dinner the other night."

Allie shoots me a questionable glance. Did I forget to tell her about that?

She whispers in my ear, "You can fill me in on that one later."

I ask George what he'd like and lean over the bar to yell his drink to the barmaid. While waiting, my eyes can't help but glance over to Brady's table. He's looking right at me, as if asking, who's that guy?

I hand George his drink and we toast, "To lovely ladies and good times."

"Cheers," we say together.

"Hey, George, I thought you were going out with some friends?" I ask, looking around him.

"Yes, over there, by the back corner of the bar."

I see three young guys and Abe standing in the corner, looking like they are having a very serious conversation.

"They seem like they are having a blast!" I say.

The three of us laugh.

"Yeah, I better head back and lighten the mood. Thanks for the drink. Maybe I'll see you two on the dance floor later." He glances back and forth between the two of us.

"Sure thing," replies Allie, giving him her sexy stare.

"Things are really getting exciting now!" says Allie, watching George walk back to his group of friends and the elusive Abe.

"Do you have a crush on the youngin'?" I tease.

"I wouldn't say it's a crush, but I would like to get my hands on him."

We both bust out laughing. I've got to slow down on my drinking. Between the alcohol and my adrenalin, I'm starting to feel a little loopy. I grab a water from the bartender and chug it down. I tap Allie's shoulder. She is already talking to the guy standing next to us.

"I'm going to go to the ladies' room. Do you need to go?"

"No, I'm good. I'll be here," she says and turns back to her conversation with the older-looking gentleman.

Chapter Eighteen

'm happy to get away from that music blaring for a few minutes. Maybe I am really getting old. I just can't stand when the music is so loud you can't even have a conversation with anyone. The bathroom is on the other side of the building. There's a nice seating area and fireplace away from the bar and the music. This place really is quite nice. I head into the ladies' room and of course, there's a line. Always. I look at the young girls adjusting their hair and makeup in the mirror. Then I think I see one of the orange skanks from Facebook. She looks at me through the mirror and has a look of recognition as well. But we leave it at that. I really just need to use the bathroom.

I wash my hands, put on some lip gloss, and I'm out the door. I look to my left outside the bathroom door and notice a patio area with portable heaters. People are sitting out there smoking. I really like this place. No wonder Allie frequents it here. For Falcon Lake, this place really is happening. As I turn back, I bump smack into Brady.

"Oh my gosh, I'm so sorry! I wasn't paying attention!" I laugh.

Brady grabs me, pushes me against the wall, and begins kissing me with a passion that I feel from my feet to my heart. It's like we are the only two people in The Bird's Nest at that moment, but we are right smack in the middle of the bathroom and smoking crowd. Brady doesn't seem to care, so why should I? I'll never see these people again after a couple of months.

"Wow, do you do that to all the girls that walk into you?" I say, smiling from ear to ear.

"Nope. Only the hot chicks," he says with that dimply grin.

Me? Hot? Oh Lord, is Brady a player? I hope not.

"Are you and Allie having a good time?" he asks, still pinning me against the wall.

"We're having a great time. How about you and your homeboys?" I grin.

"They're getting a little bored, hearing me talk about this girl that's walked back into my life. They say they've never seen me this way. I'm not sure what to do about it," he says, in a deep, sexy voice.

"I could see how that would bore them. I hope she's worth it," I say, knowing damn well he's talking about me but still trying with all my might to play hard to get. Right now though, if he wanted, he could have me; right here against this wall. That's how taken I am with him and everything he's saying. "Well, best of luck with that girl. I need to get back to Allie."

"What am I going to do with you, Laney Simms?"

"Oh, I'm sure you'll figure something out." I wriggle around him and walk away. I force myself not to turn around to see if he's watching me and put a little attitude in my walk. That's right, take that, Brady. Now the tables have turned. It's time for you to start stalking me!

When I get back around the bar where Allie said she would be, she's not there. I look around the bar and then glance to the dance floor. There she is, getting down with George. She is dirty dancing all up on that young man. She cracks me up! Oh well, guess I'll have a drink while I wait because I am not quite drunk enough to be dancing. I turn back toward the bar and a person moving toward me on my right catches my eye. I turn, and there standing next to me, is Abe.

"Hi, Laney. Nice to finally meet you. I'm Abe." He extends his hand for a shake.

"Well, well, if it isn't my elusive neighbor Abe," I say.

"Yeah, sorry I haven't been over. I've been busy trying to run our company while George is out having fun." He motions with his head to George, dancing like a madman. "And on the dock this morning, I really felt you were enjoying your moment. It was so peaceful and quiet. I didn't want to yell between the docks and meet you that way. I hope you weren't offended?" he says.

"No, not at all! So…"

Awkward pause. I can't help but notice how rugged and handsome Abe is. He's not as lean as George. He's more muscular, and his face is more chiseled. The same wavy, sun-kissed blonde hair as George, but everything about him is just more…masculine.

"Why aren't you out there dancing?" I ask, not sure what direction to take our conversation.

"Ha, yeah, I haven't had quite enough to drink yet. I'm a fantastic dancer when I'm drunk. Or at least I think I am." We both laugh.

"Me too! Maybe we should do a shot?" I suggest, while waving the bartender over.

"I guess we could. That will probably send me over the edge of sobriety." Abe hands me my shot and toasts, "To new friends."

"To new friends," I toast back and smile. Dang, that shot was strong! "That is going right to my head. Should we possibly do one more?" I ask, halfway drunk.

"Are you sure you can handle it?" Abe jokes.

"Bring it on, big boy." I say as I again motion the bartender. I sneak a quick glance at Brady's area. All the guys are gone, replaced by a group of middle-aged woman. Well, woman my age. Damn. When did that happen?

Abe toasts again, "To almost having the ability to dance."

"To dancing! Woo-hoo!" Oh, I'm there, my dancing shoes are coming alive. Part of me feels slighted. I can't believe Brady left without saying goodbye. I take a glance at my phone to see if there's a text. Nope, nothing. I hope I didn't offend him when I left him abruptly after our make-out session against the wall. Well, I'm here to hang with Allie, so hang with Allie I shall.

"Abe, you ready to dance?"

"I'm ready, neighbor. Let's do this!" he says with a hysterically funny face on and pumps his fist.

We join in next to George and Allie. George looks completely stunned to see me dancing with Abe. Abe and I could care less! We are having a blast and seem to be experts at the dance.

I yell to Allie, "Let's make an Abe sandwich!" So we converge on Abe, Allie facing his back and me facing his front. Then we turn and do the same thing to George. We twist all the way down to the floor and I lose my balance on the way back up. Abe grabs my arm and steadies me so I don't fall. Once I regain my composure, we both crack up laughing. Abe is laughing so hard he's almost crying.

"Come on, let's go get some water," he yells and guides me off the dance floor to the bar.

"Okay, maybe those shots were a little too strong," I laugh.

"I thought for sure you were going to fall on your ass. That would have been hysterical!"

"Thanks a lot!" I smack his chest. Ouch, that's a hard chest. I look back to the dance floor and wonder what the heck I must have looked like out there. Who cares? It was fun!

"Look at those two still going at it!" I motion toward Allie and George.

"George has his game face on. Looks like your friend may be sleeping at our house tonight."

"That's bullshit. Allie is supposed to be sleeping at my house!" I say, and once I realize how childish I sound, I crack up and stomp my foot like a little kid.

"It's okay, Laney, maybe Allie can sleep at your house another night," Abe mocks me while petting my head.

I know I'm going to regret those shots in the morning, but for now, I'm having so much fun.

Abe and I join George and Allie for one more dance and then we all head to the bar for one last drink.

"Laney, do you mind if I don't sleep at your house tonight? It will be like I'm there, because I'll be right next door," Allie asks with a huge grin on her face.

"You dirty old lady!" I say and smack her on the arm.

Yep, I'm drunk. Luckily, Allie is too, so this doesn't even phase her.

"Yes, you can go sleep somewhere else with a young boy that you barely know," I say with a drunken slur.

Then we both laugh. It's time for us to leave; the bar is now spinning. I check my phone again for a text. Nothing. Then I text the driver and ask him to pull up.

"Abe! George!" I yell unnecessarily because the band is no longer playing. "Do you want a lift home? I have a car outside. You two are way too drive to drunk!"

It takes a second for it to register what I just said, but when I do, I laugh at myself so uncontrollably I can barely stop. I haven't laughed like this in a long time.

Chapter Nineteen

A be and George agree and get a ride home with us. It's a quite uncomfortable ride as George and Allie make-out the entire drive back. Abe and I make nervous chit-chat and try not to look at the two of them. As we approach the houses, I lean toward the driver in all my drunken glory to give him directions.

"First, we need to stop right there at that driveway. See it? With the two cars? Yes. Then after the boys get out, scoot up a little more to the next driveway, and the girls will get out."

The driver looks at me like I'm nuts, but I'm okay with that. Allie has to come to my house anyway to get her stuff. We say goodnight to the brothers. Well, George gets a "see you in a bit" from Allie and another over the top kiss.

We walk up the driveway and notice something on the front step. A huge bottle of water and a bottle of pain relievers with a note attached. I eagerly open the note.

> Thought you might need these. Sorry I had to leave so quickly.
> Pete had to get home. Looking forward to seeing you in the
> hammock tomorrow. - Brady

I practically melt right there on the front stops. So thoughtful, so kind.

"Holy shit, that was nice," Allie says, practically falling through the front door.

"He's dreamy." I stare at the note. You bet your ass I'm going to be in that hammock tomorrow. Pretending to read a book, but really staring at you.

"Okay, love, I'll see you in the morning." Allie grabs her stuff and heads back out the door.

"You be careful, Allie. If you need to come back over here at any time, do it. I'm sure I'm going to be up all night with a headache anyway." I wait until I see her enter George's house to turn off the outside light and lock up.

I need to thank Brady for his thoughtfulness. But what if he's sleeping? Does he turn off his phone when he sleeps? Will I wake him? He has to work tomorrow. What time is it? 12:30. Yeah, that may be too late. Maybe I'll send it anyway so when he wakes up in the morning he'll get it. Sure, what the heck.

> You are so very thoughtful and I am truly appreciating your gift right now. I know for sure that tomorrow will be a hammock day for me. This old lady can't handle that much liquor! Thanks again for everything tonight.

I take a big gulp of water and wait for a response. Nothing yet. Shoot, I hope I didn't wake him. *Ding-dong.* A response.

> I had a feeling you'd get good use out of that. I saw you do your first shot and had a feeling that wouldn't be your last of the night. Glad you had a nice time. I know I did. Especially against that wall. See you tomorrow.

Shit, he saw me do a shot with Abe? Oh, I wonder if I made him jealous at all? That would be good.

I lie in bed, trying to get the room to stop spinning. Reviewing the night in my head. How about that Abe? I wonder if he is just as much fun sober? I had a great time with him. That was a pleasant surprise. But not as good of a surprise as the kissing. Brady's lips are so soft. It's like a firework goes off inside of me every time our lips meet. Maybe I was obsessed with Brady all through high school because he was my destiny. This is the guy I'm supposed to be with.

What the heck am I thinking? I'm here for two months. Two months. Not the rest of my life. My life is back in South Carolina. This is all way too much thinking for the pounding headache I have. I take a few more sips from the huge water bottle and two of the pain relievers Brady got me, and try to sleep.

Chapter Twenty

I wake at five a.m., feeling like I'm going to be sick. I know the only thing that can help this feeling right now is eating some carbs. I put just the small light on over the stove; my eyes can't handle much more. I grab the loaf of Italian bread I bought for the bruschetta I made. Shoot, I forgot to serve the bruschetta to Allie! Oh well. I break off a piece, sit at the island, and start painfully chewing on it. I know it's the only thing that will make me feel better. I drink more water, watch some news, and feel like I need to get back to bed. It's five thirty.

I turn off the light, and as I walk past the window facing the lake, I see movement down by George and Abe's dock. Someone is using a flashlight. I squint to try and figure out what I'm seeing. The flashlight shines on the kayak and I see it being lowered into the water. No way. Abe is going out in the kayak this early after drinking so much last night? He better be careful. I watch until I can no longer see his flashlight. That guy is crazy. This old lady is going back to bed.

I wake again and look at the clock. Boom! Boom! Boom! It's nine a.m. and apparently the dock boys are up and at 'em. I sit up and surprisingly I don't feel too bad. I make my way to the kitchen and fire up the coffee pot. Oh, how I need coffee. It may be a two-cup day for sure. I hop in the shower real quick. I feel so gross from last night. All sweaty from dancing and too much hair product in my hair for my liking.

The shower feels amazing. I stand under the hot water and give myself a little pep talk. "You can do this. You can have a good day and feel fine." Ugh. Double ugh. I dress in my comfy yoga pants and an oversized, old 5K t-shirt. My hair is pulled back in a ponytail, and I have just a little makeup on. I look at myself in the mirror. Woman, you can not drink that much anymore. I look like I am so…hungover.

I head to the kitchen, grab myself a cup of coffee, put on my Duke sweatshirt and flip flops, and head down to the dock. I step out the door and the sun pierces my eyes like a flame. I turn back into the house and grab my sunglasses. I walk to the end of the dock and sit on an Adirondack chair that's down there. I turn my head to the right to see how the dock boys are doing. They are both standing there looking my way, laughing, and talking about me obviously.

"How's it going old lady? Drink too much last night? Got a little headache?" Pete yells in an obnoxious tone.

I don't even look over. The Jersey girl in me ignites, and I just raise up my arm and flip them both off. Well, that cracked them up. Their laughter echoes around the cove. I giggle a little too, while sipping my coffee, then lean my head back and close my eyes.

The nausea is coming back, when I hear, "Yoo hoo! The bagel lady is here!" Allie walks down to the dock. Oh good, more carbs. "Cream cheese on an everything bagel, right?"

"Yes, you are! You know me well."

Allie hands me the bag of bagels and her coffee. "Here, hold this. Let me grab a chair." Allie brings a chair up alongside me. I hand her back her coffee and, reach in the bag, and give her her bagel.

"So tell me how it went with Junior next door," I say, taking a bite from the bagel. Yummm, I forgot how good Jersey bagels are.

"Well, it was interesting to say the least. He's a firecracker in the sack!"

"Allie!" I blush. "Really, a firecracker?" I ask, wanting to know more.

"Yes, I was pleasantly surprised," she says with a grin. "We didn't hit the sack right away. Actually ate some food and hung out with Abe for a bit. He was asking a lot of questions about you," Allie said in a teasing way.

"Me? Why was he asking about me?" I take another bite of this delicious bagel.

"I don't know, I guess he thought you were fun!"

"Did he say I was fun, or do you think he just thought that I was fun?"

"Haha, I don't know, Laney. It's hard to remember the details, but it seemed like he was into you."

Hmmm.

"You know that crazy ass went kayaking at five thirty this morning?" I alert Allie.

"Really? And what was your crazy ass doing out of bed to know this?" she asks, laughing.

"I had to get up because I felt like I could barf. I ate a piece of bread, and when I was going back to bed, I saw him leave. Isn't he hungover?"

"I'm sure he is, but George said he is extremely regimented. That's his daily workout. He kayaks the whole perimeter of the lake. That's why he's so buff."

Interesting. He really is buff. I think back to how hard his chest was. Mmmm. Then I look to the right quickly to see what the dock boys are up to.

"Is that Romeo over there?" Allie asks, craning her neck to see around me.

"Yeppers. That's him in all his dock-building glory." I stare for a bit but look away when he catches me. "Let's go back to the house. I need more coffee," I say to Allie as I stand. I look back at the dock boys and make eye contact with Brady. I raise my hand and give him a quick wave. He waves back and gets back to work.

"I feel like I got hit by a truck," I say, stretching my arms out in a big yawn.

"We need to build up your stamina!" Allie says, like a seasoned professional.

"No, thank you. I can't drink like that on a regular basis. I'm way too old," I yawn again.

"Stop that yawning! I have to go to work. See you later maybe?" She hugs me.

"Maybe. It may just be a quiet night for me." I walk her to the door and she's off to work. Wow, I can't believe she slept with George. I'm glad in a way. I felt like he may have been coming on to me a bit and that one-sided conversation we had totally turned me off. Now Abe, on the other hand, definitely intrigues me. Again, it could just be Drunk Abe that makes me laugh. I'm sure I'll get to spend some time with Sober Abe now that we've broken the ice.

The rest of the day I spend napping and actually getting some reading done. It keeps looking like rain, so I decide to stay indoors and recommit myself to playing hard to get. That decision comes easy every time I pass a mirror. "Umpf, I am too dang old for that much booze," I say, pulling my eyelids down in the mirror. "And Brady does not need to see me this way."

Just then I get a text and my heart flutters. I try to contain my disappointment when I see it comes from Grace.

Why don't you come over tomorrow? The whole family will be here and I could use your help with some of the work for the banquet next weekend.

Well, this is why I came to Falcon Lake. To spend time with my friends, not to chase a high school crush.

I'll be there bright and early!

Back to the couch for me.

Chapter Twenty-One

My visit with Grace and her family is a great one. She and Ben have raised the nicest children, and that grandbaby of hers, what a peach! Makes me excited to think I have that to look forward to. It's late and I'm exhausted by the time I get back to the lake, but there is the most beautiful full moon out. I decide to throw my blanket over my shoulders and head to the back deck to admire it and its reflection off the lake.

Sitting there staring at the moon makes me start thinking about where I am in my life. Of course, my self-doubt trickles in. Why am I crushing on this guy again? Wasn't years of my life in high school enough? He didn't want me then, why would he want me now? I take a deep breath. Okay, I am only here for two months. Just eight weeks! Do I really want to get involved with someone who I'll ultimately just leave? My home is most definitely in South Carolina. Then, let's say we do commit to each other. We're going to live eight hundred miles apart? Will I ever be able to trust him? I'd struggle with trust even if we lived in the same damn town! I take another deep breath and I can hear Allie's voice telling me to just have fun with it. He's just looking for a good time, I'm sure.

Just then I hear some splashing coming from in front of George and Abe's house. It's definitely not a fish. Too big. Then I hear someone say, "Shhhhh." And some giggling. I get up quietly and walk down the deck steps. I step gingerly behind the hedges that are between our yards and peek toward the lake.

That's when I hear a familiar voice. "Oh, George, that feels so good." I quickly cover my mouth to prevent myself from laughing out loud. It seems my girl Allie is skinny dipping with her boy toy George. That chick is braver than I could ever be. Lake water makes me nervous during the day, but in the dark? Forget about it! I walk back to the house and head for bed. That's two too many full moons for me.

**

Waking up to the sounds of the lake is the best way to wake up. I'm so relaxed here…What the?! A new text makes my heart jump out of my chest. Oh, it's Allie.

Hey we're going apple picking in a hour, come with us!

Hmmm, apple picking. Haven't done that in a long, long time. Well since no one else is texting me, I guess I'll go and be a third wheel. Fun!

Sure, I'm in!

The apple orchard is about forty-five minutes from Falcon Lake. The drive there is gorgeous. The mountains, the lakes, the farms. It's all so breathtaking. Jersey gets a bad rap. People who have never been here always just associate Jersey with the horrible reality TV shows filmed here and the airport. They couldn't be more wrong! Most of the state is beautiful!

At the orchard, an old barn has been converted into a store area where you can buy ciders, pumpkins, jams. Allie and George grab two plastic bags and hand me mine. "Here you go, honey. This bag is for your apples." Allie says.

"Thanks, Mom."

George grabs an apple picking pole and we head into the orchard.

I forgot how much I loved this part of fall. There aren't any apple orchards in Charleston. I'm carefully picking the most perfect apples I can find when Allie yells from the other side of the tree, "Hey, Laney—hot babe alert at three o'clock!"

I look to her and she nods her head over two rows of trees. There he is. Like an apple-picking god. Lucky for me, Allie yells loud enough that everyone within a four-tree radius hears her. Brady is looking right at me. He waves and I see him turn to a group at the tree behind him and say, "I'll be right back."

My face immediately feels flushed and the hairs on my neck stand up. Oh

Lord, why does he have this affect on me?

"Hey, Laney! What are you doing here?" he asks, blushing and answering his own question. "Well, obviously picking apples." We both laugh. I can see Allie and George move on to the next tree to give us some privacy.

"Yeah, Allie and George invited me along," I say, motioning toward them. "Who are you with?" I ask, looking over his shoulder, assessing his company. Please, please don't let it be another woman.

"Just my son, Jeremy, a couple of his friends, and my folks," he says, looking back. "Hey, listen, I had a great time with you the other night. Having a hard time not thinking about that kiss."

Oh my gosh. I know I'm blushing. I'm just hoping I don't look like I'm on fire.

"I'm double booked this week with work, but I should be free by the end of the week. Can we get together then?"

"Sure, I don't see why not. Don't forget, Saturday morning I kick your ass in the 5K." I say, smacking his arm playfully.

"We'll see about that. In the meantime, I'll be looking for you in the hammock." He steps in and gives me a long hug. "See you soon."

Oh my gosh, he smells like fresh, cool air. I love that smell.

"Bye!" is all I can muster.

"I hope you plan on making me something delicious with those apples!" he yells back to me.

"Oh, I will!" I say, swinging my bag of apples, trying hard not to float away. As I stand and watch him walk away, I imagine myself lying naked on the bed covered in apples. Here's your apple treat, Brady. Allie wakes me from my fantasy.

"Oh my gosh, you are so whipped!" Allie comes up behind me, throwing her arm over my shoulders while she loudly bites into an apple.

"I am not! I'm just admiring the view." We both watch Brady walking back to his group and then they are gone.

"Thanks so much for including me today," I say, still in a daze, leaning my head on Allie's.

***

Okay, I have just a few days to really prepare for this run. I tie up my laces and hit the road. The brisk morning air makes me feel so alive, so light on my feet. My thoughts are filled with Brady. I wonder if he thinks about me as much as I think about him? I have a huge bag of apples to cook up. What sweet apple treat should I make him?

First, I need to head to the grocery store to pick up all my baking ingredients. With my list in hand, I head out the door. As I reach my car, I see a Falcon Docks truck coming up the road from the right. My heart stops, of course, but as the truck brakes at the end of my driveway, I see that it's Pete.

"Geez, don't look so disappointed!" Pete yells from the truck.

"Oh no, sorry, Pete. Not disappointed at all. How are you doing?" I ask.

"Good, good. Just headed back to the job. Everything going well for you?" he asks, scratching at his beard.

"Everything is fine, thanks."

"Well, you sure do look great, Laney. You have a good day. I'll tell Brady I saw you." He chuckles.

"Okay," I say, not sure how to take Pete. He gives me the heebie jeebies.

The rest of the day I spend baking, boiling, you name it. I'm exhausted! I end up with six jars of applesauce for Grace's grandbaby, the best looking apple pie I think I've ever baked, and an apple crumble. It's pretty late. I'll have to wait until tomorrow to make my deliveries. A knock on the door makes me jump. I peek out and see that it's Abe.

"Hey, Laney. Just returning the juicer that George borrowed. It's getting in my way in the kitchen," Abe says, walking in and placing the juicer on the island. "Oh, you've been baking?"

"Yes! I'm exhausted! Not my forte like it is yours, that's for sure. But here, let me get you a piece of this crumble I made." I need to get as much of this stuff out of the house as possible.

"Great, looks amazing. Thanks! You have a good night!" Abe takes his plate and heads out the door.

"See ya." I head back to the crumble. I scoop some out, then grab the vanilla ice cream I bought, and throw some of that on top. Yum! Tomorrow, I will deliver Brady's pie. I hope he loves it!

I wake up with excitement. I get to surprise Brady with the pie today! It's so ridiculous, I know, that something so little can get me excited, but it does and

I am loving the feeling. I get back from my run, shower, and dress. I make sure I look good just in case I see him. My plan, which I thought about in bed last night, is to leave the pie on the front seat of his truck with a note.

I wrap the pie in cellophane. I even bought a fall colored bow and a special note card that has apples and pumpkins on it. Now, what should I write?

"Hope you enjoy my pie?"

No, too forward.

"This pie was baked with love?"

Hell, no. Can't come on too strong.

"Here are the baked goods I promised you.
Look forward to seeing you soon. - Laney."

Perfect.

I attach the card to the pie, look at the back window to make sure Brady is busy at work, and I head out the front door to walk down the street. I come to the driveway, where his truck is parked. He can't see the driveway from where he is. I carefully open the truck door and place the pie on the seat. I close the door gingerly and head back home before he spots me.

I get back in the house and I am giggly. Downright giggly. I feel like a kid again. Now I just wait. Every once in a while, I get up and look out the window to see if he's left the dock yet. He's still working hard. My phone rings and it's Kerry. "Hey Ma, how's it going?"

"It's going great, kiddo! How are you?"

"Wow, Mom, you sound so...happy! What are you doing up there on Falcon Lake? Or should I say, who are you doing?" She laughs.

"Kerry! Don't talk to your mama like that! I'm just having fun with my friends. It's so great to see everyone again," I say, trying to sound innocent.

"Hmmm, okay. Whatever you say, Mama. I'm glad you're having fun. Have you talked to Jake? He's got a woman!"

"What? I haven't talked to him. Who is she? Is she nice?" I ask, concerned. Jake has been known to date girls that I do not approve of. That's why I never find out from Jake that he has a girlfriend. It's always Kerry that fills me in. Which I am fine with. I'm so happy they are close and talk that way. Makes me feel that I did something right.

"She seems smarter than the rest of them, that's for sure. Pre-med. Must have half a brain, but that remains a mystery as she has chosen to date Jake." We both laugh.

"Don't pick on your brother. He's a sweet boy." He is a doll, just not a great judge of character. He must take after me.

"Whatever, Mama. You get back to your good times. Don't drink too much or sleep around. I love you and miss you!" Kerry says in her strong Southern accent.

"Love you, honey, call if you need anything!" Oh, my sweet daughter. Love her to pieces.

A couple of hours later, my phone dings. My hands are shaking.

Hi! Can you go out on the front stoop for a minute?

Oh my gosh, oh my gosh. I quick check myself in the mirror. "Good, not great," I say, fixing my hair a bit. I step out on the porch just as Brady's pulling in my driveway.

"Hey, I hope you didn't sit on the pie!" I say as he approaches. He looks amazing. A little dirty, but amazing.

"Hey." He steps toward me, puts his hands on my face, and pulls me in for the most amazing, warm kiss. I'm certain at that moment that I may faint. He takes his lips off mine. "Thanks for the pie. I'll see you soon." He steps off the porch, runs back to his truck, backs up, and pulls away smiling and waving.

My mouth is still open and I'm trying to figure out how to move my legs to get me back in the house.

"Bohemian Bling, this is Allie."

"Allie, you are not going to believe what just happened!"

***

The next morning is another clear, crisp day on the lake. I decide today will be my last run before the 5K on Saturday. I need to rest these old lady legs. As I'm running I'm thinking about the kiss. That was so unexpected. It was magical and I loved it! That man knows how to get me. I feel like a fish that's been hooked.

I remembered seeing an advertisement for an outdoor concert in the local free paper while standing in line at the supermarket the other day. I find the paper and check it out. Yes, the Falcon Lake Orchestra is conducting an outdoor concert at a gazebo in town. Sounds lovely. Part of me wants to ask Brady, but I remember he said he was double booked this week. Plus, the hard to get card I'm desperately trying to play. Allie would never. Elise, probably not on a school night. Let me see if Grace is in.

"That sounds great Lane! I'll pack us a picnic dinner and meet you there at six?"

I know for sure that basket is going to be delicious. "See you at six!"

It's a gorgeous night for a concert. It's cool out, but not freezing by any means. Even for a Southerner like me. I bring an extra blanket just in case. I see Grace across the field. She spots me at the same time. She already has the blanket all set up, and as I approach, I notice the trim of the basket matches the pattern in the blanket. "Really, Grace? Really?"

"Shut up. It was a set!" She defends herself.

"It's so you; Adorable Grace. Can't wait to see what you have in your basket! I'm starving." I lift the lid of the basket to see what she's thrown together.

"First, here. It's wine in a travel coffee cup so no one knows we're drinking," Grace says, handing me my cup.

"You are so tricky. And that's why I love you," I say to Grace as we click our "coffee" cups. The rest of the basket is full of a variety of cheeses, crackers, fruit, and pâté. She's thought of it all.

"Oh look, there's Jean and Pete." Grace nods to my right. I look over and Jean is intently listening to the orchestra. Pete sees me looking; he nods, winks, and smiles.

"Ew, Pete grosses me out."

Grace just dismisses me. "He's harmless," she says, taking a big gulp of her drink.

Maybe she thinks so, but I have my eye on him. I feel like he's up to no good.

The orchestra puts on a great concert. The sky is full of stars. Grace and I are both lying on our backs, listening and enjoying the gorgeous sky. "Gosh, what I wouldn't have given to get you girls in this position in high school." The stars are now blocked by Pete's belly hanging over our heads.

"In your dreams, Pete," I say, annoyed at him for ruining our moment of peace.

"I know of someone else who is dreaming of getting you in this position, Laney." Pete is obviously drunk, but I still want to punch him because that's the last thing Grace needs to hear.

"Bye, Pete. See you later," I say, shooing him away. Lucky for me, he listens and weaves his way back to his wife. "Still think he's harmless, Grace? He's a pig."

"Don't even tell me he's referring to Brady, Laney." She sounds like a disappointed mother.

"Oh please, Grace. He's drunk as a skunk. Just ignore him." I wave my hand in a dismissive manor. "Let's get back to listening to the music." Grace drops it. But of course, now my mind is wandering. Did Brady say that? Is he planning on just using me for sex? So they talk about me on the construction site? Oh my gosh. Am I going to have sex? It's been so long. I better shave.

***

"Bird's Nest! Tonight! Half-price drinks! We are going!" Allie yells into my ear. I move the phone away from my ear. It's too early in the morning for such an excited phone call.

"No way am I drinking. Well, not like I did last time." The memory makes me shudder.

"Okay, I'll keep an eye on you. I'll let George know you are in! See you later. I'll be at your house at seven." Allie hangs up before I can even ask any questions. My immediate thought is, I hope Brady is there.

From the moment we get to the bar until the moment we leave, I look for Brady and hope he shows up. Why am I doing this to myself? He's not there, nor does he ever show up. Is he with someone else? Are there other bars we should be going to? I don't even realize how much I'm drinking. The dancing, the shots, it all blends together once more. I'm a dummy.

Abe didn't come out with us, so George summons him to pick us up. I just want to get in my bed and forget that I didn't get to see Brady tonight. I'm so tempted to text him when I get home, but I have some of my senses left and realize that drunk texting is never a good idea.

***

The next morning is rough, but not as rough as I expected. Maybe Allie is right; I just need to build up a tolerance. Just then a wave of nausea overtakes me. I quickly grab something to eat. Maybe I should go for a walk, get some fresh air. Or maybe I'll just take a little nap, but inside, since it looks a like it might rain. Plus, I'm playing hard to get.

A text wakes me up. I look at the clock. Holy cow, I've been asleep for two hours. It's already after lunch. I look back at my phone. It's a text from Brady!

> Hey, Laney. Want to come with me to pick up our race packets, then get some dinner?

Crap, I didn't even register yet. I do need to go. I hate saving that for the morning. Alone time with Brady. That would be interesting.

> Sounds great. Do you mind if I pick you up? I'll already be out running some errands. Just text me your address and tell me a time.

Yes, I'll drive. I feel more in control of the situation when I drive.

> That works better for me. My pickup is a mess right now. How about 6? 1324 Lakeside Rd. Look forward to seeing you then! No hammock today? Bummer.

Gosh, he's cute.

> Had to sleep inside—you two were making a racket! See you at 6.

Oh my, that makes me nervous. I think back over the week and we honestly haven't had a lot of time alone. This should be interesting. I hope I like his personality as much as I enjoy looking at him…touching him…kissing him.

Chapter Twenty-Two

I hope Brady is taking me somewhere casual for dinner. I guess I should ask him before I leave.

> Hey dock boy—are we going somewhere casual for dinner? Just checking.

Dock boy...sounds demeaning. Let me delete that and start over.

> Hey Brady—are we going somewhere casual for dinner? Just checking Love, Laney

Better. Send. Oh wait, shit, did I just write "Love?" Oh no, cancel, cancel, cancel. Crap. It went through. Maybe he won't notice. So much for hard to get. *Ding-dong.*

> Yes, casual for sure. See you in a few hours. Love, Brady :)

Crap, he caught it. What is wrong with me? I do love the idea of Brady, but still, I barely know this man. He could be a total creep, under those green, green eyes and gorgeous, deep dimples. The adorable texts, the kind gestures, they can all be a ruse to get into my pants. Hopefully tonight will answer some of those questions for me.

I freshen up as much as I can, still looking ever so slightly hungover but feeling much better. I head to the next town over to do some shopping. I need to find something to wear to the banquet and get some new running socks. I have an hour to kill before picking up Brady. I'm so nervous, my palms are sweaty on the steering wheel.

After getting all I need and then some, I head back to my car. I notice a man leaning against my driver's side door. I stop dead in my tracks. Who the hell is that? Should I set off the panic button? I slowly approach the car, squint my eyes, and recognize the man standing there with his arms crossed. Abe! "Good God, you scared the crap out of me! I thought you were breaking into my car!"

"Ha, sorry to frighten you! You parked right next to me, or maybe I parked right next to you, I don't know. I saw you walking out, so I thought I'd strike a pose on the Beemer." He grins and acts like he's modeling.

"Looks like something I'd see in *BMW Monthly* for sure!" I say, laughing, then I swing one of my shopping bags and hit him in the arm.

"I see you've recovered from another night of drinking. Good for you!" he says in a mocking tone.

"Barely. Once again, I am swearing off alcohol," I say, rubbing my forehead.

"Famous last words. I'm sure Allie will have you out again before you know it! Speaking of Allie, she and George were up all night, if you know what I mean," he says, rolling his eyes.

"Really? Lord. She's a stronger woman than I…I couldn't wait to get to sleep!" There's a slight pause and some silence, but it's not uncomfortable.

"So, where you headed?" Abe asks.

"Oh, going to pick up a friend. We have to get our race packets for the 5K tomorrow and then we are going out to dinner."

"Sounds good. Make sure you eat some carbs, and it wouldn't hurt to drink a lot of water. I'm sure you're still a little dehydrated. You don't want that to be an issue in the morning." He offers advice like a doctor.

"Thanks, you're right. I still do feel a little off. I will drink plenty of water. Nice seeing you, Abe. Enjoy the rest of your day!"

"You too, Laney," He walks toward his car, gets in, and pulls away.

Hmmm. I like Abe. He seems really sweet.

I throw my purchases in the back of the car, get in, and pull down the mirror. Makeup still looks okay, check. Nothing in teeth, check. Lip gloss reapplied, check. I throw a breath mint in my mouth, enter Brady's address into my GPS, and I'm on my way! According to the GPS, I'll be five minutes late. Perfect. Nothing wrong with keeping him waiting a couple of minutes.

The lake is to my right. I can see the cove I'm staying in all the way on the other side of the lake. Brady's house is on the left, across the street from the lake. Cute one-story home, almost has a log cabin look about it. Very cozy. I wonder if he lived here with his ex? I pull in the driveway. Do I go to the door? Nah, I send him a text.

Your chariot awaits you, sir.

I'm smiling already just waiting for his response. *Ding-dong.*

It's about time! I'll be right out.

Oh, my stomach just did a flip. I'm nervous, but I'm not. Part of me feels like I already know Brady, but when I think about it logically, I realize I know nothing about him. He steps out of the house and turns to lock the door. Oh boy, he looks hot. Red and rust colored flannel, perfect fitting jeans. I'm sweating, so I quick turn up the air a little.

The door opens, and as he gets into the car, I realize he smells as good as he looks. "Well, hello there. Thanks for picking me up." He leans over and gives me a peck on the lips. "Pete is a slob, so the passenger side of my truck is a mess. I haven't had anyone but Pete or my son in that seat, so it hasn't mattered."

Interesting. No other 'dates', or does he always get picked up? I'll find out later.

"No problem. It worked out perfectly. I had to go out and pick up a few things," I say, throwing the car into reverse.

"This is a beautiful car, Laney. Is it brand new?" He asks, surprised.

"I think I've had it close to a year. Yes, it will be a year in November. I love it. It's so comfortable." I hope he doesn't think I'm a snob. This was truly my one extravagant purchase. Everything else I own is pretty simple.

"Good for you, it's great. Okay, so you know where we're going, right?"

"No, I do not…am I headed in the right direction?"

"Yes, just turn left up here. Packet pick up is right at the banquet hall where the event will be tomorrow night. It's actually the start line for the race too. The course goes right past my house, so if you get tired, I'll hide the key under the mat and you can finish the run after a little rest," he says with a smart ass grin.

"Oh, you joke, but I may just have to take you up on that offer. Do leave the key under the mat! Also, leave some drinks out and maybe a snack. As long as I don't come in last, I'm fine with it!" We both laugh.

"I'm not in that great of shape for running right now either. I hurt my knee this summer and it just hasn't been right since. So maybe I'll join you for a rest at my place."

"Sounds like a plan." I raise my hand to give him a high five. Instead, he grabs my hand, places it in his, and kisses it ever so gently. He holds it the rest of the drive to the banquet hall. I'm concentrating real hard on the sweat level of my hand. I feel good, like that's where my hand was always meant to be.

I find a spot right on the side of the hall and pull in. "Let me at least get your door for you, since you drove," he says and hops out. I watch him walk around the back of the car. He's at my door in a flash, opening it and motioning his arm down with a slight bow.

"Thank you, kind sir," I say with a British accent.

He closes the door then pulls me in for a long, hard hug. It feels so good and safe in his arms. He leans in and gives me a soft kiss. We pull apart, then just smile at each other.

"Come on, let's go get our stuff so we can get something to eat. I'm starving," He takes me by the hand and leads me between the cars to the entrance of the banquet hall.

We must be a sight because the three women running the packet pick up all stop what they are doing and look us up and down, from our hand holding to our faces and back to our hands.

One of those women is Grace! "Grace!" I let go of Brady's hand, go around the table, and give her a hug. "I know, I know, play hard to get. I am trust me," I whisper in her ear before she has a chance to yell at me.

"MmmHmm, yeah, it looks like it," she says with a disapproving glare.

"Whatever. I need to register for this fine 5K, Mrs. DeCaro."

"First, let me introduce you to Beth Pamett. Beth!" She yells over to Beth, who is already helping Brady. "I need you to meet my oldest and dearest friend, Laney McGuire."

Beth stops looking for Brady's running bib and walks over to me. "Laney, hi! So nice to meet you. Grace has told me so much about you."

A fake, forced conversation. My least favorite type of conversation.

"Yes, hi Beth. Grace speaks very highly of you." I've got nothing left to say.

Beth has already rubbed me the wrong way. Grace's face and the other lady's face, when we walked in, were faces of surprise. Beth's appeared to be a look of disgust.

"So, how long have you and Brady been an item?" she says deliberately loud so as to include Brady in on the embarrassment. Thank goodness we're the only ones in the banquet hall picking up our packets at the moment.

"Oh Beth, no worries, we're not an item per se. It's purely physical. We've been getting it on since Laney arrived in New Jersey," Brady says out of nowhere. Beth's jaw practically drops to the ground. Brady looks at me, I look at Grace, then back at Brady, and the three of us start laughing. Beth takes offense and goes right back to finding Brady's bib. She hands him his shirt and says, "Thank you for signing up for the race. We'll see you tomorrow morning."

Brady comes to the end of the table by Grace and me. "Hi, Grace. I hope you know I was kidding."

"Yes, I know that Brady. Laney isn't that easy. She's actually very picky and deserves only someone with the best intentions. She's a very special woman." Grace is and always will be my best defense attorney.

"Oh I know it, Grace. I know it," he replies, looking at me lovingly.

Just his look makes me melt.

"Okay, Grace, here's my $25. You can fill out my crap with your address, I just need my bib and shirt and we can get out of your hair." Grace grabs my things. I see Beth has stepped away from the table and is busy talking with the other woman handing out bibs. I'd love to hear what that conversation was about, but at the same time, I really don't give a shit. I actually love giving people something to talk about.

I hug Grace, as does Brady, and we walk out of the banquet hall the same way we walked in. Hand in hand.

"That was fun," Brady says laughing.

"Yeah, hysterical! Did you see their faces? That was classic. Here, you drive. You know where we're going." I throw Brady the keys and we're off to dinner.

"Wow, you're right. This car handles great. I'll happily be your driver while you're here," Brady offers.

He does look good behind the wheel. Hell, he looks good everywhere.

"You'll have to be at my beck and call. You're okay with that?" I say, grinning.

"You bet I am." He squeezes my leg, then rubs it.

Oh Lord, sweating again. Is the air blowing on this side of the car? Whew. It's amazing how he affects me.

We pull up to the restaurant. It's Vito's, the same one Allie took me to for lunch. That is fine by me. I love good Italian food!

"I've been here! I love it!" I blurt out.

"Oh no, did you want to try somewhere else?" Brady asks, looking disappointed.

"Absolutely not. I really liked it. Plus, I wasn't here with you, so it will be even better." Okay, I throw some his way. I have to; I can't resist him.

He smiles. "Okay, stay there. I want to open your door again." He winks and gets out of the car. How's my breath? Shoot, no time to fix anything, my door swings out. He reaches for my hand and helps me out. This time, no hug. Just a long, delicious kiss.

I say breathlessly, "Yeah, you can definitely be my driver." We both giggle and walk inside.

"Table for two. In the back if you have it," I hear Brady tell the maître d'.

"Absolutely, sir, please follow me this way." Brady leads me to follow the maître d'. Just him touching my lower back sends chills up my spine. He is such a gentleman. I love being treated like a lady. It rarely happened in my past life.

We are seated in the back corner of the restaurant. The lighting is low and there is a small candle on the table. The waitress introduces herself and hands us menus. I open the menu and realize I can barely make out what it says! Crap. I move the menu out to the side of the table and try to hold it out a bit.

"I don't know about you, but I can't see a damn thing on this menu," Brady says kindly, obviously seeing me struggle.

"Oh, good, me neither." I reach into my purse and get out my pink, floral reading glasses. I look over the menu and decide on a dish. Then, like second nature, I hand them to Brady. He puts them on and looks at the menu as well. Doesn't even hesitate to put on pink, floral glasses.

"That's better, thanks."

The waitress comes back to take our orders. The whole time Brady has the glasses on. I'm giggling while ordering, he looks so darn cute. The waitress takes our menus and walks away. Brady takes off my glasses and hands them to me. "I like those, but they clash too much with my shirt." We're both laughing when our drinks arrive.

"I'm not sure I should be drinking this. I think I'm still kind of drunk from last night," I say nervously. "But maybe just a little bit," I wink.

"Cheers, Laney. I'm so happy you're here."

"Cheers. Coming here was definitely a good decision." I clink my glass against his.

Chapter Twenty-Three

Dinner is wonderful. Our conversation is satisfying. I find out so much about Brady I didn't know, and I am reminded about all the things I already knew about him from my stalking days. We discussed our exes and couldn't believe the similarities between them. Especially the cheating aspect and how much it hurt.

"I just felt so naive. I think part of me always felt he was capable of cheating, but another part of me thought he would never be so stupid as to go through with it. I never thought anyone would jeopardize such a great family for sex. Why not pick up an exciting hobby, like alligator hunting, if you want a rush?" I say, trying to lighten the mood.

"That's funny. I felt that same way about Susie. She was a flirt with a lot of guys. Friends' husbands, you name it. I always just thought it was a joke to her. She wouldn't wreck a marriage for it. But she did. It's so hard to trust again, isn't it?" he asks, looking so very defeated.

"It is. Very much so," I say, taking a sip of my drink.

I tell him all about my kids, my life in South Carolina, how I got there. He tells me about his different business ventures, all in the building industry, the ups and downs of owning a company. We have that in common too. We talk, eat, drink, and before we know it, we are one of only two other tables of people left in the restaurant.

"What do you say we settle the bill and get out of here?" he asks, motioning the waitress.

Everything in me wants to pay the bill, but I'll let him get this one. With all the positives that come with having money also come some negatives, like guilt. This guy works his ass off, doesn't have tons of money, and here I am sitting on my huge inheritance, not paying. I'll let him pay this time. I wouldn't want to hurt his ego. Before we reach the car, Brady spins me into his arms for another great kiss. "Hey, Laney," he says in between kisses, "why don't we go to your place, get your running stuff, then go back to mine? The starting line for the 5K is so much closer to my house. We can walk to it. Save time."

Still kissing, I respond, "Okay, let's go."

We part and practically run to the car. We get to my place, and as I'm getting out I say, "Wait here, I'll just be a second."

I get my bags out of the back of the car and run in the house. Holy shit, holy shit. What am I doing? All I hear in my ear is Grace: "This is not playing hard to get, Laney!" Then in my other ear I hear Allie: "You only live once—do it! Do him!" Then Elise chimes in: "Don't get hurt again, Laney."

If dinner had gone any other way I would be second guessing myself, but it was really, really perfect. I like everything about him. He's romantic, he's considerate, he has amazing manners, and he makes me laugh. That's super important to me. Sorry, Grace—I'm doing this! Him!

As I'm running around the house gathering my things, I'm so very thankful that I picked up a sexy nightgown at the store today. It's short, not too revealing, but just right. I must have known what was in store for me, or my subconscious was hoping for it! I'm about to lock up and run out to the car when I get a text from Elise. Yay, my running partner!

> Laney—please don't be mad—I can't run tomorrow. I threw my back out at school today, rearranging my office. I thought I'd feel better by now, but I don't. I'm sorry. Let me know that you got this.

Crap. Running alone, very slow. Oh well. Maybe I'll meet someone on the route that I know.

> That's okay, you take care of yourself. Use some ice and double up on the pain relievers. Oh, and elevate your feet! Talk to you tomorrow.

Doors locked and I'm headed back to the car. I throw my bag in the backseat and we head to Brady's.

Chapter Twenty-Four

Brady carries my bag in and tells me to 'stay put' while he turns on some lights. The house is adorable and not too different than the one I'm staying in. Except his view of the lake is out the front windows.

"I'm going to start a fire; please make yourself at home. Would you mind pouring us some wine? There's a bottle in the island."

"Sure." I check out the selection of wines that he has stacked in a beverage cooler built into the island. "I love your house! The island, all the built in cabinets and shelving in the living room; it's beautiful." My eyes wander, taking it all in.

"Thanks. Actually built all that myself," Brady says humbly.

"No way. Wow, you have some mad skills, Mr. Gramble."

"Thank you! The bottle opener is in the drawer right in front of you and the glasses are in the cabinet behind you." Brady directs me with a nod of his head because his arms are full of firewood.

I pour two glasses and look over to the living room. Brady is hard at work, trying to light a fire. I notice a plush rug in front of the fireplace. Hmmm, looks like a rug with a purpose. I wonder if it's been used before. After Brady has the fire going, he turns and moves two big pillows from the couch. He puts them in front of the couch for us to lean on. Smooth move, smooth move. Then he goes into a hall closet and gets some blankets.

"Why do I get the feeling you've set this stage before?" I say, accusingly. Oh my gosh. Is he a player? Am I being played? Desperate woman arrives in town, thinks she knows me, still has a crush on me. I'm sure she'll be an easy lay. I feel a little nauseated.

"Nope, I haven't. Not at this house, ever. And I've been here two years. I just planned it out since that Monday morning, hoping that one day I could set this stage."

Monday morning? Aw, when he first saw me? This guy says all the right things.

"When you had breakfast with Pete? I don't remember him looking that good that morning!" I say, with a smirk on my face.

"Very funny, Laney." He laughs. He heads to the kitchen area and I hand him his drink. He grabs my hand with his free hand and leads me to 'the stage.'

"Oops, I almost forgot." Brady puts his glass on the fireplace mantel. He runs over to the stereo and tries to find a good station. "This will have to do because we only have three radio stations here."

I notice Brady's hands are a little shaky as he's adjusting the radio.

"That is fine. You okay? You seem nervous." I ask. He really does. It actually makes me feel better about how nervous I am. He grabs his glass and sits down next to me on the plush rug.

"I wouldn't say nervous. Well, maybe a little. I haven't been with anyone else since my divorce," he says as if embarrassed. So sweet.

"Well, guess what? Neither have I! We'll have to walk each other through it," I say.

He seems surprised. "You haven't? Really? I would have thought you'd be fighting the guys off."

Ha, that's funny.

"Yeah, that's never been a problem with me. If you remember correctly, I was usually the one being fought off." I remind him gently of how he never acknowledged my existence in high school.

"I want to talk to you about that, Laney," he says, grabbing my hand and putting it in his lap. "Of course I knew you liked me in high school. I almost felt, in a way, not worthy of you liking me that much. I remember thinking, what does that chick see in me? Plus, I was a jerky guy. All the attention from the slutty cheerleaders because I was the star player. It all went to my head. And I'm sorry for that, but I have to say at that time in my life, you were definitely way out of my league. You seemed very grown up, mature. I was a dumb jock with a huge ego."

That's sweet. I hope it's true. I'd like to believe that. This conversation is getting too intense.

"Flip, I knew I should have been a cheerleader!" We both laugh and take big sips of our wine. "It's okay, you made high school interesting for me Brady. Gave me a reason to want to look my best every day. You have no idea how bummed I'd be if you were out. I was a walking hormone. I'm sorry if that made you uncomfortable at all." I take a sip of wine and wait for his response.

"Hell no. I loved it. In fact I specifically remember puffing my chest out a little and making sure I did my cool walk whenever I saw you."

"What a tease! If only I knew that then; I would have put you in your place!" I say, smacking his arm and laughing.

Brady gets a serious face on and takes my glass and puts it on the table next to the couch. Uh oh. Here goes nothing. He turns back and gently runs his manly yet tender hands down my cheek while looking me in the eyes. "This may sound corny and crazy, but I swear to you, Laney, the past several days have been the most exciting days I've had in a long time. I feel so happy. And the thought of possibly seeing you each day makes me…I don't know… excited. I think I have an idea of how you felt in high school. When you weren't in the hammock the other day, I felt deflated. But the thought of you possibly coming home and me getting to see you kept me going. I hope you're not weirded out by that."

"Absolutely not, I'm flattered. More than you could know." And just then, I put my hands on his face and pull him toward me and start kissing him. A kiss that makes your toes curl and makes your stomach feel like it's doing somersaults. We are both so taken with one another, and I can feel it in this kiss.

I move my body so I have my legs wrapped around him, sitting in his lap. This feels so good. I forgot how much I missed kissing. Brady slowly runs his fingers through my hair. It's giving me goosebumps on top of everything else I'm feeling. Brady is obviously also enjoying the moment; I can literally feel his excitement. Since he told me the effect I'm having on him, I decide to take things one step further. I reach down and pull Brady's shirt over his head. I slowly tickle his chest and run my fingers up and down his stomach. Gosh, he is solid, so strong. He returns the gesture and takes my top off as well. Then he begins taking my bra off. Come on, girls, don't fail me now. Stand up tall and proud…please, I'm begging. He hardly seems to notice the ever so slight droopiness of the girls. He cups my breasts in his hands so gently and runs his thumbs over my nipples. I leave his mouth and lick his neck. He's delicious.

I realize, looking around his back, that we are pretty much out in the open. His blinds are open, but I'm sure no one can see in, can they?

"What's the matter?" He senses my concern.

I giggle. "Your blinds are wide open. Can anyone see in here?" I'm starting to feel a little self conscious.

"I don't believe so, but let me close them regardless."

"Would you mind also turning off the lights? I've always wanted to make love by the light of the fire," I say, hoping he doesn't realize my real reason is so that he doesn't get a full blown shot of this forty-eight year old body.

"Sure." He walks around the room and comes back on to the floor, this time, pushing me down on my back so that I'm lying in front of the fireplace. We kiss some more and it's feeling very hot, and not just because of the fire. Brady reaches down and unbuttons my jeans and pulls them off, along with my panties. I help him do the same.

"You're so beautiful, Laney," he whispers in my ear.

I want to tell him I love him, because I feel at that moment I do. That I always have.

But I don't. I just say, "Make love to me Brady."

And with that he enters me. I forgot how good this can feel when you are doing it with someone who feels the same way about you. I'm practically digging my fingers into his back. He kisses my neck and my shoulder, moaning. I want this feeling to last forever, but at the same time, I can't wait to reach orgasm.

"I'm getting close, are you?" Brady asks between heavy breaths. Considerate even during love making. This guy is a dream.

"I am, I am." We both climax at the same time, like a beautiful love song. "Oh my gosh, that was amazing." I pant, out of breath.

"It really was…I don't want to move," he says still kissing my neck and shoulder. "You are so sexy, Laney."

"Stop, you're embarrassing me." I see the hurt in his eyes. "I guess I'm not good at accepting compliments, sorry," I say, feeling bad.

"Well you better get used to them, Laney Simms—because you're going to get a lot of them from me!"

We kiss some more, then just hold each other for a while.

After using the bathroom, I throw on my new lingerie. I strut my best strut back into the living room. Brady has on comfy-looking pajama pants and no shirt. So sexy. He's back on the floor with fresh glasses of wine ready for us.

"You look amazing in that. I may have to throw you on the floor again," he says proudly.

I snuggle up next to him and pull a blanket on me. I look up to him. "That wasn't too bad for someone so out of practice." I wrap my arms around his chest and hug him, giggling.

"That was a lot of pressure for me. I didn't want to let you down after all these years." We're both laughing now.

We talk nonstop for the next couple of hours; however, we never once bring up the topic of me leaving.

I fill him in on the skinny dipping action I saw the night of the full moon. "Oh my gosh, skinny dipping in this cold water? You couldn't pay me!" Brady says, which is a huge relief to me.

"Oh good, I'm glad we're on the same page with skinny dipping. I honestly don't even like swimming in lakes during the day. I need to see what's swimming around me. A small piece of weed can touch my leg and I'm certain it's a fish biting me. I hate it!"

I don't want to think about leaving anyway. I want to live in the here and now and enjoy every minute I get to be with this amazing man. I look at the clock and realize it's eleven thirty. "Holy cow, it's late, Brady! How the heck are we going to get up for that race tomorrow?"

"Let's worry about that in the morning." He grabs my head and pulls it toward him. We kiss more passionately than before and make love again with the flames of the fireplace reflecting off our sweaty skin. I didn't think I had it in me to do it twice in one night, but this man makes me able. His passion, his words, his dimples. I want all of him, all the time.

Chapter Twenty-Five

Bang! What the heck was that? I shoot up from a sound sleep, nestled in Brady's arms in front of the dying fire. Brady bolts up next to me. "That sounded like a gunshot!" I yell, not having a clue what time it is or what's going on. I'm so tired.

Brady jumps up and peers through the front blinds. The sun is obviously up, as it is causing me to squint.

"What is it? Do you see anything?"

He starts laughing. "Yeah, I see something. I see people running their asses off, doing a 5K!"

"Oh shit! We are missing the 5K?" I say, panicked.

"It's looking that way. Quick, get your running stuff on," Brady directs me as he heads off to his room.

"What do you mean? It's too late!" I yell, totally confused at what's happening.

Brady peeks his head out of his room. "Trust me, Laney, get dressed."

I quickly get my bag and head to the bathroom. I throw on my running gear, favorite hat, socks, and sneakers.

"Here, pin your bib on." Brady is in his running gear, tying his sneakers.

I pin my bib on. "What are we doing?"

Brady starts laughing. "I have a perfect plan, Laney. See that line of trees on the edge of my property by the road?"

I look out the front. I see what he's talking about and now I think I know where he's headed with it.

"The 5K route passes my house, goes down about a mile and a half, then the runners turn and come back past my house. They have about a half mile to go until the finish line. Are you up for running a half mile this morning,

Laney?" Brady smiles a devilish grin.

"I think I can handle it. You are a genius!" I give him a big kiss on the lips.

He goes back to the window and glances out. "Okay, we have about ten minutes or so. We don't want to look too good."

I have an idea. "Wait, let's wet our hair so we look sweaty!" Like two little kids, we run to the bathroom and start wetting each other's hair. We put water around our necks. Brady even puts some in his armpits.

"Okay, I think we are ready. Let's go!" We sneak out the back door and walk around the back of Brady's house. I don't get to look long, but I do notice how beautifully his backyard is landscaped.

"Oh, I like your yard!"

"Thanks. I take that as a huge compliment coming from you."

It looks better than anything I've ever designed. This guy does it all!

"Follow my lead." Brady runs down along the tree line. Runners are passing, but can't see us. Brady peeks behind us through the trees and sees an opening. "Jog in place," he orders me. I do as I'm told. He bends down on the side of the road and pretends to be tying his shoelaces. I'm next to him jogging in place. A couple of runners pass us and don't even seem to be phased by us. They all look too tired to care. One runner even asks if we need help.

"No, thanks, just some shoelace issues," I yell to their back.

Brady stands up and says, "You ready to run?"

With that grin and those dimples, I am ready to do anything with him. We run that last half mile as fast as we can. It's a struggle because we are laughing and running at the same time.

"There it is! The finish line! Do you think we can make it?" I say, laughing.

"I think we can. It's going to be a struggle, but we can do it. Together!" Brady grabs my hand and we cross the finish line holding hands. Then Brady hugs me, picks me up off the ground, and spins me around. Both of us are laughing. Finally, I have someone with me at a finish line. My time has come. It is a great moment.

Brady and I grab a bagel and a bottle of water from the sponsors of the race. "Let's go back to my place for some coffee," Brady suggests. I pan the crowd looking for familiar faces, see a couple of people from high school, maybe? It's hard to tell. I just want to get back and have some coffee. That was a shock to my system getting up and running. Even if it was for only half a mile!

Brady starts the coffee pot. "So what do you have planned for the day, Ms. Laney?"

I think about it and really nothing comes to mind. I guess I can go visit Elise and check on her back.

"Not too much, how about you?" I ask as I spread some cream cheese on my bagel. Got to take it easy on these carbs.

"I unfortunately have to work a bit today. Just a couple of hours, then if you want, you can come back here and we can go to the banquet together?" he asks sweetly.

"I already told Allie I'd go with her. I'm sure once we get into the banquet, she'll dump me for some hot young thang, and then I'm all yours!" I say, then take a big sip of my coffee. Oh, how I love my coffee.

"Just as long as you don't dump me for some hot young thing," he says, looking at me over his coffee cup.

"You never know what might happen, Mr. Brady. I'm such a sexy woman," I do a comical strut over to him and wrap my arms around his neck. "I'm pretty sure I'm smitten with you, Mr. Gramble." I give him a quick closed-mouth kiss because I know we both have coffee breath.

"I'm pretty sure I'm beyond smitten with you, Laney," he says in a very serious tone.

I put my head on his chest and he hugs me real hard. Brady's hugs are all-encompassing and I feel so safe in them. Such a sense of security. How am I ever going to leave him? I shake the thought from my head. I don't want to think that far ahead. Live in the moment, Laney. Live in the moment.

Chapter Twenty-Six

I say my goodbyes to Brady and head home. When I pull in the driveway, I notice an aluminum tinfoil-covered plate on my front steps. There's a note on top.

> Thought you'd need some energy after your run.
> Freshly baked for you - Abe

I look next door to see if anyone is outside, no sign of anyone. I bring the plate inside and peel back the foil. The most delicious looking cheese danish is staring back at me. Did he really make this? I wonder to myself. It even has the decorative icing lines on it. It's gorgeous! I'll have that for lunch. I'm a lucky girl.

I get in the shower and can't stop thinking about last night and this morning. I have a huge smile on my face. What an amazing night! And not just the fabulous sex. The talking, the laughs, falling asleep in each others arms. Just all feels so natural, not forced. Brady is everything I hoped and more. I'm a little scared how quickly and how hard we've fallen for each other. It feels like we were always meant to be. It's just so natural, like two puzzle pieces that were finally brought together. Am I being realistic? How does that happen? Brady wouldn't even look at me in high school. Now we're an item? I shake the thought from my mind. I turn off the shower and begin toweling off. *Knock, knock, knock.* Crap! Someone's at the door. Shoot, they know I'm home and I'm soaked. I can't get clothes on. I wrap a towel around me, making sure every important inch is covered.

I step gingerly to the door and peek through the blinds. Crap, it's Abe. I crack the door open a little bit so just my head is exposed.

"Hello there, my friendly neighborhood baker!" I say with water dripping off my head onto my face.

"Laney, hey, I'm sorry to bother you. I was just checking into make sure you were okay. I haven't seen you around." He seems concerned, but he also seems like he's looking for information.

"Oh yeah, I spent the night out last night, but I'm back now. Thank you so much for the danish! I can't wait to dig in!" I say enthusiastically.

"You are welcome; that's one of my specialties." He boasts proudly.

"You should really consider opening a bakery. You have such a gift." "Thanks, but no thanks. Too many hours in that business. Hey listen, I know it's sort of last minute, but would you like to have lunch with me today? I know a great spot that has amazing views of the entire lake."

Oh boy. What do I do here? I do like Abe, but wouldn't that hurt Brady? I really shouldn't put all my eggs in one basket. Abe is nice enough. I really don't have anything else going on today. I never told Elise I was thinking of coming over. She probably just wants to rest anyway.

"Laney? Lunch?" Abe asks as I'm lost in my thoughts.

"Oh geez. Yes, sorry. Sure, lunch sounds great!"

"Perfect. Why don't you walk over around noon and we'll head out?"

"I'll be there!" I say, trying to convince myself.

"See you then!" Abe responds and walks back to his house.

Shit. What did I just do? Should I tell Brady I'm going out to lunch? Would Brady tell me if he was going out to lunch with another woman? Should he have to? I think if I want this relationship to go anywhere with Brady, I need to be forthcoming with him from the start. But really, what kind of relationship can I have with Brady living eight hundred miles away from me? In any case, I despised Jim's knack for being able to dispense lies with ease. As far as I'm concerned, not telling someone you care about something is the same as lying. Lying is ugly and hurtful. I wouldn't do that to Brady. He's been through too much.

I get my phone off the counter and text Brady.

Thanks again for an amazing night! I can't stop smiling. Just wanted to give you a heads up. My neighbor just asked me to lunch, so no hammock time today :(Sorry. But I can't wait to see you tonight!

I return to the bathroom and finish drying off to distract myself for the wait of the return text. *Ding-dong.* I pick up my phone.

> Deflated. I was looking forward to hammock time. Isn't your neighbor a guy? Be careful. Counting down the minutes until tonight.

Oh, that "deflated" hurt. But then I am uplifted once more…counting down the minutes to see me? Wow. He really does say the right things.

> Of course I'll be careful. I wouldn't go with him if I felt any kind of weird vibe, trust me.

I'm sure trust is a tough thing for Brady, like it is for me. In that way, we are similar. We've both been so hurt by someone we loved, we could never put another through that pain. *Ding-dong.*

> I do.

I have no words to respond with. So I just type a heart and send it. Yes, Brady, you have my heart.

***

I put on a pair of khaki pants and a light sweater. That little nap was just what I needed before heading to lunch. I walk over to Abe and George's house and before I'm even able to knock on the door, Abe walks out. "Oh, hey Laney. You ready to go?" He asks, walking toward his car.

"Sure thing. Can't wait to see the view!" We drive for about twenty minutes, up and down the hills surrounding the lake. It's a beautiful day and the sky is full of the fluffiest clouds I've seen in a long time. The conversation is great. Abe really makes me laugh. "Where the heck are we going? I didn't know there was a restaurant around here," I say, wondering if we're lost.

"No restaurant, Laney. It's better than a restaurant. You'll see!" Abe smiles. He really is handsome.

We turn right down a road with a marker that says *Overlook*. How could I have lived here all those years and not known about this place? Abe pulls the car into a dirt lot that has posts to designate the parking spots. We get out of the car and Abe pops open the trunk. "You need help?" I offer. Abe closes the trunk and I see he has a blanket and a picnic basket.

"Nope, I'm good. Come on." I follow behind Abe as we walk to a small marked trail. The trail is only about fifty feet long when we come to an opening. The view is spectacular! We can see the entire lake, shoreline to shoreline. It's amazing! "How about right over there?" Abe points to an area that's partially shaded by a beautiful pine tree.

"That's perfect!" We walk over and I help Abe spread the blanket. I kneel down on the blanket and just continue to take in the view.

"How did I not know about this place?" I ask Abe.

"They just cleared this area and made it an overlook about four years ago. This is my favorite spot. I come here a lot just to clear my mind, meditate," Abe says while taking in the view like it's the first time he's seen it too.

I get my phone out and take some pictures. The kids need to see this.

"Are you hungry, Laney?" Abe asks before opening the basket.

"I sure am! What do you have in your magical basket?" I ask, teasing.

"A little bit of this and a little bit of that." Abe begins unpacking perfectly wrapped cheeses, crackers, nuts, and figs in containers. Bottled waters, fruit, all cut.

"Holy cow, did you do all this yourself?" It's always shocking to me to see a man do anything domestic.

"I sure did. It's really nothing too fancy, Laney. Don't give me so much credit." Abe hands me a little plate and he closes the basket so we can use it as a little table. "Dig in!"

This is a perfect little lunch. The view, the food, the company. I really like Abe. I'm trying not to, but he is giving me no reason not to. He's very charming and it doesn't hurt that he's pretty darn handsome. He's so intelligent and interesting as well.

We talk about our work and schooling. I tell him that I didn't go to college. I'm always a little embarrassed to say that because it seems like every one I know went to college. Not Jim and I. We had to rush off and get married. Luckily, we had enough common sense to run a halfway decent business. Pure luck.

"I actually went to Harvard," Abe says, trying not to sound boastful.

"Are you kidding me? Harvard? That's incredible. I'm so impressed, Abe,"

I say truthfully. I respect people who have a passion to learn. Abe goes into some detail, but I have a feeling not all detail, when talking about what he's done since then. I'm curious, but at the same time respect the fact that he doesn't want to share everything about himself. I know I'm not going to tell him about Brady. Not yet.

"What are you thinking about, Laney?" Abe asks as if he can read my face.

I do have the kind of emotional face that shows every thing I am feeling. That's why I can never play poker.

"Just thinking how crazy life is. A couple of years ago, going through the divorce and all, was really tough on me. But I feel like I'm in a good place now. It's amazing how just taking a moment, to enjoy the scenery, can put things in perspective."

"I know. That's why I kayak and that's why I come here. Makes me appreciate life and living. Sometimes we all just get too caught up in things that don't matter," he says, turning his face up to the sky and closing his eyes.

"I agree." I lean back and do the same. We sit like that for a few minutes in silence. It's so relaxing here. We are both startled when a family of four comes running out into the opening. The couple has two boys and the boys are throwing a ball back and forth to each other. I think back to when my kids were little and smile at the memory.

"Well, you ready to go? Kids tend to ruin the peace and quiet of the place," Abe says, standing.

"Sure. That was really nice, thank you, Abe," I say politely, but I can't help but be turned off by his last comment. "Hey, Abe, I never asked you, how old are you?" I know he's older than George, but I cannot tell by how much.

"I am forty-three. How old did you think I was?" He asks, smiling.

"Honestly, I thought thirty-eight at the most. Ya jerk, you are aging well! It's unfair!" I smack his arm in a playful way.

"It's my weekly Botox injections; they're really doing the trick!" Abe jokes.

When we get back to the house, I give Abe a hug, thank him for lunch, and head back to my place. I'm really glad I had lunch with Abe. I don't want to deny myself meeting new people or possibly liking someone else because of Brady. I did that for three years in high school. I always regretted that. We really have only been on one true date. It's not healthy to put all your eggs in one basket, I remind myself. But at the same time, I know in my heart that once again, all my eggs are in Brady's basket.

I peek out the side window and do not see any dock boy action down the cove. Darn it. I missed him. That's okay. It only makes the excitement of seeing him again tonight build. I can't help but smile at the feelings I'm having.

Chapter Twenty-Seven

The banquet starts at seven. Allie arrives to my house at 7:10.

"Again, Laney, you look hot!"

Allie is the best kind of friend to have. She's so complimentary but also tells it like it is.

"Why, thank you, so do you as usual."

She has on a long ruffled skirt with a tank. Pretty sure no bra, but I don't stare. I found a great dress on sale yesterday. It's form fitting on the bottom but is blousy on the top and swoops down in the front to reveal the little bit of cleavage that I have. With my black strappy heels, I do feel sexy. The thought of seeing Brady makes me feel even more so.

"Are you ready to go?" I ask, feeling antsy and excited.

"Can I have a drink first, Lane? It's good to be fashionably late."

I know that's true, plus it helps with playing hard to get. At the same time, I can't wait to be in Brady's arms.

Ding-dong. A text!

Don't keep me waiting too long, I've been dying to see you all day.

Allie grabs my phone. "Let me see that." She reads the text. "Holy cow, this boy is whipped. What did you do to him, Laney? He's like you in high school!"

I smile, feeling like a winner.

"I know. It's so great, Allie. I haven't felt this way since high school. He gives me nonstop butterflies. And guess what we did last night, twice?" I say, grinning as if I made a huge conquest.

"No way, Laney! Oh my gosh, that's amazing! I'm so happy for you," Allie hugs me. "You really needed that, girl. That was way too long of a dry spell."

We both laugh and I anxiously watch her finish her drink.

"So you ready to go now?" I ask, like a little kid.

"Yes, Little Miss Ants-in-her-pants! Or should I say, Miss Brady-in-her-pants?"

Again we crack up laughing.

"I'm going to drive separately. Not sure how long I'm going to last at this gig. Seems a little boring for me."

"That's fine." I know that even if Allie leaves, I'll have Brady there.

We arrive at the banquet hall and walk in. Wow, Grace's team outdid themselves. The hall looks great and it's packed. The girl I didn't know from packet pick up is collecting our tickets at the door.

"The bar is in the left corner, food on the right. Enjoy your evening."

By the look and sound of it, that girl has said that same thing about three hundred times or more. I look around the room for Brady. I don't see him immediately. Allie walks toward a group of people standing to the right of the room. It's a bunch of people that we graduated with. Geez, everyone looks so…old. Do I look that old? Shit. We all make small talk. The music isn't so loud; you can actually speak to people. A guy I graduated with who always made me laugh, Dave Buckleman, yells over the group, "Hey, Laney, heard you finally landed Brady Gramble! Cheers!" Everyone lifts their glass and drinks to me and Brady.

I'm beet red and respond, "I don't know what you're talking about, Dave. Now go get me a drink!"

Dave laughs and walks to the bar.

Allie yells, "Dave, get two!"

I look past Dave at the bar and see Brady sitting on a stool alongside the bar with Pete and his wife, Jean. Some woman is standing directly in front of Brady and is leaning in talking his ear off. It's a little bit of a turn-on seeing another woman hitting on Brady. I know his body language already. He is obviously uncomfortable with this woman's advances. That makes me feel better. I know Brady wouldn't hurt me, or would he? I quickly get my phone out of my purse and send him a text.

Tell that bitch to back down. You are my man!

I watch Brady dig his phone out of his pocket and read my text, all while the woman is still talking a hundred miles a minute. Brady smiles and looks around the room. He spots me, and his face lightens. God, I love having that effect on him. I wink at him and he winks back.

The DJ plays a slow song and I'm interrupted from hearing about a class-mate's hysterectomy by a tap on my shoulder. I turn, expecting to see Brady, but there's Pete. In all his bearded, bellied glory.

"Miss Laney, may I have this dance?" He puts his hand out for mine.

"Sure," I say, trying not to sound too disappointed. He walks me out to the middle of the floor and spins me in a circle, then pulls me to him.

"Laney, you look fine," he says as a strong smell of alcohol blows in my face.

"Thanks, Pete, you…look fine too." I look over to the bar and see Brady smiling. He shrugs his shoulders, then goes on pretending to listen to the woman gabbing in front of him. Jean, Pete's wife, is sitting on the bar stool glaring at Pete and me. Lovely.

"So, Laney, how is it that you've been back in town for two weeks and you're all I hear about?" Pete asks through his 'needing-a-trim' beard.

"I have that effect on small towns. Happens wherever I go really," I say, smiling.

"I bet it does, I bet it does. Well, I don't know what you did to my boy Brady, but he can hardly build a dock this week, he's so preoccupied. I'm a little concerned, Laney. You leave here in two months, then what becomes of Brady? I hate to have to help him through a broken heart again. Pissed the hell out of Jean last time because I spent more time with him than her!"

Oh my, I'm taken aback by what Pete's saying. It's so hard to think of the future when what you have in the present is so deep and amazing.

"I don't know, Pete. I haven't given it much thought. I don't want to think about it. It makes me sad." My face must be visibly showing my concern and how the direction of our conversation has changed. I see Brady excuse himself from the talker and head toward us on the dance floor.

"Pete, I think it's my turn to dance with Laney now," Brady says sternly as if he knows what Pete is up to.

Pete knows that Brady is on to him. He stands back and says to Brady, "Wasn't it enough to have your heart broken by Susie, man? Why are you wasting your time? She's out of here in two months, bro. Get out while you can." Pete looks at me with disgust.

I feel like I've had the wind knocked out of me. This is too much.

"I should be going." I begin to walk away. Brady grabs my arm and pulls me back into the huddle of him and Pete.

"Listen, Pete, I appreciate everything you have done for me. You've been a great friend to me when I needed one. If you can't be a great friend to me during the bad times and the great times," Brady looks at me and squeezes my hand, "then maybe you're not as good of a friend as I thought you were." Pete looks down at the ground, obviously caught off guard by Brady's confrontation. "And Pete, if you speak to Laney like that ever again, you know I'm going to have to knock the shit out of you, right?"

Pete says, "Sorry man, sorry. Maybe I just had too much to drink. I dunno. Sorry, Laney." Pete walks off the dance floor with his tail between his legs. He sits next to Jean at the bar and looks defeated. Brady pulls me into his arms and dances with me slowly, just hugging me.

He says in my ear, "I'm so sorry, Laney. He's a stupid, drunk, jealous man. Part of me even thinks he's not over you from eighth grade. He hasn't been supportive of us at all."

I think about everything that Pete said. It was true in a way. I will be hurting Brady when I leave. But I'll be hurting me too. Just thinking of that moment makes me sick.

The song finishes, but I really don't want to let go. Neither does Brady, so we just stand in an embrace. Then, with people starting to fast dance around us, Brady leans in and kisses me. A long, delicious, 'take-that-Pete', kiss.

Brady walks back with me to the table of my former classmates. Dave starts clapping for us, hands me my drink, and shakes Brady's hand. I spend the rest of the night with Brady's arm around my waist, chatting it up with old friends. It is a blast! We never even see Pete leave, but I have a feeling it wasn't long after the dance floor incident.

"I'm heading out, lover girl," Allie says in my ear and gives me a hug.

"Okay, I'll talk to you tomorrow," I say with a wink.

"Get it on, girl," she says in my ear. She hugs Brady and gives a few of the others goodbye hugs and leaves.

We stand around for probably another hour, when I lean up and whisper in Brady's ear, "You want to go back to my place?" I read his face. He gives me a huge dimpled smile and nods his head yes. We say our goodbyes and head out the door of the hall.

We get back to my house and there is another wrapped treat on the front steps. Oh boy, not a good time, Abe. I carry it inside and put it on the counter.

"I'm suspecting that's not your first delivery?" Brady asks.

"Nope. Been getting some yummies almost daily. It's the guy next door. He seems very nice, but really, I'm going to gain a hundred pounds while I'm here if I keep eating his baked goods. Do you want it? Take it." I say and push the plate toward him.

"There's a note, here." Brady hands me the note and begins eating a delicious looking piece of German chocolate cake.

I read the note to myself.

> Thanks for joining me for lunch today.
> We should do it again some time soon. - Abe

Oh, Abe, I'm not so sure about that.

"Come over here. You need to taste this. I think something is wrong with it," Brady says with a horrible look on his face. He gets a spoonful and I lean into the spoon to smell it first. Brady smears the icing and the cake all over my face. I can't believe I just fell for that. He starts laughing, then begins to lick the cake off my face. He is so sexy and fun. I take a handful of icing and smear it all over his mouth and face and proceed to lick it off as well.

"Very funny, Brady, very funny. The cake is good, though I like it best on you." Our licking turns into a passionate kiss. We quickly take all that passion into the bedroom, where we make love once again. I can't get enough of him. I feel like I can spend every day of my life making love to Brady Gramble.

Chapter Twenty-Eight

When I wake the next morning, I reach over to touch Brady and he is not in bed. I can smell the coffee brewing. I stretch and think about what a lucky girl I am. Brady is obviously cooking breakfast. I forgot that he rebuilt this place, so he obviously knows his way around.

I yell out to him, as I make my way to the bathroom to freshen up, "Good morning, gorgeous!"

"Right back atcha, hot stuff!" he yells back.

Smiles. All I see are smiles every time I look in the mirror. I feel like I've smiled more this past week than I have in my lifetime. The scary part is that I feel like I am truly in love. How can that be? It's only been a couple of weeks, I remind myself. I would be so pessimistic and doubtful if someone came to me and said they were in love after two weeks. A part of me thinks we are truly destined for one another.

I look back in the mirror. This is as good as it's going to get this morning, I think to myself. I throw my sweatshirt and my yoga pants on and walk to the kitchen.

"There she is!" Brady walks toward me, wraps his arms around me, and gives me a huge bear hug. He then holds my face in his hands, gives me a soft, gentle kiss on the lips, and says, "I couldn't wait for you to wake up! I missed you, and I've only been awake for thirty minutes!"

I'm melting. Who says things like this? No one has ever said such loving things to me.

"You are so darn cute. I'm having so much fun with you," I say, while Brady pulls me into a giant hug again.

"I'm so disappointed in myself that I was such an ass in high school and never approached you. Makes me wonder what would have happened if I had," He looks a little sad.

"Oh my goodness, I don't know. Things happen the way they are supposed to. So what did you make for breakfast?!" I ask, changing the subject. I don't want to think of what might have been. "It smells delicious!"

"For you, madam, I have some scrambled eggs, toast, and coffee. Sorry, I didn't have much to work with. We need to get you some groceries today. Oh, and I guess we can have this danish. Is this from the guy next door too?" Brady asks, holding out the plate.

"Yeah, he brought that yesterday morning," I say, totally uninterested in Abe's danish as I fix my coffee.

"Geez, Laney, I think this guy has a crush on you. Is this the guy you had lunch with yesterday?" he asks with a hint of jealousy.

"Yes. Besides the baked good deliveries, I really don't get that vibe from him." That's the truth. Before sleeping with Brady, I found Abe attractive and funny, but then it kind of fizzled when I realized how bad I have it for Brady. Turned into more of a friendship feel.

"Where did you go for lunch?" Brady asks while sipping his coffee.

Shit.

"Well, he said we were going to a spot that had a great view of the lake. I couldn't imagine what restaurant had that kind of view..."

Brady says, "The Overlook? He took you to the Overlook?"

"Yes. He packed a picnic lunch. I honestly had no idea; otherwise I probably wouldn't have gone. But truly, he didn't make a move on me. It was very platonic."

Brady looks down at the newspaper on the island.

"Brady, look at me. Please."

He looks up and stares me straight in the eyes. I can see the pain behind his.

"I have been so hurt by dishonesty and cheating. It killed a part of me. You have been hurt the same way. In a million years, I would never, ever inflict that kind of pain on you or anyone. You need to believe this. I never really had an opportunity to fill you in on lunch, and to be honest, it didn't cross my mind. The whole time I was up at that overlook, there was only one person on my mind."

Brady looks at me and says, "Pete?"

We both bust out laughing.

"Yes, Pete and his sexy beard." I walk, practically run, toward him and hug him. I can no longer play hard to get with this man. I am his and he is mine.

We spend the rest of the morning just relaxing and talking. About our kids, our exes, our childhoods. I didn't know that he was in fourth grade when he moved to Falcon Lake. I thought he had always lived here. He didn't know that I've been friends with Grace since first grade. It's so easy to be with Brady and the conversation is effortless. Brady decides he is going to cook dinner for us this evening. I don't think I've ever had a man cook me dinner before! We shower, get dressed, and head to the super market.

We look like any other married couple food shopping together. Brady is picking out what he needs for his meal, and I'm picking up my usual odds and ends. We turn down the third aisle and I recognize immediately the man standing in the aisle, looking at baking supplies. Abe. Oh boy, this should be interesting.

"Abe—hey, how are you?" I say before he sees us. I can see Brady's body stiffen.

"Hey, Laney! Good, how are you?" he asks me, but he is looking at Brady.

"Great, thanks. Abe, this is Brady Gramble. Brady, this is my neighbor, Abe Olsen."

They shake hands and exchange pleasantries. I know Brady is a little jealous that I had lunch with Abe.

"Uh oh, buying more baking supplies? I'm going to have to have elastic bands put on my pants," I say with a nervous giggle. This is a very uncomfortable situation.

Then Brady chimes in. "Oh, hey, you made that German chocolate cake? That was delicious! We really enjoyed that, didn't we, babe?" Brady looks at me with a smart-ass, dimpled grin on his face. I want to punch him in the gut at that moment, but I refrain. For now.

"It was my favorite so far. Thanks so much, Abe. Well, I hope you have a nice day. See you soon." I quickly push the cart past Abe, who is still standing there, looking shocked.

I turn around to the next aisle and smack Brady's arm. "That was not nice!" I quietly scold him.

"Why not? You said you didn't get a vibe that he liked you. What's the big deal?"

"Well, of course, there's a chance he may have liked me. Between the picnic and the baked goods! He just was not making any physical moves! Oh my gosh, so embarrassing," I say, shaking my head.

"Relax, at least now he knows for sure that you are mine," Brady says with a sexy smile, wrapping his arm around my waist.

"That's true, but what if he stops baking for me? I really liked his goods," I say, pretending to pout.

"You can have my goods, baby."

Brady is making me get the chills all the way down to my feet. This man makes me sweat. We hurry through the rest of the store so we can get home. I'm eager to try out Brady's goods once more.

Chapter Twenty-Nine

Dinner was fabulous. Beef tenderloin, steamed broccoli, and a rice pilaf. I'm pretty sure if Brady made me peanut butter and jelly I would think it was fabulous at this point. I'm cleaning up the dinner dishes when Brady comes up behind me and wraps his arms around my waist.

"Hey, it's getting late. How about you drive me home real quick. I'll get my stuff and my truck, and come back here for a sleepover? Then tomorrow morning I just have to roll out of bed to get to work," he says, while kissing my neck, giving me chills all over my body.

"Well, all of that sounds fine except the rolling out of bed part. I wish you didn't have to work!" I turn and face him. "I loved being with you all day today. I can't believe I've only been here two weeks. I feel like my whole world has been turned upside down." I wrap my arms around his neck.

"Laney, I know this may sound ridiculous to you, but I swear it, I think I'm falling in love with you." My heart just jumped out of my chest. "I'm sure of it." He looks even more beautiful after hearing those words come out of this mouth.

"Really?" I ask, blushing.

"I mean it. I don't know if you're feeling that way, too, but it's like nothing I have ever felt. It's so intense," Brady says with a look of sincerity in his eyes.

"I feel the same way, Brady. It seems crazy that it could happen this fast, but at our age, I guess the heart knows what the heart wants." I kiss him. We lean back and look at each other, and we're wearing the biggest smiles ever.

The drive back to Brady's house only takes ten minutes. "You want to come in with me?" Brady asks before getting out.

"No, that's okay. I'm going to head back and do a couple of things. I'll see you back there. Hurry though, because I'm going to miss you."

Brady smiles and gives me a reassuring kiss on the lips.

"I'll be right behind you!" He jumps out of the car and heads in his house.

On the drive back to my house, I'm reliving the moment of Brady Gramble telling me that he loves me. Did that really just happen? I am floating on a cloud. I'm so deep in thought I don't even see the deer that just runs in front of my car. I slam on my brakes and miss hitting it by inches. Wow, my heart is racing. Forgot about the damn deer up here. Especially around the lake. The lake. The lake that I'm leaving in less than two months after falling in love. What the heck am I doing? How will this ever work? I am not moving back here and he most definitely will not move to Charleston. What have I started and how is it going to end without both of us getting hurt? I shake the thoughts from my head and remind myself to live in the here and now.

I focus on the road and pull into the driveway. Hmmm, that's weird. I don't remember leaving my bedroom light on. I know I didn't. Just the light over the sink. Something doesn't feel right.

I call Brady. "Brady, hey, I just pulled up to the house and the bedroom light is on. Did you leave it on?"

"No, I wasn't in the bedroom. Do not get out of your car. Understand?"

"Yes, yes. Of course. I can't see anything moving in there. I'm sure we just left it on by mistake."

"Maybe we did, but don't take any chances. I'm on my way, stay put. Laney?" I'm trying to see if I can see anyone in the house from the driveway. I'm sure if they were in there, me pulling in the driveway scared them off.

"Okay, I'll wait in my car. Should I call the police?" I ask, starting to get a little nervous.

"No, I'll check it out. I have a gun. I'll bring it with me." Brady has a gun… hmmm…not sure if I like that, but I'm used to guns coming from the South. We kept a gun locked in a vault in our house for emergencies.

"Okay, good. See you in a bit. Watch out for deer, I almost hit one."

"Lock the car doors and just wait."

I sit for what feels like an eternity until Brady shows up. He gets out of his truck and comes to my door. "Give me the key, Laney."

I hand him my keys and he heads to the front door, motioning at me to stay in the car. Oh my gosh, this is terrifying. I don't think anyone is in there, but if anything happens to Brady, I'm not sure what I'll do. He goes in the house and closes the door. I can see his shadow making its way around the house. I'm thankful he knows the whole layout of the house. Every nook and cranny. He's in the house for about seven minutes; I'm watching the clock. He comes out, walks to my car, and opens my door. "There's nobody in there. I'm not completely convinced that someone wasn't though. Come on in and see if anything is missing or out of place." Brady helps me out of the car and we head into the house together.

I walk around the entire house, not really noticing anything out of place. "Did you lock the back door, Laney? It was unlocked." I try and remember.

"I honestly can't remember. Maybe I forgot to lock it. Why would someone come in here and not take anything though? My laptop is sitting right there," I ask Brady as if he's a detective.

"I don't know. Maybe you messed up their plan when you pulled back in the driveway," Brady suggests.

"Or maybe I left the light on to begin with and totally forgot. That wouldn't surprise me either!" I laugh and try to get Brady to relax. He seems pretty uptight. "Why don't you put the safety on that gun and put it away? I have a love/hate thing with guns. I know how to shoot them, but they scare the crap out of me."

"Laney, since you know how to use that, why don't you keep it in the table next to the bed? Just in case. For when I'm not here. It scares me to think someone was in here and could have harmed you." My initial thought is, no I'll be fine. I'm not used to having someone worry about me. Jim never worried about me. I really hated that about him.

"That's not a bad idea, Brady. That would make me feel a heck of a lot better. Plus, I'm probably a better shot than you, so it's best if it's on my side of the bed," I say, teasing him.

Crime is rarely an issue here. Growing up, we never locked our doors; everyone knew everyone else. There was such a great sense of security. I guess I need to be careful and pay closer attention to what's going on around me. Brady and I get ready for bed. All this excitement has worn us out. We snuggle under the blankets and face each other. Brady pushes my hair off my face and puts it behind my ear.

"I love your eyes."

He is so sexy. He's not even trying to be sexy, he just is.

"I love your dimples," I say, running my finger over them.

"I don't want this to end, Laney. What are we going to do?" he says with such concern in his voice. I guess it's been on both of our minds.

"I say we cross that bridge when we get to it, Brady, and just enjoy what we have right here, right now." Brady takes my face in one hand and puts his other hand behind my head. He pulls me in for an amazing kiss. We make love again, but this time it feels so much more intense. So full of love and passion. Sharing our feelings with each other has created an intimacy between us. I want to scream at the top of my lungs that I love this man. We reach our climax at, again, almost the same moment and just fall into each other's arms.

Brady says softly in my ear, "I love you, baby."

"I love you, too, Brady."

Chapter Thirty

Morning comes too fast. Brady's alarm goes off and I watch him, through one eye, make his way to the bathroom. For a man approaching fifty, his body is tight. Great ass. And that ass is all mine. Lucky girl. While Brady is in the shower, I force myself out of bed and make a pot of coffee. I'm still half-asleep and drop some of the coffee grounds on the floor. Damn it.

I grab a wet paper towel to pick them up and notice a small little sticky note pad on the floor under the cabinets. That's weird, where did that come from? I open the drawer right above it, which I remembered is a "junk" drawer, and put it back. I haven't opened that drawer since I first got here. I'll have to ask Brady about that later. First, I have to make him a nice breakfast for all the hard physical work he's about to do. An omelet with spinach and cheese and a side of toast should do. I put so much care and love into this omelet and I have to say, I'm proud of myself. I hear Brady finishing up in the bathroom. I have his seat all ready with his breakfast. He walks out of the bedroom with a great big smile on his face.

"Well, this looks better than Henry's!" He gives me a bear hug and a kiss on the forehead. "I could get used to this!" He sits down and takes a taste of his coffee. "Fixed perfectly, thanks babe."

"You are so welcome. I hope you like it," I say, proud of my omelet. He's already digging in and nodding his head yes.

"It's delicious. Aren't you going to eat, babe?"

"I'll eat later; it's a little early for me yet. I'm actually thinking of going for a run this morning. It's been almost a week since I've exercised and I feel like crap."

"Hey, don't forget we ran that 5K on Saturday morning!" He winks at me while sipping his coffee.

"Oh, I know. I'm still sore," I say, smiling at the memory of it. "Maybe I'll find a gym instead of hitting these hills again," I say, rubbing my knees like I'm in pain.

"There's a gym right on Piedmont. It was the old tennis club."

"Oh yeah, that's right. Perfect. I think I'll go there, get a temporary membership."

"Why don't you get a permanent membership?" Brady asks in a serious tone. It breaks my heart.

"Because I'm living in the here and now, and here and now, I just need a temporary membership. Please, don't make me feel bad," I say and put my head down.

Brady reaches across the table and lifts my chin up. "Laney, I'm sorry. I have no intention of making you feel bad. But know this, I also have no intention of letting you go." And just like that, he goes back to eating his breakfast.

"Okay, gotta head out. Pete is waiting on me over there." Brady gets up and grabs his keys.

"No, I don't want to let you go," I whine and hug him, putting my head against his heart.

"Sorry, baby. I've got a dock to build. How about lunch?" He pulls my head away from him so he can look me in the eyes.

"Fine." I stamp my foot. I want to tell Brady he doesn't have to work anymore if he is mine. We can be together all day long. But I know it's too early to let him in on that little tidbit about myself. Besides, I don't think it would stop him from working. He seems like the kind of guy that likes to keep busy. We share one last hug and kiss, then he's out the door.

Before I head to the gym, I call Grace to see how she's doing. She decided that she wasn't going to be needed at the banquet the other night and wanted to stay home and rest. I get that. She works hard. Grace sounds well-rested. "Hey, Laney! How was your weekend? I heard the banquet was a huge success."

"It really was. You outdid yourself as usual, Grace." She really does go above and beyond in everything she does. It's annoying, really. But I still love her.

"Let's do lunch this week, though. I want to catch up on what's been going on with you," Grace says in a suspicious way. I wonder what she knows. I'm sure her little spy, Beth, told her she saw me dancing with Brady.

"Oh, I've been busy, Gracie. I'll bring you up to speed this week. Any day is good for me, just let me know your schedule. Talk to you soon!"

I put on my workout clothes, throw my hair up in my ponytail and hat, and head to the gym. Before I leave I make sure everything is locked up. It only takes me five minutes to get to the gym and my is it beautiful, and full of beautiful people. I get a month by month membership from a girl who looks very familiar, but I don't feel like doing the small talk to figure out where I know her from. I hop on a treadmill, put my headphones on, and start running.

I'm about a mile in, and in the mirror that's against the whole wall of the gym, I can see that Abe has walked in. He walks directly to the free weights and starts his workout. I don't think he sees me. Which is fine. That scene in the grocery store was completely uncomfortable. Obviously he may have been interested in me. I mean, who packs a picnic lunch for a friend? Then Brady has to say he loved the cake. Jerk. But he still makes me smile. I would have done the same thing if the scenario played out the other way around.

I'm about two miles into my run when Abe walks in front of the treadmills to use some of the machines there. He still doesn't see me; at least he's not making eye contact with me. That's okay, I'm sure I look close to death. You take one week off running and forget it. It's like you have to start training all over again. It's exhausting. Two miles is all I have in me today, so I reduce the speed of the treadmill and do a fast walk for the next mile. I finish up and do a quick scan of the gym. No Abe. I get off the treadmill and open the door to exit the gym and practically walk right into Abe who is headed back in.

"Well, hey neighbor! How's it going?" I ask casually.

"Oh, hey Laney. Good, good. Just forgot my headphones in the car. How are you doing?" He asks, but not sincerely at all. He's barely making eye contact with me.

"Good, happy to have my workout over with," I say, still out of breath. An awkward silence ensues.

"Well, gotta go. Have a nice day," I say and scoot past him.

"See ya."

Oh boy. Looks like I may have pissed him off. I'm sorry for that, but I don't think I gave him any kind of signs that I was interested in him. I know I didn't lead him on. He'll have to get over it. I have a hot lunch date I need to get ready for.

On the drive back home, I think back on my interactions with Abe. Just to make sure I never led him on. I know I didn't. I found him attractive certainly, but nothing more. I hope he lightens up. I don't want to spend the next two months avoiding him or having to feel uncomfortable around him. I pull in the driveway and see George returning from a run.

"George! How have you been? Haven't seen you since Thursday night." I yell to him.

"Hey, Laney...sorry, still catching my breath. I'm doing better now. Came down with a stomach virus Friday afternoon. Just got out of bed yesterday. It was horrible."

"Oh no, George. I'm so sorry. You probably shouldn't be running just yet." I dish out my motherly advice.

"Yeah, I realized that about a half mile in. Didn't get very far," he says with his hands on his knees, trying to catch his breath.

"Well, take it easy. Let me know if you need anything."

George thanks me and I head back into the house.

I get my phone out and text Allie.

Your boy toy had a stomach virus. Hope you are okay.

Yes I know- he texted me. So far I'm okay, but just
thinking about him puking is making me feel nauseated.
How are things with you and lover boy?

Had an amazing weekend with him. I'm totally in love with him Al.
Am I crazy?

Absolutely not! You can't control love.
It has a mind of its own. Just enjoy. He's hot.

Let's do lunch this week—I'm free every day but today so far.

How about tomorrow?

Sounds good to me, I'll come to your shop at noon?

I'll be waiting!

I peek out the kitchen window to see if the dock boys are busy at work. Hmmm. I don't see anyone. Weird. Maybe they're out getting supplies. I decide to get showered so I can go to the store and buy some lunch. Before I get in the shower, I make sure the doors are locked. I'm still feeling a little paranoid, I guess. I forgot to ask Brady about the sticky note pad I found on the floor. I'll ask him at lunch.

Chapter Thirty-One

The shower feels great. I blow out my hair, put my makeup on carefully. I throw on this cute brown knee-length skirt, a poncho sweater, and my great Italian leather boots. It's amazing how being in love makes you feel so much more confident in everything. I have been feeling so sexy lately, so desirable. It's really been an ego boost for me to be here.

I head straight to this sandwich shop that I have been to a few times over the years. As I walk in and see the board filled with choices, I realize something. I really don't know what Brady likes. Crap. Well, of course I don't. I've only known the guy two damn weeks.

I play it safe and order three different kinds of sandwiches. I'm bound to get one right. A woman walks in while I'm waiting. Again, another familiar face, but I can't place her. She is very pretty but looks a mess. Clothes wrinkled, hair all over the place. But you can see in her face a beauty that once was.

"Hey, Susie," the guy behind the counter says. "What can I get you today?"

Susie. Hmmm. I don't know anyone named Susie. Wait a second, all the pieces are coming together now. Susie! Holy crap, I'm in the same room as Brady's ex. She glances over at me and gives me a look that says, "What are you looking at?" I glance at my phone, trying to pretend I wasn't just staring at her. When she turns away, I check her out with different eyes now. How could she take a chance losing such an amazing man? What an idiot! And with her son's teacher, no less? Well, her loss is my gain.

"Ma'am, your sandwiches are ready." The young kid behind the counter breaks my stare.

"Oh thank you. Have a nice day!" I shoot Susie one last look. She looks like a lost soul. I don't feel sorry for her—you play, you pay, biotch.

On the drive home, I try to decide if I want to tell Brady that I saw his ex at the deli. I know it's the right thing to do.

"Honey, I'm home!" Brady walks through the door like he lives here.

I run into his arms, and he picks me up and swings me.

"I missed you! How's the dock going?" I ask after kissing his luscious lips.

"It's going. Sorry, I'm a little sweaty." He puffs his shirt to air it out a bit. I don't even notice dirt or sweat. Love is blind. He looks perfect to me.

"Come have a seat. I have a couple of choices for you today," I say, leading him to his lunch.

"Let me just wash my hands real quick. Wow, Laney, you went all out." Brady glances over his shoulder at the buffet of sandwiches.

"I know. I wasn't sure what you liked, so I got a little bit of everything. Would you like to sit out on the deck? It's so beautiful out," I ask.

"Sounds good to me, as long as I'm with you I can eat out in the canoe." He says, smiling with his dimples looking deeper than ever.

We grab the sandwich pieces that we want, I put them on a tray along with a pitcher of homemade sweet tea and some fresh fruit.

"You are spoiling me, Laney. First breakfast and now this amazing lunch. I can't wait to see what's for dinner!" He jokes.

"Don't hold your breath. I usually max out at preparing two meals a day. Besides, I thought we'd take the boat out and maybe go to that restaurant on the lake. Is it Sammy's still?" The place used to change owners so frequently I could never keep track.

"Nope, now it Smoky's Bar and Grill. Pretty decent food, though. Sounds like a plan to me. I'll just have to run home and get cleaned up first. Can I sleep over again tonight?" he asks, raising his eyebrows.

"Oh, you can try, but I'm not sure how much sleep we'll get," I say in the sexiest tone I've got.

"How am I supposed to concentrate on work the rest of the day? You're killing me." He squeezes my leg and leans over and kisses my neck.

Oh my. He gives me chills all the way down to my toes.

"Oh, Brady, I thought of two things I need to tell you about. First, did you open any of the drawers in the house the other night? The night we thought someone was in the house? There was a sticky pad on the floor yesterday morning that fell out of the junk drawer. I know I didn't drop it. Did you?"

Brady thinks back. "No, I never opened a junk drawer. I've only opened the silverware drawer and the drawer that has the cooking utensils in it. Are you sure you didn't do it?"

"I really don't think so. It made me think that if someone was in here, they were opening drawers, looking for something." I fill Brady in on my detective work.

"But what, I wonder?" Brady's face turns serious.

"I don't know, but I hope they found it the first time and don't come back to look for it again," I say, hoping that it's true.

"What was the other thing you wanted to tell me?" Brady says before taking a big bite out of one of the sandwiches.

"Oh, I think…I'm not 100 percent sure…that I saw your ex at the sandwich shop in town." I take a bite out of my sandwich, waiting to see Brady's reaction.

"Really? How do you know it was her?" He looks a little flustered.

"Well, I knew what she looked like from Facebook stalking her years ago. Ya know, I wanted to see who my high school crush ended up with. Then the guy behind the counter said, 'Hi, Susie.' That's when I connected the dots." I look at him over my glass of sweet tea.

"She's a mess, isn't she?"

"Yes, yes she is. In the South, she'd get a big old bless her heart."

Brady laughs. "I guess it's karma. She brought that all upon herself. As long as she takes good care of Jeremy until he graduates, that's all I care about." He shrugs his big, broad, gorgeous shoulders. "Speaking of Jeremy, you know I get him tomorrow after school and Wednesday after school. So no sleepovers those nights." He rubs his hand up and down my arm.

"That's right. And this weekend coming up too?" I ask, starting to feel very sorry for myself.

"Yeah, the weekend too. Maybe we can all do something together this weekend?" Brady asks, trying to make it seem more hopeful.

"Do you think it's too early for us to meet? Would he be okay with that?" I ask. I feel very hesitant about it.

"It's not like he's a little kid, Laney. He's practically a grown man. I'm sure he'll be fine. I'll run it past him tomorrow."

That makes me think of my own kids. I'll need to call them and tell them what's going on. I kind of dread it in a way because the last thing you want is for your kids to call you crazy and question your judgment. I do that to myself enough.

We finish our lunch and just talk a little while longer. "Gotta head back, Lane. We should be finishing the dock this week. Next week we're off to another spot on the lake," Brady says, filling me in on his schedule.

"No, you're killing me…first tomorrow and Wednesday, then the weekend, now you're going to leave the cove? You're bumming me out!"

"Come here." Brady grabs me and pulls me in for a delicious kiss. "I'll see you later, baby."

"I'm going to stalk you from the hammock in a little while," I warn him.

"I'll be stalking you right back." He smiles and heads out the door.

Ah, he makes me happy. I feel like we're an old married couple already. I really am sad that I won't see Brady for two nights, and to be honest, I'm a little nervous to sleep alone. What if there really is someone out there looking for something in this house? The thought gives me the creeps and the chills. Not going to think about it. Just like I'm not going to think about the fact that two weeks are gone and I only have six left.

Chapter Thirty-Two

I clean up the house a bit, check email, then call my kids. "Hi Jake, it's Mom," I say nervously.

"Hey, Mom, what's going on? Having fun up there?" He asks, like he knows something.

"I am, I really am. Hey, Jake, I met someone. Well, really I already knew him, but we've been hanging out and I really like him." I cringe, just waiting for his response.

"That's cool. I hope he's good to you." Then Jake changes the subject and fills me in on his life and his new girlfriend. That was easy. We end our conversation with "love yous" and "miss yous."

Okay, one down, one to go. "Kerry, I've met someone and I think I'm in love." I hold my breath and wait.

"I knew it! I thought you sounded ridiculously giddy on the phone that day! Tell me everything!"

I hit the highlights but do not go into too much detail. There are some things a daughter does not need to know.

"He makes me very happy, Kerry. I just don't know what happens when I leave."

"Well, Mom, when you start a relationship with someone that lives twelve hours away from you, that's something you need to face. I guess just wait and see. I don't want you getting hurt again, Mom. You deserve only the best."

Her caring warms my heart. I know it was a hard pill for the kids to swallow; knowing their dad had cheated on me. They felt violated as well, like he cheated on them. And he did. He cheated on all of us. Our conversation ends with the same "love yous" and "miss yous." I close my eyes and thank goodness for my wonderful children. Not sure how I would get through life without them.

Time to head to the hammock with my book. I laugh every time I look at this book. I think I've restarted it three times now. I hope today I at least get a couple of chapters under my belt. It's a beautiful, crisp, clear day. I glance to my right while walking down to the hammock and give the dock boys, well really only one of the boys, a wave. They both wave back and get to work. Well, I see Brady pause for a moment and watch me. Pete smacks his arm and they are back to work. I'm actually reading my book. Elise recommended it. A murder mystery. It's supposed to grab you as soon as you start reading. But I've been distracted.

I'm deeply concentrating on my book when I hear, "Hey, Laney." I jump and drop my book on the ground. It's Abe. Standing along side the hammock with an aluminum foil-covered plate.

"Holy crap, Abe. Sorry, you scared me! Actually, it was more the book. It's intense. How are you? Oh boy, what do you have under that foil?" I say, sitting up in the hammock.

"Do you mind if I pull up a chair?" Abe asks.

I hesitate for a second because I can feel Brady's eyes looking this way.

"Sure, grab a chair." I try and position myself into the least provocative position I can in the hammock. It's not easy. When I try to roll onto my side to face him, my legs keep rolling and I almost fall off. Then I try to place my head up on my hand, but again, the hammock tilts. I change my mind and sit up instead.

Abe pulls a chair up and hands me the plate. "It's a slice of lemon poppy cake. My grandmother's recipe," he says proudly.

"Oh, I love lemon poppy cake! Thanks, Abe." I break off a small corner of the cake to sample it. "Oh my, that's good. I'll save the rest for later." I cover the plate back up and place it next to me.

"I guess I should have brought two slices," Abe glances at Brady, who is trying not to be too obvious about his stalking. "Seems you two are pretty tight." Abe looks down, then looks up at me again.

"Yes, it's been a long time coming, Abe. I've had a crush on that man since I was fourteen," I say, glancing over at Brady. "We ran into each other a couple of times since I arrived in town and just had an instant connection, like it was fate." I try not to be insensitive to Abe, but at the same time, I want to make it clear that I am off the market.

"Yeah, he's a good looking guy. I enjoyed watching him while he was rebuilding this house." He motions back at the house I'm staying in. Wait, what?

"What…he is…you did…what?"

Abe laughs. "Yes, Laney, I'm gay. I was stressing about how to tell you, but knew I needed to."

Holy crap, I almost fall off my hammock. Again.

"You are not!" I say with my hand over my mouth, trying not to laugh.

"Yeah, I'm pretty sure I am. I've been sure since about the eighth grade."

I can't believe it. Usually my gay-dar is pretty good. I totally didn't see this coming.

"Well, what the hell, Abe? I thought you were coming on to me! All the baked goods, the picnic…crap, I should have known better!" Now we're both laughing. I get serious for a second and say to Abe, "Well, you better keep your eyes off of Brady; he is taken!" We both laugh again and Abe assures me he will behave.

"He's not my type anyway, but he's definitely nice to look at." We both look at Brady at the same time. He's looking at us like we're crazy. We catch each other's eye and laugh again.

"I have to be honest Abe. I'm relieved. I did not want to hurt you if you did have feelings for me."

"I had a feeling that you were concerned about that. As well as your hunk of burning love over there. It seemed he was declaring you his property at the grocery store. Thought I'd bring you both some relief. I do have feelings for you, Laney. I could tell when I spent that time with you at The Bird's Nest that you were going to be a great friend for me."

"I'm all in, Abe Olsen. I'm here if you need me," I say, reaching out my hand to shake his. We shake on our new platonic relationship. Abe heads home and I break off another piece of cake, give Brady a quick wave, then dive back into my book.

An hour or so passes when I glance Brady's way and smile. I keep catching him looking at me. I decide to text him.

Quit stalking me, I'm trying to read.

I watch him dig his phone out and respond.

I can't help it, you're beautiful.

Ahhh, really? He's killing me.

You are too sweet Mr. Gramble.

Speaking of sweet, what was that Abe guy doing over there?
Looked like he was hitting on you. I was about to come over there
and give him a beating.

I look up at him after reading that and I can see, even from a distance, he has his smirky grin on.

He was just showing me his goods. And making me aware that he plays for the other team. So you better watch out, Brady. It may be you he hits on.

I watch him read the text. I can see by his reaction that he's surprised.

I didn't see that coming. Well, I don't mind Abe now. He can keep bringing by the baked goods. I'll be over around 5. Love you!

Five o'clock can't come fast enough. I can't wait to hold that gorgeous man in my arms again. He's all I think about. I freshen up and put on a pair of jeans and a comfortable sweater. I'm sure it's going to be cool out on the boat tonight. Brady arrives and looks so handsome. Jeans, hiking boots, and a flannel. He sure does like flannels, and it's no wonder. He looks rugged in them. I go outside to meet him.

"Hey handsome—you look great." I grab him at the waist and kiss him.

"So do you, baby. Let's go inside." Brady practically pushes me through the front door. "Work was hell today," he says while kissing me. "I just wanted to be with you. And when I saw that dude over here, I really got jealous."

We finally come up for air.

"Wow, you did miss me!" We laugh and hug. "You ready to go?" I ask.

"Sure. You better bring a blanket; it may get chilly out there." Brady, always thinking of me. So caring.

Brady starts the boat up. It's a pretty nice speed boat with a small cabin in the front. Stacy and her husband must do pretty well financially. We slowly pull away from the dock. Brady is standing to drive and I'm sitting in the seat next to him. I see Abe outside on his deck and I give him a wave. He gives a big old wave back. Wow, I still can't believe he's gay. I never saw that coming. Hmmm. Well, maybe I'm not such a babe magnet after all. That's okay. I have the only one I want.

The houses around the lake always look so different when you see them from the lake. I haven't been out here in many years. There are a couple of new homes, some fixed-up older homes, and some that need TLC for sure. It's a pretty lake, still plenty of untouched shoreline.

I help Brady tie up the boat, then we walk hand in hand inside. "Should we sit inside or out?" I ask, noticing Brady glancing around the bar.

He exits the bar in a hurry. "I was thinking outside. Sometimes it gets smoky in here, plus they have portable heaters outside if it gets too chilly." Brady leads me to a table on the back deck of the bar. "Is this okay?" he asks, not acting himself.

"It's great. What's going on, Brady?" He pulls out my chair, then takes a seat.

"Nothing, Susie was at the bar. I wish I never had to see her, but unfortunately we live in the same town."

I try to crane my neck a little to see her, but I can't. "Was she with someone? I didn't see her."

"Yeah, she was with her dirtbag of the week. She gets around a lot these days. I'm starting to think she's on something. I feel bad for Jeremy. She usually brings these losers home with her. That's another reason he spends so much time in his room or at my folk's place."

I squeeze his hand. "Would you rather find another place to eat? I don't mind leaving if you're uncomfortable at all."

"No, no. I'm fine. Every time I see her it initially makes me angry, but I'm over it. Waitress," Brady calls and orders our drinks and an appetizer. "It just really annoys me that she ruined a big chunk of my life. She's obviously ruining her life, but now she's dragging Jeremy into it. It's amazing how much someone can change over the years. I feel like I never really knew her."

I squeeze his hand again and then pull him toward me for a gentle kiss. "I'm sorry. I know how it hurts. But you can't change Susie or how she's going to behave. You can only change how you're going to react to her and do your best to be the proper example to Jeremy."

"I know, you're right. She just frustrates the hell out of me. So back to us. Tell me how Abe told you he was gay." Brady grabs both my hands and holds them, leaning in to hear the story.

"Let me think…oh wait, it's all coming back to me. He mentioned that he thought you were hot."

"What?" Brady almost chokes on his drink, laughing. I hope that Susie is watching this whole thing. This is what true love looks like, Susie. Take it in.

Dinner was just okay, not the best food in the world, but the company was wonderful as always. "I'm getting this one Brady," I say, grabbing the bill. "No arguments." I quickly grab the check and put my card on it.

"That makes me uncomfortable, Laney."

"Well, get over it," I say in a joking way, but I can see he is bothered by it. "No, really, I'm not trying to make you uncomfortable. I can afford it and I want to." I hope he leaves it at that.

"I've been wondering how you are able to take two months off of work and the car. Did you do that well in your divorce?" he asks, but not in a prying way. I'd be curious too, if the tables were turned.

"No, actually by the time we got divorced, there was nothing left to split but debt. Jim took some major risks with our business, some loans that I wasn't aware of. Just about ruined my credit along with his. Then about a year after our divorce, I came into an inheritance. I think my grandmother was waiting to go until she knew I was divorced from Jim so he wouldn't see a red cent! I'm very blessed, Brady. My grandmother took good care of me. And now that I am able to, I want to help take care of the people around me. That includes you. So please, don't feel uncomfortable, embrace it. Because I'm not going to stop."

"Good for you, Laney. I'm so happy for you. I'll try my best not to feel uncomfortable, but it's going to be hard, I tell ya."

"We'll manage. Let's not think about it." I kiss him on the lips, just a soft closed-mouth, restaurant-appropriate kiss. I stop when I hear someone coughing. I look up from Brady's eyes and there's Susie, in all her glory.

"So sorry to interrupt you two lovebirds. Brady, can you make sure Jeremy gets to his dentist appointment after school tomorrow? He can't miss it again."

"Yes, Susie, I'll get him there. I've already spoken to him about it." Brady turns away from Susie and looks at me, trying to ignore her.

"Hi, I'm Susie Gramble, and you are?" she asks with her hand out.

I pull my hand away from Brady and shake her hand. "Hi, Susie, nice to meet you. I'm Laney McGuire."

"You from around here, Laney?"

"I am, grew up here. You?" I ask, trying not to give up too much information.

"For now. Got stuck in this crappy town when I married this guy." She points her thumb at Brady. "Now I'm just waiting for my son to graduate so I can get out. Getting tired of running into the same old people all the time." She sounds a little tipsy, so I don't want to push her too much.

"Well, sometimes the grass is greener on the other side," I say, offering her some unsolicited advice.

"Whatever. See ya." She walks back into the bar.

"I'm so sorry about that." Brady looks totally humiliated.

"Oh, please Brady, don't give it a second thought. I can handle that kind of girl, no worries. She's obviously got some major issues. I feel bad for her in a way. She lost out on an amazing man. She's a fool," I say, rubbing my nose against his.

"Ready to go?" Brady stands up and leads me down to the boat. We untie, hop in, and take off. It's starting to get dark, so Brady slows down and puts the lights on. I notice we're not going back toward my cove.

"Where are we headed?" I ask, intrigued.

"You'll see."

Brady leads the boat into a small cove where there's only a couple of houses. We're the only boat around. The lake is so quiet and peaceful. Brady turns on the radio real low, but loud enough to hear that it's a slow song playing. He pulls me up from my seat. "Dance with me, Laney?"

There's not a ton of space to dance per se, but we manage to sway back and forth a little bit, along with the boat. When the song is over, Brady leads me to the bench seat at the back of the boat. He sits down and is waiting for me to sit next to him. Instead, I grab the blanket and throw it over my shoulders. The blanket covers my whole body, but I leave the front open. Standing, facing Brady, I begin to take my clothes off. This man makes me do things I never thought I would have the nerve to do. But I want him so bad, all the time. Brady catches on to what I'm insinuating rather quickly. He glances around the cove and slides his pants off quickly. When he's done, I straddle his lap, wrapping myself and the blanket around him as well.

The sex is so hot. The thought of people being able to see us is even more of a turn on. I want to scream, but I know it will echo around the entire cove. And I want this moment to be just for us. "Oh my gosh, Laney, oh Laney." Brady moans. We both finish, but I remain on his lap, with my arms wrapped around him and my head on his shoulder. Looking out at the lake with the moonlight sparkling off it, I can't imagine it can get any better than this.

"I love you so much, Laney."

It just got better.

After a short ride around the lake, we decide to head back home. I help Brady tie the boat up and cover it. We walk back into the house.

"Oh, it's chilly in here," I say, rubbing my hands together.

"Want me to start a fire, baby?" Brady asks.

"That sounds nice. Would you like a glass of wine?"

"Sounds good to me, I'll be right back."

Brady heads outside to get the firewood. I go to the cabinet to get out the glasses and notice a dish towel on the ground. I know I left that by the sink. I am starting to freak out that someone keeps coming in here while I'm gone. I open the refrigerator to get the wine, and I almost vomit from the smell. What the hell? It's a small container of dead bait fish. I pull my shirt over my nose and mouth and put it out on the front porch. Okay. Someone is messing with me. But why and who? What do they want?

Brady comes back in with some wood and I jump. "Sorry babe, did I scare you?"

"I'm a jumpy person, sorry. Would you believe that someone was in here? I know for sure now. They left some dead fish in my refrigerator."

"Why the hell would anyone do that? Let's call the cops." He heads over to put the firewood down.

"No, no. I'm not getting the cops involved. The cops around here will do nothing; write it up and file it away. I don't feel like causing a scene. Let's just see where this goes. Obviously someone is just trying to freak me out. I'm not going to let them win." I bring the glasses over to the coffee table, get the blanket that I used on the boat, and snuggle up on the couch. Brady finishes with the fire, snuggles in next to me, and hands me my wine.

"I don't agree with you, but I will honor your wishes for now. In the meantime, I'd like to propose a toast," Brady says formally, "to a beautiful, loving woman, who has shown me more love in one week than I have felt in a lifetime. Cheers."

"Cheers. You are so darn sweet and make me so very happy," I say, leaning over to give him a kiss.

As we lay in bed, Brady holding me from behind, I can't help but think that I never want to leave here. I wonder to myself how I can stay. What would my kids do during break? Would they come up here or just head to Jim's? It would kill me not to see them. Plus, I do have my dream house in South Carolina, and some really good friends. How can I just pick up and leave that? And the winters in New Jersey. Just the thought depresses the hell out of me. What am I going to do? Just then Brady brings me back to the here and now by gently kissing my neck. I drift off to sleep.

Chapter Thirty-Three

Brady's phone alarm wakes me up and I see him go into the bathroom. I hate alarm clocks. I like my body telling me when it's time to wake up, not some obnoxiously loud beeping. I put my robe on and head to the kitchen to make Brady his coffee and breakfast. I look outside, hoping to see rain, but no. The sun is shining bright off the lake. Darn it. I was hoping for a rainy day so I could have Brady to myself all day.

"Good morning, sunshine." Brady walks out of the bedroom and comes up behind me, hugs me, and kisses my cheek.

"Good morning, doll. Coffee is ready and I'm making pancakes," I say, trying to sound cheerful. Even though, on the inside, I'm crushed because I know he won't be back to spend the night until Thursday.

"Yum, I love pancakes. You need any help?" He's so thoughtful.

"Nope, I'm good," I say, carefully flipping the pancakes. "So what is your schedule today?"

"Well, Pete and I are going to put some finishing touches on the dock down the street, then we have an estimate not far from Smoky's Bar at noon. I have to get Jeremy early from school for his appointment. After that, Jeremy and I will probably get some dinner, then go home and relax." I put the plate in front of Brady and he digs in. I sit down across from him with my coffee. "These are delicious. Aren't you having some, babe?"

"In a little while, I need to wake up first," I say, still half-asleep.

"So what is on your agenda today?" Brady asks. "Well first, work out, then I think I'm having lunch with Allie. Not sure what I'm doing later, besides missing you," I say and stick out my bottom lip, pouting.

"I know, it stinks." Brady reaches over and moves his hand over my cheek.

I grab his hand and kiss it.

We share a long stretched-out goodbye like a couple of teenagers. "Just one more kiss," Brady says leaning in.

"Okay, okay, get to work! Maybe if you have time we can meet for lunch tomorrow," I suggest.

"Sounds good. See you soon!" And he's off. I close the door and lean back against it. This house sure isn't as cute without Brady in it. Time to get to the gym.

***

My run kicked my butt today. After getting showered and dressed, I text Allie to see if she's still up for lunch.

Yes! I need to get out of here for a while. Pick me up at noon.

Hmmm, wonder what's going on with her? I'll find out soon enough, I guess. Then I text Grace to see what she's up to tonight and if she wants to come over for a sleepover.

I wish! I need more notice! Got the grandbaby tonight. Maybe tomorrow?

Works for me.

That will be fun, maybe we can go to the movies. I sit at my computer and send the kids emails, then notice I have a new one in my inbox from Stacy.

Hi, Laney! Hope you're enjoying the house and time with your friends! Just wanted to check in and see how things are going and if you have any questions. I also wanted to give you a heads up on the guys next door. I'm sure you've met them already. They are good neighbors, but I would be cautious and keep them at an arm's length. I don't want to go into any details, but we've had problems with them in the past. Nothing for you to worry about! :) Enjoy your day! Stacy

Really, nothing to worry about? What kinds of problems? Geez. Who writes crap like that and doesn't expect someone to worry? I wonder if George mentioned anything to Allie? I'm going to ask her at lunch. This is too weird. I peek out the kitchen window to see if the dock boys are working. They are and just seeing Brady from a distance makes me smile and feel all tingly inside. I think some hammock time is in order. I go in the bedroom to grab my book, when there's a knock on the door. Oh crap. It's George. Before that email I could care less that it was George, but now I am leery. I open the door and try to act natural.

"Hey George. How's it going? Feeling better?"

"Hey Laney, yes. Thank goodness I'm better. That was horrible. Do you mind if I come in for a second?"

Oh Lord. Why? Why do you need to come in? Today of all days, George, really?

"Sure," I say with hesitation. "What's up?" I ask, positioning myself behind the kitchen island, so as to have a barrier.

"I was wondering if you've spoken to Allie? I've left her a couple of messages and texted her a few times, but I haven't really gotten a response. Did I do something wrong?" He asks with puppy eyes.

"Oh gosh, George. I honestly have no idea. I haven't spoken to Allie about you. I know she's been super swamped at the store. Maybe that has something to do with it." I know damn well that has nothing to do with it. I know Allie; she's not interested in George. If she was, she would most certainly be in touch with him. But I don't have the heart to tell George that.

"Okay, well, if you see her, tell her I was asking for her." He sounds like a broken-hearted school boy.

"I will, for sure." I walk to the door to lead George out.

"What have you been up to, Laney? I've been seeing that dock truck here a lot. Does Laney have a boyfriend?" He jokes with me.

I'm not sure how much information I want to give up. That email has me on edge.

"Oh no, just getting an estimate for Stacy on some dock work." I wink.

"I'm sure you are." George winks back. "Have a nice day, Laney." George walks out and I close and lock the door behind him. Damn email.

Chapter Thirty-Four

I head down to the hammock and gingerly get in. Once I'm confident and safely positioned, I glance over to where Brady is. He is so caught up in a serious conversation with Pete, he doesn't even notice I'm in the hammock. I see Pete lifting his arms up and down as if he's frustrated or upset. Brady looks just as intense. I can hear their voices but can't make out what they're saying. This discussion goes on for a few more minutes. Brady turns his back, walks away from Pete, and heads toward his truck. What is going on? I can no longer see Brady, but I hear his truck start and pull away. Pete goes back to straightening up a pile of leftover scrap from their job. He does a double take when he spots me in the hammock. Oh crap, he caught me staring. He gives me a quick, unenthusiastic wave and gets back to work.

I want to text Brady and find out what happened, but I know he's driving. And I don't want to call because I know Pete will catch on. I pretend to be reading my book once again. When I glance up, I see Pete walking along the water's edge, through people's yards, coming toward me. Shit. Are you kidding me? What's up with today? I do not need this. Before you know it, Pete approaches me.

"Hey Laney," he says, a little out of breath. I notice he shaved his beard and got a haircut.

"Hey Pete, like your haircut." I'm trying to be nice, but I'm still quite pissed at the way he talked to me at the banquet.

"Thanks, I was starting to look like a farmer." He smirks, but I'm not amused.

"So what's up, Pete? Have you come over to lecture me again? I'm not really in the mood and I think you've said everything that I care to hear." I'm hoping he catches on to how pissed I am. He was my boyfriend for a short time, but we remained friends all through high school. I expected his support.

"Sorry about that, Laney. I didn't mean to piss you off. You know I care about you. Part of it is caring about Brady, too, but more so you. You chased that guy for three years, Laney, three years. Now all of the sudden he's interested in you? Makes no sense to me. Maybe he's after your money. He's always talking about starting his own company. I don't know. I think you're both going to get hurt, but I think it's going to be you hurting more than him."

Pete sits down in the chair next to the hammock and I get in a defensive position.

"I'm a big girl, Pete. I can handle my relationships on my own, thank you." Pete looks at me, uncertain about my statement.

"Really, Laney, can you? I just think you're chasing a dream with Brady, an ideal. You barely know him and now you two are in love? Come on! That doesn't happen in real life, Laney."

"Who says it doesn't happen in real life, Pete? Just because you've been with the same woman since birth doesn't mean other people can't have more than one relationship. Or love more than one person in their lifetime." I cross my arms. He's really pissing me off.

"I know that. I've loved more than one person in my life, Laney." He reaches over and rubs my leg.

I push it off in disgust. "Pete, what the hell are you talking about?"

"Oh please, Laney. I've loved you since the eighth grade! Then we get into high school and all you talk about is Brady this and Brady that. Now it's happening all over again!"

He's loved me since eighth grade? Is this some kind of joke? "You have got to be kidding me, Pete! You don't even know me, so how can you say you 'love' me? I've had two actual conversations with you in the past thirty years and they've both happened in the past couple of weeks!"

"If my love for you isn't real, then your love for Brady isn't real," Pete says, crossing his arms.

"Are you trying to prove a sick point, Pete, or are you just playing head games with me? Either way, I would like very much if you left," I say sternly. Who the hell does this guy think he is? Is this what he and Brady were arguing about? Holy crap.

"I just think you are both making a huge mistake and you are in over your heads. Just trying to prevent two people, who I love dearly, from getting hurt.

But you have it your way, Laney. Best of luck to you two lovebirds," Pete says as he stands to walk away.

"Thanks, asshole, appreciate your kind words. Now do me a favor and never speak to me again!" I yell to his back.

It happens in a flash. The words leave my mouth and in an instant Pete is back at the hammock, on top of me. Kissing me so hard that it hurts. Squeezing my breasts. Grinding his hips against mine. I can't believe it is happening. I try to fight him off while trying to balance myself in the hammock at the same time. I keep thinking that if it flips, Pete will crush me.

"Kiss me, Laney, kiss me! You know it's me you want to be with. Please, Laney." Pete continues kissing me, harder and harder. I can barely breathe between the weight of him and his mouth covering mine.

"Get the fuck off of me, Pete. What the hell are you doing?" I manage to get out.

Pete loses his balance and puts one foot on the ground. At this point, I am able to pull my knee up as hard as I can into Pete's crotch. I can see the pain in his face. I then use all my strength and push him over. He falls to the ground moaning, and I quickly get out of the hammock and run to the house. Up on the deck, I look back at Pete, still lying on the lawn.

"Hey Pete, who would you rather face—the cops or Brady? Your choice. I'll give you that, you dick head."

Pete looks up from the lawn and starts crying.

"Please, just Brady, not the cops, Laney. I'm a stupid, stupid man. I'm so sorry." He goes back to crying with his face planted in the grass.

I get in the house and lock the door. I call Brady, no answer. Are you kidding me? I don't leave a message. I wait for him to call back. I look back at the lawn and see Pete walking to the worksite. I can't even believe that just happened. Is this some kind of nightmare? The whole thing sinks in and I start to cry and shake. Just then my phone rings and it's Brady.

"Hey babe, what's up?" Just hearing his voice makes me break down crying. I try and get the words out between the tears. I'm barely making any sense. Brady interrupts, "I'll be right there. I'm one minute away." And he hangs up.

I wait for him at the door. He runs to the door and I open it.

"Tell me exactly what happened."

We sit on the couch, facing each other, and I tell him the whole thing. I see his jaw and hands clenching in anger. He looks like he's going to explode.

"Calm down, Brady, we need to approach this sensibly," I say, rubbing his fists.

"Sensibly? How about I sensibly go beat the living shit out of that dirt bag?" Brady stands up and storms toward the door.

"Brady, wait! You can't get in trouble, Brady. You have Jeremy; he needs you!" I yell at his back.

He stops at the door. I can see he realizes that physically harming Pete is not the right response.

"Shit, Laney. You're right." He turns around and hugs me. "Are you physically hurt?" He's holding my face in his hands.

"No, no. He just scared the crap out of me. I need to wash my face." I head to the bathroom and Brady follows.

"So this happened right after I pulled away?" Brady asks, trying to get every detail.

"Yeah, I heard you pull out and started reading my book. When I looked up, not a minute later, he was walking my way. He looked deranged when he was on top of me, like a lunatic." I shake at the thought, and Brady holds me. "I don't think he was going to rape me. It seemed like he had only kissing and groping on his mind."

"What the fuck is wrong with him?" Brady asks as if I know.

"It seems he's lost his mind."

"I'm not even sure what to do right now. Do I go over there? I'm afraid if I do I'm going to kill him. I almost don't even want to see his face again." Brady rubs his hands together.

"This is a nightmare. I wish I hadn't even come here now," I say and start crying.

Brady quickly pulls me into his arms, "Don't you dare say that. Besides having Jeremy, you are the best thing that's ever happened to me. If you hadn't come here, I wouldn't have seen Pete's true colors, and I would've been stuck in this crappy business with him the rest of my life."

"Oh, great, now I've ruined your business?" I put my face in my hands.

"Hey, Laney, listen to me." Brady pulls my hands from my face and is looking me straight in the eyes. "You didn't ruin anything. Pete and I have been butting heads for a while now. I've been looking into other options on the side. I wanted out of business with him way before you got here, Laney. I swear it." Brady tries to reassure me.

"You swear?" I ask in between sniffs, remembering what Pete said about Brady using me for my money to start his own business.

"Yes, I swear." Brady softly strokes my face.

"Okay, that makes me feel a little bit better. I need to get a tissue." I get up and walk to the bathroom.

When I come back, I see Brady looking at his phone.

"What is it?" I ask.

"It's Pete. He sent a text. Says he's sorry, blah, blah, blah. Wants to talk. I'll be back in a bit."

"I'm supposed to go to lunch with Allie," I say, realizing it's almost twelve.

"That's not a bad idea. Get out of the house and have some lunch. I'll be here when you get back." Brady walks over to me and gives me one last hug and kiss. His kiss is soft and gentle. "I'm so sorry he hurt you, Laney. I'm so sorry. I can assure you, it will never happen again." And with that he walks out the door, gets into his truck, and drives off.

I go to the bathroom and try and freshen up as much as I can. Did that really just happen? Pete could go to jail for assault if I reported him. What a disgusting pig. I would love to send Jean an anonymous letter telling her what a dirt bag she's married to. I'm sure she knows. I scrub my face as hard as I can. I don't even realize how hard until I look in the mirror again and see how red my face is. Shit. I look like a clown. I decide there is no way I can leave the house. I look horrible. I call Allie and give her a synopsis of what happened.

"Holy shit, Laney! I'll pick up lunch and bring it over. See you in fifteen minutes." I'm glad she's coming here. I know when I talk about the whole thing again I'm going to cry, and I do not want to cry in public. It's amazing how one minute can change everything for you. This past week I've been floating on a cloud, butterflies in my stomach, and now I feel like the rug has been pulled out from under me. What made Pete think it was okay to do that to me? Even if he did think that he loved me. I feel sick just thinking about it.

There's a knock on the door and I jump. I am so deep in thought I don't even realize how much time had passed. It is Allie.

"What the fuck just happened here? Please tell me Brady is beating the crap out of that loser? Have you called the cops yet? Where are they?" Allie throws her stuff on the counter and gives me a hug.

"Can you believe it, Al? What the hell is wrong with Pete?" I ask her, still utterly confused about the whole situation. "I'm not calling the cops, Allie. I can't, I just can't. There's obviously something wrong with him."

"Sounds to me like he's lost his mind, Laney. No normal person behaves that way. He could have crushed you to death for Christ's sake!" That makes me smile a little. Leave it to Allie to lighten the mood. "It's not too late to call the cops if you change your mind."

"Come on, let's eat. I brought some wine too. You need it." She walks around the kitchen opening drawers and cabinets. I sit at the table like a lump and just wait for her to serve me. I hate to be so rude, but I'm just so numb. And I know Allie understands.

"The whole thing is like a bad dream. I keep waiting to wake up," I say, rubbing my forehead. I feel a headache coming on. A migraine even. "I'm sorry Allie, I don't think I can eat or drink right now. I feel sick."

"I'm sure you do. No one should have to experience anything like that. Where is Brady now?"

"He got a text from Pete and went to meet with him. I hope he doesn't do anything physical. He can't get in trouble. He has a son to support." I put my head down on the table and let a big sigh out.

There's a quick knock on the front door and it opens. It's Brady. "Hey, girls." He walks over to where I'm sitting and kneels next to me. "You okay, baby?" He pushes my hair behind my ear.

"Yeah, I'm okay. Just still shocked it even happened. What happened with Pete?"

"Don't you worry about that. It's fine. Hopefully, I'll never be speaking to that asshole again." Brady looks at Allie. "Thanks for coming here."

Brady fills us in on his exchange with Pete. Although a part of me thinks he's leaving out some of the details. They basically agree to no longer be in business together. Brady is giving him the Falcon Docks name.

"I didn't want that name anyway. Limits you. People think you only do docks." Then he goes on to say that he told Pete if he even looked at me again, he was going to call the cops and report the attack.

"I don't know how you resisted beating the crap out of him," Allie chimes in.

"Well, there was one quick punch. Sorry baby, I had to. He knew he deserved it," Brady says, looking at me apologetically.

"It's okay. I'm just glad you didn't put him in the hospital. I could see that jerk pressing charges against you for battery. He has no conscience."

Brady and Allie have lunch, but I still feel too sick. "Babe, you should eat something. Let me get you some pain medication." Brady makes his way to the bathroom medicine cabinet.

"He is so good to you, Laney," Allie says taking a sip of her wine. "Is he like this all the time, or is he just putting on a show for me?"

Allie makes me smile. "Nope, he's this sweet all the time." Brady comes back into the room.

"Here, take this." Brady hands me a pill and some water.

"I think I'm going to go lie down. Do you guys mind showing yourselves out?" I'm beat. I just want to rest.

"Absolutely, I need to get back anyway. Busy today. Love you, Laney. You rest." Allie hugs me and we both turn and look at Brady.

"You're kidding, right? You think I'm leaving you after that? I'll lay down with you." Brady rubs my back.

"You can't. What about work and Jeremy's appointment?" I ask, concerned about Brady's responsibilities.

"Work is taken care of, and my parents are taking Jeremy to the dentist and bringing him back to their place. They love having him. No worries, you are stuck with me for the rest of the day."

Allie leans in my ear. "Lucky you." We smile at each other and I squeeze her hand.

"Thanks for coming, Allie. I'll talk to you tomorrow."

Allie heads out and I head straight for my bed. I hear Brady cleaning up the lunch mess and putting things away. Then I hear him kick off his work boots and take off his dirty jeans. He gets under the covers and holds me from behind.

"I am so sorry to have put you in that position, Laney. If I had any idea Pete was such a sick bastard, I would have gotten him out of my life a long time ago." Brady kisses my cheek and hugs me.

"It's okay, there was no way of knowing." I need to close my eyes. I can feel a migraine growing in the back of my head. A total stress headache for sure.

Chapter Thirty-Five

When I wake up, I'm unsure of where I even am. I was dreaming of South Carolina. I reach behind me, but Brady is not there. I lay back and assess my headache. It seems to be okay. Geez, I wonder how long I was sleeping. I get up, go to the bathroom, and head into the living room. Holy cow, it's four o'clock already. I can't believe I slept that long. I glance around and see Brady out on the deck, on the phone. I grab a bottle of water from the refrigerator and head outside.

"Okay, Mr. Silverstein. Yes, that sounds good. I'll see you then." Brady hangs up and stands up to greet me. "There's my sleepy head." He hugs me, then holds me back to see my face. "How are you feeling?" I'm still a little groggy, probably slept too long, but my headache is much better.

"I'm feeling a lot better, sorry about that. I never nap that long."

"Don't apologize. Of course you slept that long, you went through a very traumatic situation Laney."

Oh crap, that really did happen? I was hoping that was just a nightmare.

"Yeah, I guess so. I wonder if Pete took a long nap, too, after all the crying he was doing?" I ask.

"Let's not talk about Pete or bring his name up again. I'm done with him," Brady says.

"Okay. So, what should we do for dinner? I'm pretty hungry." I take a big sip of my water.

"What do you feel like having? I can cook you anything you like or go get something or we can go out. It's all up to you," Brady says, holding me by the waist. "Want to pick up some Italian and we can have it back here? Maybe start a fire outside?" Brady asks with a cute, dimply smile. Just thinking of it makes me feel better.

"That sounds terrific. Let's go check out some menus online."

Brady takes me by the hand and we walk inside.

We go to the store together to get some wine, then pick up our food. I feel a little guilty taking Brady away from his son for the night, but I'm so glad he's here. He makes me feel safe. We get back to the house and Brady gets everything ready for us to eat outside by the fire.

"No, I don't want you lifting a finger. You just go out by the fire pit and wait for me." Brady practically pushes me out the door with a big glass of wine in my hands. I take a sip and get a chill. It's amazing how cool it gets as soon as the sun starts to go down. It feels good, but I am shaking a little bit. I sit by the fire pit and glance over to the hammock. My sanctuary has been ruined. My spot for relaxation. Stupid, stupid Pete.

Brady interrupts my thoughts by bringing out a tray with our food on it. He sets it down on the table in between the two chairs that surround the fire pit. Then he's off to the shed for some firewood.

"You are spoiling me, Brady!" I yell to him behind me.

"You deserve to be spoiled, Laney," Brady says back. I smile and take a bite of the most delicious garlic bread ever. "Mmm, you better hurry up! This bread is delicious and I'm afraid I'll eat the whole loaf."

"Almost done. There!" The fire sparks up almost instantly.

"I've never seen anyone light a fire so fast!" I say in amazement.

Brady sits down and grabs a piece of garlic bread, "Well, I wanted to make sure I got some bread!" We both laugh, say our cheers, and clink glasses.

After a delicious dinner, Brady pulls the table out of the way and puts our chairs right next to each other. He pours me some more and has a seat next to me.

"So, what's it like in South Carolina?" Brady asks while staring at the flames of the fire.

"It's beautiful, like here, but different. So different. Different foods, the ocean, palmetto trees, tons of humidity and heat in the summer, but beautiful falls, winters, and springs. Construction workers can work year round down there." I give him an elbow in the arm.

"Is that right?" He smiles at me, dimples sparkling. "Part of me would love to try something new, but another part of me feels so safe here. This is all I know. Every time I go into a store, I know someone there. Every time I drive down the street, I recognize someone driving in the opposite direction," he reflects.

"Doesn't that get boring to you though? I like seeing new places and new faces." After I say it, I realize that might be insulting.

"I guess. I don't know." Brady seems to have had enough discussion on the topic.

"I would definitely like to see where you live, Laney."

"I would love for you to come down. You'd love my house," I say, squeezing his hand.

"So, what happens now with work for you?" I ask, changing the subject.

"Well, I already have two jobs lined up. Pete and I split the jobs we had left, and I already contacted some other people I had leads on. I have an estimate tomorrow for a third job."

"Wow, that's great! Will you hire someone to help you?"

"Yeah, I've got to work on that part tomorrow. Can't do it alone, that's for sure." Brady takes a sip of wine and stares at the fire as it dies down. "Should I put more wood on the fire, or are we about ready to go in?" Brady asks while kissing my hand.

"I think I'm just about ready to go in. Are you ready?" I'm still so worn out.

"I am. You head back in and I'll clean up down here."

I look at Brady from the deck and think of how lucky I am to have him.

Chapter Thirty-Six

No annoying alarm clock waking me up this morning. Just the smell of fresh brewed coffee. Just like every day when I wake up, I can't wait to see Brady. I go to the bathroom, freshen up, then head out to the kitchen. A coffee cup is waiting for me on top of a note.

> Hey, gorgeous. Had to run out and do some errands. I'll be back around lunch. Love you - Brady

Bummer. I didn't even hear him leave. I turn on my phone to send Brady a text. As soon as it powers up, there's a text from Grace.

> Are we still on for tonight? I'm bringing dinner!

Oh, yum. Grace is a great chef.

> Yes! I am so looking forward to it!

Now on to Brady.

> What a horrible way to start my day without seeing you. :(Thanks for the coffee!

I pour my coffee and anxiously await a return text. *Ding-dong.* My heart flutters. Oh shoot, it's from Grace.

> Me too! See you around 5!

That will be nice; spending some quality time with Grace. I'm debating on whether or not to tell her about the Pete incident. I know I should. I would want to know if something horrible like that happened to her. But it's such a small town. If word gets out, Pete's name will be tarnished forever. What he did was really wrong and stupid, but I think the key word is that Pete is stupid. In my heart I don't think he was going to hurt me. I almost feel like, in his head, he was trying to prove a sick point. What that was I'll never understand.

Ding-dong. I'm so deep in thought I jump a little. New text from Brady.

> Sorry, baby, you looked so peaceful I didn't want to wake you. I thought for sure all the noise I was making would wake you, but you obviously sleep like a rock! Believe me, I was crushed not being able to give you a hug and kiss goodbye. I'll see you in a few hours. Love you!

He's so sweet. It's such a wonderful feeling to have a man take care of you. I've never had that. Well, my dad. He took care of me. Jim, forget it. I was on my own.

There's a knock on the door and again I jump. Gosh, I guess I'm a little on edge. I can see through the door window that it's Abe.

"Hey Abe! Is that an aluminum foil covered plate I see?!? Come on in!" Abe walks through the door and places the plate down on the counter.

"How are you doing, Miss Laney?" he says in an attempt at a Southern accent.

"Well, I'm doing just fine. Whacha got under that there foil?" I ask with an even stronger accent.

"Just some cannolis," he says modestly.

"Just? Just? Only my favorite, Abe Olsen! Thank you so much! I guess if I go to the gym I can eat one right now for breakfast, right?" I ask, taking a bite out of one.

"That is fine. Just make sure you save the other one for Brady," he says and winks at me.

"I'll think about it." I smirk.

"Well, gotta get to work. You have a great day, Laney!"

"You too, Abe. Thanks again." As I'm closing the door I see a green pickup truck drive by slowly. I squint, I think out of shock, but I can clearly see that it's Pete. He's looking at Abe, then looking at me. He gets a sick ass smirk on his face, then drives off. I hope for Pete's sake that was just a coincidence that he was driving by. If I find out he's stalking me now, I'm going to kick his ass. I quickly walk over to the side window in the kitchen to see where he's headed. He's lucky. He pulls in the driveway of the house he and Brady were working on. I wonder if Brady knows he's there. I'll mention it to him at lunch. Did Brady tell Pete that Abe was gay or not? If not, I'm sure he's got some ideas running through his head right now. He sees me in my bathrobe with an attractive neighbor leaving the house. Let your imagination run away with you, Pete, you asshole.

I get dressed and head to the gym. As I enter, I see a sign advertising a special for a massage hanging at the front desk. I could use a massage right about now for sure. I bet Brady could too. Hmmm.

"Excuse me, where is the masseuse?" I ask the woman behind the counter.

"She should be here in about a half hour. Her name is Natalie and her office is right down the hall on the right." She points in that direction.

"Thank you!" As I run on the treadmill, I think about what a great surprise it would be to have a couples massage. I wonder if Brady would even be into that? I don't see why not. I'm so excited to see Natalie, the masseuse, when my run is over.

"Excuse me, Natalie?" I knock on her half-open door.

"Yes?" She turns to greet me. "How can I help you?"

"Oh hi, I was wondering if you offer couples massages?" I ask, hoping she says yes.

"We do!"

"Wonderful. Now, another question, do you ever come to people's homes to do massages?" I ask, really hoping she says yes to that question too.

"Hold on one second," she directs me in and closes the door behind me. "We do, but of course, those fees are not related to the gym. When are you thinking?" she asks, flipping open her schedule.

"This might sound crazy, but today at noon?"

She looks a little taken aback.

"Okay, short notice, let me see. Well, I'm open. I'll have to check with my partner, Amanda. Hold on, let me give her a call."

Natalie calls Amanda and I can tell Amanda seems a little annoyed about the short notice. "I'll ask her," Natalie says into the phone. "The cost is $250 for the hour. Does that work for you?"

"Money's not an issue," I say back with confidence.

"Yes, okay, talk to you soon." Natalie hangs up with Amanda. "Noon works fine for us. Just write down your name, address, and phone number and we'll see you then." She pushes a piece of paper and a pen in front of me.

"Great, thanks. See you at noon." I walk out of the gym feeling very full of myself. I ran three miles in record time and used my disposable income to get something I wanted. I'm feeling better already!

I stop at the grocery store on the way home to pick up some lunch, dessert, and wine for tonight. Grace and I have a favorite chocolate chip mint ice cream we have to eat whenever we are together. As I'm waiting in line, looking very sweaty and I'm sure smelling pretty darn bad, I glance over at the magazines next to me. My eye catches someone looking at me. I look up, and like a deer in headlights, I see Jean, Pete's wife, staring back at me from two aisles over. Holy shit. Did Pete tell her? How do I react to her? She gives me the same stern look she always seems to have on her face, then turns away. Okay, she knows something because if she didn't, I'm sure she would have at least waved. I feel sorry for you, Jean, being married to such a loser and all.

***

The shower feels great. I'm so excited to surprise Brady with the massage. I wonder where we should set up the massage tables. Maybe on the back deck? No, not private enough. I'll just rearrange some of the furniture in the living room. I get showered, throw on my bathrobe, and put my hair in a ponytail. I always like to shower after a massage, so no need to do my hair and makeup.

I head to the living room and take a look. Okay, if I slide the couch against the windows and put the chair back against the wall, two massage tables should fit comfortably in here. I start pushing the couch. Damn these things are heavier than they look. I get one side of the couch against the windows, now to the other.

Wait a second, what's this paper on the floor? It's folded like a note. I look around before opening it, feeling guilty, like I'm invading someone's privacy. I can see through the paper that it's handwritten. Probably just a shopping list or something. I open it and read in big, bold letters:

STAY THE FUCK AWAY FROM MY WIFE OR I SWEAR TO GOD I WILL KILL YOU!

Holy shit. What the hell is this? Oh my. What was going on in this house before I got here? I'm starting to think this place is cursed or something. I quickly fold the note up and put it in my robe pocket. Hmmm, so Stacy's husband was being unfaithful? And she still went to Germany with him? Or has Stacy slept around? Yuck. Cheaters. I shrug it off and get back to my rearranging.

The girls arrive fifteen minutes early to set up the tables, which is perfect, because then Brady will totally be surprised when he walks in. Natalie's partner, Amanda, is quite cute. I think I'll have her massage me. The thought of her touching Brady gets me a little jealous. Amanda lights some aroma therapy candles along the fireplace mantel and Natalie sets up soft, relaxing music. The setting is perfect.

I hear Brady's truck pull up and the door slam. I walk to the door and greet him. He's smiling from ear to ear and his dimples look deeper than ever.

"Look at you in your bathrobe. Now that's the way I like to be greeted." He picks me up and carries me in. He immediately sees we have company. His eyes glance between the massage therapists and the tables.

"Surprise! We're getting massages!" Brady slowly places me down.

"What…what do you mean?" He looks confused. Oh shit. Did I mess up?

"I've arranged for us to get massages. This is Natalie and Amanda. Natalie will be massaging you today," I say, arranging that politely.

"Hi ladies, nice to meet you. Lane, can I talk to you for a second in the bedroom?" Brady leads me by the small of my back to the bedroom. He speaks in a low tone to me so the women can't hear. "Laney, I've never had a massage before. Should I shower? Do I leave my underwear on? What?"

I start giggling. He looks like a little kid.

"Well, I don't know, Brady. Do you smell? Have you been sweating? You look good to me, but if you're unsure, go take a quick shower. There's a robe waiting for you." I smack him on the ass as he walks to the bathroom. "And get naked. Natalie will cover you up. No worries." I laugh and walk back out to the living room. The girls look a little confused. "It's his first time. He's going to take a quick shower and be out in a minute. Can I get you something to eat or drink?"

Brady comes out to the living room in his bathrobe. I have to remember to wash that. I found it in Stacy's closet, but it must have been her husband's because it fits Brady fine. "There he is. You ready, honey?" I ask, hopping on my table.

"I guess I am." He turns to Natalie. "Laney told me to take off my underwear. Is that right?" he asks.

We all laugh a little and Natalie tells him that's fine. They look away while Brady and I drop our robes, lay down on our stomachs and pull the blankets up to cover our backsides. He looks at me and mouths, "I love you," and I mouth the same back to him.

Natalie turns up the music and the girls get to work. I feel every ounce of tension leaving my body. I hope Brady is enjoying this as much as I am.

"How are you liking it so far, Brady?" I say through the hole my head is sticking through.

"Oh my gosh, it's amazing. Thank you so much, Laney."

I smile, "Don't thank me, thank Natalie."

"Thank you, Natalie," he says half moaning.

I giggle to myself. I have found my new passion. Giving Brady things he's never had before. It makes me so happy.

When the massage is over, Natalie tells us to relax, and when we're ready, to get up and dress. She and Amanda will be waiting outside. I hear the door close and turn my head to look at Brady. His eyes are closed and it almost looks like he's drooling. "You okay over there, Brady?"

His head slowly turns toward me. "I can't believe I never had a massage before. I want to get one every day now."

I laugh. "I know. They can be addicting. I think every two weeks is good. I think I'll book them now if that works for you."

"Laney, I can't have you treating me to a massage every other week," Brady says with pride.

"Brady, it's not up for discussion. Remember what I told you. I can do it. Please let me do it. You have no idea how happy I am right now that you loved the massage. It means the world to me, really. So just accept it and say thank you."

"It's not easy for me, but thank you. And when these ladies leave here with their tables, I'm going to repay you the only way I know how," he says with his devilish grin.

"Bring it on, big boy," I say with my own devilish grin.

I go outside and tell the girls we are dressed. They quickly pack up their tables and belongings. I hand Natalie three hundred dollars and book her three more times.

"Just three more visits?" Natalie asks, being a good salesperson.

"For now, yes. If anything changes, I'll let you know." I hold the door open while they shuffle out with their tables. I close the door behind me and lock it.

Brady is standing in the bedroom doorway with his robe open. Oh my, oh my. He makes me sweat. I quickly make my way to him and he moves me to the bed. We take each other's robes off. We are so smooth and slick against each other from the massage oils. Our bodies glide against each other. I don't know if it is the oils or the massage, but we have some of the best sex I have ever had in my entire life. I give him everything I have; all of me.

When we both reach climax, we collapse into each other's arms. So relaxed and so full of love. I start to cry happy tears.

"Oh no, baby, what is it? Are you okay?" Brady wipes the tears off my face.

"I'm just so happy. That was so beautiful." I feel a little embarrassed, but Brady always makes me feel better.

"That's love, baby. That's what it's supposed to feel like. I love you, Laney, so much." And he hugs me. We hold each other for a little while longer, then decide to shower. I love soaping Brady up. His body is so beautiful. I can hardly believe that it's the body of an almost fifty-year-old man. He's so solid and thick. Gosh, what is he thinking about my body? You know what? I don't want to know.

We finish showering and I quickly get dressed and get out the salads I bought for lunch. "Eat this, Brady, before you go. I almost forgot to feed you!" I say, like a mother hen. "What time is your next appointment?"

"No worries, baby. I have to pick Jeremy up at school at two." Oh crap, that's right. He's leaving for the night. "Let me help you put the furniture back."

Brady easily puts everything back in its place.

"Oh hey, that reminds me. Let me show you what I found when I moved the couch." I go back to the bedroom and get the note out from my robe pocket. I hand the note to Brady. He reads it and looks confused.

"Wow, that's bizarre. It was under the couch?"

"Yes! So it seems like someone in this house is cheating," I say, like a detective that found a huge clue.

"People suck, don't they? If you're going to cheat, get out of your marriage first," he says, like a seasoned veteran.

"I know. It's sad. Cheaters suck, not people. Cheaters." I say, thinking of how bad Jim sucks.

"Agreed. Well, let's dig into those salads, I'm starving."

Brady hands me back the note and heads to the kitchen.

"I can not thank you enough for today. That was amazing, Laney. I truly appreciate it." Brady gently kisses me on the lips. "Love you so much." He rubs his nose against mine.

"Love you, too, Brady. I guess I will see you tomorrow? What time, so I can count down the hours?"

He smiles and leans his head back. "Let me think. I can't do lunch. Gotta meet with Jeremy's math teacher; he's having a hard time. Then I have to go back to my new job and work until dark. So six or six thirty?" I feel like every minute I have here is so precious and I hate spending them away from Brady.

"That sucks," I say, like a twelve-year-old.

"I know, sorry. I've got to get that job done. The guy says he has other people he can refer me to. Referrals are huge." He explains himself when he shouldn't have to.

"I know, trust me, I know. I just hate being away from you. But I am looking forward to spending some time with Grace."

"Tell her I said 'hi' and be safe. Are you girls just planning on staying in?" he asks, concerned.

"I think so, but maybe we'll hit up The Bird's Nest. I'm sure Grace hasn't been to a bar in years. I like doing things like that to her," I say smiling.

"Just be careful, okay?" he says, lifting my chin with his fingers.

"Yes, Dad." I say and we both laugh. One last kiss and he's out the door. I sigh. A massage, amazing sex, and salad. Does it get any better than that?

I decide to take a nap. This has been one heck of a day. The massage and sex wore me out. I so badly want to head to the hammock, but I'm not feeling it right now. I plop right on the couch and cover my eyes with a pillow. It's so hard for me to shut down my thoughts. I keep thinking about the note I found…Pete…Brady…wait, what about that locked closet? I wonder what's in there? Was this note supposed to be in there? It's none of my business really. I need to let it leave my brain. But I am super curious. I wonder why

I should keep the boys next door at an arm's length, according to Stacy? What happened between them? George acts like they are buddies. Abe's never mentioned Stacy and John, has he? Hmmm. I wonder. Who the heck keeps coming in here? Why dead fish? I again try to nap; then I think about Pete. What a jerk. He's always loved me? Gimme a break. How could I not notice something like someone loving me? Was I that engulfed with Brady all those years I didn't notice that Pete was in love with me? The only thing I remember is Pete always being with Jean. Makes no sense. Now I have Grace coming here for dinner. Do I tell her or not? I guess I have to. I just need to swear her to secrecy. Okay brain, stop now. Take a nap.

Chapter Thirty-Seven

The nap is exactly what I needed. Just thirty minutes and I feel completely refreshed. I get online and decide to check emails and Facebook. Both of my kids emailed me, checking in on their mama. That makes my day! I peruse Facebook, pretending I'm not interested. Oh, an inbox message. I click on the box. Holy shit, it's from Pete.

> Hey Laney. I'm sure I'm the last person you want to hear from. Just want to tell you how sorry I am for the way I acted. I'm not sure what came over me. Just tired of hearing Brady go on and on about you two. Guess I got a little jealous or something. I don't know. Would just appreciate if you kept it to yourself. It's a small town and if that gets out, it could ruin my marriage and my business. Thanks, Pete.

I'm shaking as I read his words. I don't even know what to say, so I decide to not even respond to him. He isn't worthy of a response. Let him sweat it out. Jerk.

I decide to do a little stalking online. I check out Pete's wife's page. I know it's public because I've looked at it before. She has nothing new. Darn it. Let me check out Brady's ex, see if she's put up anything new. Bingo. Tons of pictures of her at the bar with her arms around different men. Good God, she is really a mess. Poor Brady.

I look at some of her other pictures to see if I can see Jeremy. She doesn't have one picture up of him. What the heck? I click through her pictures quickly, they all look the same. I pass one, but have a hint of recognition, so I click the back arrow. What the flip? It's a picture of her hanging all over Abe! He's really hanging all over her too. He looks the furthest thing from a gay man in this picture, that's for sure. I click forward to see if I can find any others. Nope, just that one. I click back to it and examine it. It looks like it was taken at The Bird's Nest, but I can't be sure. How bizarre. Who knows, maybe Susie was just wasted at the bar one night, sitting on guys' laps. I quick enter Abe's name in the search to see his page. He's blocked. Then I try George. Nope, he's blocked too. Darn it! What a small, small world.

Ding-dong. Oh, a text. I grab my phone off the counter. I get butterflies in my stomach. It's from Brady.

I miss you so much already.

Not as much as I miss you!

Send me a picture of you.

Oh my gosh. I blush at Brady's request. I put my phone in front of me and snap a few pictures. I review them and they all look horrible. I change my pose a little bit and make kiss lips at the camera. I'm laughing with each shot. I see one that is halfway decent and send it to Brady.

You are so damn sexy! I wish I could be there kissing those lips.

Even his texts get me hot.

Okay, now you send me one.

I can't wait for this. I'm so glad I'll be able to look at my phone whenever I miss his face now. *Ding-dong.* I'm starting to sweat a little in anticipation. My heart, a big dimple filled smiling picture. Ah.

You know what those dimples do to me. I love you!

Love you too, baby!

It's amazing the effect Brady has on me. I don't want this feeling to ever go away.

***

Grace is on time and appears very excited to be out of the house. "Woo hoo, girls' night!" she yells when I open the front door.

"Come on in, wild woman!" I grab some of the bags out of her hands.

"What the heck did you bring and how long you planning on staying? A month?"

"Oh my gosh, look at this place, Laney! It's so perfect!" she says with wide eyes.

"I know, isn't it? I'm loving my time here."

"Oh my gosh, that hammock! I need to spend some time in that!"

"It is all yours." I offer up in a put-off tone.

"Why? What's the matter with it?" Grace asks curiously. Oh boy, here we go.

"Let's pour some wine and have a seat, and I'll tell you my tale." I grab two glasses and begin to fill Grace in on the hammock debacle.

"What? No way. Pete? What the hell is wrong with him?" Grace is shocked.

"I think it's fair to say that Pete has lost his mind," I say while taking a big sip.

"I'm just stunned, Laney. Thank God you're okay. That must have been terrifying for you. I'm torn on whether or not you should report it though. What if he tries this with someone else? You think you should just let him get away with it?" she says, teary eyed.

"I know. It wasn't an easy decision. This is the best decision for the circumstances. I don't think Pete would pull that on anyone else. I believe he really thinks he has feelings for me. If my opinion changes while I'm here, I'll report him. Until then, I'm going to push the horrible memory of the experience from my mind," I say, getting chills just thinking about it. "But let's change the subject. I don't want to waste another thought or word on that asshole."

"Cheers to that," Grace says while raising her glass.

We spend the rest of the night drinking, eating, and talking. I fill her in on my relationship with Brady. "Grace, I'm the happiest I've ever been. He is so kind, romantic, and thoughtful. I've really fallen hard for him and I know he feels the same way about me." I worry about her reaction.

"Laney, all I want is for you to be happy. If Brady Gramble makes you happy, so be it. But I do insist you bring him to the baby's christening."

I smile. "Of course we'll be there." Just then I hear the familiar noise. "Let me get that." I head to the kitchen for my phone. A text from Brady.

> Just wanted to say goodnight. Hope you and Grace are enjoying yourselves. Can't wait to see you tomorrow. Sweet dreams, baby. Love you.

I read it aloud to Grace.

"Oh Laney, that's sweet. I guess you've come full circle with that guy."

"It's looking that way."

Grace and I drink a little too much and stay up way too late. But it is fun. When I wake up, I notice a little headache. Nothing too bad. I go to the bathroom, then head out to the kitchen to make some coffee. By the sounds of it, Grace is still asleep. I quietly shuffle through the house so as not to wake her. I take a look at my phone. No new messages. I quick look at Brady's picture he sent me. Ahhh, and he's all mine. For now.

Grace and I talked about what happens when my time is up here. I hate even thinking about it, but I know I'll have to face it eventually. I'm not ready to leave South Carolina. I can't. It's my home now. It's my children's home. I can't ask Brady to move there. He has his whole life here. I shudder at the thought of what will be, but suppress it. I just want to enjoy the here and now. I fix my cup of coffee and quietly head out to the deck. It looks like a beautiful day. I know it will be at six o'clock. What to do until then? Hmmm. I'll see what Grace has planned. I really don't want to just sit around. That will make the day drag out even longer.

Grace finally appears on the deck with me about thirty minutes later. "Good morning! Guess I needed that sleep. I haven't slept that long in years!" Grace says, while sitting down next to me.

"Good morning. What a beautiful day, isn't it?" I say, looking at the lake.

"It's so peaceful here. You should buy this house from Stacy. Come spend your summers up here rather than in that humidity," Grace suggests.

"What would Jake and Kerry do? I doubt they'd come with me. They have all their friends and their dad in South Carolina," I remind Grace.

We just sit in silence, enjoying our coffee. That's a great thing about good friends. No awkward, silent moments. We just allow ourselves our own private thoughts.

My thoughts only seem to be about Brady these days. I still can't believe what has happened here. I only wish I had an idea of where it is headed. After some deep conversation with Grace last night, I'm beginning to wonder if getting into a relationship with Brady was the right thing to do. It was hard to avoid because we were both so overcome with an instant attraction to one another. But should I have stopped it from becoming anything more than that? I mean, really, where do I think it's headed? It's not a fling. I have legitimate feelings for him. Are his feelings just as true? Am I being selfish like Pete said?

I am going to hurt Brady. Eventually. Because I'm not staying in New Jersey. Especially not with winter right around the corner. Shit. What have I done? I try to stop myself from thinking this way. Things will happen the way they are supposed to.

Chapter Thirty-Eight

Grace has to head home for babysitting. Darn it. Now what am I supposed to do until six? I check the movies that are out. Nope. I do need to get some groceries for dinner. I should also hit the gym. I'm not in the mood, but I know I have to. I throw on my workout clothes and head to the gym. I arrive later than usual and it is pretty quiet. I head to my favorite treadmill and begin my run. Every muscle in my body is sore. This is going to be a tough one. I try to distract myself by looking around the gym. I see a woman on an elliptical across the gym that looks familiar, but I can't place her. Everyone in this town looks familiar.

In the far corner of the room, there's an office with a window that is tinted so you can only see shadows, not actual people. There's something going on in that office that intrigues me. It's definitely two people. I can see their shadows intertwining. I guess they could be doing some kind of workout, but it really doesn't appear that way. Times like this, I wish my vision was better. Another joy of growing older.

Wow, whatever those two are doing, it is truly distracting me from the pain I'm feeling doing this run. It seems pretty darn hot, but I'm sure if it is what I think it is, it can't be two people who are supposed to be doing that together. I'm guessing they don't realize everyone in the gym can see their shadows either.

The lady on the elliptical sees me staring in that direction and has a look. She watches for a moment, then looks back at me and mouths, "Oh my gosh." I mouth back, "I know!" And we both chuckle.

Suddenly, the light goes out and we are no longer able to watch the shadows intertwine. I continue running, trying to keep my eyes on the screen in front of me because I know the two shadows will be exiting momentarily. Luckily,

I'm in the far corner of the gym, and unless they walk back this way, they will not even see me. The door opens and a woman walks out, closing the door behind her. I almost fall off the treadmill. Holy crap, it's Brady's ex, Susie. Susie the floozy. I wonder who her latest conquest was. I'm so caught up in this drama, I don't even realize how fast I'm running or how far. The wait is killing me, who is Susie doing at the gym? I see the door open slightly…oh boy, here it is. The big reveal. The door swings open and he emerges. Looking disheveled and freshly laid.

Oh my goodness. What the hell is going on in Falcon Lake? Pete! Mother freakin' Pete! I have to grab hold of the handles of the treadmill and slow it down. My knees are shaking. First off, what the hell is Pete doing in a gym? Second, he's married and he's banging his ex-best friend's ex-wife? Holy shit, I can't breathe.

I get off the treadmill and put my hands on my knees to try and catch my breath. What the hell is wrong with people? Poor Jean. Brady's ex? Wow. Pete. I was starting to feel a little sorry for you. Not any more. You are by far the biggest loser I have ever met. Feels like my skin in crawling. I decide to stay at the gym a little while longer. I do not need either of those two seeing me leave. They'll know I'm on to them. I decide to hit the sauna, try to steam out of my memory what I just saw.

I head down the hall to the steam room and hear the hammering of nails. Before I can put two and two together, bam, there's Pete. On a ladder, right in front of me.

"Well, lookie here, it's Laney Simms. Aren't you a sight for sore eyes?" Pete says in the most arrogant tone ever. I quickly turn on my heel and walk right back from where I came from, not even uttering a word to Pete. I feel like I may even vomit. "Really, Laney? No hello? Nothing?" Pete yells to my back. I stop in my tracks. I know I should keep walking, and I tell myself to keep walking, but I can't. I turn and walk back to Pete.

"I'm going to say this once, Pete Murdough, so are you listening?" I look at him with the most evil look I can conjure up. "I don't want you to speak to me ever again. Not a hello, nothing. In fact, I don't want you even looking my way. So help me, if you do, Pete, I'll be marching my ass right over to your dear Jean and filling her in on your infidelities. Then, I'll head to the police department to press charges. Do you understand me, Pete?"

Pete nods his head and looks stunned. I turn and walk away. I'm glad I didn't slip and say that I saw him with Susie. I want to keep that one in my back pocket. I'm sure he thinks Brady has filled me in on his wandering eye. Oh Pete, what has become of you? Such a loser.

My knees are shaking the whole ride home. I'm dying to call Brady and tell him about what I saw. I'll save that for tonight. Gosh, I miss him. Can't wait to see him. I pull in the driveway and send Brady a text.

I am counting down the hours—can't wait to see you!

Time to go shower and do some food shopping. Hmmm, on second thought, I think I want to go out to dinner. Out of Falcon Lake.

When I walk in the door, it catches my eye. One of the kitchen drawers is open. Just a little bit, but open. The hair stands up on the back of my neck. Shit. Someone has been in here or is still in here. I quickly make my way to the nightstand and grab the gun. At that moment I received a reply text, making me jump. Brady's text will have to wait. I walk through the entire house checking out every closet, every inch. I check the lock on the back door. It's locked. Who the hell is coming in here? What are they looking for? They obviously aren't trying to rob me. They also know when I'm not here. So they are nearby watching. The guys next door?

"Keep them at an arm's length." Stacy's words echo in my head. Breaking and entering doesn't seem like their style. Maybe this has something to do with the note I found. Maybe I'm just letting my imagination get the best of me. Grace probably left that drawer open. Yes, I'm sure that's what happened. Then it catches my eye. A magnet on the refrigerator. It's a South Carolina magnet that most definitely wasn't there before. What the hell? Someone's trying to freak me out. But who and why?

Having a bad day, can't wait to see your beautiful face—always makes me happy. Love you!

Oh no, he's having a bad day. Yeah, me too, Brady. Me too. Hmmm, what can I do to make it better? I go online and do some research. Most romantic restaurants in the area, best views, best food. One restaurant keeps popping up in all my searches. Alejandro's. I wonder if Brady will even feel like going out. The restaurant sounds amazing with its views of New York City. I can totally go for that. Let me text Brady.

> Are you up for an adventure tonight? It would require getting dressed up. If you're too tired, it's okay.

> Baby, I'll do anything as long as I'm with you. I'll be wrapping up a little earlier than I thought. I can be showered, dressed, and at your place around 5.

That's perfect because the restaurant is about forty-five minutes away. I'm still looking at their website. Outdoor patio/dance floor, overlooking the skyline, with outdoor band. Okay, yes, we are going. Sounds amazing. Now what to wear? I only brought one dress and I'm unsure about it. It's pretty, but it doesn't represent the way I'm feeling these days. It's not…sexy enough. I want to blow Brady's socks off. I text Allie.

> Feel like flying the coop for a couple of hours? I need a new sexy dress.

> YES! Get me outta here! And I know exactly where to go for that sexy dress! Come and get me whenever you are ready!

I love Allie. Always so reliable. I pick her up about a half hour later. "Lane, there are days I just want to throw in the towel with that store. So much stress. Huck better make it to the pros soon so I can retire." Allie had Huck just five weeks before I had Jake. They are best friends. They've always considered themselves cousins, even though they haven't seen each other in a long time. That's where social media steps in. Huck has always been athletic, but he took a keen interest in ice hockey. He plays in a league right below the professional level up in Canada. He's hoping to be called up to the NHL at any moment. And he will; he's that good.

"I'm sorry, Allie. What can I do to help? Do you need some money?" I ask, truly concerned.

"No, no. I'm getting by just fine. It's just the little crap. Plus, I'm tired. Didn't sleep well last night," Allie says with a smirk.

"Oh Lord, who now?" I ask giggling.

"Believe it or not, it was George again. Decided to give the kid another shot. I couldn't take his whining and thought it would shut him up for a bit." We both start laughing.

"So? Any better this time around?" I ask, hoping for some details.

"Actually, it was. I think he's starting to grow on me," Allie answers with a smile on her face.

"Well, just be careful. Stacy says those two are not to be trusted and should be kept at an arm's length. I would have told you that sooner, but I didn't think you'd be seeing him again."

"I'm not worried. From what I hear from George, it's Stacy that should not be trusted. Seems she was a little loosey goosey if you know what I mean."

"No way! Well that explains the note!" I tell Allie about my find under the couch. Then, I tell her about someone coming into the house. I make her swear not to tell anyone, especially George. "I need to set some kind of trap to prove that someone's coming in. What are you doing this weekend? Maybe you and I can do a little detective work and get to the bottom of this."

"That sounds exciting! Count me in!"

Chapter Thirty-Nine

My friends are really the best shoppers. Allie picks out a sexy red dress for me. A little more form-fitting than I normally like, but I feel like a million bucks in it. My stomach has butterflies as I put the finishing touches on my hair and makeup. My ear is peeled, listening for Brady's truck to pull up. Oh, how I've missed him. One last spray of perfume, and there he his. Perfect timing. I want to run out and greet him at his truck but decide to play it cool. I peek out the window and watch him get out of the truck. He reaches back in and grabs a suit jacket. Oh my, oh my. He looks hot. Then again, he looks hot in everything. And nothing. Woo, calm down girl. I'm starting to sweat. I try and fluff my dress a little to get a breeze going and to cool me down.

I walk to the door and open it. "Well hello, gorgeous," Brady says as he pulls a bouquet of flowers from behind his back.

"Hello right back at you, gorgeous," I say while leaning up to kiss him.

"I missed you so much. You look amazing," Brady says to me in between kissing. He pushes me into the house, then closes the door. He places my back against the door and kisses me so passionately. I'm really sweating now.

"I don't like being away from you," Brady says, leaning his forehead against mine. He looks so sad.

"I don't like it either. You okay, babe?" I say, putting my hands on his cheeks.

"Yeah, just stressed out. Having a hard time finding reliable help." He throws his jacket over the kitchen chair and gets the flowers ready for a vase.

"I'm sorry. I wish I could help. I can put an ad in the paper for you, be your secretary." I hug him around his waist.

"You're sweet. That's okay, someone will show up. I have the word out. The problem is Pete grabbed some of the best guys before I had a shot at them. You snooze, you lose, I guess."

"It will be okay. You ready to head out for our romantic night and forget all our problems?" I ask, kissing him.

"Yes, I am. Let's go." I hand him the keys and we're off.

The restaurant is over-the-top beautiful. I reserved the best table in the place. The views of the city are amazing. Brady holds my hands across the table. "I have heard about this place but have never been. It's amazing." He glances around in wonder. All the trees surrounding the outdoor patio and dance floor are covered with white lights. It's such a romantic setting.

After a delicious meal, Brady stands up and holds his hand out to me. "May I have this dance, my lady?" I put my hand in his and we head out to the patio. Brady pulls me into his arms and we begin to dance. A slow, soft dance. "Did I mention to you how absolutely beautiful you look tonight?" Brady asks me, then dips me.

"Yes, you have and thank you. You make me feel beautiful, Brady," I blush.

"I love you, Laney Simms," Brady says with an intense look in his eyes.

"I love you right back, Brady Gramble." It's one of those moments you want to last forever. The lights in the trees, the city in the distance.

After the song is over, we head back to our table for dessert. "I don't know if I have room for dessert."

"There's always room for dessert, baby. Don't worry, you're going to work it all off later," Brady says and winks at me.

"Bring it on then." I squeeze his hand. I think I'll wait until morning to tell Brady about what I saw at the gym. I don't want to ruin his good mood.

"I do love this dress on you, but I can't wait to get it off of you," Brady says, hugging me from behind and kissing my neck while we walk to the front door.

"Stop, I'm going to trip!"

"I wouldn't let you fall. Hold on, let me make sure of that." Brady spins me around and throws me over his shoulder.

"Brady! Put me down! You're going to break your back!"

"Relax, Laney. You're light as a feather!"

"Oh Lord, Brady. I wouldn't go that far!"

Brady fumbles, trying to get the keys in the lock. We get in the door, and he kicks it closed behind him and carries me into the bedroom. He places me gently on the bed.

"You okay? I don't want you complaining tomorrow that your back is out," I say smiling.

"Oh, my back might go out, but not from carrying you." He unzips my dress and begins kissing my neck, chest, and stomach. I feel chills traveling from my toes to my head. I feel dizzy. We spend the rest of the night making love, and it's magical. I still can't believe this is happening to me. To me! Wow.

Chapter Forty

M orning comes way too fast; as it always does when Brady sleeps over. I know this weekend is his weekend with Jeremy. I'm so bummed, but I know it's important for him to be with his son. We talked about all three of us doing something together, but ultimately agreed to wait on that.

"So lover boy, when am I going to see you again?" I say, sipping my coffee.

"Well, Jeremy comes by my house tonight and stays until school on Monday morning. So I guess Monday night?" The thought of not seeing him kills me.

"That stinks. Big time. Speaking of stinking big time, there's something I need to tell you."

I pull out a chair and sit next to him at the kitchen table.

"Oh no, sounds serious. What is it?"

I tell Brady what I witnessed at the gym with Pete and Susie.

"You have got to be fucking kidding me!"

"I wish I was. Because then I tried to sneak out of there without them seeing me and ran into Pete. He said something arrogant to me. I told him to never talk to me again, or I was going to tell Jean about his infidelities."

Brady's eyes practically popped out of his head. "You said that to him? Holy shit, Laney. Threats do not sit well with Pete."

"Well, too damn bad. I've known him a long time and I know he's really a big wuss. He better just stay the hell away from us," I say in my tough Jersey girl voice.

"Susie? Really?" Brady says while sipping his coffee.

"I know. I couldn't believe it when I saw it. Of course, my initial shock was: Pete is in a gym? But then when I realized he was there for the sex and the construction, it all made sense."

"I wonder how long that's been going on?" Brady asks in a serious tone, as if thinking back.

"Oh, Brady, I'm sure it's new. Pete is a slimeball, but I doubt he was doing anything with Susie while you were still married. Right?" Oh shit, what have I unleashed here? I should have never said anything. Crap.

"Well, I guess it wouldn't totally surprise me. I know Susie is easy, and I guess I didn't know the real Pete until he attacked you. I guess anything is possible, isn't it?"

Brady looks like he's been punched in the gut. "I'm sorry, honey. I was going to tell you yesterday, but I didn't want to ruin our night. It sounded like you were having a tough day already. Look at me, Brady." I pull his big rugged jaw toward me. "You're not going to be hurt like that ever again. I promise. Not by me. I love you." I give him a reassuring kiss on the lips.

"Thanks, babe, love you too. I guess I gotta go. Come here and sit on my lap so I can give you a big hug." I hop over to his seat and sit in his lap. "I'm so thankful you came back into my life. When I needed you most, it seems. Everyone around me is really showing their true colors. Love you, Laney." We say our goodbyes for our four torturous days apart and he leaves. Now I feel deflated.

I know that I can't just lie around and wait for Brady to return. I have to keep busy. I'm really not in the mood to go to the gym. I decide to walk around the lake and grab some breakfast at Henry's. It's a beautiful, crisp morning. I pass many walkers, runners, and bikers. Someone in a car beeps and waves at me, obviously thinking I am someone else. This makes me laugh to myself. I've done that many times.

I have a spring in my step this morning. What a wonderful night with Brady. I still feel like I have to pinch myself. I am really with him. In love with him and he is actually in love with me. It feels surreal. I'm starting to realize this is how I was meant to be loved. To be treated. I feel like a new person. These past few weeks have changed my life. The days have been so full. Not all good, though. Especially the episode with Pete.

I will never forgive him for that. Crap, I hope he isn't at the diner. I didn't even think about that. But I have the upper hand on Pete, so he doesn't scare me in the slightest. All I have to do is make one phone call and I can change his entire life. Jean. What does she see in him? I guess I shouldn't judge her. I'm sure some people thought the same about Jim.

I call Allie while I'm still walking to confirm our plans for the weekend. "I'm going to ask Elise and Grace too, a real Girls' Weekend," I say to Allie.

"Sounds good to me! The more help, the better to get to the bottom of who is breaking into your house." She's right. If the four of us put our heads together, we are sure to figure this out. I text Elise and Grace. They respond quickly. Grace can stay tonight, but not tomorrow night. Elise is in for both nights. So exciting! Not only am I going to get to spend time with my closest friends, but it will keep my mind off missing Brady so much.

I walk into Henry's, quickly glancing around to see if I recognize anyone. It's pretty crowded, so it's hard for me to take it all in. The waitress seats me immediately. I pick up my menu and glance around, using my menu as a shield of sorts. I start at the counter. Hard to tell if I know anyone. They all have their backs to me. Then, I look to the area where I first saw Brady that morning. The memory of it makes me smile. Focus, Laney. I glance over my shoulder and low and behold—in the back corner of the restaurant—Pete and Jean. It seems they are having an intense conversation. In fact, I don't even think they saw me walk in. Looks like trouble is brewing for sure.

I turn back to my menu and jump. Abe is sitting across from me. "Good morning, Laney!"

"Holy crap, Abe. You scared the shit out of me," I say, putting my hand on my chest.

"I'm so sorry. I saw you walk in. I had just sat down, so I thought I'd join you. Is that okay?"

"Oh, absolutely. I appreciate the company. How the heck are you? Where have you been? More importantly, why haven't you been baking?"

"Ha, yeah, I've been out of town this week. I guess the last time I saw you was Monday? I left Tuesday morning, just got back last night. I'll be baking again this weekend."

"Oh, good. I'm having a Girls' Weekend at the house, so we'll be needing some sweets." Crap. I shouldn't have told him that. He is one of my main suspects. Now, if he knows I'm having a houseload of people, he won't break in. "I think we are all going out on the town tonight, though. Getting my dancing shoes ready," I say, hoping he'll go back to his plans of breaking in. Well, if it's him.

"That sounds like fun! You seem to be really close to your friends. That's nice."

"I am. They have known me almost my whole life. They mean the world to me."

"Well then, Allie must have told you about her and George?" he says, like he's about to unload a whole bunch of juicy dirt on me.

"Yes, she told me they hooked back up. Did something else happen?" Abe looks left, then right; as if he's about to give away the world's best kept secret.

"Did Allie tell you George asked her to marry him?" The expression on my face must have answered his question. Just then the waitress came to take our order.

I wait for her to leave before bursting out, "What? What the heck are you talking about? I just talked to her ten minutes ago and she didn't say anything!" I'm trying to keep my voice down, but I'm shocked that Allie hasn't let me in on this huge piece of information.

"I guess, in the heat of passion, George asked Allie to marry him and she said yes."

I just about choke.

"I don't believe it. Were they drunk? Allie just met George!" My hands are shaking, and I can't wait to leave the diner so I can call Allie immediately.

"Who knows? They think they have some cosmic connection." Abe waves his hands in the air.

I'm having a hard time believing what I'm hearing. I look off toward the door when someone walking past our table catches my eye. It's Pete and Jean. They both look exhausted and stressed. I wonder if Pete has come clean. Nah. He's too much of a coward.

He turns to pay at the register and spots me. Jean sees him looking my way and does the same. We are caught in a stare. I'm not sure what to do here. Jean leaves the register and walks toward me. Fuck. What is she going to say? It can go either way here. Oh Lord, why do I always find myself in these predicaments?

"Laney, good morning. I just want to tell you how very sorry I am for my husband's horrible behavior. I'm not sure what got into him, but I want to assure you it will never happen again. I hope you can keep this matter to yourself for the sake of our kids," Jean says with a stern, unwavering tone. Almost like a robot, or like the speech had been rehearsed. She does not even look at Abe or acknowledge that he's there.

I stutter, "I-I-I appreciate it, Jean. I know Pete was not of his right mind when he pulled that stunt. I think he may need therapy to deal with some issues though. I hope you two are able to work it out."

Jean just turns and walks away. Pete opens the door and looks back to me, like a beaten little puppy. Jean should kick his ass. Does Pete think I don't have anything on him now? I still have Susie the floozy in my back pocket, Pete. What a jerk.

"What the heck was that about?" Abe asks with inquisitive eyes.

"Too long of a story. I'll save it for another time. Now back to Allie and George. When did this proposal happen?" I ask, hurt that Allie hasn't mentioned it to me.

"Last night. I got home around midnight, bumped into George on the way to the bathroom, and he told me. Seemed like it had just happened."

"Were they drunk? Allie had to be drunk; she would never agree to get married again. She barely likes your brother. No offense," I say, sipping my coffee.

"None taken." Abe digs into his omelet. "I was surprised as well. George has never proposed to anyone before. Then he meets Allie and a few weeks later, proposes. Weird if you ask me."

"Beyond weird. I can't eat. I have to call Allie and find out what the heck is going on." I throw a twenty down on the table. "I'll see you later, Abe. Don't forget the baked goods. I have a feeling we're going to need a bunch."

I call Allie's number and get her voicemail. Crap. Did she turn her phone off? Is she still at George's? I decide to run back. What is Allie thinking? She doesn't even know this guy.

Who am I to talk? If Brady asked me to marry him right now, I probably would say yes too. But that's different. Right? Yes, of course it's different. I am nauseated and decide to walk. I try calling Allie and her phone is still off. It's almost nine. Her shop opens at ten. What the heck is she doing? I start running again after the sick feeling passes. I arrive, sweaty and barely breathing, at George's front door. I ring the bell and knock on the door.

"Allie!" I take a deep breath. I hear movement behind the door. George opens the door, wearing just a pair of boxer shorts.

"Hey, Laney, what's up?" George says acting coy and innocent.

"Where's Allie? I need to speak to her." I say, still trying to catch my breath.

"Allie, Laney's here," George calls behind him. Allie arrives at the front door with a men's bathrobe on.

"Laney! What are you doing here? Excuse me, George." Allie steps outside and closes the door behind her.

"Holy shit, Allie! I just talked to Abe and he told me you're getting married?" I'm still catching my breath.

"Oh frig, Laney. I fucked up. It was in the heat of passion. I thought he was just caught up in the moment. I said yes, but I was referring to the sex, not marriage! How do I get myself in these situations?" Allie rubs her brow. "Now this morning, it's all he's talking about. So excited, destiny shit. What am I going to do?"

"You're going to tell him the truth. That it's too soon. You said it in the heat of the moment." I tell her with certainty. Allie is looking me right in the eye and I can see her thinking.

"I know, I did think about doing that. But I do kinda sorta love him. And he's very successful, very hot. I could do worse for sure." Allie's eyes leave me and look off.

I want to shake her at this point, get some sense in her, but who knows? Maybe this is the way it's supposed to be for her. "Allie, I think you should clear your head and think this over. Then, at that point, have a talk with him. Follow your heart, girl. But give it a little time. You barely know this guy."

Allie responds, "You're right, Lane, I need to spend more time with him. Really get to know him. Thanks for caring. I need to get back in there and get ready for work. I'll see you tonight?"

"Absolutely. And Allie, don't look so sad. You have a hot young man in there that is madly in love with you and wants to spend the rest of his life with you. Things could be worse, my friend. Remember what you told me—you can't control love. It has a mind of its own!" She nods her head in agreement, smiles, and walks back in the house. What the heck goes on when I'm not here? I'm beginning to think this town is a little crazy.

Chapter Forty-One

I head back to my place and get in the shower. My head is spinning with everything that's happened in the few hours I've been awake. I need to call Brady and fill him in. I hate interrupting him at work, so I decide to text him.

> Hey honey, busy morning here so far. Had words with Jean and Allie's getting married. How's your day?

I laugh to myself, imagining his face when he reads this text. I start blow drying my hair, waiting for his response. I see he's responded and put the blow dryer down.

> I'm jealous of Allie. I want to marry you, Laney.

I almost pass out on the bathroom floor. Wow. I just got done lecturing Allie, and now Brady is saying this to me? What the hell is in the water here?

> In time my love, in time.

I take a deep breath and exhale, waiting for his response. Oh my gosh, this is taking longer than it should. Is he insulted by my response? Come on, come on. Respond. *Ding-dong.* I jump yet again.

> I know, but don't keep me waiting too long.

Whew! Okay, that makes me feel better. *Ding-dong.* Another text.

Want to meet me at the *Overlook* for lunch? I know that's your and Abe's special place, but I'd like to go there with you, too. Let me know. We can meet at noon?

I'll be there! What would you like me to pick up?

You seem to know what I like already, which is anything that you choose for me. See you soon.

Yay! I'm so excited! Bonus time with Brady! This day is turning around!

I pull up to the *Overlook* and see Brady leaning against his truck, pretending to be looking at his watch and insinuating that I'm late.

"You don't even have a watch on!" I yell from my car window. We both laugh. He comes over, opens the door, and helps me out of the car.

"Hey baby." Brady hugs me and gives me a kiss.

"Well, hey there, gorgeous man of mine." I'm smiling from ear to ear. "Everything is in the trunk." I pop open the trunk and we carry our lunch and blanket to a remote spot. No one else is around, which is nice. Although lately, I never see anyone but Brady when we are out. I guess I only have eyes for him. Just like high school. But different, yes, different. I'm an adult. I know the difference between love and a crush now. Don't I?

"This deli makes the best sandwiches." I say, biting into a sandwich. I forgot I didn't eat breakfast and I'm starving.

"They are good. So tell me more about your morning. Start with Jean." Brady says in between bites.

"Yes, Jean. Our poor dear friend Jean who is being taken advantage of by a psycho. Well, she said that Pete has made her aware of what happened, apologized for his behavior, and said it would never happen again. I would have loved to have been a fly on the wall to hear that conversation go down," I say, taking a bite of my sandwich.

"Wow Laney, it's still amazing to me how much has changed in just the couple of weeks you've been here. I mean, think about it. It seemed like everything was just going with the flow—then all of the sudden Pete jumps you, you see Pete with Susie, it's just crazy." Brady continues eating his lunch. His words sting me. Does he think I'm the root cause of all these things?

"Happy to add some excitement to the place. It seems like it was Boresville, USA without me," I say with a chip on my shoulder. Brady doesn't seem to notice that I'm hurt. He keeps on eating his sandwich, staring at the lake.

"Do you think I'm a trouble maker, Brady?"

"Don't be ridiculous! None of the things that have happened have been under your control. I was just thinking out loud how weird it is. Things change fast don't they?"

I nod my head 'yes' as he continues. "I can't believe it was just a few weeks ago that I was spending my whole day with Pete, and my whole night alone, with the exception of when Jeremy was over. I was alone and not feeling like I would ever meet anyone. Then all of the sudden, there you were. Sitting in that diner alone.

I remember looking over at you and thinking, gosh, now there's a pretty girl. I wonder why she's alone? Is she in the same boat I am? Me staring at you is what made Pete look your way. He recognized you immediately. Then I felt intimidated. I knew what I was to you in the past, but knew you were well over me by now. I was just going to be a single, almost fifty-year-old, dock builder in your eyes. I worried that you'd feel relief when you saw me, like, 'oh, thank goodness, I didn't end up with that loser.' But then when we approached you, I felt so much hope. You lit up when you saw me. Then, when you told Pete you were divorced, well, it made me light up too.

So, do I think you are a trouble maker, Laney? The answer is no. You are my destiny. The love of a lifetime that I've been waiting a long time for. Thank you for coming here and changing my life."

Brady calmly takes another bite of his sandwich and goes back to staring at the lake. I can't even speak. That was so beautiful. I place my sandwich down and sit down on his lap so that I am straddling him, and wrap my legs and my arms around him. He returns the hug. We just hold each other. I never want to let go of this man. Ever.

Brady needs to get back to work. We pack up our lunch and fold up the blanket. "That was just about the best lunch ever. Thanks honey," I say to Brady, leaning up and kissing him on the lips. Just then my phone *ding-dongs*. I pull it out of my pocket and see a text from Allie.

Can you come to the shop? I need to talk to you.

I wonder if Allie had a talk with George. Hope she's okay.

Sure I will be there in a bit.

"Everything okay?" Brady asks as he closes the trunk of my car.

"Yeah, Allie needs me. So, I guess this is goodbye until Monday? Have a great weekend with Jeremy. Maybe we'll get lucky and bump into each other around town." I hug Brady's waist.

"No such luck. I've decided to take Jeremy away for the weekend. We're going to go visit my sister, Jane, this weekend out in Pennsylvania. She just called last night and invited us up. Normally I would say no, but she needs some help around the house that I've been promising to do. I was going to head to her house right after Jeremy gets out of school. I hope that's okay?" Brady asks me, like he needs my approval.

"Oh please, Brady! Of course! Have a great time with your family! I'm going to be busy here with my girls. I'm looking forward to it. We always have so much fun when we are together."

"Well, be safe. Make sure you lock up. Bunch of creeps obviously live around here."

"No kidding. I love you. Have fun and be safe yourself. Text me when you get to your sister's so I know you're okay." We give each other one final kiss and hug goodbye. I hate goodbyes.

The drive back into town goes by quickly. My head is just so full of Brady. Just like high school. I wish I had the guts back then to talk to him. Maybe we would have been together sooner. But then I wouldn't have had my kids and I can't imagine that. I guess things happen the way they are supposed to.

What's going to happen next? Brady and I rarely talk about what happens when I go back home. I know he's dreading it as much as I am. We'll make it work. I have the ability to fly back whenever I want. We can vacation together. It can work. It won't be your typical long distance relationship. We'll be different. I'm sure of it. My eyes fill with tears at the thought. I pull up to Allie's shop, wipe my tears away, and go inside.

Allie is on the phone and holds her finger up as if to say one minute. I glance around her shop. That necklace that I love is still there. Hearts intertwined. That's Brady and I now.

"Hey girl!" Allie hangs up the phone and walks around the counter to hug me.

"Well, hey there yourself, Mrs. Olsen."

"Quiet. You know darn well if Brady asked you, you would say yes."

I'm not going to tell her that he already mentioned that he wanted to marry me, and she's right. I probably would say yes if he did it formally. What is wrong with me?

"I know, it's so crazy. There is something defective with me for feeling this way after a few weeks. I'm so worried, Al. I have never felt this way, ever. But how do I know for sure that I am in love with Brady and not in love with the idea of Brady? The Brady infatuation from high school?"

"Good God, why are you so whiny this morning? This is supposed to be about me! Stop over-thinking everything, Laney, and just live your life." She teases me.

"I know, you're right. This is supposed to be about you. So tell me, have you picked out a date yet?" We both laugh and head to the back room of the store.

"Come get some tea and I'll fill you in, old friend."

"Is June off today?" I ask about her one and only employee.

"Yeah, she's away. I cut back on hours this week. I feel like I almost get more done when she's not here. I get lazy when she's working." Allie sits down and joins me.

"Does she ever fill you in on what Adam is up to?" I ask taking a small sip of the very hot tea. I always liked Adam; he was just definitely not for Allie.

"Between her and Huck, yes. They both fill me in. He's dating a woman from work. She's actually closer to his age, so it sounds like a good match." Allie blows on her tea.

"Well, that's good. So, what's cooking sister? Did you have a talk with George?"

Allie takes a deep breath. "Yes, we talked. He agrees we need to get to know each other better, but he says he's never felt this way before. He said he knew when he saw me at your house that night that I was the one for him. We are going to start spending some major time together, starting with this weekend. We are actually leaving tonight. Going to head to the city."

"Oh no, so you're going to miss our detective work weekend?" I ask, pouting.

"Yes, sorry. I hope you understand. You'll have Grace and Elise there. You girls can get to the bottom of it without me, I'm sure. You better text me with updates," she says, shaking her finger at me.

"I will. I'm hoping we find nothing out. I'm sure it's just someone goofing around, trying to scare me." I grab Allie's hand. "I'm happy for you, Al. Go for it. Let your guard down and take a long hard look at George. He seems like a genuine person. Do what's best for you and don't worry about what anyone thinks."

"Thanks, Lane. You know I never give a crap what people think. I'm looking forward to being out of Falcon Lake for the weekend, that's for sure. I'm getting so bored here. I think that's what I like about George. He's different for sure. And so young! His body is so hot, Lane! Woo hoo!"

I leave Allie's shop and head home. I straighten up the house a bit, do a load of laundry. I think I'm going to suggest to the girls that we go out to dinner. That way we can set up a trap while we are gone and see if anything has been moved. I decide to head to the store and stock up on snack foods and alcohol. There's a great new upscale market about twenty minutes away that I heard about from Allie. I think I'll try it out. It's a beautiful fall day in New Jersey. No humidity; just clean, crisp air to breathe in. Makes me feel so alive. I have the windows and sunroof open and the radio up loud. I feel like a teenager again, but this time, I have the hot guy. These familiar roads and the wind blowing through my hair gives me such a sense of freedom. I'm so glad I went online that day and saw the ad for this house. It has been life-changing for me.

***

I follow the directions on the GPS and I'm at the market in no time. It's pretty crowded. I have to drive around a while to find a parking spot. When I walk into the market, I immediately wish they had a place like this in South Carolina. It's amazing! Fresh meats, the cheeses…it's all so much to take in! I take my time meandering up and down each aisle.

I'm barely paying attention to the people around me when I hear, "Oh, hi Laney." I look over and see Beth Pamett standing next to me. I haven't seen her since the night Brady and I picked up our race packets. She seemed really put off by us. Quite annoyed. But I know she's buddies with Grace, so I have to seem a little nice.

"Oh hey, Beth, right? How are you?" I say between my teeth.

"Yes, it's Beth. I'm good. How are you? Still spending time with Brady?"

There it is. She didn't take long at all to get on that subject.

"Pretty much day in and day out. It's like we're joined at the hip!" Beth brings out the bitch in me like no other. She just really seems to have her panties in a knot about me and Brady, and I can't help but push her buttons for some reason.

"Well, that's nice. I'm glad your dreams from high school are coming true. You are a patient one." She reaches for an item on the shelf nonchalantly.

Oh boy, those are fighting words. I take a deep breath. I guess Grace has filled her in on my history with Brady.

"And how exactly do you know Brady, Beth?"

"His ex-wife was sleeping with my husband. We were there for each other during our divorces, consoled each other. I guess you can say we were joined at the hip then."

Holy shit, this woman is relentless. What a royal bitch! I'm furious. At her. At Brady. How could he not tell me? I can't let her win this. I say the first thing that comes to my mind.

"Well, I guess I'm living my dream and yours." And with that, I walk away. I'm shaking, but I quickly compose myself. I don't want her to see that she got to me. This has turned into a very interesting afternoon. What the hell? Brady didn't tell me this information when we saw Beth at packet pick up. Why is he hiding it? I'm so pissed I've allowed her to get under my skin. I'm pissed at Brady too. Not telling is the same as lying.

I finish my shopping; buying several bottles of wine, some great cheeses, and breads. I try my best to avoid Beth the rest of the time I'm in the store. Part of me is dying to text Brady and ask him what the hell she was talking about. But I resist. I'll wait until he's back from his sister's. What the heck, why hasn't Grace told me about them? She's supposed to be one of my best friends. I'll be having that discussion with her this evening for sure. I load my groceries into my car and drive back home. My windows are closed and my radio is off. This time the drive feels stifling.

When I arrive back to the house, I see Allie and George packing up the car for the weekend. George runs over to help me carry my groceries in.

"Hey Laney, I was hoping to see you." He grabs a bag and follows me to the front door. "I just wanted to let you know that I would never hurt Allie.

I'm just crazy about her, Laney. From the second I met her, I haven't stopped thinking about her."

I unlock the front door and walk into the house. I put my bag on the counter.

"That's great George, because if you do hurt her, there will be hell to pay," I say in no joking manner. I'm not in the mood to joke anymore.

"I know that. I plan on treating her the way she deserves to be treated." "Good. You two have fun in the city and I'll talk to you when you get back." I lead him to the front door. I see Allie standing by the car, waiting for George. "Bye, Al! Love ya! Have fun!" I yell.

She blows me a kiss and gets into the car. She waves excitedly to me as they pull away. Be careful, Allie girl.

I put away the groceries and decide to venture to the hammock for a nap. I'm not going to let what happened in that hammock ruin it for me. I'm not going to let people like Pete, Beth, and Floozy Susie ruin my time here. I paid for the right to nap in the hammock and damn it, I'm going to. I'm hoping the nap will change my mood, too. I've got to shake this before Elise and Grace get here.

I take a quick look to my right to make sure Pete isn't at the house they were working on. Looks like everything is cleaned up and completed. Good. One less thing to worry about. I carefully climb into the hammock, try to relax, and close my eyes.

Of course, my mind is going a mile a minute. Beth and Brady? Really? Attached at the hip? What did she mean by that exactly? Were they intimate? She really doesn't seem like Brady's type. I guess since he was in such a vulnerable position that she was able to manipulate him. But why didn't anyone tell me? Maybe she's full of shit. Jealous, I'm sure. I've got a dream guy. Who wouldn't be jealous? My phone does a *ding-dong*. I open one eye and look to see who it's from. Brady.

Just wanted to tell you one more time before I leave how much I love you.

You too. Safe travels.

Do you really, Brady? I take a deep breath, close my eyes, and drift off.

Chapter Forty-Two

I wake up thirty minutes later and feel refreshed. Still pissed, but refreshed. The girls should be here in about an hour, so I decide to shower and freshen up. I'm hoping Grace arrives first so I can talk to her about Beth. After getting ready, I pour myself a glass of wine and start checking restaurants online. Maybe the girls have a good idea of where to go. I hear a car pull up. I jump up and peek out the window. Perfect! It's Grace.

I open the front door to greet her. "Well, hello there Gracie!"

"Laney! I am not kidding you; you need to buy this place. I would love to have this place to escape to!" She gives me a big hug and we head into the house. "I beat Elise and Allie?"

"Well, you beat Elise. Allie is no longer coming. Let me get you some wine and get you caught up. Before we talk about Allie, I need to tell you what happened to me today with one of your buddies." I proceed to tell Grace about my run-in with Beth and how she insinuated that she and Brady were an item.

"Oh, Lane. I'm so sorry about that. I didn't mean to tell her how you felt about Brady in high school. I just told her how you had come full circle with him. It is a great story. As far as Beth being with Brady; this is the first I'm hearing of it. I find it very hard to believe that she wouldn't have told me that. Sounds odd." Grace takes a big sip of wine. "The fact that it was Beth's husband that slept with Brady's wife was a known fact. I'm sure I told you that. I know I did. It was the same time you were going through your crap with Jim. I'm sure it went right over your head. Who would even remember that? I barely knew Beth then," Grace says calmly.

She's right. I was an emotional basket case then; caught up in my own world. I guess now that I'm thinking back it sounds vaguely familiar. "Hmmm, I just don't remember that, I guess. It didn't matter, so I just discarded it from my memory. Can you believe she threw that in my face? She was vicious! What is her deal?" I ask, hoping Grace can solve the Beth mystery.

"Based on her reaction at the packet pick up and now this; sounds to me like she had it bad for Brady and then you swooped in and got him. Pure jealousy, my friend. I've never made a strong connection with her, and now I know why."

There's a knock on the door. "Elise!"

"Hey girls!" Elise has a bottle of wine and a couple of overnight bags. "You don't mind if I stay for a week do you? Wow! Look at the view!"

I take Elise's bags and put them in the spare room. Grace pours Elise a glass of wine and we move our little party out onto the back deck.

"Laney, this is awesome!" Elise says.

"I know, I'm loving it." I raise my glass. "Cheers, girls! Love you both so much!"

"Cheers!" We all clink our glasses and drink up. I run into the house and get the platter of breads and cheeses I prepared earlier. The three of us sitting outside talking is just like old times. I fill them both in on recent events, including Allie's marriage proposal.

"You have got to be kidding me!" Elise says in shock.

"She told him she needs to get to know him better, but she's pretty smitten. He is a catch. Good looking, successful. I'm hoping it does work out for Allie. She deserves it," I say, trying to be a supportive friend. The way Allie always is to me.

"Well cheers to that!" Grace raises her glass again.

"Cheers!" We all clink glasses.

"So girls, where should we go tonight?" I explain to them that someone is trying to spook me. The fish, the magnet. I tell them about the note too.

"That's scary! I'm not sure I want to stay anymore!" Grace exclaims. "Have you called the cops?"

"No, no cops. There's nothing for them to work with. Whoever is doing it has a key or knows where one is hidden. Someone is trying to scare me and I'm not going to let them," I say, standing my ground.

"As far as Stacy is concerned, I barely remember her from high school. They don't have any kids, so we definitely do not run in the same circles," Grace says.

"Yeah, I'm not sure what their story is. I'm hoping to figure it out before I leave," I say while swooshing my wine in the glass. *Ding-dong.* "Oh a text!" I shout. I think this wine is going to my head quickly.

"Awe, it's from Brady: 'Arrived safely. Have fun with the girls. Love you.' Isn't he a doll?" I say with a big smile on my face, not letting them know that part of me doesn't trust Brady right now.

"Isn't young love adorable?" Elise asks Grace. We all laugh and toast once again.

***

We decide to stay in town and go to the Italian restaurant.

"Are you sure you don't mind going here? Haven't you been here twice?" Grace asks.

"Yes, I'm fine! Please, I am not picky and I really like the food here," I respond as we walk in the door. Again, I glance the whole restaurant to see if I recognize anyone. Of course Grace does. She is busy talking to a couple when Elise leans over and whispers, "And this is why I moved out of town. I can't stand running into people from high school."

I do not recognize the couple she's talking to. Do I? I guess their faces look somewhat familiar.

"Laney, you remember Coleen and Mike Venero from high school?" Grace pulls me by the arm and reminds me of who they are.

"Oh, of course, hey guys. Great to see you," I say, giving them fake hugs. I haven't seen these people in thirty years.

"Hey Laney. Saw Brady a couple of days ago. He mentioned you were in town," Mike said, raising his eyebrows. "Sounds like that guy has it bad for you."

My stomach gets butterflies. It's so reassuring to hear that Brady is out there telling people about us. It is real.

"We all know you've always had it bad for him," Coleen chimes in and she and Mike laugh.

"Yeah, yeah. I know, nothing has changed. You can take the girl away from Brady, but you can't take the Brady out of the girl." I say that again in my head and realize it didn't sound right. "Wait, I didn't mean it like that." Everyone is laughing now. I even have to laugh at myself.

Thank goodness our table is ready and I can get away from Coleen and Mike before I say something else stupid. We say goodbye to the Veneros and are seated at our table.

"Elise, you were quiet back there. I remember you and Mike having some major make out sessions at that one party at your house," I rib Elise.

"Yes, thank you, Laney. And that is why I moved out of town—so I do not have to see guys that have shoved their tongues down my throat in high school."

"Well, I could live here, because the only guy that really shoved his tongue down my throat is in South Carolina!" I say, raising my water goblet. "Where is our waitress? We need some drinks!"

"Hey Elise, how's your back feeling? You seem a little quiet tonight," I ask, knowing she's not being herself.

"It feels better. It's always something these days," she says, not even looking up from her plate.

Grace and I look at each other with concerned faces.

"How's Scott? He doing okay?" I ask, hoping to get her to open up, which she's never been great at.

"I guess he's okay. To be honest, we don't talk too much these days." Elise puts her fork down and clasps her hands together. "He's been drinking a lot these past few years, girls. Recently, it's been even more than usual. I'm sorry I haven't been open with you about it. It's easier for me to deal with it on my own."

I'm shocked, but not completely. I knew Scott was a heavy drinker, but it never seemed to affect them as a couple. Her back injury enters my mind.

"Is he violent with you, Elise?" I ask, afraid to hear the answer. If he did hurt her, I couldn't imagine she would stay. She's too strong. She doesn't need Scott. Elise looks down at her plate.

"No. But I am always there to pick up the pieces for him. Whether it's dragging him from the car into the house or lying to his boss about him being too sick to come to work. I hurt my back last week getting him in the house after an all weekend binge. Now, before you all start telling me what to do, I know. I'm going to leave him. I'm just finalizing the plans on where I'm going and what not."

Grace and I are stunned. How could we not see this coming?

"Wow, Elise. How is it possible for us to not know this? We talk all the time." Part of me is hurt that she doesn't share everything with me.

"Honestly, I didn't want to burden anyone with my problems. It's my issue and I have to deal with it. No one can help and everyone has their own stresses in life. They don't need mine. Now, please, let's get back to having fun. You can judge me later. Cheers!" Elise raises her glass, waiting for Grace and I to do the same.

I clink her glass but am still shocked. I feel so blindsided. Am I that self involved that I didn't even hear my friend in pain on the other end of the phone, or is she that closed off?

The subject gets changed and we talk about our kids being in college or married, and Grace being a grandmother. It's all so surreal. Time really has flown by. I feel like it was just yesterday I was sitting with these same girls in the pizzeria talking about 80's music and boys.

"I'd like to make one more toast while we are here," Elise says, clearing her throat. "I know Grace agrees with me, so I'll speak for both of us." Elise turns to Grace and they nod at each other. "Laney, it's a beautiful thing to see you this happy. You've deserved this your whole life. I feel horrible that you and Brady have missed so many years together, but cheers to what lies ahead for you two."

We clank glasses. "Thanks girls, that means a lot to me." My eyes fill with tears, mostly from guilt. I'm happy and Elise is miserable.

"Don't you dare cry. You'll make us cry!" Grace yells. "Now, let's go back to your place and see if anyone has broken in!"

Elise drives my car back to the house. "I'm going to beep just to let them know we're back and to get the hell out."

"I'll go in first. They work fast, so I'm sure they have been here and are gone." I say protecting the girls. I walk in and turn on the lights. Everything that we set up—towels hanging over the drawer, book against the back door, light on in the bedroom—is the way we left it. No one has been here while we were gone. "All clear. They must have had plans tonight," I say, taking a few last glances around.

We all get comfy in our pajamas and watch a movie that Grace brought. One of our all time favorites from high school. These women always have a way of making me feel like a kid again. There is nothing in the world like childhood friends.

Chapter Forty-Three

The next morning, we all take our time getting up. I'm up first because I want to make sure I have coffee ready for the girls. Looks like it's going to be a beautiful day. I know Grace has to leave this morning, but maybe Elise and I can do some kayaking or just float around on the lake. I saw some inner tubes in the storage shed. In my head, I've already made our plans for the day. Hope Elise agrees.

Within a half hour, both Grace and Elise are up and we are back on the deck, drinking our coffee.

"This is good living, girls. I am tempted to make Stacy an offer on this place. It can be all of ours. Our little escape to paradise whenever we need it."

Grace looks out over the lake.

"I would most definitely spend time here and keep an eye on the place for you. Lord knows I never get a moment's silence," Grace says, sounding exhausted.

"You're the one that can't say no to anyone! What did you expect?" Elise jokes with Grace. We all laugh.

Elise takes a sip of coffee. "I would love to escape here too. Don't get me wrong, my house is quiet with the girls gone. Sometimes, though, I would love to be alone and not feel the pressure of always making sure Scott is okay. It almost seems like now that the girls are gone, we have even less in common. Who knows? Maybe the girls are the only reason we stayed together."

"No, don't say that, Elise. You and Scott were an amazing couple at one time. Scott has an illness it sounds like. That's not always something you can control," I say, feeling sad for Elise.

"I guess so."

Grace chimes in. "Elise, this weekend away will be refreshing for you. It will give you a nice clear head. You and Scott just need to talk and figure out which direction your relationship is going. If you both don't see it going anywhere, then it's time for you to focus on you. You deserve that. Life is short."

Elise nods in agreement. "Thanks, girls. You're right. Time to start making changes. For now, I just want to enjoy this weekend! Cheers!" We clank our coffee mugs and giggle.

Before lunch, Grace packs up and heads out. "If I don't see you during the week, I'll see you both next Saturday, right?" she says, raising her eyebrows.

"Of course, we'll be there. I'm so excited to have a date for the christening!" I give Grace a hug goodbye.

"I'll be there too. Do we have to do the church part or can we just come to the food part?" Elise asks Grace.

"Just do the food part. The church is so small and can just about accommodate our immediate family; there are so many of us. I'll see you girls then!" Grace walks out to her car while Elise and I stand in the doorway and watch her. I notice an unfamiliar car parked in George and Abe's driveway. I guess Abe had a sleepover last night. I wonder who the lucky fellow is?

Elise and I get dressed and head out to the lake. We decide to kayak since the water has gotten too cold for this southern girl. I grab the hose and wash out the kayaks. They are full of cobwebs. I guess Stacy didn't have time to kayak with all her drama. Elise grabs two life jackets out of the shed and we are on our way.

It's a beautiful day on the lake. Lots of boats are out, so it's making kayaking a little difficult. We try to stay close to the shoreline and in the coves, where it's less wavy.

"Girl, we are going to be feeling this tomorrow. Last time I kayaked, I could barely lift my arms for two days," I yell back to Elise.

"I'm feeling it already! Hey, look out, there's a boat coming toward us."

I look over and see a speedboat slowing, making its way toward us.

"Hey, Laney, is that you? Hey Elise!" Behind the wheel of the boat is Mike Venero.

"Well, hey Mike! Long time no see!" I yell back to him. He's alone on the boat and not looking half-bad. I can feel Elise's lack of enthusiasm at seeing Mike again.

"Hi, Mike," she says without emotion.

"Hey Elise, good to see you," Mike says, smiling. Mike is really caught up with Elise. I can see it in his face. I'm glancing back and forth between the two of them and can feel some sort of tension. Can this still be from high school? Seems weird.

"What are you up to, Mike?" I ask to break the silence.

"Oh yeah, I'm headed to Jimmy Scanlon's house to borrow a big cooler. Hey, I'm having a party tonight at my house. Why don't you two come on by?" he asks. "Bunch of people from high school, it will be a blast!"

I can almost feel Elise's skin crawling. Of course, I am excited. I play it cool though, because I know I will more than likely not be able to talk Elise into going.

"Maybe we'll stop by. Thanks, Mike!" Mike slowly starts to pull away from us.

"Hey Elise, come by. It will be fun, I swear."

Elise rolls her eyes and continues paddling.

When Mike is far enough away, I turn to Elise. "What the hell was that all about?" I can see her face getting red.

"Oh fuck, Laney, I screwed up."

I almost flip my kayak. "What are you talking about Elise?" I stop paddling and grab her kayak so we are side by side.

"A few years ago. I couldn't tell you because you were just finding out about Jim cheating on you, and I knew you would think I was a total loser." Elise has her head down.

She looks up at me. "I had a fling with Mike Venero," she says and scrunches up her nose. I can't even believe it. My straight as an arrow, doesn't seem to be very adventurous, friend had an affair?

"You are joking." I hope she says yes.

"I wish I was. Listen, you don't know what goes on behind closed doors. My marriage has been bad for a long time, Laney. I was so lonely and horny, damn it. Scott barely even looks at me, let alone touches me. We haven't had sex in like, five years, Laney."

I am about to fall out of my kayak. I can't even believe what I am hearing.

"Again, Elise, how did I not know this? Why haven't you talked to me about it? I'm more upset by the fact that you don't feel close enough to me to share shit. This is huge, Elise!" I feel so offended and I'm taking this personally now.

"I was ashamed, Laney. Embarrassed. I was raised in a family where you didn't share your emotions, and if you did, that meant you were weak. You stay married to a man even though there is nothing left. I just swallowed the pill I was handed and figured I had to stay with Scott, no matter how horrible." Elise pauses.

"Then, like I said, a few years ago, I was at the big teacher's convention in Atlantic City. The one they have every year. That's where I hooked up with Mike. That was the most exciting week of my life, really.

Sadly, it started there and ended there. I haven't been with him since. I sure do think about him a lot though. Every time I see him, it's like a knife in my heart. He was one of the guys in high school that treated me so nice. We had more than that make out session at that party. You remember how I felt about him, don't you?"

I nod my head yes.

"We had notes, smiling glances in the halls of school, late night phone calls." Elise smiles and reminisces. "Then we left for college and went our own ways. I think if we had the technology then that we have today, Mike and I would probably be together today."

I am totally caught off guard with everything Elise is saying. I never suspected any of this. She always played things off as being good at home. I guess I was so caught up in my little world I didn't notice. In my defense, though, Elise has always been hard to read. I remember she and I having a huge fight in high school all because I had no idea that she was upset about something. She didn't talk to me for a whole week, then finally I was able to get it out of her. Totally annoying. I can't even remember what it was now.

"Wow, Elise. I have no idea what to say. I didn't see this coming. I'm sorry it's been so bad for you. I wish you would have shared that with me. Of course I wouldn't think you were horrible for cheating on Scott if I knew how bad your relationship was."

We just sit in silence for a few moments, letting the waves gently rock us.

"Yeah, well such is life, I guess." She sounds defeated.

"No. No, it isn't. Look at me. I'm a perfect example. I thought 'such is life' too! Things can change with the flip of a coin, Elise. You shouldn't just settle. Life is too short. Plus, do you want to be that example to your girls? You should always want the best for yourself. In time, it will happen, but you have to go look for it, Elise. Not hide from it." I'm regurgitating everything that

Elise said to me while I was going through my hell. Maybe she was trying to convince herself too.

"I know you're right. It's just a hard pill to swallow."

Elise is a stronger woman than I.

"Well, I say we go shopping, get your nails and hair done, buy you a kick ass outfit, and go to that party tonight, Elise." I let go of her kayak and we begin paddling again.

"Oh, I don't know about that," Elise replies. "I don't want to stir the pot with Mike again. He and Coleen seem to be working things out."

"What do you mean? Were they having problems?" I am so intrigued now.

"They were. When Mike and I were together, they were separated. They had been for about a year. Last I heard about a year and a half ago, they were giving it another go."

"You never know, Elise. He seemed to really want you at that party." I'm hoping she says she'll go, but I don't want to push.

"I don't think I want to be put in that position. Cheating is a horrible thing."

It is a horrible thing, I'll give her that. To me though, her relationship seems different. If one person in a relationship is still emotionally involved and vested, then it's cheating. It sounds like Scott and Elise both checked out a long time ago. It disappoints me that she made that choice, but part of me understands. No touching? No affection for that long? That can't be easy. Jim at least saved some hugs and kisses for me. He was such a great actor that way.

"Are you happy, Elise?" I ask her bluntly. She takes a minute to answer.

"No, Laney, I'm not. Scott has really gotten so mean over the past few years. He flies off the handle so easily. He scares me sometimes."

Her answer breaks my heart. How could I be so oblivious? My poor friend has been suffering and I've had no clue.

"You need to find your happiness again, Elise. Wherever that may be."

"I know I do Laney, I know."

We are almost back at the house.

"You know what, Laney? Let's do it. Let's go shopping and get me all dolled up. I want to go to that party. I need to find myself. I used to be a lot of fun. I want to be that girl again."

Elise's enthusiasm excites me. "Woo hoo! Let's do it!" My yell echoes in the cove. We both laugh.

I love nothing more than shopping with my girls and getting dolled up. For women in our late forties, I think we still have it. Elise is super petite; but with the heels we got her today, she looks about six inches taller.

"Wow, Elise! You look amazing!" Her meticulously colored blonde hair, her new outfit. She looks ten years younger.

"Thank you, Laney! I feel amazing! I needed that. Thank you." She gives me a big hug. Another luxury of having money is being able to treat your friends. My favorite thing to do.

"Are you ready to go have some fun?" I jump up and down, trying to get her excited.

"Yeah, I guess so. I may puke if I see Coleen and Mike making out; be there for me to hold my hair."

"Will do, friend, will do." We head out to the Beemer and cruise to the other side of the lake.

Mike and Coleen's house is gorgeous. They have luminaries down the entire walkway that look so beautiful. The backyard is even better. Lights in the trees, an outdoor fireplace, huge stone patio, built-in barbecue grill, flat screen television, surround sound. It's magical.

Elise and I look at each other and mouth, "Wow." We stand at the entrance of the backyard for a moment just taking it all in. There's already a fair amount of people here. I do a quick glance of the crowd to make sure Pete isn't here. He and Mike never really hung with the same crowd, so I'm hoping to get lucky. Not in the mood to see him or his sad wife. Looks like I'm in the clear for now.

"Hey girls! I'm glad you could make it!" Mike runs up to greet us. He gives me a quick hug and then turns to Elise. "Elise, you look beautiful." He leans in and hugs her an extra long time.

Elise pulls away. "Thanks Mike, you look very handsome as well." She fidgets with her hair.

I can feel the sexual tension between them. I interrupt their moment. "You and Coleen have a beautiful home here, Mike. This is truly stunning." Mike does not want to take his eyes off of Elise, but he turns and looks at me, confused.

"What, Laney? I'm sorry. No. I live here alone. Coleen moved out about two years ago. I did all this after she left." I quickly look at Elise's reaction to this news. I have no idea how to read her face. She looks happy with a hint of terrified.

"I'm so sorry, I had no idea. I assumed when we saw you last night at dinner that you were together," I say, hoping he clears that up.

"Oh no, we tried for a long time, but it never happened. We have dinner once every few months to catch up on what's going on with the kids. Stuff like that. We are very good at communicating and co-parenting. We always loved each other, but I'm not sure we were ever in love with each other." He does the air quotes around the 'in love' part.

"I know what you mean," Elise chimes in.

Mike looks at her with a sad, compassionate face. He grabs her hand and squeezes it.

"Let's not think about all that crap tonight and have some fun. What can I get you ladies to drink?" We give him our drink orders and he takes off.

I look at Elise and she looks back at me. I see her take a deep breath and then smile the biggest smile I've seen on her ever.

"Thank you for making me come out tonight, Laney. Whatever happens, I feel alive tonight."

"I know that feeling! I've felt that way ever since I bumped into Brady!"

We begin mingling and I realize there are so many people here I know. Some of the people from the banquet are here, including Crazy Dave. He yells when he sees me, "Hey, there's Brady's lover girl! Where's Brady?"

I crack up laughing and fill him in on Brady's whereabouts. It's so great to reconnect with all these people from my past. People who were such a huge part of my life growing up. I'm spending so much time talking with other people, I realize that I haven't seen Elise in a while. I crane my neck looking for her. She's cuddled up in a corner, sitting with Mike. They seem to be having a very deep conversation. They are sitting knee to knee, leaning into each other. The music is a little loud, but they are definitely closer than they need to be. Good for Elise. It makes me sad that she's been unhappy for so long. Who knows? Maybe she'll find happiness with Mike.

I turn to continue mingling and bump right into Paul Laryn.

"Oops, sorry," I say, not realizing at first that it is Paul.

"Laney!" He's had a few drinks. "I haven't seen you since you treated us all to drinks at The Bird's Nest! Thank you for that, that was really sweet. How are you doing?" he says, regaining his balance.

"I'm doing great, thanks. How's everything with you?" I'm hoping he doesn't bring up the Pete and Brady break up. I'm sure he knows. He's good friends with them both.

"I'm doing good, keeping busy. Working on Wall Street, so doing the whole commuting thing, which sucks, but the money is decent. Hey, I talked to Brady the other day. He told me what a douche Pete was. Sounds like they had a major falling out. That's too bad, they've been buds a long time." Paul takes a sip of beer, waiting for me to respond.

"Yeah, that is too bad. So, do you still live in town?" I'm desperate to change the subject.

"Oh no, no. Next town over. Right by the train station. Makes my commute more bearable. So what happened between Pete and Brady, any idea?"

Please drop it, Paul.

"Yeah, it's a story not worth repeating, but trust me, Brady is better off without the likes of Pete Murdough in his life." I take a sip of beer and glance around the party looking for an out. Damn it, Elise. She's still knee deep with Mike. He's rubbing her leg now and she's laughing. Maybe discussing the old times back in Atlantic City?

Paul brings me back. "Well, that's too bad. I'm close with both of them, hate to see that."

"I'm going to keep mingling, Paul. Great to see you!" I lean in and give him a hug, then walk around him.

I don't know where I'm going, but I know I need to get away from him. I walk over by the lake and notice a single chair, away from the party. I decide to give my feet a break and have a seat. Mike's house looks stunning from the lake. I try to envision Elise living here with him. I can see it, almost. I look back at the lake with the moonlight reflecting off it. I wonder how Allie is doing with George. I hope they are having a great time. I also wonder how Brady is doing with his sister. Does she look like him? I'll have to find her on Facebook.

Then my thoughts can't help but to go to the end of October. When my rental is up. I pack up my car and just head back? How am I going to manage that? I stretch and close my eyes and try to force the thought from my head. Live in the here and now, Laney.

With my eyes still closed, my ears zoom in on a voice from the party. I know it so well. It's Brady. I sit up and look back. There he is, drinking a beer, talking to a woman I do not know. He looks like he's flirting. My heart stops. I stare towards Brady so confused and so hurt. He was supposed to be at his sister's. Did he tell me that so he could come to the party without me? To be with her? I feel like I'm going to vomit when I see Elise approaching me.

"Laney, would you totally disrespect me and hate me if I spent the night here tonight? With Mike."

"Well no, but at the same time, I would like you to be honest with yourself and honest with Scott. I don't like the fact that I know this and he doesn't. When I think of all my friends that knew Jim was screwing around and didn't tell me, it is so hurtful," I say with my fist clenched, just staring at Brady, shaking.

"Would it make you feel better to know that Scott has been unfaithful much more than me?" Elise says with tears in her eyes.

"What are you talking about?" I'm not sure how much more of this I can handle. I'm learning more about people the past two weeks than I have in years. "Yes, Elise, two wrongs make a right. Go for it. Listen, I have to leave. Now. I'll talk to you tomorrow."

I don't even give Elise a chance to stop me. I walk through the neighbor's yard to avoid talking to Brady. I can't talk to him because all I want to do is scream at him. How the fuck could he do this to me? After everything we've both been through. Lies. I hate them. I'm sure Elise will tell him I was there, that's if she can tear herself away from Mike. I get to my car and pull out of there as fast as I can. I can barely see the road through my tears.

I'm so happy to be home. Part of me wants to pack up all my shit and get the hell out of this town. I quickly flip on the light and lock the door behind me. I glance around at the traps. Shit. The book has been moved by the back door. I know Elise put it up against the door when we left. It's clearly not there anymore.

I run to the nightstand. I grab the gun and begin my search. I'm so pissed and hurt that I feel like shooting everything around me. Shit, shit, shit.

I need to calm down. Do I call the cops? No. These local yokels aren't going to be able to do anything. Once again, the back door is locked. Someone most definitely has a key. But who and why? Then I see it. A note on the counter.

Go back to South Carolina where you belong.

Believe me asshole, I just may.

Chapter Forty-Four

I wake up in the morning and lay in bed for a while, thinking things over. I glance at the clock and realize it's already ten. Just then, there's a knock on the front door. Crap. Who the hell is that? I look like shit, I'm sure. I jump out of bed and peek out the front window. I see Elise standing on the front steps and Mike sitting in his truck parked in the road. I quickly open the door.

"Good morning, sunshine!" Elise gives me a big, enthusiastic hug. She turns and waves to Mike, giving him the okay to leave. "I'm glad you're up! I called, but your phone was off."

I stretch my arms up to the sky and yawn. "I just woke up. Good timing. Let me put some coffee on."

"You seemed upset with me last night? Is everything okay with us?" Elise asks, concerned.

"Yeah, we're fine. I wasn't upset with you. You just caught me at a bad time. Did you see Brady there last night?" I ask, hoping she told him off for me.

"I did. It was uncomfortable, to say the least, when I told him that I had arrived there with you. He looked like a deer in headlights."

"I bet he did, because he lied. I'm starting to think our whole relationship is a lie," I say, slamming drawers and throwing spoons.

"He said he came back early and didn't want to bother you because you were with your friends. I don't think he's a liar, Laney. He looked pretty upset." Elise defends Brady.

"Well, he wasn't upset enough to call me. Let's change the subject. Tell me, lover girl, how was your night?"

"Oh, Laney. It was so great! Mike had no idea that I didn't know he and Coleen had broken up. He said he was a little hurt that I hadn't reached out to him. I told him that I tried to work things out with Scott after our affair, but he had already checked out, so I just had to wait for the girls to finish high school." Elise is talking a mile a minute.

"So what now, Elise? Are you going to end it with Scott?" I ask. I know that Elise feels Scott checked out a while back, but that still doesn't justify what he did or what she's doing now.

"I think that's the next step." She falls onto the couch. "He's not going to see it coming at all. I'm sure he assumed it would be him pulling the trigger on our marriage, not me. I think he'll be relieved in a way."

Elise crosses her legs and hugs a pillow.

"What does Mike say?"

"He thinks I should leave Scott immediately, of course. I told him it's not that easy. We've been together over twenty-five years. Oh Laney, I'm scared." I walk over to the living room area and place our cups of coffee down on the table. I sit next to Elise and put my arm around her.

"I know it's scary. Being with Scott is all you know. But here's what I know. You are super successful in your career, and you have been super successful in raising two amazing daughters. Now it's time for you to be successful in a happy relationship. You deserve that Elise. Happiness. It's what we all deserve. Life is too short to waste it with someone who obviously doesn't deserve you. I say you tell Scott immediately. Tell him you'd like him to move out and call an attorney in the morning. The longer you drag it out, the harder it will be. Call the girls. I have a feeling they won't be too surprised." I hand her a tissue from the end table. This is the first time I think I've ever seen Elise cry. She's always been such a rock.

"I know they won't be surprised. Are you kidding? They tried to convince me to leave Scott a while ago. They knew what was going on. They heard our fights." Elise blows her nose and asks for another tissue.

"Okay, enough crying over Scott. I'm only going to smile, thinking about last night. It was so special to be with Mike after all these years. I feel like he was waiting for me. He said he had dated a couple of people, but no one serious because he always thought of me when he was with them," Elise says, wiping away her last tear.

"That's great, Elise. That's the kind of man you deserve."

Elise and I drink our coffee and talk some more. She gathers up her things and decides to go.

"No time like the present to start your future. I texted Scott and told him we need to talk. He's at home waiting. Wish me luck, Laney."

We hug.

"Good luck, stay strong. I guess I'm saying that to the wrong person!" We laugh. Before she walks out, she turns back and looks around the house.

"There's something magical about this place, Laney. I'm with Grace; I think you need to buy it."

I smile. "I'll think about it and let you know." I stand at the door until she pulls away. Good luck, friend. That's a tough position to be in, but I know she'll be okay. I'm sure Scott sees it coming. He has to.

It seems like all my friends are happy. Grace has always had an amazing family and Ben has been the love of her life. Allie seems to be finding love with George, and now Elise with Mike. Everyone's pieces seem to be falling into place and mine feel like they are starting to fall apart. Maybe it was too good to be true.

Chapter Forty-Five

I spend the rest of the day relaxing. Reading, talking to the kids, catching up on emails, and of course, Facebook. Brady's tried calling a couple of times, sent several texts. I'm not ready to talk to him just yet. I need some alone time with my thoughts. I decide to watch an old movie that Stacy has in the cabinet, but first, I pour myself a glass of wine and make myself a little plate of leftover cheeses and bread. I'm snuggled as comfortable as can be on the couch, watching the movie, when there's a fast frantic knock on the door.

"Laney!" I hear Allie yelling.

"I'm coming. Hold your horses!" I yell, trying to untangle myself from the blanket. I look at the clock. It's only five. I didn't think Allie would be back already. Hope everything is okay. I open the door and can immediately tell that everything is not okay.

"Laney, sit down." Allie pushes her way through the door and practically shoves me down on the couch.

"Holy shit, Al, what is it? Is it my kids? Al?" I'm getting frantic now. I can feel the panic in Allie's tone.

"Laney, when is the last time you saw Elise?"

My head is spinning. Oh my gosh, Elise. "Why Al? What's wrong?" I say, losing my breath.

"Laney, what time?" I can't think straight. I know something bad has happened.

"I-I-I don't know. I think she left here around eleven. Why?"

"Laney, Elise is dead." With that, Allie's head drops, her hands cover her face, and she sobs.

I can't even begin to wrap the words around my head. Dead? What? No, no. Elise is alive. She's going to be with Mike. "I don't understand, Allie. No, she's alive. You're wrong," I say, shaking my head emphatically.

"Lane, Scott killed her. He shot her, Laney. He shot her." Her sentence trails off into a hysterical cry.

I can't believe this. I feel like the walls are crashing in on me. I was just sitting on this couch with her. She was in this spot. Here. With me. Alive. How can this be?

"What…how…why?" Oh my goodness. Why! I close my eyes and begin to scream. I know why. She told him that she wanted to divorce him. "No!" Allie grabs me and we just hold each other, rocking back and forth. "I know what happened, I know what happened," I say sobbing.

"What, Laney? Why did he do it?"

"She was telling him she wanted a divorce." We continue hugging and sobbing. "Did they arrest him? Is he in jail?"

"No, Lane. He killed himself." Allie is shaking.

"Oh my god, the girls! Who is going to tell the girls? They need their mom and dad. What the fuck Allie?" I can't breathe.

***

I feel so numb. I have no tears left. Grace is on her way over. Mike. Someone needs to tell Mike. Allie and I are just sitting on the couch. How could Scott do this? Leave those beautiful girls without parents? If he was that miserable, why didn't he take his own life? Leave Elise here with us. Elise was so happy this morning…so excited about what lay ahead. Now it's gone. All her hopes and dreams, gone in an instant.

There's a quiet knock on the door. Allie gets up to see who it is. It's George. I don't even turn to say hi. I can't turn my neck. My whole body hurts. Like I've been hit by a truck. I hear them quietly speaking to each other. George leaves and Allie places some things on the kitchen counter.

"George and Abe got us some food, Lane. Why don't you come eat?" I hear Allie opening aluminum foil-covered plates.

"No. I can't. It feels like someone is stabbing me in the stomach," I say without moving.

It's been almost two hours since I found out one of my dearest friends has been murdered. I can't imagine this pain ever subsiding. Grace comes flying through the door. She stops and looks at Allie, then looks at me.

"What are we going to do?" she cries. I get off the couch and run to her. Allie does the same. We all stand, hugging, leaning on each other's shoulders, crying for what feels like an eternity.

I am finally able to fall asleep around three in the morning. Allie and Grace sleep over, which I am so thankful for. I can't imagine being alone now. I wake at eight and head out to the kitchen. I'm the only one awake. I put a pot of coffee on and stare at the lake. I picture Elise and I washing out the kayaks. Did this all really happen, or is it just a nightmare?

I turn my phone on and receive four new texts. One from Elise's sister. I texted her the night before because I could not speak to her. I am not ready to hear her pain. It would kill me.

> I'm picking up the girls from school today and bringing them to my house. We'll start making the arrangements and get back in touch with you with the details.

Poor Emily. She and Elise were somewhat close. They struggled with their relationship, but they were sisters.

I quickly respond to Emily.

> Please text me your home address. Again, so sorry.

It's all I can type. I have no words for my own pain let alone theirs. Emily sends her home address. She lives about thirty minutes away. I go to my checkbook and write her a check for ten thousand dollars and put it in an envelope. I'm hoping that will help with some of the costs of the funeral.

I remember I have three other texts. One is from Brady.

> I'm so sorry, Laney. I just heard about Elise.

I'm not sure if I'm ready to see him. I do not feel like talking. I just want to crawl into a ball. The other two texts are responses from my kids. Their kind words make my eyes fill with tears just when I thought I didn't have any left.

I fix my coffee and head to the deck. The morning sun makes my tired eyes squint. I close my eyes and tilt my head back. I still can't imagine that this is real. My sorrow has turned to anger. I'm so furious with Scott. How could he? I'm also mad at myself. I should have never pushed her to go to that party. I should have told her not to tell Scott anything. She'd still be here.

Allie and Grace come out a short while later. We all just sit on the deck in silence. Allie is the first to speak. "Well, I need to open the shop. I can't sit around anymore. I'm going to go crazy."

I have nowhere to go. Just here, where Elise was still alive twenty-four hours ago.

"Yeah, I have to head home in a bit too. You going to be okay here alone, Laney? You want to come over to my house?" Grace asks.

"No, thanks. I'm just going to stay here. I'm feeling so weak. I just want to rest."

We sit a little while longer; talking more about Elise and what the arrangements might be. How will the girls be? What about their house? So many loose ends. I guess, between the girls and Elise's family, they'll sort it out. Eventually. Such a nightmare. Allie and Grace say goodbye to me. I can't even stand up.

"Sorry. Hope you don't mind showing yourselves out. I'm going to hang out here for a while."

Allie kisses my head. "You stay put. I'll call you later."

"Do you want another cup of coffee?" Grace grabs my mug.

"Nah, that's okay. I'm good." We say our goodbyes and they leave. I think about the relationships between Elise, Allie, Grace, and me. I was definitely closest to Elise out of all of us. Their relationship with Elise just grew over the years from me visiting and insisting we all do things together. Then years ago, I noticed them all getting together even when I was back in South Carolina. This made me a little jealous, but I was glad they all got along so well. They are all so important to me in different ways.

My thoughts are interrupted by the sound of a boat. It's coming right toward my dock. I shade my eyes with my hand to see who is behind the wheel. Shit. It's Mike. He docks the boat and ties it up. I still can't stand. He walks up the back steps and stops when he sees me. There is a silent stare between us for what feels like forever. I push my chair back and stand up. He walks to me and we just hug. I can feel him crying. His whole body is shaking. I feel like I'm holding him up. I push him away from me.

"Sit down. Do you want a cup of coffee?"

He nods his head yes, sits down, puts his elbows on the table, and wipes his eyes. I go into the house and pour him a cup of coffee, grab a spoon, the creamer, and some sugar.

"Laney, please tell me what happened," Mike says between sniffs. This is a man who is in agony. I put his coffee down in front of him.

"Mike, I don't know. Obviously, Scott was a very sick man. I know Elise didn't see this coming. She did just tell me he was angry and sometimes she was scared, but who could ever imagine?" I'm glad Grace brought a box of tissues out on to the deck. My nose is starting to run and I see that Mike has already grabbed two.

"She came here so excited yesterday morning, Mike. You really meant so much to her. She was going home to tell Scott she wanted a divorce. I'm not sure if she told him about you or what. He did know she wanted to talk because she sent him a text, giving him a heads up. Maybe he saw it coming. Maybe he wanted to be the one to pull the plug. Sick fucker. Ruined everyone's lives. Especially his own daughter's lives," I say, rubbing my temples. My head has been pounding since last night.

"Not to be selfish, but my life too. I really saw a future with Elise, Laney. She was my girl. I just know it. Now I won't know what could have been for us." Mike begins to sob again. I reach over and rub his shoulder.

"I know, Mike, I know. She was in love with you; that I know. She said you made her the happiest she's been in a long time." I try to console him. Try to console myself. I start to think what life would have been like for Elise with Mike. She probably would have moved to Falcon Lake. I can't really her see wanting to hang out with people from town, but I guess she would have done anything to make Mike happy. I shake the thought from my head. It will never be, so I don't even have to try and imagine it. It's too painful.

After an hour, Mike heads out. We exchange numbers so I can send him the funeral info. I can't wait to get into the shower. I use my arms to push me up from the chair. My legs feel like jelly after talking with Mike and thinking of what could have been between him and Elise.

As I head back in the house, there's a knock on the door and I see someone walking away from the house toward George's. I open the door and look down to see an aluminum foil-covered plate. Oh, Abe. I grab the plate and head inside. Abe attached a little note to the plate.

So sorry for your loss. I'm here if you need me. - Abe.

That's so kind. I open the foil to find some fresh baked bread. It's still warm. I should eat something. I need some strength. I get out the butter and start spreading it.

I realize, even though I am physically buttering bread and eating it, all I can see or think about is Elise. I need to shower and get in contact with her girls. I dread it. I hate seeing people hurting. It makes me feel so helpless. I'm sure they want to talk to me. Besides their Dad, I was the last one to see Elise alive.

***

I spend the rest of the day on the phone with various friends of mine and Elise's; answering texts from other friends and Brady. I can tell he's worried about me. I'm glad he couldn't come over earlier in the day. I wasn't ready to see him. But by the sound of his texts; there's no avoiding him coming over.

I hear his truck pull up and I take a quick look at myself in the living room mirror. I look like I've aged about ten years in two days. Oh well, take it or leave it, Brady. I open the door before he reaches it. He stamps his boots out. I didn't even notice it had been raining.

"Hey, how are you?" He gives me a quick kiss on the lips. "Let me put this stuff down. It's nasty out there." He places the bags on the counter, takes off his wet jacket, hangs it on the back of the chair, and turns to me, grabbing both of my hands. "I really don't know what to say to you, other than I love you, and it hurts me so badly that you are hurting."

With that he grabs me in his arms and hugs me. The kind of hug I needed, making me feel so safe and loved. His words, his warmth make me crumble, and once again, I am sobbing.

"It's okay, baby. Let it out, let it out," he says softly in my ear while stroking my head. My face is buried in his chest. I didn't think I had any tears left. I sobbed in Brady's arms for a few more minutes while he just held me, rocking me.

"I'm so sorry," I say between sniffles. "I can't handle this. It's all too much." I wipe my eyes.

"No need to hold it together for me, Laney. Let me get you some tissues." Brady walks over to the coffee table and grabs a box of tissues for me. I blow my nose and clean up my face. "Oh good, you've got our drinks ready. Come sit down and let me get your plate ready. Have you eaten today? You need to eat," Brady says, guiding me to my chair.

"I had some bread that Abe made." I plop down in the chair and take a sip of wine. Brady opens up containers of Italian food. It smells delicious. "I got this from our little Italian restaurant, where we had our first date, a whole three weeks ago." He almost makes me smile.

We spend the rest of the night talking about Elise. Well, I'm talking about Elise while Brady massages my feet, my legs, my shoulders. I'm glad he's here, even though I've been hurt by him. It would have been horrible to be alone. *Ding-dong.* A text. I pick up my phone and see it's from Emily.

The girls would like to see you tomorrow. Can you come by?

Oh, Lord. Brady can see my breath leave me.

"What is it Lane?" Brady asks concerned.

"Elise's girls. They want to see me tomorrow. This is such a nightmare, Brady. I have to be the one to tell these girls about their mom's final moments." I cover my eyes and rub my forehead.

"I know it's going to be hard, Lane, but at least you get to tell them how happy she was." He rubs my back.

"I know, I know."

What time should I be there?

I sit, waiting for a response. Emily texts back that ten in the morning works best. I tell her I'll be there and spend the rest of the night picturing the whole scenario of seeing the girls for the first time in my head. Will they be falling apart? Will I have to console them? I dread it.

I pull away from Brady. "I know Elise told you I was there at Mike's the other night." I wait for his reaction. I feel like I have a built in lie detector in my body now. I'm a pro with liars.

"I swear Lane, I didn't plan on going to the party. I got back early and didn't want to tear you away from your girl's night."

"Whatever, Brady. I can't even think about it right now. I just want to go to sleep," I say, bringing my glass to the sink.

"Is it okay if I stay, Laney? I'd rather you not be alone."

"That's fine. I'd rather not be alone either."

Chapter Forty-Six

Morning comes way too fast, as usual. I hear Brady in the shower. I look at the clock and it's only seven. I stretch and contemplate going back to sleep, but decide to get up and get ready. I want to go to the store and buy some things for Emily and the girls anyway. I open the bathroom door and make Brady jump.

"Whoa, you scared me."

"I have that effect on people first thing in the morning," I say, then bend over the sink to brush my teeth.

"I wish I could take your pain away. I hate to see you like this." Brady says, giving me a hug.

"Thanks. I guess with time I'll feel better. I can't imagine it now." I pull away and get ready to get in the shower. "You're not leaving right away, are you? I can wait to go in the shower."

"No, go shower. I'm going to make us some breakfast." He continues toweling off. Part of me is starting to believe that Brady didn't want to ruin my girl's night. But the way he was acting with that woman. I mean, he seemed a little too comfortable with the flirting. I felt he was looking at her the way he looks at me. I start to cry at the thought of losing Brady, and then quickly my thoughts turn again to seeing two beautiful young women who lost both of their parents in the blink of an eye.

Brady has breakfast waiting for me on the deck when I'm done getting ready. He has my coffee prepared just the way I like it.

"Well, don't you look pretty!" Brady scoops some scrambled eggs on my plate.

"Thanks, Brady."

"Nervous about today?"

"Yes, very much so. I just don't like seeing people in pain. Makes me fall apart. I know I need to be strong for them, so I'm going to try my hardest to keep it together. Kind of defeats the purpose of me being there if I'm blubbering." I sip my coffee and stare at the lake.

"Well, you need your strength, so eat up. You'll do great, I know you will." We finish up breakfast and clear the table.

"I assume the services will be tomorrow and Thursday?" Brady asks while putting dishes in the dishwasher.

"I assume that as well, but I'll call you after I leave Emily's. You have Jeremy tonight?" I ask, still drinking my coffee.

"No, he's staying with Susie. I told her and Jeremy what happened and they both agreed that I needed to be here with you." I think about how that conversation went down. I can't really picture Susie the Floosie being so compassionate as to care about me, but I guess you never know.

"That's really sweet. I'll be happy to have the company." Brady finishes up and comes over to give me a hug goodbye.

"It's getting harder and harder for me to be away from you, Lane. I can't help but think about October 31. I think about it a lot. One of these days, we are going to have to come up with a game plan because I do not see a future without you being with me. I don't," he says, putting his forehead against mine.

I smile. "Thanks for everything. I'll see you around dinner time. Want to go out?" I'm not purposefully trying to change the subject. I just do not have the strength emotionally to deal with this right now.

"Going out sounds good. Call me if you need me after your talk with the girls. It's going to be okay. Stay strong." Brady kisses me and then he's out the door. I close the door and lean against it and close my eyes. Is it going to be okay?

I make the bed and finish straightening up before I head to the market. I decide to hit the fancy one I went to the other day, since it's on the way to Emily's. Lucky for me, this time I do not run into Beth. I still need to talk to Brady about that. That will have to wait for another time. I pull up to Emily's house and get the bags of groceries and pre-made gourmet frozen meals out of the trunk. Emily's house is cute. As I'm walking up the sidewalk, I try to remember the last time I saw Emily. Gosh, it's been a while. Maybe a graduation party for one of the girls? Everything is a blur, so there's no sense trying to remember right now.

After ringing the bell, my knees shake a little bit. Oh, how I dread this. Emily opens the door. "Laney, hi! Thanks so much for coming. Let me help you with those bags." Emily grabs a bag and we walk toward the kitchen. I nervously glance around to see if I can spot the girls.

"How are you all holding up?" I ask Emily, trying to make conversation.

"Ya know, Laney, we're doing better than I thought. I'm sure we're in shock, but overall, we are doing okay." That makes me feel a little better.

"Hey, Emily, before I talk to the girls, here." I reach into my purse and get out the envelope with the check. "Please use this toward Elise's funeral. The last thing you all need to worry about right now is money." I place the envelope in her hands.

"No, Laney, I can't." Emily rubs my arm. "That is so sweet of you."

I can tell by her reaction that the money is needed.

"Just take it and use it any way you see fit. One less thing to have to think about. Please. I want to do this for the girls and Elise," I say with a huge lump in my throat. I take a deep breath and pull it together. Emily gives me a hug just as Riley and Rachel walk into the kitchen. As expected, when I see them, their sad faces, I begin to cry.

The three of us just stand hugging in the kitchen.

"Hi, Aunt Laney," they say almost in unison.

"Girls, take Laney into the living room and I'll bring out some drinks," Emily instructs them.

We sit down in the living room. The girls are on one couch and I'm across from them. We make some small talk until Emily comes back to the room with a tray of drinks.

"I have iced tea or lemonade."

"Lemonade is fine, thanks." I say, not feeling like having a thing, but trying to be polite. "So girls, I guess you have some questions for me?" I say, trying to start off this conversation that I'm dreading so much.

Riley begins, "Well, yeah. First off, who is Mike?"

With that our two-hour conversation begins. The girls listen intently and even smile at times when I tell them about their mom's run-in with Mike, what the party was like, how happy Elise was.

"I only wish she didn't wait so long to reach out to Mike. She could have had happiness so much longer." Rachel puts her head down and puts her hands over her eyes. Riley rubs her back.

"We tried to get mom to leave dad a long time ago. We even tried to set her up on a date with our old swim coach," Rachel says. The girls giggle a little thinking back on what was obviously a funny memory.

The girls tell me that they are going to have two separate services for their parents. Scott's will be tomorrow and Elise's on Thursday. They have both been cremated already.

"Girls, will you be highly offended if I don't attend your dad's service? Be honest. I'll be there for you if you need me, not a problem," I say and take my last sip of lemonade.

"No, no, we understand. I think there is going to be a low attendance rate at that service," Rachel says while looking at her sister.

"We aren't going, Aunt Laney." Riley confesses. "We are so angry with him. We have been for years. He gave up on our mom and on us a long time ago. Shut us out. Why couldn't he have just killed himself?" Rachel cries and Riley embraces her. I squeeze in next to them and lean on Rachel's shoulder hugging her.

"Girls, we'll never know why and we have all been robbed. You, your mother, me, your Aunt Emily, everyone. Look at me, girls." I sit up and look at these poor girls' faces. They both turn toward me. This is my moment to be strong. "Your Mom was an amazing woman; a very strong and determined woman. I'm saying this for her. You mourn your loss, your horrific loss, but you keep living, live life to the fullest. Follow every dream and know your Mom is watching you and cheering you on. Don't you dare give up on your dreams. She would never want that. Do you hear me girls?"

They both nod their heads.

"One more thing before I go. You need to know that if you need anything, and I mean anything, you better call me. I'm just a phone call away. Do you understand? You need to get away, call me. You need money, call me. I mean it. Got it?"

They nod their heads again and thank me. We give each other another group hug.

"I'll see you girls on Thursday. You make your Mom so proud, okay?" I get out to my car, get in, and sob. All I can see is the pain in their eyes. The sheer agony of losing their parents.

I hit a drive-through on the way home for a large, extra-thick chocolate milkshake. This will be my lunch today. I'm too tired to even chew. As I'm waiting in line for my shake, I see a car pull up and park outside the fast food joint. It catches my eye because I remember seeing the same one in George and Abe's driveway a couple of days ago. I straighten up in my seat when I see Susie get out of the driver's side. Luckily, I'm far enough away that she can't see me. There's someone in the passenger seat but I can't make out who it is. Maybe it's Jeremy? It's twelve thirty though, he should be in school. Hmmm.

As I get closer to the pick up window, Susie's car is getting closer. The guy looks too big to be a seventeen-year-old. The drive-through line is barely moving. Susie makes her way back out of the restaurant. She's got two drinks in her hands. I watch her walk to the passenger side window. The guy puts the window down and reaches out for his drink. She leans in and kisses him. I'm able to move up one more spot in line. I just need to get a little bit closer. I'm squinting, trying to make this guy out. Then, as Susie puts the car in reverse, I catch a glimpse of him in the side view mirror. I only see him for a second, but that's all I need. Pete. He's at it again. What a low life. What is the deal with those two? Gross.

Chapter Forty-Seven

I get home and decide I'm going to venture out to the hammock again. I'm not going to let Pete ruin that spot for me. Bastard. The sun feels so good. All this crying has made me so exhausted. I close my eyes and quickly fall asleep.

My dreams are vivid. Elise and Mike pulling up on the boat, me and Brady meeting them on the dock. The four of us having a barbecue. Laughs, drinks, fun. I'm taken away from this pleasant dream by the buzz of my cell phone telling me I have a text. I almost don't want to look at it. It's from Allie.

You are not going to believe who just left my store.

Oh Lord, please no drama. I can't handle it today.

I'm afraid to ask.

Just tell me, Allie. It must be a doozy if she's making it so suspenseful. *Dingdong.*

Jim.

Jim who?

I'm trying to think of a Jim we went to school with.

Your Jim. McGuire. Sound familiar?

I almost fall off the hammock. I'm shocked. What the hell is he doing here? Holy crap. I guess he heard about Elise. Is that why he's here? Shit, does he know I'm here? I'm sure the kids told him. This is not good. Jim always hated, and I mean hated, Brady because he knew how I felt about him. Oh, why Jim, why? I hope Allie didn't tell him where I was.

Call me right now, please, if you can.

My phone rings a few moments later.

"Can you even believe he is here, Laney?" Allie asks immediately without even saying hello.

"What the fuck, Allie? What did he say?" I'm so pissed.

"He said he came up because he heard about Elise and Scott. He said he drove all night. He's going to stay at his cousin's house and go to the services."

Oh shit. I forgot about his cousin, Rob. He and his wife Christine still live in Bear Creek, I guess.

"Does he know I'm here?" I ask, but I already know the answer. I'm sure he heard from the kids. I didn't feel the need to inform him of my whereabouts, but I'm sure it came up in conversation. Plus, word of mouth back home. It didn't even cross my mind that he would come up here for the services. I'm wondering what his real motives are. He's not that compassionate of a guy.

"Yes. He asked how you were doing, if you were holding up okay. He wants to come see you. He went for a walk down the street and said he'll be back in five minutes. Asked me to call you. What are you going to do?" I feel the hairs on my neck stand up. I really do not want to see him, but maybe if I get it over with now, I can relax when I go to Elise's service.

"He's such an asshole. Tell him I'll meet him in front of your store. I'm leaving now. Thanks, Al, see you in a few."

"Okay see you in a bit."

I lie there for a second. Close my eyes and take a deep breath.

"What a way to ruin another day." I say out loud as I get out of the hammock.

"Hey, I heard that. Are you talking about me?" Abe yells from his back deck.

"Not today, Abe. How are you doing?" I shield my eyes with my hand so I can look at him on his deck.

"Good. More importantly, how are you?" Abe stands and walks to the railing. "I'm okay. I think I'm still shocked, ya know?" I answer, scrunching my nose.

"I can only imagine. Let me know if you need anything."

"Thanks, Abe, appreciate it." I walk up to the house, grab my keys and bag, and head to Bohemian Bling.

***

As I pull up to the store, I see Jim outside on the phone. Just seeing him makes my stomach flop. I often wonder what I ever saw in Jim. He's totally not my type. His hair is on the long side, blonde, and unkept. He's fair-skinned, tall, and very thin. If he were any guy standing on the sidewalk right now, I probably wouldn't give him a second glance. I park across the street and walk over.

Jim is finishing up his conversation. "Okay, Bud, gotta go. I'll see you tomorrow. Hey, Laney, how are you, honey?" He leans in and gives me a hug, which I do not return. He steps back from me. "I'm so sorry about Elise. You doing okay?"

"No, I'm not doing okay, Jim. What are you doing here?"

"I got a call from Pete Murdough. He told me about Elise, said you were having a real hard time. He told me all about Brady and you too. Thought I'd take a ride up, make sure you are okay. You are the mother of my children after all, Laney." He rubs my arm. I pull away.

"First off, if you even knew what Pete Murdough pulled on me, I'm sure you wouldn't be having phone conversations with him. I'll save that gem of a story for another time. Second, you never gave a shit about my friends when we were together, all of the sudden you care?" I can see Jim is shocked at my reaction.

"I cared about your friends, Laney, I did. I just felt at times they were more important to you than I was," he says with a puppy dog face that I'm not buying.

"I call bullshit on that, Jim. I think the real reason you came up here is because you heard about me and Brady. Had to see it for yourself, did you?" I'm shaking now. Jim has that effect on me.

"I guess that was part of the reason, yes. Especially since Pete told me that Brady was just after your money. Thought you should know that piece of information, Laney."

I feel like I just had the wind knocked out of me.

"Go the fuck back to South Carolina, Jim," I say, slowly poking him in the chest.

"I'm not going anywhere, Laney. I'm staying for the services. I guess I'll see you and your money-hungry boyfriend there." He turns and walks away.

I run into Allie's shop.

"Holy shit, what the hell was that about?" I walk to the backroom and begin sobbing. I fill Allie in on what just transpired.

"Laney, Jim is a jealous asshole. Don't listen to a word he says. You know Pete just made that up because he's a jealous asshole too. Ignore it. It's not true," Allie says, trying to comfort me.

"But what if it is true, Al? Brady never even looked at me in high school, never acknowledged my existence, now all of the sudden I'm his dream girl?" I blow my nose and can't even believe I had tears left to shed. "Shit. This is the last thing I needed right now."

***

I leave Allie's shop once I calm down. What do I do? Do I confront Brady right away with what Jim said? Or do I watch and see what happens? I feel like I don't have the strength right now to deal with it all. My stomach is killing me. Damn extra thick shake. The ride home can't be fast enough. I just want to get in the house, lock the doors, and think about my next step with Brady before he gets there.

Shit. We're supposed to go out to dinner. I don't think I'm up for that. The last thing I need is to bump into Jim in town. I still can't believe he is here. Why does that man insist on ruining everything?

Once I get home, I get a text from Brady.

Be over in an hour. Where are we headed for dinner? Miss and love you.

Do you mind if we order in again? Rough afternoon. Not sure if I feel like heading out. Sorry.

I plop on the couch and lie down.

> Sure thing. I'll pick something up on the way over. Any special requests?

> I need wine and I'll eat whatever you bring. Thanks.

I stare at the ceiling, trying to think of any signs that Brady is just after me for my money. There really hasn't been a thing that I can think of. Damn it, Elise. I wish you were here. She would definitely be my go-to girl in this situation. I miss her so much.

My phone rings and it's a number I do not recognize.

"Laney? Hi, it's Natalie, the masseuse. Just wanted to make sure we are still on tomorrow for noon?"

Shit, I forgot about that.

"Natalie, thanks for calling. Is there any chance we can do it another day? Maybe Friday?" As bad as I need a massage, I can't think about doing anything until after the service on Thursday.

"That should be fine. If it's not, I'll give you a ring back. Otherwise, just plan on seeing Amanda and I at noon on Friday."

"Sounds good, thanks Natalie." Yeah, Friday will be good. I have to remember to tell Brady that.

I must have fallen asleep again. Brady opening the front door startles me. I sit up, completely unaware of where I am for a second.

"Shoot, I'm sorry. Did I wake you up?" Brady asks, carrying a few bags in and closing the door behind him.

"Yeah, it's okay. I must have fallen asleep again." I stand up and stretch. Brady walks over and gives me a hug and a soft kiss on the lips.

"You okay, babe?" Brady asks, rocking me in his arms.

"I'm as good as I'm going to get." I pull away from him. "Jim is in town."

This catches Brady off guard.

"What? Why? When? Did you see him?"

"He says he's here for the services. Your buddy Pete called him. He also told Jim about us," I say, walking to the kitchen.

"Oh shit. What the hell is wrong with Pete? So you saw Jim, or he called you?" Brady follows me.

"Oh, I saw him. Met him in front of Allie's shop. He had Allie call me. He didn't care about Elise; he's here because he knows you and I are together." I fill two wine glasses all the way to the top.

"Why though? Why does he care so much that we are together?" Brady asks, acting confused. I want to blurt out what Jim said, but I pause. Not yet.

"Who knows? I guess he always knew that I had the hots for you. It's always bugged him, so maybe he wanted to see us together first hand?" I feel guilty not telling the truth, but I know for now I need to protect myself.

"All I know is he is an asshole and I'm not going to waste another breath on him." I hold up my glass to clink Brady's. He hesitates but does it.

"So what is he going to do? Start a fight with me or something? I don't get it," Brady says, taking a sip of wine, obviously consumed by Jim's sudden appearance.

"Me neither, but I can tell you this; I could care less that he's here. My focus on Thursday is going to be Rachel and Riley."

Brady and I eat dinner and spend the rest of the night talking. I tell him about my meeting with the girls and he talks about the job he's doing right now on an addition to a house.

"Sounds like a good job. I'll have to come by and see it some time," I say, trying to be supportive and push all the negative thoughts to the back of my mind. I'm having a real hard time being present in this conversation. I'm also trying my hardest not to believe what Jim said about Brady. When I think of all the small things Brady has done—the talks, the love making—I can't even fathom that any of that was not real.

"Laney? You with me honey? Are you okay? Talk to me," Brady says, turning my face toward his.

I can't lie to him and I feel like I'm a pretty good judge of character. I'll be able to tell by his reaction whether or not he is lying. Won't I?

"Pete told Jim that you are with me for my money." There it is. I put it right on the table, and now I watch. See if there's a nervous laugh, any sign of it being true.

"Are you kidding me?" Brady looks very, very hurt. "Well, I know you didn't believe that for one second, did you Laney?" he says with tears forming in his eyes.

"No, I didn't believe it. Well, I worried for a flash because I started thinking, how you never even looked at me in high school or anything, and now..." I pause, taking in his reaction.

His head is down and his hands move up to cover his face.

"But then I started thinking about us and how it's been, and I knew that it wasn't possible. This is real, right, Brady?"

He takes his hands off his face. "Of course this is real, Laney! I'm in love with you. You! Not your fucking money. I am a simple man, Laney. I don't need a lot of money to be happy. I am very content with my life and even more so with you in it." He grabs my hands. "Please believe that. That is not who I am."

I wipe the tears that have fallen from his eyes and run down his face. Not even the best liar in the world could pull off a performance like this. "I believe you, Brady. I do. Come here." I embrace Brady and he hugs me so hard. I know the words left my mouth, but they are ringing in my head. I believe you. Do I? Do I really? Can I?

"I can't believe Pete would do this to me. Why is he out to get me? I don't understand. We've been friends for years."

"I don't know. He's not a well person. Obviously some mental issues." I pull back from Brady so that I'm looking him in the eyes. "I saw him again today with Susie. They were in her car."

"I don't understand that either. What the hell do they see in each other? It's sick. Poor Jean," Brady says and pulls me back into another hug. "Laney, I'm starting to think we are the only honest people left in this world." I stare off when he says that; hoping and praying that it's true, but worrying that, maybe, it's not.

Chapter Forty-Eight

The next morning I am awakened by Brady's alarm. I really hate alarms. He gets out of bed and heads to the shower. I stay in bed, staring at the ceiling. Another day to face my truths. Elise is gone. I'm losing faith in my and Brady's relationship. I'm losing faith in Brady. And I hate that. I hear Jim's voice telling me Brady just wants me for my money. I know my money means everything to Jim, so it does not surprise me that he is so pissed about Brady and me. And Pete, well, Pete is a jealous asshole as well. Those are two people that belong together—Jim and Pete!

Brady comes out of the bathroom all showered and dressed. He sits next to me on the bed and begins running his fingers through my hair.

"I love you, Laney Simms. So very much. I know the next couple of days are going to be hard, but I'm here for you." Brady rubs his nose against mine.

"Thanks. I appreciate it. I dread tomorrow," I say, looking down, thinking of Elise. "It's going to make it real. I think I'm still in shock."

"I'm sure you are, and maybe that's best for now." Brady leans in and gives me a kiss on the forehead. "Well, baby, sorry to say, I've got to hit the road."

I'm watching him get his boots on when I realize I'm going to have to hit the gym today. It will be a good stress relief, I guess, but every part of me just wants to stay in bed.

"I'll see you tonight?" Brady asks.

"I'll be here waiting," I respond, still under the covers.

"Right there? In bed? Hmmm, I may be home early." Brady winks. "Try and have a good day."

"I'll try. Don't forget the christening at Grace's on Saturday. I did. I need to get a card." I wonder if Grace will still have the christening. I'm sure she will. Elise would want her to, that I know.

"I may have to be a little late for that. Not sure. I'll know by Friday night. Love you. Call me if you need me and I'll see you later." One last kiss and Brady is out the door. Shoot. I've let so many things slip my mind. I almost forgot my confrontation with Beth Pamett. I still need to ask Brady about that.

After coffee, I force myself to go to the gym. My legs feel like logs, but I know I need it. I'm so paranoid when I head into the gym now. I do not want to see Pete right now. I don't know what I might say. Now that he's got Jim involved in my private life, it may be nearing a time when I need to tell his wife about what I've seen. I shake my head. It sounds so evil, but I'm so tired of Pete. I feel it's only fair that Jean knows what he's been up to. Luckily, there is no one that I recognize at the gym and my run is much less painful than I thought it would be.

I head home, shower, get dressed, and do my hair and makeup. Maybe if I look better, I'll feel better. I text Riley and Rachel to see how they're doing, my kids and Allie. Everyone checks in. Allie wants to do lunch. That might be a good idea. I need to get out of the house. I text her back.

That sounds good. Should I pick you up?

As I'm waiting for her response, there's a knock on the door. Shit. I hope that's Abe with baked goods, otherwise; I'm not interested. I look out the window and see a car that I don't recognize. I glance to the door. Double shit. It's Jim. I open the door just enough for my head to show.

"Jim, what the hell are you doing here?" He's all dressed up.

"Hey, Laney. I just wanted to check on you. I was headed to Scott's service, but thought I'd stop by here first, make sure you're okay."

"I'm fine Jim, but I'd be better if you were not in this state." He makes my blood boil.

"Laney, please, I'm really sorry about what I said to you. I should not have told you that, but I felt like you should know what I heard. I'd want you to do the same for me. And I guess I'm just really jealous. I know you always had a thing for Brady and now to hear that you are with him, it hurts." Jim puts his sad face on again.

"Why do you care, Jim? You didn't give a shit about me when we were married. Now that I'm in love you do? Or is it about the money for you too, Jim?" I'm fuming now.

"Oh, Laney, how can you be in love? It's been a few weeks. Gimme a break! It's not real, Laney. Don't you get it? That's what Pete was trying to tell you."

Oh Lord. Can of worms: opened. Now I open the door and step out on the porch, closing the door behind me.

"Did Pete share how he tried to tell me that, Jim? Huh? Did he tell you how he fucking assaulted me? Grabbing my tits, trying to shove his tongue down my throat? Pinning me down on the hammock? Did he tell you that fun story, Jim? Fuck Pete and fuck you, Jim!"

I don't realize how loud I yelled that last part. Jim takes a step back. It's obvious by his response that he must not have heard that story. I hear a noise to my right and see that Abe has stepped outside.

"You okay, Laney? Need me over there?" Abe yells, concerned.

"I think I have this situation under control, but thanks, Abe. Keep an ear out though." I'm shaking now.

"Laney, no. I'm so sorry. I didn't hear about that. Did you call the cops on the bastard? Why isn't he locked the hell up?" Jim says, acting like he's really concerned.

"No, I didn't call the cops. Look Jim, please, I'm begging you. Stay out of my business. You put me through hell with all your whores. This is my time to have happiness, and I have it with Brady. Leave me alone!" I turn back to the door.

"Laney, wait!" Jim reaches for my arm and turns me around. "Laney, I'm so sorry. I know I hurt you. I hurt the kids too, and I am forever regretful for that. I loved you, Laney. I still do. I miss you; I miss us. You are all I've been thinking about lately and I hoped that maybe there was still a chance for us."

His words make me want to vomit.

"Then I get this call from Pete. He tells me about you and Brady, and well, I got scared. I knew how you've always felt about him and I thought if I didn't come up here and see you…I would never have a second chance with you. Please Laney, let me come in so we can talk. I'm begging you. I am a stupid man Laney. I messed up real bad. I see that now. I have nothing without you. You are my everything." Jim pleads with me, tears in his eyes. I look at him and all I feel is disgust. He broke my heart and tore apart my family.

"Too little, too late, asshole." I go in the house and slam the door behind me. I quickly lock the door and sink to the floor. I hear his car door slam. I put my hands over my face and just sit there in utter disbelief.

I'm still sitting on the floor, when there is a small knock.

"Laney? It's Abe. You okay in there?" I push myself up and open the door.

"Hey Abe, yes. I'm fine. Thank you so much for keeping an eye out for me. I really appreciate it. Would you like to come in?" I say, stepping back.

"No, no. Thanks anyway. I need to get back to work. I'm glad you're okay. Who was that guy? If you don't mind me asking."

"That was Jim McGuire. My ex-husband." I shake my head and rub my brow with my hand. "Thanks again, Abe. I appreciate you caring." Abe steps off the porch,

"No problem. And Laney?"

"Yes?"

"You look much better with Brady than with Jim McGuire."

I smile and thank him.

***

I need to get out of this house. Before I leave, I text Brady.

> We are definitely going out tonight. Let's go the Bird's Nest and dance and drink.

> Sounds good, but hope everything is okay with you. Love you.

> I'll fill you in when I see you.

I head to Bohemian Bling to pick up Allie. I park right in front of her shop and she walks out not a minute later.

"Hey Lane, where are we headed?"

"I don't know. Want to just go to Henry's?" I pull away from the curb and head in that direction, not waiting for her to answer. I just start ranting about Jim's visit. "Can you believe that jerk?" I say, pulling into a parking spot in front of Henry's.

"Doesn't surprise me, Lane. I knew you being with Brady would drive him nuts."

We go into the restaurant and I automatically do my scan of the place, making sure I don't see any of the usual suspects. Part of me would love to run into Pete, but I'm sure he's probably at Scott's service.

"Can we have a table in the back corner over there?" Allie's asks the waitress.

"How are things with George?" I feel bad I haven't asked, but it's been so crazy.

"They're going pretty well. He's been at my place just about every night. We're really getting to know each other and it's good." Allie looks over the menu.

"Just good? Not great?" I ask.

"Yeah, just good. There are times when I can really tell how young he is. I love it and hate it at the same time. But he's super passionate and really seems to dig me, so I guess I can't complain."

The waitress puts our drinks down. "Plus, he's great in the sack."

"Would you and Mr. Great-in-the-Sack like to go out with Brady and I tonight? I was thinking Bird's Nest…dinner, cocktails, dancing." I say, taking a forkful of salad.

"Oh yeah, that sounds good. We need that. I'll text George and ask him." My eyes veer to the doorway as I watch a few women walking in together. There are four of them, and after one of them steps to the side, I see Jean. Poor naive Jean. The waitress sits them on the other side of the room and she cannot really see me. I wonder who those other women are. Maybe it's a support group for women with horrible husbands. I needed one of those at one time.

"George is in! What time should we be ready to go?"

"Want to leave at, like, six?" I think that should give Brady plenty of time.

"Yay! I'm so excited to be going out. I need some happy times. The past few days have been such a nightmare!"

I agree with Allie. We all need happy times.

Allie and I finish up lunch. We walk to the register by the door to pay and I'm trying to stay out of view of Jean. Seeing me I'm sure only upsets her, poor woman, stuck with such an awful husband. Allie gets a call. "I'll meet you outside."

While waiting for the bill to be rung up, I glance at the table Jean's sitting at, trying to see who she's with. Oh Lord. Beth is one of them, but I don't recognize the others. Beth spots me and I quickly look away. Please hurry up, cashier. I glance back and see Beth saying something to Jean, then all four of the woman look over at me. I focus on the cashier and the problems she's having with the credit card machine.

"Ya know what? Here, I have cash." I quickly grab my card from her and hand her money. "Keep the change." I quickly exit the place. I can only imagine the conversation at that table right now. That's one thing I despise about a small town. You can't go anywhere without seeing someone you know.

The rest of the day is uneventful. I'm awaiting Brady's arrival and trying my hardest to look good for tonight. I feel horrible on the inside; might as well look nice on the outside. Nice pair of jeans, cute top, sexy heels. I need this. I'm glad Brady is getting here a little early. I want to talk to him about Beth before Allie and George come over.

I hear Brady's truck pull into the driveway. I peek out the window. Damn, he looks good. Button down, black dress shirt. Yum. I open the door just as he steps on the porch.

"You look so good," I say, trying to control my urge to jump Brady right there. That shirt, with his dark hair and light eyes.

"Well, thanks, you don't look so bad yourself," Brady says in between kisses. "Let's take this mutual appreciation of each other inside." Brady grabs my ass and guides me back through the front door. "It's nice to see you smiling again." He closes the door behind him but still has his arms wrapped around my waist.

"It feels good to smile, but at the same time I feel guilty," I say, thinking of Elise.

"Well, I didn't know Elise very well, but I do know she would not want you to feel that way."

I agree. Elise would be pissed at me. "You're right. Gosh your eyes look greener than ever in that shirt." Focus, Laney. "I actually need to talk to you about something."

I grab his hand and lead him to the couch. "Have a seat." I sit down and pat the cushion next to me.

"Why do I feel like I'm in trouble again?" Brady asks, sounding a little nervous.

"You're not. Just wanted to share with you a little run-in I had with Beth Pamett last week." I proceed to tell Brady how Beth told me that they were joined at the hip at one time and how my high school dreams were finally coming true.

"Wow, that was pretty nasty of her."

I nod in agreement.

"To say we were joined at the hip is a complete lie. We went to dinner once and I think I talked to her on the phone once. I swear, Laney. I didn't do anything with her, nor do I consider her a friend. The only thing we had in common was that our spouses did each other," Brady says with certainty, and I think I believe him. Beth is so not Brady's type and I know Brady's type. Me. Right? I'm his type.

"I believe you. I can tell when someone is talking out of anger and jealousy and that's exactly how she was behaving."

"Can we just run away from here? I'm getting sick and tired of all these assholes." Brady grabs my face in his hands and kisses me.

"Yes, we can. We can run away to South Carolina. I know someone there that has this cute little house." He makes a frustrated face.

"You know I can't leave here, Laney. Not with my business and Jeremy. My whole family is within an hour's drive." So, he has thought it over and obviously has decided he's never leaving here. Not even for me.

"So it's me moving here or nothing at all? I'm happy to know where you stand, Brady. Thank you. That will make leaving that much easier on me. I'm not having a long distance relationship. Especially if…" I stop myself before I let pure evil out of my mouth. I walk away to try and control my emotions.

"Especially if what, Laney?" Brady says, still seated on the couch. Just then there's a knock on the door and Allie enters. Very typical Allie.

"Oh, did I catch you two in the middle of something?" she asks.

"Nothing that can't be finished another time." I shoot Brady a look. "Come on in. Where's George?"

"He's on his way, just finishing up an email."

"Would you like a glass of wine before we head out?" I ask, grabbing the glasses out of the cabinet.

"Thank you for already knowing the answer." Allie smiles.

I glance at Brady. He is sitting there, looking stunned.

"Brady, would you like some wine?"

"Yeah, sure." He still looks blindsided. I'm starting to feel bad.

"Brady, how's it going?" Allie sits down next to him on the couch.

"It's going okay." He looks over at me in the kitchen with sad, puppy dog eyes. "How are things with you and your fiancé?"

"Well, it's not official yet. We are going to take our time. Get to know each other a bit. Why rush, right?" she says, sounding like she's convincing herself. I hand them their wine and then head back to the kitchen to pour George and myself a glass.

I return to the living room and catch the second part of Brady's response.

"Part of me thinks that life is too short, and sometimes you just have to go for it. If it's meant to be, it will be." He takes a sip of his wine. "Right, Laney?" he asks.

"I guess so. But it takes two people willing to make sacrifices. You both need to give 100 percent."

Allie looks back and forth between us. Another knock on the door. Perfect timing.

"Come in!" Allie and I yell in unison as if we are both trying to escape the conversation. George walks in, looking very handsome as well.

"Hey George, you look handsome." I get up and give George a hug and hand him his wine. We sit and talk until we are all finished with our drinks. "Ya'll ready to hit the road?" I say, standing up. They all giggle a bit.

"I'll never get used to you saying ya'll Laney, I swear." Allie stands up to join me.

"I'll drive." Brady heads to the kitchen with the glasses.

"No, that's okay, I'll drive." I grab my coat and keys. George follows Brady and Allie follows me.

"You okay?" she says in my ear.

"I'll be okay."

"That answer isn't good enough for me, but we'll talk more later." She puts her arm around me and squeezes me.

When we arrive at The Bird's Nest, there aren't many people there. It is early and it is only Wednesday night. I'm sure by the time we finish dinner, more people will show up. The waitress seats us at a table in front of a beautiful stone fireplace.

We're all looking through the menu when Allie blurts out, "So Brady, how are you handling the competition in town?" She winks at me. Oh Lord, here we go.

"Competition? You mean Jim? I don't consider him competition, Allie." Brady squeezes my hand and smiles.

"I don't know, the way he was begging Laney to come back to him; he's come to Falcon Lake with his game face on." Allie laughs and I shoot her a dirty look.

Brady pulls his hand away from me. "You saw Jim again?"

"Yes, I did. It was so meaningless to me I forgot to tell you." I turn to Allie, "Thank you Allie, for reminding me." I glare at her and she turns a little red.

"Oops, sorry about that." Allie sips her wine.

"No need to apologize. I was going to tell you about Jim's visit before we left, but we ran out of time," I say to Brady. That is the truth. I'm not trying to hide anything. Just then the waitress arrives to take our orders.

Brady takes my hand back after I'm done ordering and holds it in his lap. He leans in and says in my ear, "I'm sorry about before. I don't want to seem unreasonable. I know it has to be a give and take. We'll work it out." He smiles and kisses me on the cheek. I'm not so sure we will.

"Glad you two lovebirds have kissed and made up; now let's eat!" Allie says just as the food arrives.

Dinner is delicious and the conversation is stimulating. It feels so good to be out. Tomorrow is a day I know Allie and I are dreading. This is a great distraction. Plus, I've had three glasses of wine and I'm feeling pretty loose. We hear a band start playing in the other room. We settle the check and Allie and I take a trip to the ladies' room and tell the guys we'll meet them at the bar.

"Sorry about what I said at dinner, Lane. Hope I didn't cause any problems for you. You know I lose my filter when I'm drinking. They might as well call that stuff truth serum," Allie says, fixing her hair in the mirror.

"No, no problems. Horrible timing, but I'm kinda glad you said it. Get that man a little jealous. Keep him on his toes!" I laugh while trying to apply lip gloss. I miss my top lip by a quarter of an inch and Allie and I crack up laughing, not realizing that someone is in a stall.

Just then the stall door opens. "Sounds like your relationship is off to a great start." Beth Pamett. She's everywhere. She goes to the sink alongside Allie. Big mistake on Beth's part.

"Now who the fuck are you?" Allie says with her hands on her hips.

"She's nobody, Allie, just ignore her." I pull at Allie's arm. I do not want her to lose it on Beth.

"I'm Beth Pamett. I've met you two times already, Allie. Through Grace.

Why don't you head to the bar and have another drink?"

"Why, you bitch!"

It takes all my strength to hold Allie back.

"Allie! Stop! She's not worth it." Beth gives us both a snide smile and walks out of the ladies' room.

"What the hell is her problem, Lane? Holy shit, what a nut bag!" Allie says, straightening her shirt and hair.

"Relax, she's bitter because she has the hots for Brady. Wait until I tell you what she said to me at the market." I grab her arm leading her out of the ladies' room.

"Why the hell is Grace friends with that wench?" Allie asks.

"That's a good question. I have no idea."

We head over to the bar area. The place has really filled up. Allie and I are both craning our necks, trying to spot our guys. Oh Lord, I spot Brady in the corner of the bar and Beth has his ear. He looks extremely uncomfortable and she is laying it on thick. Really hanging on him. I motion to Allie to look that way.

"What is wrong with that chick? I'm going to kick her ass!" Allie says heroically.

"No, no. Let her be. I feel sorry for her in a way; so bitter. It's sad." I watch Beth Pamett hang on my guy.

"You're crazy, Lane. I'd kick her ass if I were you."

"I am kicking her ass. I've got Brady," I say, winking at Allie. We laugh.

Allie spots George waving from the bar and heads toward him. I head over to save Brady from the likes of Beth. I squeeze in between them and wrap my arm around Brady's waist.

"Beth, so great to see you again!" I say with a big obnoxious smile on my face.

Beth leans into Brady and says loudly over the music to make sure I can hear, "When Laney goes back to South Carolina in a few weeks, call me. We can get together." With that she walks away before Brady can even respond.

Brady looks at me. "What was that all about?"

"I don't know, but if you go out with her I'll kill you," I say with a serious face. With that, Brady takes my face and starts making out with me, like no one else is in the bar. It's the kind of kiss that takes your breath away.

When he's done he says, "I'm never going out with anyone but you. From now on."

I smile and almost forget where I am (and all the tension between us) until I hear Allie say, "Why don't you two get a room?" She and George join us and bring us each a beer.

We see a few people from town, but most of the time, I keep my eye on Beth. She's with one of the women from Henry's that I didn't know. The band starts playing a slow song. Brady grabs my hand and leads me to the dance floor. We sway back and forth, just hugging each other.

Brady says in my ear, "Remember our first dance here?" I nod my head yes, trying not to cry. "I can't believe it was just a few weeks ago. I feel like we've been together forever. Let's not discuss the future for now. It's all too much to handle. Agree?" He looks at me and gives me a soft, gentle kiss.

"Agree, but we will have to face it eventually," I say back to him, reminding him. Then we hug and sway again. I'm lost in the moment, melting in Brady's arms, when I spot Jim walking in with Pete. Are you kidding me? Why?

"We need to get out of here, Brady." I stop swaying and go in total panic mode.

"Why?" He says looking around. Just then he spots them too. He grabs me and holds me tight, and goes back to dancing with me. "I'm not leaving because of those two assholes. Let them leave."

My buzz has vanished and I feel the hairs on my neck standing up. "I can't imagine this ending well." I say, hoping this convinces Brady to leave with me.

"It will be fine. Relax." Brady takes my face in his hands again and plants another kiss on my lips. I'm having a hard time enjoying it, but he's right. I have nothing to hide from Jim and I sure as hell do not give a shit what Pete thinks. It bothers me that Jim would still even want to hang out with Pete after what I told him Pete did, but it doesn't surprise me. Jim never had my back.

The song comes to an end and Brady leads me back near the bar where Allie and George are. They were able to get a table, which is good. I need to sit down; my knees are shaking.

"Can I get you a drink?" Brady asks.

"No. I'm good."

Brady walks to the bar and I can't help watching his every move. I do not want him getting near Jim or Pete.

"Holy crap, Laney, do you want to leave?" Allie asks.

"I would love to, but Brady says we should stay."

"I'm with Brady," George chimes in, taking a sip of his beer.

Brady comes back to the table with a drink for me. Even though I said no, I'm glad he did. Hopefully, it will take the edge off. I try my hardest to relax and have a good time. It's not easy. I can hear Elise in my ear telling me to get out of here. There is nothing good that can come of this situation. Brady moves his chair so he is right next to me and puts his arm around me.

"I'll never let anyone hurt you, Laney." He kisses me on the cheek. George starts talking about some new work project while my eyes glance around the bar. I can't help but notice Beth and Jim dancing. They're practically taking up the whole dance floor. Why the hell is Jim dancing with Beth? I see Pete standing against the wall, watching them. Then he looks my way and gives me a sick smile. Like it's something he's arranged to mess with me.

"You know what? I'm pretty tired and would like to get out of here. You all can stay. I can call a cab or something." I'm listening to Elise's voice telling me to get out. I've concluded that Pete is mentally ill. You shouldn't mess with someone who is mentally ill.

"I'm ready to go too," Allie says, supporting me. Brady stands and pulls out my chair like a gentleman, grabs my hand, and leads me out of the bar.

We're almost to the exit when I hear, "Laney! Laney, wait!" I do not even want to turn around. I know that voice and I feel nauseated. I stop and turn. Jim is fighting his way through the crowd to get to me.

"Laney! Hey, you're leaving already? I was hoping you could save me a dance, for old times' sake," he says, putting his hand on my elbow.

"No Jim, you go dance with Bitchy Beth and have fun with Crazy Pete." I can feel Brady's hand tightening around mine.

"Please, Laney, don't leave. Not with him," Jim says, finally making eye contact with Brady. "Brady, quit using her man. The jig is up. She's too good of a person to be hurt the way you plan on hurting her." Oh my goodness. Here we go.

"Gimme a break, Jim. Laney knows the truth. The only one who has ever hurt her is you, Jim." Brady pokes Jim in the chest.

"Brady, please, let's go." Jim has a short fuse and I know that poke did not go unnoticed.

"Hey, Brady, how about we take this outside and settle it like men!" Jim yells to our backs as we walk away.

Brady stops and turns back to Jim. "I am being a man and I'm taking MY lady home." We walk out and I glance back at Jim. He looks very upset and frustrated. This makes me smile.

"That was a close call. All we would have needed was a brawl!" Allie says, jumping in the back seat with me. Brady gets in the driver's seat and George jumps in the passenger seat.

"Did you see Jim's face when you said you were being a man? I thought his head was going to explode!" George chimes in.

"He's a dick." Brady looks back as he backs out of the parking spot. He's about to pull forward when I see Jim standing in front of the car.

"Brady, watch out!" I yell from the back seat. Jim bangs his hands on the hood of the car and heads to the driver's side door.

"Oh shit. Don't even open your window, Brady, just get the hell out of here!" I yell from the back seat. Another thing I love about Brady—he listens to me. I see him flip Jim off and we pull out of The Bird's Nest.

Allie and I look back and can hear Jim yelling, "He's using you Laney! Wake up!!" Allie and I look at each other, then we both look at Brady.

"Laney, you know that's not true," Brady says looking straight ahead, focusing on the road.

"I know, Brady," I say, then grab Allie's hand.

"It's never a dull moment going out with you ladies," George says, getting out of the car.

Brady opens my door for me and helps me out. "You okay honey?"
"Yeah, I guess. I just really wish Jim would leave town. This is turning into a nightmare." I bury my head in Brady's chest. "I just want to go to bed. Allie, George, see you in the morning. Thanks for coming out with us tonight." I give them each a hug, and Brady and I head into the house. I go straight to the bedroom to get changed and brush my teeth. Brady does the same.

"Would you like some water?" I ask.

"Sure," Brady says, getting into bed. I grab two glasses of water and head back to the bedroom.

I toss and turn for what feels like forever. I can't shut my brain down. It is swirling with thoughts. Maybe Brady really does care about me, for me. In the meantime, I have created nothing but hell in his life. Everything was good for him before I came here. Everything was good in everyone's life before I got here. Elise. Her kids. What have I done? I try and pull myself together. I know I need to get some sleep. Tomorrow is the service. I lay in bed just looking up at the ceiling, knowing there is no sleep in sight.

Chapter Forty-Nine

I wake up with only a couple of hours of sleep under my belt. Brady has left already and I didn't even hear him go. I wish he could have driven with me, but I know he has work obligations. I need to get my act together. The girls are counting on me today. Rachel and Riley need me. I drag myself to the shower with the hope that it wakes me up a little bit. I put my head under the shower and begin to cry just thinking of Elise again. How can this all have happened? Poor Elise.

George and Allie pick me up for the service. The drive there is awfully quiet. Allie and I both know that today is going to be so hard.

Allie turns to me as George pulls into a parking spot. "You ready for this?"

"Nope, but we have no choice." With that, we exit the car and walk arm in arm, holding each other up.

Elise's girls decided to have her service in a park near their home. It has a small waterfall. In front of the waterfall is a small field shaded by trees. I knew people had wedding services here, but this is first time I have heard of a memorial service here. It is so beautiful and I know Elise would have loved it. The girls greet us and walk with us to sit in the front row. Grace and Ben are already there waiting for us. We all hug, but no words are spoken. My throat hurts from the baseball-sized lump that is stuck in it.

At one point during the service, I turn, hoping to see Brady. He is coming right from work. In the few hundred or so people crammed into this small area I only see one face. Jim. I quickly turn back, but not before catching him smiling at me.

When the service ends, the girls lead everyone to a park building near by that has a catered lunch. Jim approaches me as Allie and I walk toward the building.

"Hey, Laney. Anything I can do for you, honey?" he says, putting his arm around me, acting as though he's consoling me.

"Yeah, you can get your hands off of her," a voice says from behind. It's Brady. I duck under Jim's arm and fall into Brady's arms.

"Brady, I'm so happy you're here."

He gives me a long, hard hug. He puts his arm around me, and we walk right past Jim; ignoring the fact that he is even there.

I stay at the luncheon as long as I can. Grace, Allie, and I huddle together for one last cry. Between being emotionally drained and having to be in the same room with Jim for two hours, I've had enough.

"Allie, I'm going to have Brady take me home if that's okay. I'm worn out." I give her a hug. "I already told the girls I was headed out."

"George and I have some errands we have to run anyway. I'll see you at Grace's on Saturday," she assures me.

"Grace, you need me to bring anything?" I already know her answer, but I ask anyway.

"Nope, just yourself. Oh, and the man of your dreams." Grace motions to Brady. He's talking with Ben but keeping an eye on me.

"That he is, girls. I don't know how I'm going to leave him." I squeeze their hands and walk away.

"Wow, you cleaned your truck for me?" I ask as Brady gets into the driver's seat.

"I did, just in case I need to give you a lift." Brady smiles and grabs my hand.

"That was a beautiful service. Elise would be proud of her girls," I say, looking out the window. "I'm so glad that part is over. Now I want to just try and have happy memories of her." I wipe more tears from my eyes.

"This has been a crazy couple of weeks. I bet it makes you glad you left here in the first place," Brady says, rubbing his thumb over my knuckles.

"I've never had so many things happen to me and to those around me in such a short period of time, that's for sure. It's been such a roller coaster of emotions. I'm hoping now the roller coaster stays up for a while. How about you?" I ask.

"That would be nice." Brady smiles and squeezes my hand. The rest of the ride is quiet.

Brady drops me off and heads out. He has work to finish up and something to do with Jeremy. I'm fine with that. I need some alone time. I'm exhausted.

I'm deep in thought, lying on the couch, when there's a knock on the door. It catches me off guard and I jump. Oh, please, just let it be some baked goods. I peek out the window and recognize the car right away. Shit. Jim. I open the door just a crack.

"What is it, Jim? Haven't you annoyed me enough for one day?"

"Wow, I'm sorry I annoy you so much, Laney. I was actually just checking in on you to make sure you're okay. I'm leaving town in the morning, thought we could have a drink." He holds my favorite wine in his hand and his face looks optimistic.

"Fine, Jim, come in. I swear to God if you try anything, I'll kick you out of here so fast," I say, my fist shaking at him.

"Calm down, Lane. Jeez."

I walk over to the cabinet and get two glasses.

"This sure is a nice place, Laney. Are you thinking of moving back here?" he asks, opening the bottle.

"I haven't given it too much thought, and even if I did, I doubt I would share that information with you, Jim."

"Relax, Laney. I'm sorry you have so much hatred for me, I really am. But I get it. I messed up in the worst way possible. For a long time. Can you come sit down with me? I need to talk to you about something." Jim walks over to the couch.

"I swear, Jim. If this is a I-know-I-screwed-up,-I-swear-I-can-do-things-better kind of talk, I'm not interested. My ship set sail a long time ago, Jim. I am over you!" I do not feel bad at all saying these words to Jim. He deserves them.

"Laney, sit down please. It's not that kind of talk." He pats the couch.

I roll my eyes, but play along.

"Laney, there are two reasons I actually came up to Jersey. One was for the funerals and to check in on you, absolutely. Another reason was to come up and see some of my family I haven't seen in a long time. I'm going through a rough time myself right now."

Oh brother, here we go. I'm supposed to feel sorry for him?

"I have cancer, Laney. "

Well I wasn't expecting that. "Really? What kind?"

"It's prostate cancer."

"Okay, well that's curable, right? When do you start treatment?" I ask, trying my best to act concerned. Not that I wish cancer on Jim. I've just lost my compassion for him. Part of me even wonders if it's true.

"I start radiation on Monday. It was caught very early, thank goodness. I'm still scared though, Laney. I know I have no right to ask this of you, but can you come back, Lane? Please? I don't want to go through this alone." Jim asks in a horrible, begging, pathetic tone.

"Oh lawd, Jim. Really? You're going to make me the bad guy in this situation? That's really not fair. I have a rental here that I paid for, and frankly, I need to see where my relationship with Brady is headed. I have very strong feelings for him. So, I'm sorry. No, I won't be there for you." I have instant guilt after the words leave my mouth, but I can't handle this. Not what I needed. I wonder if he'd be there for me if the tables were turned. I know the answer to that already.

"Okay. Well, I guess you really do hate me."

"Don't play that card, Jim. It's pathetic. I'm not sure why you thought after everything we've been through that I would be willing to drop everything for you."

"I guess I just hoped, Laney. Well, I better hit the road. Hope you find happiness, Laney. I really do. Just be careful. For the sake of our kids, be careful." Jim gets up and walks to the door. He turns before walking out, "I love you, Laney. Always have and always will."

I say nothing in return. He opens the door and leaves.

Shit. What the hell can happen next? There is a shit storm of emotions swirling around me. I feel almost dizzy. How much can I possibly take? I'm not strong enough for this. I pour myself another glass of wine and plop down on the couch. I text Brady.

> Do you have time for a massage tomorrow? The girls are scheduled to come at noon. Let me know.

I start looking around the house. Shit. I should pack up, drive home, and pretend none of this even happened. Then I hear the *ding-dong*.

> Can't make it tomorrow, sorry. But maybe you can massage me tomorrow night?

Deep breath. He makes me feel better.

> I will gladly massage you and look forward to it.

Next I text Allie.

> Please tell me you can come here at noon for a massage tomorrow.

> If you twist my arm I can come. You okay, sista?

> I'm not okay. But I have wine, so I will survive. I'll fill you in tomorrow.

Chapter Fifty

Thanks to the full bottle of wine I polish off, I am able to sleep pretty soundly. A text wakes me.

Would you like to walk to breakfast with me? – Abe

Hmmm. That sounds good. I could use the exercise.

Sounds good. Be outside in 10.

Some fresh air and a spinach omelet is just what I need. I drag myself out of bed and get ready. Abe is already outside waiting for me when I step out of the house.

"Good morning!" he yells cheerfully.

"Look at you all chipper and full of energy!" At that moment, I am thankful I chose to take a couple of pain relievers before I left the house, because my own voice echoes in my head and it hurts.

Abe and I talk the whole way to Henry's. He fills me in on a new love interest. Some art dealer who has a summer house here. Lives in Williamsburg, Brooklyn but comes out to Falcon Lake on a regular basis. Abe sounds very happy and I'm happy for him. "Hey Laney, I wasn't going to ask, but the curiosity is killing me. What happened yesterday with your ex? Saw him pull up to your house." I take a deep breath and fill him in on all the drama.

"Now that I've shared with you, how about you share with me?"

"Sure."

"I noticed a car in your driveway the other day that I didn't recognize."

"Maybe my cleaning lady?" Abe says, guessing.

"Maybe. Is her name Susie by any chance?" I say, holding my breath waiting for the answer.

"Sure is. She cleans Stacy's house too. Well, before they left for Europe. You know her?" I stop dead in my tracks.

"Okay, wait. So Susie probably has a key to my place?"

"I would assume so. She has one for mine." Abe continues to walk.

"Well, that makes sense. Now I know who's been coming in my place while I'm not home, snooping around, and leaving me little gifts and messages. Susie!"

"Really? I guess that sounds like Susie. She has very few morals and definitely does not know boundaries."

"You know she's Brady's ex, right?" I ask, assuming Abe knows this already.

"No!" Now he stops in his tracks. "Wow, now that's surprising. Maybe she looked better in her prime?" We both laugh.

I then fill Abe in on Pete and Susie.

"I've seen her with that guy. He makes more sense than Brady, that's for sure."

With all the new information floating in my head, the walk to the diner flies by. Abe holds the door open for me and I scan the place. Abe does too, and waves at some family members in the kitchen. There they are, in the corner. Pete and a couple of guys I don't recognize. Maybe some of his new employees. Who knows? I quickly point him out to Abe.

"Good God, he's gross," Abe says then looks over the menu.

"Order me up a pot of coffee and a spinach omelet, will ya? I have to go to the ladies' room." As I turn down the hall to the bathrooms, I see Pete give me a shit eating grin. I shoot him the dirtiest look possible in the short amount of time I have before clearing the corner. That man disgusts me.

As I walk out of the bathroom, I practically bounce off his belly.

"Wow, how nice of you to help out your cancer ridden ex. You're not as nice as I thought you were, Laney. Brady better hope he never gets sick. Lord knows you'll leave him to deal with it alone too."

Something comes over me just then; a pure hatred for another human being. My foot, like it has a mind of its own, raises up at bullet speed, and kicks Pete right in his nuts. He buckles over in pain and gasps for air.

"I told you never to speak to me again you piece of shit." And with that I walk past him, back to my seat where my coffee is waiting for me.

"Everything okay?" Abe asks.

"Yes, everything's great." I throw my napkin on my lap and take a big sip of coffee. "Just let me know when you see him come out of there. I want to make sure he's headed back to his table and not over here."

"What did you do to him? It didn't sound too good," Abe asks with a smile on his face.

"Oh, I didn't do anything. It was my damn spastic foot. It's been an issue for a long time. I should really see a doctor about that." We both laugh and clink coffee mugs.

"Oh, there he his." Abe motions with his head toward the bathroom hall. I turn and glare at Pete with disgust. He looks like a beaten puppy. He quickly sticks his tail between his legs and heads back to his table. "Shit, Laney, I'm beginning to wonder if anything happens in this town when you're not around."

The rest of the morning flies by and I realize it's approaching noon. I hear a door slam and see the masseuses getting out of the car and gathering their things. Where's Allie? I call her. No answer. Frig, I hope she didn't forget. I send her a text and await her response.

I let the girls in to set up and run next door. I'm hoping George knows where Allie is. I ring the bell and bang on the door.

"Hey, Laney!" George opens the door in his boxer shorts.

"George! Jesus, put some pants on." I shield my eyes. "Is Allie in here with you?"

"Yes, she's just getting dressed and ready to head on over." George grabs my arm. "Laney, you coming here was the best thing ever for me. Without you, I wouldn't have met Allie. I'm so thankful." I needed to hear that my visit has been good for someone.

"Thanks George, I really appreciate that." I'm almost in tears when a thought pops in my head. "George, you got an hour to spare?"

"I do! I'm on my official lunch break now."

"Why don't you head over to my house with Allie and get a couples massage? I have errands I have to run anyway."

"Are you sure, Laney? Gosh, that would be great." George sounds like a little kid. Allie walks out from the bedroom.

"I'm ready, Lane. Sorry to keep you waiting," Allie says, winking at me as if

I don't know what just happened in the bedroom.

"Well, guess what? I'm giving my session to your lover boy. So you two go and enjoy!"

"Are you sure, Lane? I know you really need a massage."

"No, really. Go ahead. No worries." I give a wink right back to Allie. I head over to the house with them, explain the change to the massage girls, grab my things, and head out. "Just lock up when you're done!" I say, grabbing Natalie's attention and putting cash in her bag for the massages.

I hadn't given much thought to what I was going to do today. Oh, I know! I'll go to that fancy little market and buy a nice dinner for Brady and me. I need to pick up a card for the christening tomorrow as well. I hope Brady can go with me.

The market it a little bit out of the way, but so worth it. I hit the floral department first. Since Grace never lets me bring anything, I might as well take her some flowers. While looking through the bouquets, I hear a voice.

"Laney Simms, is that you?"

I look up and see one of my oldest friends from elementary school, Jenna Shawn. Jenna moved away in seventh grade. At the time it felt like she was moving out of state. Found out through Facebook that she had actually just moved to the next town over. We hadn't seen each other since then, but kept track of each other's lives; thanks to modern technology.

"Oh my gosh, Jenna! How are you?" We give each other a hug, like I just saw her yesterday.

"Great, how are you? What brings you up to Jersey?"

I tell her a brief synopsis of my adventure. Not all the details, because part of me believes someone would think I was crazy if I told them everything that has happened in such a short period of time.

"That sounds great for you! I feel like all I ever do is take care of everyone else around me—cooking, cleaning, driving kids all over. I would love a little 'me' time like that."

I do forget what it was like to be part of all that. A family. Part of me aches for that again, but life marches on.

We make a little more small talk, then Jenna says, "Oh, dear, so sorry about Elise and her husband. What a nightmare! It broke my heart when I read that in the paper." She consoles me by rubbing my arm.

"Nightmare is the perfect word," I say, accepting Jenna's sympathy.

"I guess that's why we have to live life to the fullest."

"Yes, you are right, my friend," I say with a forced smile.

"So, how's your love life?"

"Wow, that's one way to change the subject!" I wonder what she's heard. "It's actually pretty good right now. Bumped into a guy from high school and we've been seeing each other."

"Look at you! That a girl! Anyone I would remember?"

Gosh, I'm nervous to say it. It's such a small town; it feels like everyone knows everybody and everybody has a story. I crinkle my nose and say, "Brady Gramble? You probably don't remember him!"

I see the light in her eye and realize right away that she knows him. Oh shit, here we go.

"Oh my gosh, I do know Brady Gramble! He's totally gorgeous!" Phew, I breathe again. "He actually dated my sister-in-law for a while before he got married. I was devastated when they broke up!" We both crack up laughing.

"Well, he's still a babe," I say, still laughing.

"Oh, I know, I just saw him the other night at Smoky's. He's getting better with age, that's for sure!" My laugh turns into a smile, then fades to a question mark.

"What night was that?" I ask, trying not to sound hurt or surprised.

"Oh, geez, I don't know. A few nights ago?" I quickly run the days through my head.

"Oh yes, that's right! I forgot he went out that night," I say, acting as if I have it under control and that I knew Brady was going to Smoky's that night. We make a little bit more small talk, then go our separate ways.

I guess Brady doesn't feel the need to tell me everywhere he's going. That's fine, right? We've only been together three weeks or so. Why should he tell me everything? Maybe he just stopped in quickly and forgot to tell me. No big deal. I didn't tell him I went out to breakfast with Abe. I will tell him, but I haven't yet.

I'm almost done with my shopping when I see Jenna again. She pulls her cart up alongside mine and speaks in a low voice.

"Listen Laney, I wasn't going to say anything, but I would want to know something like this. I'm sure it was nothing."

That's all she has to say and my heart sinks into my stomach.

"The other night at the bar, some woman was really throwing herself at Brady. It didn't seem like he was reciprocating, but Laney, they left at the same time."

She must have seen the ache in my eyes. "I'm sure nothing happened. Really, he didn't seem interested at all. She was very aggressive though."

"What did she look like?" I say.

"Heavy set, blonde. I couldn't really see her face too well. It was dark."

A face immediately comes to mind. Beth Pamett.

"I'm sorry, Laney, I didn't mean to hurt you. Just thought you should know some other woman is after your man."

"No, thanks, Jenna. I appreciate it. I have a pretty good idea who it is, and I'm not too concerned." I smile and walk away, trying to stay calm and level headed. I have to believe that Brady didn't do anything with anyone, especially not Beth. Who the hell knows anymore? Maybe he did do something. My knees feel a little weak and I'm immediately brought back to the pain I felt when I found out about Jim's affairs. I shake that memory from my head and know that speculating isn't fair to me or to Brady. I'll ask him tonight when he comes over. I finish up my shopping and head back to the lake.

***

By the time I get back, everyone is gone. I carry the groceries in and start unloading when I receive a text.

> Sorry babe, have to cancel for tonight. Jeremy needs me. I'll call you later. Love you.

My initial feeling is of utter disappointment. Then that leads right into suspicion, and I hate that. I don't want to live this way again.

> No worries. Talk to you later.

I'm suddenly not in a "love you" kind of mood. I drop my phone on the counter, grab my lunch, and sit on the deck. I'm trying my hardest not to let my imagination get away from me. I'm sure Jeremy really does need him and Jeremy should be his priority. Then I hear Jenna telling me about him leaving the bar with a woman. I can't help but hurt a little. Not that I expect him to tell me where he is at all times, but I feel like him not telling me about this is the same as lying. Not a great start to a relationship as far as I'm concerned.

I decide to pour myself a glass of wine and relax a little. I'm sure Brady has a very reasonable explanation. Time to dive back into that book I've started, over and over again. After about an hour of reading and a quick nap, I decide to make myself a nice dinner with all the groceries I bought. No reason to just sit around and do nothing because Brady can't be here.

I text Allie and see if she wants to join me. Nope, she's busy with George. I scan through my contacts and see Elise's name. I pause and sigh and think of how much I would love to have her here with me. Just then, there's a knock on the door.

I peek through the curtain. Abe. "Hey, Abe!" I swing the door open.

"Hey Laney, baked some cookies, thought I'd bring some over."

"Oh, they look great. Can you come in?"

He walks in and places the cookies on the counter.

"Whacha got going on tonight...hot dinner with Brady?" Abe asks, winking.

"No, he blew me off tonight. I was just about to make some appetizers. Why don't you join me?" Before Abe can even answer, I'm reaching into the cabinet for his glass.

"Well, sure, sounds good."

Abe has a seat at the island while I prepare some food. I fill him in on my run-in at the market with Jenna. With what she told me and now, Brady canceling on me, I am so suspicious.

"You should most definitely not jump to conclusions. With that being said, once the sun goes down, I say we hop in my car and do a little spying on Brady. See what he's up to." Abe raises his glass to toast me.

"I love the idea, don't get me wrong. But doesn't it seem a little high schoolish? Plus, that's me saying I don't trust Brady. And I do...well, I really want to." I take a big sip of wine. "Okay, let's do it. You just better hope I do not see anything that hurts me because then you'll be responsible for consoling me for the rest of my stay here." I raise my glass again.

"You got it," Abe says, clinking my glass.

With everything telling me it's wrong, I hop in the car with Abe and travel to the other side of the lake. As we approach Brady's house, I see a car in the driveway that I do not recognize and my heart stops. We pass slowly with Abe getting the best view.

"I definitely see people moving around in there, almost looks like they're dancing. Slow dancing," Abe says cautiously.

"What the hell? I feel sick. Is it Brady? Can you see? Turn around so I can see!" I begin sweating and feel the hairs on my neck standing up. Abe turns around at the next driveway and begins his slow drive-by, this time with his headlights out.

I see him. Brady. Slow dancing with a much shorter blonde woman. I can't see her face, just the back of her head. But I see his face clearly. Smiling down at her, laughing. I put my hand on my chest because I'm certain I just felt my heart break.

"Take me home, Abe." I sink down in the seat and just stare out the window. Abe tries to speak to me, but I silence him. Abe barely stops the car in his driveway when I bolt out of the car and run back to my house.

"Laney, I'm so sorry! I never thought that's what we would see! Maybe it's better you found out now rather than later!" Abe yells to my back. I run straight to the bathroom, feeling like I may vomit. I then sit on the bathroom floor and sob. I've been duped again. What is wrong with me? Why do men think they have the right to treat me like this? Why aren't I good enough? I drag myself to bed and continue my pity party there. Alone. Again.

I'm lying in the dark, just staring out the window, when my phone rings. I know who it is immediately. He said he was going to call. If I don't answer, he'll pretend to worry and maybe even force himself to come here. I answer, trying to sound my best but knowing there is no disguising the pain in my voice.

"Hello?"

"Laney, you okay, honey? You sound horrible."

Yeah, I look horrible, too, I can assure you.

"Yeah, I have a sick headache, went to bed early." I lie.

"Oh no, I'm so sorry. You should've called me. Do you need anything?" he says, all caring and loving. What an act.

"Nope. I'm good. Just need some sleep." I say, coolly.

"Okay, honey. You rest. I'll see you tomorrow. Sorry again that I missed seeing you tonight. I love you. Feel better."

My eyes well up with tears. "Bye." I hang up. I close my eyes and try for hours to fall asleep. Maybe I should go back to South Carolina. There is nothing here holding me back. Four weeks left of my rental, but who cares? Grace can come use the place whenever she wants. Or Allie. I'm starting to wish I never came here.

Chapter Fifty-One

I wake in the morning not feeling much better. Then I remember I have to go to the christening and try and put on a happy face. I'm not sure I have the strength. I sit on the back deck enjoying my coffee and the cool fall morning. It's overcast but still so bright on my tired eyes. I get a text and glance at my phone.

> Good morning, honey. Hope you're feeling better. I'll have to meet you at Grace's and be a little late. Running behind on the work site. I'll see you there! Love you!

I fling the phone back on to the table and do not respond just yet. Love. What a word. Some take it so lightly.

I hear a door open next door, and I see Abe step out on his deck.

"Laney! I'm coming over." I hear him gallop down his steps and up mine in no time. He pulls out a chair and sits down. "How are you doing?"

I look at him over my coffee mug. "Stupid question."

Abe frowns. "I'm sorry, you're right, it is stupid. But so is jumping to conclusions, Laney. You have no idea what was going on in there. It could be something so innocent and you're blowing it out of proportion. Get the facts first before you hang the poor guy," Abe says, rubbing my arm.

"I don't see how that can be blown out of proportion. It is what it is. He was dancing with another woman. Seems clear to me."

Abe sits back in his chair and lets out a deep breath. "I was an idiot to drive you past there and instigate that whole thing."

"It's okay." I sip my coffee. "It's best that I find out now instead of later. It sure will make it much easier to leave, that's for sure." Even saying that pains me and I feel like the wind has been knocked out of me.

I decide to take Allie up on an earlier offer to drive me to Grace's house. I'm in no mood to even go to the party, but I have no choice. Allie suspects right away that something is wrong on the car ride but does not question me too much in front of George. Once at Grace's, I get the greetings out of the way and try my best to seem happy. I am happy for Grace and her beautiful family; I'm just not happy for me. Allie grabs me by the elbow and leads me into the laundry room.

"What the hell is wrong with you? Give it up, chickie," she says with her hands on her hips. I don't want to tell Allie because I know she'll give Brady an earful, but I need to get it off my chest.

"I'm going home, Allie. Brady is seeing someone else, and frankly, I'm tired of being a victim of scumbag men. End of story."

Allie looks like I just smacked her with a frying pan. "You're talking like a crazy person. What did you just say?"

I tell Allie everything. She takes a second to let it all sink in and then offers her opinion.

"Okay, first off, no. You are not going home. You have a month left on your rental and I need you here. Second, shouldn't you talk to Brady before making all sorts of crazy assumptions? Laney, I know it's hard for you to trust, but this I know—Brady is a man in love. So very in love. And he's been hurt, just like you, Lane; so I doubt very much he would put you through such an ordeal. We'll get to the bottom of it. So in the meantime, chin up, chest out, smile on your face. Be positive, woman!"

Allie's words do lift my spirits for about thirty seconds. I may have jumped to conclusions, but I feel like there are too many conclusions to come to. I want full disclosure, not secret trips to parties, bars, and now a woman in his house. I will not be made a fool of again.

As we exit the laundry room, there she is. Beth Pamett.

"Well, well, how nice of you two to help Grace with her laundry." She laughs. This bitch really cracks herself up.

"Put a sock in it, Beth," says Allie, looking like she wants to throw a punch.

"Oh my goodness, Laney, did your dear Brady tell you how he saved me the other night?"

I play dumb. She's not going to hurt me. "He did. Good for you, Beth." I had no idea what she was talking about, but I suspect it was her hitting on him at the bar, like Jenna said.

"It was great watching a tall, dark hunk like Brady change my tire. I could get used to that, and I'm sure I will once you're gone." Holy crap, this chick is relentless!

"What a kind thing to say, Beth. I'll be sure to share your opinion with Grace." I see Beth's face get serious. God forbid she look bad in Grace's eyes. Grace protects me even more than Allie.

"Simmer down, Laney. I was just pulling your chain." She walks off quickly.

"I'd really like to pop her in the mouth," Allie says, making a fist.

"She's a real piece of work, but no threat to me. I know how Brady feels about her. Allie, do me a favor? I don't want Brady to know I was stalking him because I don't want him to think I don't trust him."

"Well, you don't, do you?"

"Not completely, no. Crap. I'm just so insecure, Al. Jim really put me through the ringer. How do I tell Brady why I'm so hurt without him thinking I'm a psycho?"

"Hmmm, how about you just tell him the truth? You have to, Laney. You know that."

She's right.

"Why can't things go smoothly? I always seem to run into problem after problem," I say, putting my head down.

"Here comes a super hot and sexy problem, looking at you with eyes full of love and want."

I look in the same direction as Allie and there's Brady walking through the front door. Dressed in khakis and a light blue, button down shirt with just the right number of buttons undone. His eyes brighten and twinkle when he sees me. Just his facial expression alone lifts my heart back into place.

"Damn, Brady, you clean up nice!" Allie says and walks away. Brady wraps his arms around me and I breathe him in.

"I missed you so much, baby. How are you feeling?" He kisses me before I can answer.

"I'm okay. Still not great." I'm hurting and he can sense it.

"What is it, babe? Talk to me."

"Do you mind if we talk later? At my place? This isn't the appropriate time or place."

"Yeah, sure. Guess I'll sweat it out until then," said he says, looking nervous. "Let's just enjoy ourselves. Want some lunch?"

***

The ride back to my house feels like an eternity. I keep stalling because I want to have our conversation back at my house and Brady is losing his patience with me.

"Enough small talk. Tell me what's going on, Laney. You are not being fair to me!" Brady finally loses his cool.

"Fine! I'm afraid when I tell you this that (a) you'll think I'm crazy, or (b) I will be right."

"What is it? You have me nervous."

"Well, last night, when you cancelled so unexpectedly, Abe came over and he said, 'Let's go see what Brady is up to.' I didn't expect to find anything, but then I saw you; dancing with another woman." That didn't come out the way I wanted it to, but I am trembling. I'm so afraid of what he might say.

"So you saw me dancing. With a blonde, right?"

I nod my head yes.

"So then you let your imagination get away with you, didn't you?"

"Yeah, I guess I did. But it wasn't my imagination. I saw you." I say, shaking.

"Oh, Laney. I wish you would have told me last night when we spoke. I could have saved you all this worry. That was Jeremy's date to the fall formal dance at school. Jeremy has no clue how to dance, so she came over and the three of us practiced. It was mostly the two of them, but every once in a while, I had to jump in and give him a visual."

Shit. I feel like such an asshole. I'm glad we're getting close to my house. I want out of this car.

"I'm sorry. I assumed the worse. Just like when you showed up at the party when you were supposed to be at your sister's. And when I heard from someone I hadn't seen in years that you were at Smoky's and left with someone. It's just too much, Brady. I can't live like this. It's not fair to me and it's not fair to you. I can't trust you, Brady. I can't trust anyone!"

Brady pulls into the driveway and slams on his brakes. "You are crazy, Laney. I've done nothing to deserve this. I've been completely honest with you. Maybe I forgot to tell you where I was for dinner when fucking Beth

Pamett was hitting on me as usual, and then asked me to change her fucking tire! I'm sorry for that. I haven't been in a relationship for a long time. Guess I forgot all the rules! Or are they just your rules, Laney?"

I stop for a second and turn to him. "This was never going to last anyway, Brady. We both know that. I'm leaving here. I don't know what we were thinking. You and me; it's so unrealistic. I love you, and I wish you the best in life, but this is never going to work, Brady. I'm so very sorry." I'm shaking, but I'm not crying. That's not like me. For once I feel strong.

"That's really too bad, Laney. I thought you were stronger than that. Good luck to you." Brady never looks over at me. He stares straight ahead. I open the door and step out. He backs out of the driveway without even looking at me. I put my hand over my mouth and begin to cry. I struggle to see through my tears to find my keys in my bag. I walk through the front door and there, in red lipstick on the big beautiful window overlooking the lake, is my last message. "Leave already, bitch. No one wants you here!"

That's it. I'm done. Elise, Brady. I'm done with all this drama. I need to be back home. This isn't my home anymore. I clean the ugly message off the window, then begin to pack. I ask Allie, Grace, George, and Abe to come over in the morning. So I can say goodbye.

Chapter Fifty-Two

"I can't believe you're leaving, Laney." Grace blows her nose. This is affecting her more than I thought it would.

"I'm sorry, Grace. I'll be back to visit more often and you know you always have a place to stay with me down South. Come escape some of the winter up here. I'd love to have you," I offer, grabbing her hand across the table. Just then, there's a quick knock and Allie and the boys walk in.

"You sure there's nothing we can do to change your mind?" Allie says, hugging me from behind.

"No, I'm sorry. I need to go home. Between Elise and all this relationship drama, which I'm obviously not ready for, I've had enough. I was thinking about it in bed last night. I'm going to go home and start a foundation for women who are abused, whether it be mentally or physically. Give them a place to stay, get counseling. I think I'll call it Elise's House, or something like that. I don't know. I need to refocus my energy onto something positive. Something that lifts me up. Helping people will do that for me."

"I think that sounds great, and Laney, if it's okay with you, I'd love to visit sometime," Abe says, rubbing my shoulders.

"I would love nothing more, Abe. Make sure you bring your recipes."

We all laugh.

I say my final goodbyes, get the place looking like it was when I got there, then pack the car. I take one long hard look at the lake before I leave. I'll never forget my time here. So many emotions I've never experienced in such a short amount of time. Some I wish I never experienced and some that I will cherish. My thoughts immediately go to Brady and I close my eyes. I'll always love him. We just weren't meant to be.

Chapter Fifty-Three

Home sweet home. There's nothing like it. Now time to face the worst part of a trip. Unpacking. Seeing all the new outfits I purchased makes all the memories flood back in. The romantic dinners, the first night at his house. Crap. How am I going to get over him?

It hurts so bad. I guess time will help. Maybe my true destiny is waiting for me here in Charleston. I'm going to start putting myself out there more. If he's not going to find me, I need to make more of an effort to find him.

***

I'm so glad I've decided to start this foundation. I'm staying busy which is making the days go by faster and keeping me too busy to think. To remember.

Allie keeps me updated on the goings on up North. She and George are still hot and heavy but have slowed the wedding plans down.

"I'm still not ready, Lane. He's a young guy. What if he changes his mind and wants kids one day? I do not want to deprive him of that. I'm just going to see where this goes, reevaluate in the new year."

"Wow, that's very level-headed of you, Al. I'm proud!"

"I know, right? So not like me. I'm getting old and boring. Maybe we'll elope!"

We both laugh.

"You doing okay?" she asks, concerned.

"I'm okay. I've been real busy. I rented a building for the foundation. Signed the lease yesterday. I've already hired a full time counselor and a cook. Still looking for a maintenance man and volunteers. It's getting there."

"That's amazing, Lane. Elise would be so proud of you."

"I hope so. Once it's done, I'd like to get her girls down here for the ribbon cutting. Maybe you and Grace can come down too. It will probably be after New Year's."

"We will be there!" Allie declares. "So aren't you curious if I've seen Brady? Or heard anything?"

"Of course I am, Allie, but I need to move on. If I keep asking you about him, I'll never heal." I pause for a moment. "Why, have you seen him or heard anything?"

"Well, that was easy! Yeah, I've heard bits and pieces. Nothing major. He's just down in the dumps; missing his girl."

"This is coming from the town grapevine?" I find it hard to believe our relationship is the talk of the town.

"Nope. Heard it directly from him. He stopped by the shop to say hi. He looked like hell, Laney."

I take a deep breath. "That's sad and I feel horrible, but I had to get out, Allie. He wasn't ever going to leave, and I couldn't stay. I couldn't. It wasn't fair to either of us."

"I know, I know. Wish things would have turned out differently for you, Lane. You two seemed perfect together. Someone's walked in the store, gotta run, girl. Love you!"

"Love you too. Talk to you soon." I hit end on the phone and just sit there for who knows how long, thinking of Brady. I never did receive a call or text from him. I'm sure I hurt him more than I ever wanted to. I still feel a pit in my stomach every time I think of him. Which is all the time.

I shake my head. This is exactly what I didn't want to do. Back to work on the foundation.

Chapter Fifty-Four

It's Thanksgiving week and both of my kids are home. It makes me happy to have them around me. I only share with them part of the reason that I left Falcon Lake early. No need to tell them all about Brady when they, more than likely, will never meet him. Besides, I haven't heard a word from him. No text, email, letter, nothing. I thought he'd reach out in some way.

I guess he is over me already. I think about him every day. I read his old texts just to feel again. To read I love you, to see his face. I'm guessing those were just words. Not how he really felt.

"Mom, you need to find your happiness again," Kerry says, while folding laundry. She brought home a car load. "The way you sounded while you were up in Falcon Lake; that's what life is all about."

"I'm happy, Kerry. This foundation, doing this work for women who need help; it makes me feel complete. I see Elise's face smiling down at me and I am happy."

"You need someone to share that happiness with, Mom."

"I am. I'm sharing it with you. Which reminds me, I would like to share some of the work with you and your brother. Can you make time this week to come to the foundation to do some cleaning and painting?"

"I guess, gosh, haven't you hired a maintenance guy yet?" she says, jokingly, stomping her foot.

"No, and if I want to open by mid-January, I'm going to need help. I think the girls are planning on coming down. You'll have to plan a trip back." I wince a little when I think of the "girls." It's still so hard for me to grasp that Elise isn't part of that group anymore.

"Of course I'll come back, Mama. Wouldn't miss it for the world!" Kerry hugs me.

**

Thanksgiving passes in a blur. This foundation is all-consuming of my time. That's good. I need that. Today is a big day. The town inspector is coming by to see if we are close to opening. These town inspectors drive me nuts. In my history with them, some are real sticklers and make sure every T is crossed and I is dotted. Others just drive by and say you're good. I'm hoping for the one that drives by.

My office space at Elise's House is a mess. Files and stacks of paper everywhere. I'm a mess too. Hair up halfway in a bun, dirty clothes. Elise's House is actually an old historic house that was once used as a bed and breakfast. The floor plan is ideal. Large kitchen, large living room, and small bedrooms. This place is meant to be a home to get these women back on their feet. Not to have them stay long term. Women who have homes can come here for free counseling or to just get a hot meal and have someone to talk to. Just then there's a knock on the door.

I get to the front door and do a quick peek out the window. Oh crap. It's the inspector. An even bigger oh crap, he's handsome. I've lived in town a long time and I do not recognize this guy. I quickly try to salvage my bun and dust my clothes off.

"Hi, how are you? I'm Laney Simms. You must be the inspector?"

"Yes, good morning. Jason Speer. Just here to check out your place, make sure everything is up to code."

"Yes, please come in." I open the door and hold my arm out to direct him in. I hope he overlooks what a complete disaster I am. "Help yourself, I'll be back in my office."

"Know the place well. Stayed here on my wedding night," he says, filling out some information on his clipboard. Well, there you have it. He's married.

"Oh neat. Have fun reminiscing!" I walk back to my office, but I hear him say something under his breath.

"I'm sorry?" I say, stopping at my doorway.

"Oh nothing. Just said it was a night I'd rather forget. Marriage only lasted two months. Expensive learning experience." He grabs his flashlight from his holster and starts walking upstairs.

The old me would have probably followed him upstairs and continued the conversation. I'm officially too worn out emotionally to pursue him or his story. I focus instead on my pile of paperwork that I need to address.

The inspector walks around for what seems like forever when he finally knocks on my office door. "I'm all done here. This is a list of safety hazards that I found that need to be repaired before we can give you the okay to operate. When they are taken care of, please give me a call so I can reinspect. Once you pass that, assuming you pass that, you can open this place about three days later."

He hands me a list which feels like it's a mile long. I glance it over and just put my head down on my desk.

"You okay, ma'am?" he asks, sounding more scared than concerned.

"Yeah, I'll be okay. Thanks for stopping by." I sit up. "I'll call you when we are ready for you. It may be a year, but we'll call ya." Maybe I bit off more than I can chew with this project.

"It's a great thing you are doing here. Don't give up. Maybe advertise in the paper that you need help. People love helping around the holidays for a good cause."

He's right. Why didn't I think of that?

***

The help comes flurrying in. People are so kind, especially around the holidays. Church groups, school groups, entire families! It's just astounding to me, and at times, I need to go to my office and close the door; I'm so overwhelmed with emotion.

It's Christmas Eve already. My kids are both home for Christmas break, but I keep encouraging them to spend time with their dad.

"He needs you now. Go take him shopping or out to dinner. Cheer him up!" I say, sounding like a cheerleader.

"Don't you need us at the foundation, Ma?" asks Jake, in his man voice (which always shocks me), pouring himself a bowl of cereal. I still can't get over how grown up my kids are.

"I'm in good shape, Jake. I'm going to head over there today for just a little bit, but according to the inspector, we should be able to open right after the new year. Just a few small jobs to wrap up. It's so exciting!"

"Well, when we are done with dad, Jake and I were both invited to the Spencers' house for a Christmas Eve party. You okay if we do that? We shouldn't be back too late," Kerry chimes in from her cereal bowl.

"That would be fine. You can't miss the Spencers' Christmas Eve party. The views of the river from that plantation house are amazing."

We used to go to that party as a family. It's been awhile for me.

"Well, I hate leaving you on Christmas Eve, Mama. Do you promise you'll be okay?"

My kids are so sweet.

"I'll be fine. Go and have fun!"

Chapter Fifty-Five

After a full day of work at the foundation, I can't wait to get home. Christmas Eve is my favorite night of all. Every Christmas Eve, our entire neighborhood lines the streets with luminaries. It's beautiful! People drive from all over just to see it. I love to sit on the front porch with a big ol' glass of Bailey's Irish Cream and watch the cars go by. Some neighbors invited me over to their bonfire, but I would rather be alone. Reflect on what has been my both my best and worst year ever.

I finish lighting the luminaries and head to my mini bar to fix my drink, when my doorbell rings. Probably one of the neighbors trying to get me to come over.

"I'm not interested," I say quietly.

I open the door and there is no one there. I look to the left and the right. No one. Then I look down and there's a red box. What the heck could that be? I see a little tag hanging off the ribbon. It reads, "Merry Christmas, I know how much you wanted this."

I cautiously step outside, still looking. Whoever left this for me is more than likely watching me. I rip the paper off and open the lid to the box. I gasp and begin to shake. It's the necklace from Allie's shop. The one with the hearts intertwined.

"I can't believe it!" I say out loud. "Allie, how did you get this here?"

That's when I hear it. Him.

"It wasn't Allie." Brady steps into the light on my front walkway. I almost drop the box. I can't believe what I'm seeing.

"Oh my gosh, Brady. What are you doing here?" I have my hand on my heart because I feel like I need to hold it in my chest.

"I'm here for the maintenance worker position at Elise's House. You still hiring?"

He skips all my steps and is in front of me in an instant. He gives me a kiss that shakes me to my core. I can barely stand.

I push him back. "What do you mean? I don't understand. I haven't heard from you since I left. Now you're here? What's happening?"

He put his hands on my face. "I'm here, Laney. I'm not leaving. I hope you'll have me. My truck and all my things are parked around the corner. I've come to be with you. To help you with the foundation, to love you, Laney. I couldn't live without you in Jersey. It wasn't possible. I know trust is an issue for both of us, but I know we can make it, Laney. I just know we can." He kisses me again.

"Wait, what about Jeremy? And your business? Your house? Your family?" I manage to get all of that out in between kisses.

"Jeremy pushed me to come. He lived with me being miserable every day. He had enough, I guess. He's going to stay with my parents mostly. We'll have him here for holidays if that's okay, and he says he wants to go to college down here. I thought maybe we can spend some time at the lake over the summer, since it gets so hot down here. Have your kids up to the lake. Laney, you are my family. I love you and want to be with you always."

We are forehead to forehead now. I close my eyes and reopen them to make sure I'm not dreaming. Is he really here? I didn't think I would feel such happiness again.

I look Brady in the eyes. "I love you, Brady. I am yours. Forever."